The Astoria Chinatown Conspiracy

A Novel

by

Richard B. Powers

Credits for the book cover:

Wēijī (Crisis). Calligraphy by Dr. Yang Ji Yu, Wisdom Arts Academy, Portland, OR.

Cover design and concept by Mar De Ycaza, graphic artist.

Sailing Gillnetters (Butterfly Fleet). Image courtesy of the Columbia River Maritime Museum, Astoria. CRMM # 168-3073. Photo: O. W. Whitman.

Disclaimer:

The expulsion of the Chinese from Tacoma in November 1885 and from Seattle in February 1886 was real enough. But this is a work of fiction, not history. The events and characters, aside from major historical figures, are the products of the author's imagination.

"The Astoria Chinatown Conspiracy" ISBN 978-1-60264-897-5 (softcover).

Manufactured in the United States of America.

Dedicated to the Chinese who lived in America during the
exclusion years: 1882-1943

ACKNOWLEDGEMENTS

False starts and the cul-de-sacs I stumbled into made this book much longer to complete than I ever imagined. Rodger Larson, gifted writer and teacher, saved me from even more wrong turns with his knowledge of writing and his gentle critiquing style. Thanks, Rodger. The members of Rodger's group always gave helpful feedback. Special thanks to Brenda Buratti for sharing her insight about who my protagonist should be.

The guidelines used by Rodger in his group served as a model for Nancy Slavin and me when we started our critique group. Our "meat locker" writing group has operated since 2000 and those who've joined us over the years soon learn that praising a writer's good writing and providing encouragement when a writer is "blocked" is the heart of our approach. Thanks again, Rodger.

Our writing group makes Tuesdays the most stimulating day of the week for me. Judy Allen, our trailblazer, guides us through the "do's and don'ts" of self-publishing and has been head cheerleader in urging me to publish. Phil Blanton has been unfailingly kind when pointing out the logical flaws or other "implausibles" in my plot or writing. The story owes much to his detailed and thoughtful suggestions. Karen Keltz often prefaces her critiques by saying that her comments are only those of an English teacher. But I need and welcome her "English teacher" comments. Besides, her comments are often much more substantive than pointing out errors in grammar or phrasing. Sue Griffith is a knowledgeable editor and copyedited the entire manuscript. Thanks, Sue. Thanks also to Judy, Phil, and Karen for proofing the final manuscript as well. They saved me from an embarrassing number of errors of omission and commission.

Nancy has read and critiqued every chapter of this book several times and then read the completed book once again. She challenged me to flesh out my characters and to show not tell. More importantly, her love of words and good writing has pushed me to abandon my "darlings" and to search for the word or phrase that sparkles.

Lee Shore gave valuable feedback on several chapters and then read and commented on the entire book. Thanks, Lee.

Joan Cutuly, Elia Feely, and Sondra Kelly-Greene read and critiqued several early chapters. Their constructive feedback helped me say what needed to be said with fewer words.

The librarians and staff of the Astoria Library were always generous of their time and knowledge in helping me search the "Astoriana" section. Their collection of Sanborn fire insurance maps of the 1880's proved invaluable for they allowed me to construct accurate and detailed historical places for my characters to inhabit. It is reassuring to learn that these wonderful maps are still available through Environmental Data Resources, Inc.

For eight years, Helen Hill offered us space to meet along with a large pot of coffee at the Bay City Arts Center. Thank you, Helen and the Bay City Arts Center. Thanks to Sarah Beeler and Sara Charlton for making us feel welcome at our current meeting site in the Mark Hatfield room of the Tillamook County Library.

Liisa Penner, archivist of the Clatsop County Historical Society, and Jeffery Smith, curator, and of the Columbia River Maritime Museum, gave generously of their time in helping me select potential photos for the book cover. Eileen Houchin, assistant curator of the Columbia River Maritime Museum, went out of her way to ensure I received the photo of the Butterfly Fleet as quickly as possible.

Ten thousand thank yous to Dr. Yang Ji Yu, calligrapher, and Mar De Ycaza, graphics designer, for the gift of their art.

Finally, I thank my wife Elki for her patience and understanding over the years this book took to be born. She cheered me when I came down from my "lair" after having a good writing day and consoled me on those days when nothing worked. She is a lover of a good mystery and paid me the ultimate compliment one day while reading my novel and I interrupted her. She looked up, more than a little irritated, and said, "Don't bother me now–I need to see how this ends."

"The Astorian would deem it a blessed thing if to-morrow's sun did not shine upon a single Chinaman within the limits of its circulation.

But it is plain to any one, that to remove them this season would entail ruin, or at least enforce almost total cessation, on the cannery business for 1886."

Daily Morning Astorian, Feb. 11, 1886, p. 2.

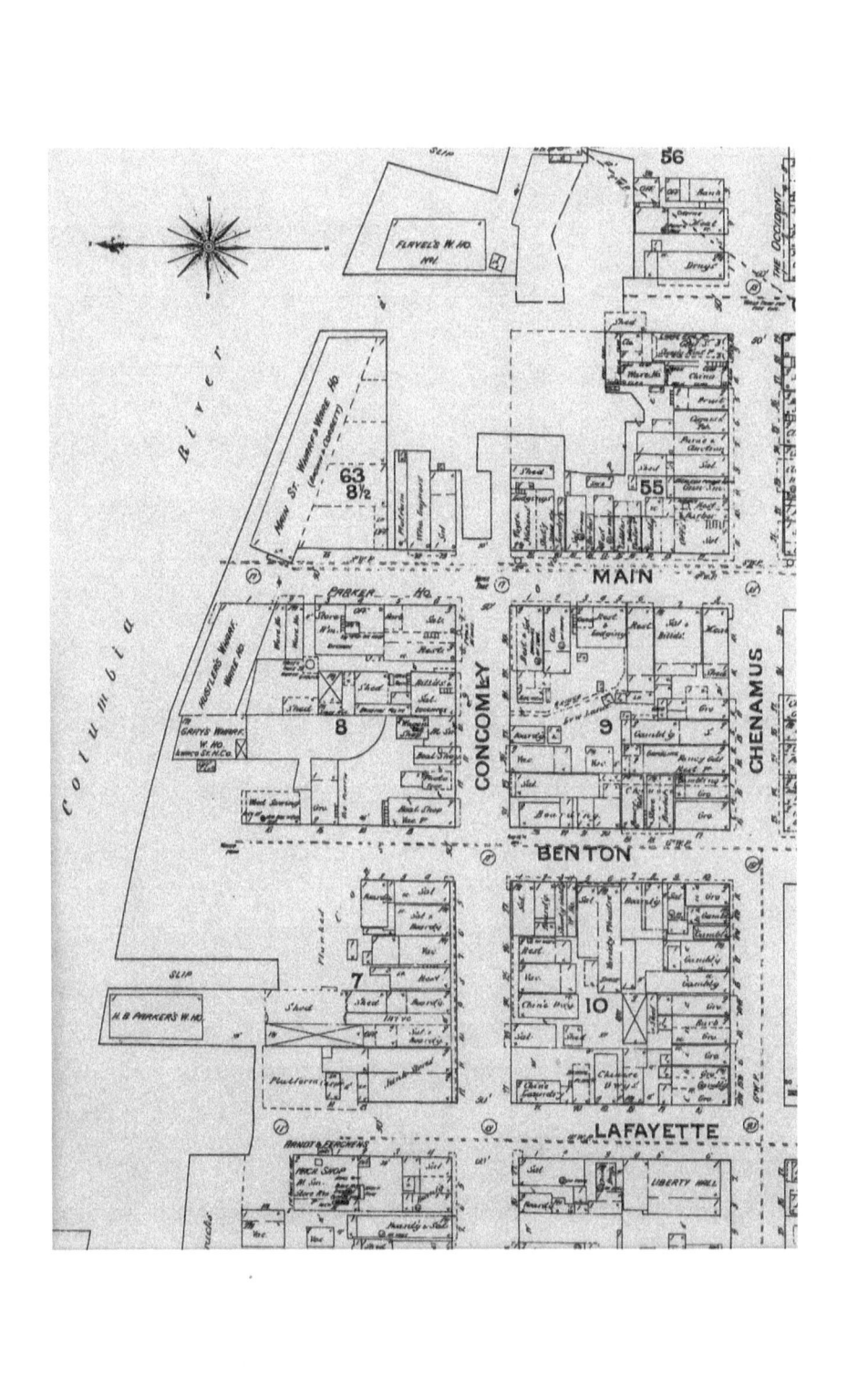

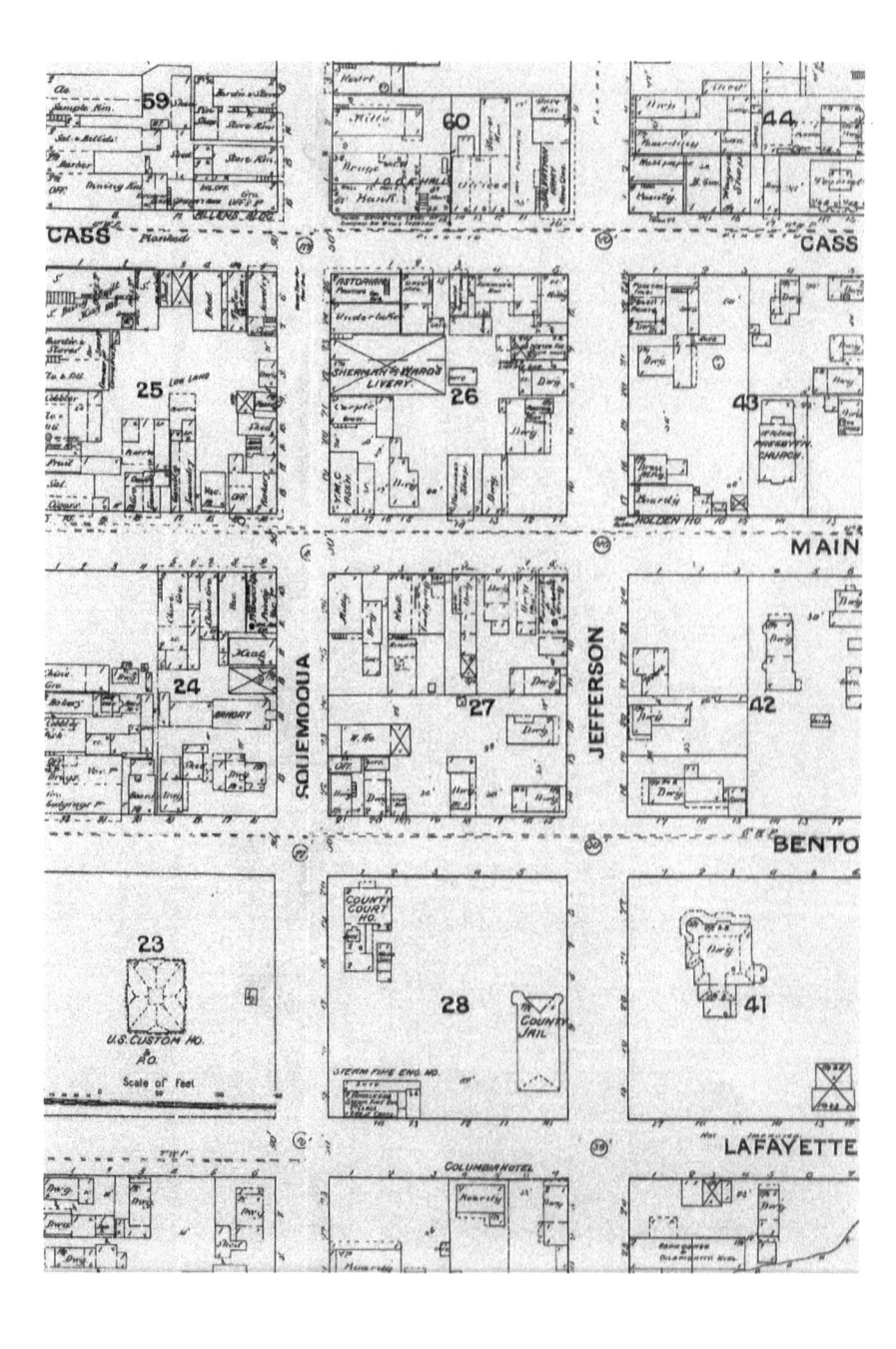

PROLOGUE

Seattle, Saturday, Feb 6, 1886

A loud noise interrupted Hop Li's dream. He woke up enough to hear rain pelting the tin roof of the laundry and the rattle of a loose drain spout. He turned over on his bed mat and pulled up his blanket, hoping to return to his dream. But then he heard a shout followed by a loud banging. He forced his eyes open and turned his head toward the front room where customers brought their dirty clothes. Another bang, this time accompanied by someone shaking the front door.

"Hey John-John! Open up," a voice shouted—a voice the god of thunder would be proud of.

Hop Li sat up and rubbed his eyes.

"Hey you, Chinky-chink. Open the door!" A different man mimicked the voice of a singsong girl. A fist pounded the door and a hand rattled the lock. Hop Li slipped on his pants. *Too early for customer*, he told himself. *Besides laundry is closed. Cousin Sing celebrates laundry's first year today, remember?*

Fists banged on the door.

Must be white devils with bellies full of whiskey wanting some fun.

He got up, lit a candle, and stumbled over a basket of clothes as he made his way to the counter.

Outside, torchlights illuminated the window shade and Hop Li saw shadows dart back and forth.

"Hop Li?" Sing whispered from halfway down the stairs.

"Yes. Do you keep Sunday hours now?"

Before Sing answered, the god of thunder roared, "Open the goddamm door or we'll break it down!"

Sing hollered back, "Go home, please! We not open!"

A second of silence followed Sing's words and then a brick crashed through the front window that read SING LAUNDRY in red and gold letters. The brick skittered across the floor and struck the counter wall. Hop Li jumped as a piece of glass hit his shin. Glass crunched under his bare feet when he took a step. Outside, men shouted and pushed against the door. Within seconds the door's lock and hinges gave way with a ripping sound. The door flew open and a group of white men burst into the room.

A gust of wind blew out Hop Li's candle. Two men carried torches and the flickering light played on the floor, walls, and faces of six white men, lighting up their noses and cheekbones while leaving their eyes in shadows. Water dripped from the their hats and slickers.

A man with a thick chest and broad shoulders stepped to the front. He glared at Hop Li from under bushy eyebrows. A nose broken more than once combined with a scar across his upper lip put a sneer on his face that his black beard couldn't hide.

The man pointed a finger at Sing. "Git down here."

Sing stepped down the stairs while clutching the railing with both hands. When Sing stood next to him, Hop Li said in Cantonese, "What do the demons want?"

"They must be drunk," Sing said.

"Shut yer mouths!" Blackbeard yelled.

The knot in Hop Li's stomach spread to his bowels. His mouth and throat were dry. He couldn't swallow.

Blackbeard had a gun stuck in his belt, as did the man next to him. The two men not carrying a torch held clubs. Blackbeard looked from Sing to Hop Li and settled on Hop Li as the one to speak to. He walked up to Hop Li and then said over his shoulder, "Big for a Chinaboy, ain' he?" He grinned but then his look turned hard. "I got something to say so listen close."

"All Chinee hafta leave Seattle. Today!" his voice boomed. "That means now, John!" He shoved his face close to Hop Li's.

Sing and Hop Li lowered their heads and stared at the floor.

"Pack only what ya can carry. We'll be back in an hour. One hour, Chinamen. Yer gonna take a little trip!" He laughed but it was more grunt than laugh. Blackbeard crossed to the open door and his men formed a circle around him.

Sing turned to Hop Li, eyes fixed on his cousin's face. "My laundry is here. I can not leave." He shook his head from side to side. "The grocer, Ah Yick, warned me that this time the *fan gway* (white ghosts) mean business. I thought him an old fool, hnnnn!"

"Maybe the talk is true, eh?" Hop Li's eyes searched his cousin's face.

Blackbeard wheeled round and faced the two Chinese. "Enough talkee-talkee. Git to packin'!"

"Why we must go?" Sing asked.

"Ya steal jobs, Chinaman! We've asked ya to go, agin and agin. But yer're mule stubborn, ain't ya? We're tired of waitin' for the law to do somethin.' Yer goin'! Git packin.'"

"Have customer. Must give laundry back," Sing said in a soft voice.

"Goddammit to hell!" Blackbeard shouted. He stepped between Sing and Hop Li, leaned over the counter, and grabbed the closest brown package. In one move, he cut the string with a hunting knife and shook the clothes out of the package. Men's white underwear and a starched white shirt spilled onto the floor. Only a few inches separated the white shirt from the man's boot, wet and caked with mud.

Sing kneeled down and reached for the white shirt. Blackbeard stepped on the shirt with his boot and, while staring at the kneeling Sing, wiped the shirt back and forth on the wet floor.

Sing moaned and covered his head with his arms.

Blackbeard grabbed Sing's queue and lifted him off the floor so that their noses almost touched.

"Still ain't listening, are ya John? Yer finished here!" Blackbeard spoke through his teeth, "Understand? Finished! Through! Done!" Blackbeard kicked his foot to the side and the starched shirt flew across the room, landing in a pool of water near the door. Blackbeard put his hand against Sing's chest and shoved. Sing flew backward, hit the counter, and slid to the floor.

Hop Li saw nothing but the face of the huge barbarian. With a yell, he charged and rammed his shoulder into the white man's chest.

Blackbeard stumbled backward, almost went down.

Shouts. Hop Li's arms were yanked behind him. Hop Li twisted his head, looking for the arms that held him. A club struck him in the ear and shoulder. He twisted his head to the side to avoid another blow from the upraised club but Blackbeard's fist found his mouth. Stunned, Hop Li sank to his knees. He tried to get up but a boot pushed him down and kept pushing until he lay flat on his back.

Hop Li ground his teeth, fighting the pain. *Be still. Do not let the dogs know they hurt you.* His lips were swollen and blood trickled from his nose and down the side of his head. He opened his right eye and saw Ti-sue, Sing's wife, on the stairs, a hand over her mouth. She ran down the stairs and knelt beside her husband. Hop Li turned and looked into the barbarian's face.

"Got some spit in him, don't he?" Blackbeard said to his men.

A short, thick-necked man with fat cheeks came up to Blackbeard. The man pushed his coat back and rested his hand on the butt of his gun. "Want me to finish him, Mr. Kephardt?"

Blackbeard looked at Sing and Ti-sue, smiled, then looked down at Hop Li. "Got a better idea." He straddled Hop Li with his legs, leaned down, and touched the tip of his knife to Hop Li's throat. "Grab his pig tail."

The fat-cheeked man yanked Hop Li's queue up. Blackbeard reached down, sawed through the yard-long queue, and then waved it over his head as his men whistled and catcalled.

Hop Li tasted bile and blood and wanted to vomit into the white dog's face.

Blackbeard stood up, tucked Hop Li's queue under his belt, and said, "Only yer pig tail this time. Next time…" He drew his knife across Hop Li's throat breaking the skin in places and drawing blood. Blackbeard turned and walked through the doorway followed by all but Fat Cheeks.

Ti-sue lit the overhead coal oil lamp then ran into the laundry room and came back with a wet towel and piece of cloth. She bent over Hop Li and wiped the blood from his lips and head with a soft touch.

A blast of wind lifted the window shade and it flapped up and down before Fat Cheeks raised it all the way up. Rain poured into the room. The white man took Sing's three-legged stool to a corner furthest from the broken window and sat down. He pulled out a plug of tobacco, cut off a chunk with a large knife, and then shoved the piece in his mouth. His cheeks stretched and twisted as his jaws struggled with the plug.

The sounds of glass shattering came from further up the street. Voices shouted and cheered. It sounded to Hop Li as if the *fan gway* were on holiday.

"Better—git—to—packin,'" The white man said and spat a stream of tobacco juice on the floor.

Sing dropped to his knees and let the underwear slide out of his arms. Ti-Sue squatted next to him, rested her hand on his shoulder, and whispered, "shu-shu." Hop Li lowered his eyes. Such touching between husband and wife was not for the eyes of others. "We must get started, eh?" Hop Li sneaked a look at the white man.

"Go, husband!" Ti-Sue pleaded. "Bring our baskets, the two large ones, then work things, but only what we can carry." She paused and glanced upstairs, "I will bring rice, tea, fruit, and jam." She put a finger over her lips and looked from Sing to Hop Li, "And no banging of tubs or pans, please. I do not know how but my A-haun still sleeps. I will not wake him until…until I must." Her eyes teared up and she covered her mouth with her hand.

The gray morning light showed broken glass scattered over half of the wet and muddy floor. Hop Li went back to his bed under the stairway, dressed, and packed his cigar box and two notebooks. The cigar box held brushes, an ink stone, and an ink stick—the tools of the scholar. One notebook was full, the other two-thirds full, with Chinese characters and their English words. He looked around a last time. Satisfied, he reached behind to coil his queue. His fingers touched the rough hair at the back of his head and he felt his bare neck. His queue—gone; the mark of an honorable man—gone. A sour taste filled his mouth and his hands shook as he pulled his bamboo hat down as far as it would go. He tightened the thong under his chin until it pinched.

"Hop Li?" Sing yelled.

Hop Li went back out front and sat down with his back against the counter. Ti-sue came down the stairs, arms loaded with clothes. Sing's flatirons, washboards, and wood washtubs were stacked on top of the counter. Piles of clothes overflowed one large washtub.

"Can I help, Cousin?" Hop Li asked.

Sing pointed to a full basket of clothes. "You can carry that one."

Hop Li pulled the basket off the counter and set it down beside him.

"The shrine!" Ti-sue tugged on Sing's sleeve.

"Aii!" Sing yelled and bolted up the stairs. He returned a minute later with a bright red tablet. The names of two of Sing's ancestors and five of his family members were written in gold letters on the red tablet. Sing folded the outside leaves onto the center leaf and wrapped the shrine in a piece of cloth. He laid the shrine on top of a bundle of letters, a photograph, and his immigration papers. He closed the suitcase and tied it with a piece of clothesline.

Hop Li's heart sank as he watched his cousin pack his shrine. He'd been given the weekend off from his work camp, some ten miles distant, to help celebrate Cousin Sing's first year of operation. He knew the white devils would never let him return to the camp to retrieve his shrine. *Maybe someone will see it, know it is mine, and...*he stopped himself...*fool, your shrine is lost.* He touched his lips with his tongue, tasted blood, and spit.

Upstairs, A-huan, the Sing's eight-month old baby, fussed. Ti-sue left off packing and came back in five minutes with A-haun in an oval basket. The suitcase and three baskets were full.

It is happening to us, what happened in Tacoma last year. And then Hop Li remembered the coal miners, almost thirty, slaughtered in their camp by white miners in Rock Springs, Wyoming Territory. *Why did I think Seattle would be safe from the white demons?*

He had less than three dollars in his pocket and he couldn't return to his camp to collect the pay due him for over four moons of work building dikes. But fishing season in Astoria started soon. At the end of last year, the Chinaboss told him he'd been promoted to number one butcher. So this year he would earn one dollar and fifty cents a day— fifty cents more than everyone but the Chinaboss. He had lost little of importance except his shrine. His heart ached for Cousin Sing and his family who had lost their laundry and home. And what of A-huan? Work hard, do not show your face, and swallow bitterness—that is all they could teach A-huan. True, but he no longer believed that lesson alone was enough to survive in *Gum Shan* (Gold Mountain).

Outside Hop Li heard horses and the creak of a wagon. Within seconds, a column of Chinese trudged past the broken window. A wagon with a dozen singsong girls and three older women, the wives of merchants, braked to a stop in front of the laundry to pick up Ti-sue and the baby.

Hop Li's throat tightened as the image of Blackbeard's face crept into his head. He closed his eyes and thought of his father's father, Chen Wei Chu, tortured and then killed by a bandit chief because he dared fight back. The face of *Guan Di*, God of War and Justice, replaced Blackbeard's face. One of the God's hands rested on the hilt of his sword, the other played with the long strands of his beard. *Guan Di's* head looked up, as if asking a question. Hop Li touched his lips with his tongue, tasted blood, and spit. *No matter the cost, I will fight him. Next time, the barbarian tastes his own blood.*

Fat Cheeks stood up. "Time to go."

1

Chinese men stood three deep around the Clouds of Heaven's gaming tables and stretched their necks to follow play or shout encouragement to the gamblers fortunate enough to have a seat. At 6' 4," Sheriff TJ Stone towered over the heads of the Chinese in the room, the tallest of whom wasn't over 5' 4." TJ caught the eye of a pock-faced dealer and the man held up his hand for TJ to wait. The dealer scattered two handfuls of polished, black stones in the middle of the table. He scooped them up, four at a time, with a smooth, easy motion. With only one stone left, he paused and paid off the two players with markers on number one. The dealer slid the losers' coins into a tray and made his way over to TJ.

"Yes? You play fan-tan, policeman?"

"Are you Wing?"

"Master Wing upstair." The man nodded at a stairway at the back of the room.

"I'm Sheriff Stone. He wanted to talk to me."

"Yes, yes." The dealer waved a young boy over and said a few words to him. The boy bowed, and then made his way towards the stairs, squirming between bodies, a minnow swimming through a school of fish.

"You wait," the dealer said and went back to his table.

TJ looked around for a spot less crowded but didn't see one. The window above the door of the saloon was shut and the room stunk of smoke, sweat, and a stale, acrid smell he couldn't put a name to. As a man moved to a table, he pushed against TJ. The man looked up and smiled by way of apology and sent a blast of wine-soaked breath into TJ's face.

Too many people in here—too godamm many. With each second, the stench grew stronger and the room smaller. Beads of sweat broke out on his forehead and a twinge of his closed-in feeling swept over him. Just after they married, he tried to tell Lucy Ann about his affliction, as he called it. At first, his head and chest got warm and then he broke out in a sweat. After that, he had a sense of not having enough room to move and the waves of nausea began, a desperate time and the instant he had to get outside. If he didn't or couldn't leave, he'd puke, start coughing and choking and, shortly after this, a dead certain feeling that he would suffocate overcame him. It hadn't gotten to the coughing-choking stage for years—he hadn't let it. The last time had been a Saturday night when his Dad came home liquored into meanness beyond understanding, beat him, and then locked him up in the coal cellar before going after Molly, his wife. Dad left the family for good a week later and they'd had no word from him since.

Three men pushed their way into the saloon. More bodies. Sweat trickled down the sides of his face. He pulled his watch out and glued his eyes to the minute hand. He'd give Wing another minute and then he'd have to go outside for open space and fresh air. Just then the boy called to him. TJ pushed his way through the bodies to the boy.

"Please, you come," the boy said and bowed.

At the top of the stairs, the boy turned into a long hallway. The rough plank wall on TJ's left had no openings, no pictures, nothing to relieve the starkness. On his right, he saw a row of crib-sized rooms each marked with a Chinese character. A curtain of threaded bamboo covered the opening of the first room and he caught a whiff of opium, a pungent, too sweet smell. In front of the next room, an old woman, bent over at close to a right angle, talked in a harsh voice to a pretty China girl with black hair that fell to her waist. The girl leaned against the door sill, arms folded across her chest, and stared above the old woman's head. As they approached, the old woman twisted her head around and glared at the boy but as she noticed TJ, her face softened. The boy spoke to the old woman who wrinkled her nose in annoyance and waved them on.

The lamps above the doors of the cribs were not lit and the only light came from a dirty window at the far end of the hallway. The harsh light, the long plank wall, the cribs, the opium stink, increased TJ's closed-in feeling. Sweat ran down his temples and he felt queasy. He told himself he wouldn't stay but five minutes.

The boy came to the end of the hall, looked back at TJ, and bowed. The contrast between the drab hallway and the doors to Wing's quarters couldn't have been greater and the sudden change shocked him. He stared at a pair of fire engine red doors shiny from countless coats of lacquer. The doors rivaled church doors in size with the handle of each door a large semi-circle of polished brass. The boy tapped with the back of his hand and the right door opened to reveal a gray-haired, thin man, a servant by the rough cloth of his clothes.

"Please," the servant said and motioned for TJ to wait in a narrow anteroom. A small oval window at one end of the anteroom admitted enough light for TJ to examine the flowers, birds, lizards and snakes cut out of the wood wall facing him. The wall extended from floor to ceiling and had a full moon opening, which led to another, larger room. He smelled incense, a flower scent, and heard running water behind him. He turned and saw a thin stream of water spurting out of the mouth of a stone lion into a basin. The sound soothed him and the tightness in his chest eased. He wiped the sweat off his forehead with his handkerchief and took a long, deep breath.

When he turned around, he found a Chinese man staring at him through rimless glasses. The man wore a red vest over a blue robe and a black silk skullcap with a red button, the dress of a wealthy merchant. The Chinaman's head and face, framed by the moon gate, seemed too large and too wide for his short stature. Though he was plump, the skin over his cheeks and throat was firm and smooth.

"Welcome, Sheriff. I am Wing Ti-sen." Wing stepped into the anteroom and extended his hand.

TJ shook his hand. "TJ Stone. Folks call me TJ."

Wing had a firm grip though his palm lacked calluses. TJ took another deep breath and ducked his head as he followed Wing through the moon gate. Everywhere he looked he saw things that said money: vases, statues, paintings, and tapestries. In a Portland rug store, TJ had seen a thick Persian carpet with a design in reds and purples just like the one he walked on. At the back of the room, a bust of a Chinese god smiled from an altar. A wood lattice formed the top of the altar and a canopy of red silk covered the lattice. Joss sticks burned in a slender vase underneath the bust of the god. The room smelled and felt like the insides of a church. He took his hat off.

"Please, Sheriff TJ, sit. Whiskey?" Wing sat down behind a black lacquered table.

"No thanks." TJ sat down facing Wing.

"Eh? No whiskey?" The thin eyebrows raised and then creased in a frown. Wing cocked his head. "Cigar? I have good cigar," the voice was pleasant, insistent.

"I'll take a cigar." TJ thought to counter the strange smells with a familiar one. Wing reached under the table and brought out what looked like a music box. He set the box in front of him and twisted the knob at the top. The music box turned, the notes of the Blue Danube played, and the doors of the six-sided box swung open. Cigars, an Upmann corona, a

Partagas double corona, a Hoyo de Monterrey Rothschild, and three European brands he hadn't smoked, stood upright behind their doors like soldiers in sentry boxes. TJ took a short Dutch cigar.

Wing poured tea into two small white cups and then slid a cup and saucer across the table to him. TJ lit his cigar, leaned back in his chair and waited. And waited. Just when TJ found the silence uncomfortable, Wing spoke.

"Sheriff TJ, you busy man. You come right away. Many thank you." Wing's fat lips smiled and his eyes turned into thin lines in the round face.

Again, TJ waited while Wing sipped tea. He wasn't sure what to do. Doc Hinkel, TJ's best friend and chess partner, said it wasn't polite in a meeting with a headman to get down to business right off—you had to act like you had all day. He no longer felt closed in but Wing had wasted enough of his time.

"Now then, Mr. Wing, what can I do for you?"

Wing set his cup down and folded his hands over his generous belly.

"This morning…ah…bad thing happen…very bad thing. Yes." He pursed his lips. "Brother Wah Fong robbed. Killed. In own store. Most unfortunate. Please, you find killer." Wing studied him over his glasses.

TJ sat up. A robbery and murder were serious, sure, and deserved his attention but the way Wing told him about it bothered him. The Chinee messenger that talked to Sketch, TJ's deputy, could have given Sketch the details. *Why does he want a sit-down with me?* Like most whites, TJ knew little of what went on in Chinatown. The richness, beauty, and strangeness of Wing's furnishings had caught him off guard, made him uncomfortable, and he felt more of an outsider than ever.

"You just come from his store, did you?" He studied Wing through his cigar smoke.

"No. Not been Fong store today."

"How the hell did you…I mean who told you about the robbery and murder?"

"Ah yes, yes. I see. Old Kao, Wah Fong helper, bring bad news. Most upset. I tell Kao lock door. Stay at store." Wing poured more tea into his cup.

"Good. That's the right thing to do." TJ ran his hand over his chin. "Wing, something' about what your tellin' me doesn't sound right."

The muscles around Wing's mouth tightened. "What not right, Sheriff TJ?"

"How come you're askin' me to look into this? This isn't how you do things here. We both know that." He challenged the impassive face with his stare.

"China Association think best. Maybe white man kill Fong. So we catch white man, what we do, eh? No. This not way. Bring much trouble for Wing, all Han brother, hnnnn!"

TJ nodded as Wing spoke but the words seemed too pat, as if rehearsed, and for that reason alone he didn't believe him. But then he remembered what happened in Washington Territory two months ago and guessed that the Chinese were testing the waters, to make sure the law would help when asked. "All right, I'll look into it."

"Ten thousand thank you, Sheriff TJ." The tightness around Wing's eyes left and the corners of his fat lips turned up in a smile.

"Guess I better go over to the store, see what this Kao has to say." TJ pushed his chair back but then stopped. "By the way, does Kao speak English?"

"Ah...not good, his English. But number one boy go with you. English very good."

"Thanks. By the way, you speak our lingo pretty good."

"Most kind, Sheriff TJ." He inclined his head a fraction, a slight bow. "But not so good, I think." Wing got up and motioned for TJ to follow him. The boy jumped to his feet as they came out. Wing put an arm around the boy's shoulders and pushed him forward. "This Sung Gee. Help you talk Kao. Come."

Wing led him and the boy through the hall and then downstairs. At the sight of Wing, the gamblers at the tables quieted, and men gave way, creating a path for Wing and his party to move through. Men inclined their head as Wing passed but he acknowledged no one. Wing led them across the street and onto the boardwalk before stopping.

"Again, ten thousand thank you, Sheriff TJ. You, Sung Gee, go now. Please, you need any thing, you ask Wing Ti-sen, eh?" he said and bowed.

As he crossed the street, Wing lifted his robe and sidestepped out of the way of a loaded beer wagon, forcing the teamster to pull up on the reins. The driver cursed and flicked his whip at the Chinaman. Wing ignored the man, taking quick, sure steps in his rubber soled, canvas-topped slippers. TJ had never seen a man that fat move so fast and so deftly. He'd misjudged Wing's physical prowess and his error in judgment reminded him of Doc's first rule in tactics: underestimate your opponent and you lose.

2

Sunday, April 4

A thin, middle-aged Chinese man squatted under an awning and rose as TJ and Sung Gee turned onto Main Street. The man walked with a limp, which caused his queue to bounce back and forth like a loose piece of rigging.

"Kao?" TJ asked as the man approached.

Kao bowed twice and then walked them back to Fong's grocery. A piece of wood nailed over a broken pane of glass in the store window showed how the killer gained entry. Though there were no shards of glass on the boardwalk, the inside of the store looked as if it had been hit by a storm: broken glass piled beside the door, tins of food shoved against the base of the counter, and a mound of rice swept up against a sack that had been slit open.

TJ waved Kao over. "Where's the body?"

Kao looked to Sung Gee who spoke to Kao and then translated. "Master Fong upstair. Room three. Kao show."

TJ looked down the narrow aisle toward the stairs and caught the outline of a bloody footprint, and another further on. "No. Stay put. Kao, let me have your slippers."

Kao removed both slippers and gave them to TJ who walked over to the first footprint and placed a slipper alongside it. It matched. He looked back at Kao.

"Aii-yee! No! No Kao!" Kao hurried up to TJ, grabbed the slippers out of his hand and crept towards the stairs in a crouch, eyes on the floor. Soon he paused, yelped, and pointed to a spot. When TJ came over, Kao placed his slipper next to the footprint and stood back. The pattern of this print looked similar to Kao's but dwarfed his.

"All right." TJ handed Kao his slippers and turned to Sung Gee. "Are any rooms upstairs locked?"

Kao listened then went over to the counter and brought back a key ring with four keys. "Four room upstair," Sung Gee said and held up a key. "This key, Master Fong room.

"Thanks." TJ put his hand on Sung Gee's shoulder. "I want you both to sit down and wait right here. And tell Kao not to touch anything. Understand?"

Sung Gee nodded.

TJ stepped around footprints as he went up and stopped at the top of the stairs to take in the layout of the rooms. The only light came from the open door of the room on his left. When his eyes adjusted to the darkened hall he saw that the room numbers were painted on the doors in English and Chinese. He stood facing rooms one and three, the doors of which were closed. Most of the bloody footprints were in front of room three but Kao would have stepped all over the prints as he went in and out of that room. Those prints wouldn't tell him a thing.

The footprints were thicker here than downstairs and easier to read. Three large ones pointed toward the room on his left. He stepped into the hall and stayed close to the wall as he followed the footprints into room two. He opened the door and, mindful of where he stepped, entered Fong's bedroom. He found a wood frame cot with a pillow, a crumpled blanket, Chinese clothes hanging in an open closet, and an Ohio safe with its door open.

He knelt down in front of the safe. The top shelf only held some official papers in Chinese but yellow tins, each the size of a cigar box, filled the bottom shelf. He counted fifteen tins in all and noted the U.S. custom stamp on each. He picked up a tin and pried the lid open with his fishing knife. The knife had nothing special to recommend it except that it had belonged to Tug, TJ's Swedish fishing partner and father in all but biology.

Twelve clay cups, each covered with a paper coated in paraffin, fit snugly inside the tin. He lifted the cover off a cup and sniffed the dark brown tar. Opium. No surprise in finding opium in Chinatown and the custom stamp meant the drug came in with the law's blessing. He studied the rest of the room. Nothing tipped over, clothes hung neatly in the closet, and an altar on a corner table told him there'd been no struggle here.

He retraced his steps out of Fong's room and unlocked the door to room one, directly across from Fong's. The furnishings were Spartan, no different than what could be found in any cheap hotel in town except for the Chinese flavor. Six opium pipes, bamboo with brass bowls, stood in a rack on a small table against the back wall. A fat-bellied, stone Buddha sat on a back corner shelf and, next to it, a tin cup full of sand held several fresh joss sticks. An extra wide bunk bed allowed two or three smokers to lie down on each bunk. Neither the top nor bottom bunks had pillows or bedclothes. The two fresh towels on the towel rack and a clean, dry washbasin told him the room wasn't occupied yesterday. He raised the shade over the back window and left the door open to allow more light into the hall.

He went into room four and like room one, it didn't look as if it had been occupied yesterday. He lifted the window shade and left the door open.

With the hallway better lit, he found another large print close to the stairwell. "What the hell..." he muttered and studied the print. This print pointed into room three. Like all footprints so far, it had been made with a smooth sole, like the rubber soled, canvas-topped slippers Chinese men wear when off work. He recalled that Wing wore such slippers as he darted across the street.

On the second step below the landing, he found another print, faint but clearly made by the large slipper, pointing upstairs. The pattern meant that the wearer of the large slipper had left room three and then returned. But why? Once the killer had taken the money in the safe and gone downstairs, why did he come back? He took out his notebook and wrote down what he'd learned so far: the yellow tins of opium in the safe, the two sets of footprints, one large, one small, and that both sets pointed into and away from room three. Just as he slipped the notebook back in his pocket, he heard angry voices downstairs.

He hurried downstairs, careful not to step on any footprints. Sung Gee and Kao stood with their arms out blocking the way of a skinny youth.

"I say no go upstair. He no listen," Sung Gee said.

Daines, a reporter for The Star, shook the lank of blonde hair off his forehead and grinned at TJ. "Mornin' TJ. Got word somethin' goin' on in Chinatown. These stupid Chinee won't let me pass."

TJ nodded his thanks to Sung Gee then reached up and grabbed Daines by the collar. He dragged the squirming youth out the door and ten yards down the boardwalk. "Don't ever bust in a place while I'm workin' it." He lifted the kid, not much over 110 pounds, off the ground so that they were eyeball to eyeball. "You hear me?"

Daines' eyes widened and his head bounced around like a cork in the river.

"Say it, son. Say you hear me."

Daines squeaked, "I hear you, sir. "

TJ lowered him and let go of his collar. "How'd you find me?"

"Deputy said you got called out to Wing's place. A Chinee at Wing's said you was here. Don't see nothin' wrong in comin' over." Daines jerked his hair out of his eyes, looked at the ground, then over TJ's head, and finally back to the ground. Daines couldn't keep his eyes from roaming for long.

"But you know different now, don't you?"

"Yes sir. But TJ, can't you least tell me somethin,' gimme rough idea what's goin' on? I don't hafta say where it come from."

"When I got somethin' to say, I'll let you know. And don't call me TJ. Now git—while you can."

Kao and the boy squatted in front of the counter and kept their eyes lowered as TJ stomped past. Upstairs, he stood with his hand on the doorknob of room three, steeling himself to open the door, his insides still churning at Daines. *Let it go. The kid was just doing his job. Go in this room all steamed up and you'll miss something.*

He slowed his breathing and thought of water lapping against the hull of the *Lucy Ann* on a calm day. In seconds, his anger melted and he opened the door. The room had been closed since Kao found the body, three hours at least, and the stench of blood, shit, and opium struck TJ with the force of a blow. His gorge came up. He backed into the hall and tied a handkerchief over his nose and mouth. After his stomach settled and his eyes adjusted to the dark, he took another deep breath and went in.

A crumpled body, one arm sticking out to the side, lay on the floor. He maneuvered around the body and crossed to the window, lifted the shade and opened the window. He saw no stairs or ladder from this floor to the alley below. Potholes and ruts in the alley were full of last night's rainwater and any recent buggy or carriage tracks would be washed out. The cool April air smelled fresh and sweet and he filled his lungs before turning back to death and its stink.

Fong's body lay on its side with the head twisted so that it faced up, eyes staring at the tasseled lamp overhead. The lower teeth had bit into the upper lip hard enough to draw blood and together with the wide staring eyes gave the face a look of surprise. One arm extended out at a right angle from the torso, the other bent back with the hand next to the head. The straw slippers on his feet and the white nightshirt, stained red-brown from the chest to the stomach, told him Fong was dressed for bed when killed. The nightshirt had been slit open and the grocer stabbed several times in the chest and twice in the gut. He knelt down and leaned over the body for a close look and saw slash wounds at the neck. The grocer was pot-bellied and had no calluses on his palms. Fong wouldn't have put up much of a fight against a worker, a man hardened by cannery or dike work.

He looked over the mess in the room. *One angry son of a bitch did this or else wanted to make sure he killed Fong…hold on, you're jumping the gun. Look the whole board over before you make your move like Doc says.*

He stood up, took out his notebook, and faced the back window. Starting on his left he noted: the extra wide bunk bed, a pair of wire-rimmed glasses on the floor with one lens broken, a brass candle holder next to the glasses, the top bunk bare, and the bottom bunk with a mat, two pillows, and a yellow bed cover with a brown stain the size of a dinner plate. He went over to the bunk, sniffed the stain and smelled blood.

In the right hand corner: a serving table tipped over, a scrunched up rug, and a teacup and saucer on the floor. The shelf above the rug and serving table held a statue of Buddha, a chipped teacup with stubs of burnt joss sticks, and several bamboo opium pipes in the rack next to Buddha. To his right, TJ saw a washstand, a towel rack with one towel, and a dry wash basin. He noted a blood splatter, maybe five feet long, against the wall next to washstand.

He turned to the front of the room and faced an open closet, empty of clothes. He finished his notes, put his notebook away, and bent down to pick up the broken glasses. As he did, his hand touched the four by four post that supported the corner of the bed extending into the room. His fingers came away sticky with half-dried blood. The post had been blackened over most of its length from years of opium smoke and made the blood hard to see.

He lifted the yellow bed cover and what looked like a rectangular vase tumbled out and landed at his feet. Only the object had no opening so it wasn't a vase. The white and blue porcelain object, about a foot long and three inches wide, had one concave side with smooth edges. He took the towel from the washstand and wrapped it around the object.

Behind the upturned serving table in the corner, he found a strange looking opium pipe, a long needle with a wood handle, and a clay bowl of opium like those in the yellow tins. He picked up the pipe and studied it. Its etched ivory stem magically turned into a lady's hand about three-fourths of the way down and supported a bowl made of ebony. The small opening in the bowl had a thin crust of opium. He guessed the pipe belonged to the wife or mistress of a rich merchant.

On a fresh page he made a list of things that didn't fit, seemed out of the ordinary, or bothered him. Who occupied room three over the weekend? Who smoked the ivory opium pipe? What was that porcelain vase-like thing? And why did the large prints lead away from and into room three? The amount of blood bothered him—so much spilled and in so many places. Why? The bloodstain on the bed cover along with the blood on the four by four post said Fong had been killed on or near the bed. But that didn't jibe with the blood splatter on the wall next to the washstand or the pool of blood next to the body.

If Fong had been smoking opium when attacked, he would have been killed on the bed and killed easily. With blood in so many places though, it appeared that he'd put up a long, tough fight. But the grocer looked like he'd lose a fight with TJ's grandmother. TJ stopped himself. He realized he didn't even know why Fong had come into this room. Why wasn't he killed in his bedroom?

His confusion grew with each question so he pocketed his notebook. As his eyes came to rest on the jumble of furniture and crockery in the corner, the corner took on the appearance of an altar where some hasty worshipper had left an offering to Buddha. He shook himself, made his way out of the room, and shut the door.

Downstairs, Kao sat on an overturned box of canned goods holding his head in his hands while Sung Gee squatted next to him. TJ unwrapped the porcelain object and held it up. "What's this?"

"For rest head when smoke pipe. Keep face cool," Sung Gee giggled, "but this one for rich man." He pointed over TJ's head at the counter. "That one for poor man." Six or seven headrests of the size and shape of the porcelain one but made of wood and leather sat on a shelf to the right of the counter.

TJ held the glasses up with the broken lens.

Kao nodded and Sung Gee said, "Yes. Master Fong."

"Did Kao sweep up the broken glass in front of the store?" TJ asked.

Sung Gee translated and Kao nodded yes.

"When did Kao find the body?" He studied Kao as the boy asked the question.

"Today, when come work, 7 o'clock."

"When did he last see his boss alive?"

"Saturday, when close store. Maybe 8 o'clock."

"All right. What did the killer take?"

"From downstair, maybe five dollar. From safe, not know." Sung Gee shrugged and looked to Kao who added a few words. "Kao say Master sometime keep thirty, forty dollar upstair."

"Anything else taken?"

"Knife. Fong family knife."

"Knife?"

Both men pointed to an empty glass case on the wall with the front panel broken. A scroll with Chinese characters hung next to the case.

"Is the knife valuable?"

"Ah, please, not understand."

"The knife, did it cost lots of money?"

Sung Gee and Kao talked back and forth, then the boy said, "Knife long time, Fong family. Handle pearl, also jade. Not for sell."

"All right. What did Kao do when he found his boss? And tell him not to leave anything out."

Sung Gee and Kao talked again.

"When Kao come, Master Fong not downstair. Kao think, Master sick. So Kao go upstair. Door open, Fong room. Safe open, money gone. Master on floor, number three room. Kao not know what do. But Kao remember headman—headman always have answer. Kao sweep floor, nail board on window, lock door, go Master Wing."

"Uh-huh." TJ made some notes then asked, "How come the killer didn't take the opium in the safe?"

Kao broke into a laugh as Sung Gee translated and started to speak before the boy finished. Sung Gee grinned as Kao continued speaking and then told TJ, "Opium all same like money. Much money in safe. Why robber no steal, eh? Robber stupid, like ox, Kao say."

"Did Kao move things around upstairs?"

Kao crossed his arms over his chest and looked at the door after Sung Gee translated.

TJ waited and then said, "The bed cover had a big blood stain on it. I need to know if he moved the body off that bed."

Kao mumbled his answer.

"When Kao come in, Wah Fong face on floor, like this." Sung Gee placed his hand on the floor, palm down.

TJ nodded, "Go on."

"Kao turn Master over. Maybe Master live? No, Master dead. Bad death bring bad luck. Much bad luck. So Wah Fong spirit angry. Kao much afraid. He sorry."

"That's all right. It's what anyone would have done. Did he take anything from the room?"

Kao's face stiffened as he listened to Sung Gee. He shouted his answer, "No. Bad man steal. No Kao." Sung Gee's volume matched Kao's.

"Tell him to calm down. I'm not accusing him of anything." He looked from Sung Gee to Kao. "Not yet anyways."

"Who rented room three this weekend?"

Kao and Sung Gee talked at length before Sung Gee turned to TJ.

"Not know. Friday, Master Fong very happy. Tell Kao clean all room. So Kao think rich man come, rent all room. But Kao see no people." Sung Gee paused then added, "Maybe robber hide in room after Kao clean, yes?"

TJ looked up from taking notes. "Is that what he said?"

Sung Gee smiled and said, "No. I ask."

"Don't do that, Sung Gee. Just tell me what Kao says."

Sung Gee nodded and then lowered his head.

TJ tried thinking of Kao as the killer but couldn't make it work. Kao seemed upset by Fong's death, had called attention to Fong's knife, and admitted moving the body. Kao acted guilty when TJ asked if he'd taken anything so maybe he helped himself to a tin or two of opium but he didn't come across as a killer.

"All right, Kao you can go. But stay close to home so we can talk again. Understand?"

Sung Gee translated. Kao bowed and then limped out.

After Kao left, TJ asked Sung Gee, "You know where the courthouse is?"

The boy nodded.

"Well, my office is at the back. It's the only one open." He pulled a nickel out of his pocket. "My deputy's name is Sketch. I want you to bring Sketch back here with the buckboard." TJ held up the nickel. "This is yours if you come back in twenty minutes. Think you can do that?"

Sung Gee's face lit up at the sight of the nickel. "Yes. Bring Master Sketch. Bring buckboard. Come back twenty minute." He bolted out of the store.

After Sung Gee left, TJ sat down and thought over what he'd learned. The large footprints were as large as his own, size 13, and meant they belonged to a large Chinaman or at least one with big feet. And if the killer were as big as his footprints suggest, killing the grocer should have been easy and any blood found would be close to where he was killed. Instead, blood was all over the room. But the main question nagging him was why Fong left his bedroom to go into room three.

In less than twenty minutes, Sketch and Sung Gee rode up in the buckboard. Sketch, a skinny six footer with a full head of stringy blond hair was twenty-six. Unlike TJ, who knew only the life of a fisherman before he became sheriff, Sketch had drifted from job to job much like a butterfly flitting from flower to flower. Before Astoria, he eked out drink money on the streets of Portland doing quick studies in charcoal. His drinking buddies had christened him Sketch and the name stuck.

TJ thanked the boy, tossed him the nickel, and sent him on his way. TJ gave Sketch a rough outline of what Kao told him and then they went upstairs. TJ pointed out the tins of opium in the safe and made sure Sketch saw the large footprints going in both directions.

Each covered his mouth and nose with a handkerchief before going into room three. TJ waited while Sketch looked over the room, the body, and saw the blood on the walls, bed cover, and floor. Fong's twisted body lay as before with one arm out to the side. After ten minutes, Sketch told TJ he'd seen enough and they covered the body with the bedspread and picked it up. But before they had taken two steps, Sketch shouted, "Hold on, boss." He lowered Fong's legs and then picked up something from the floor.

"Lookee here." He held up a small jewel, possibly a diamond.

"Good man." TJ took the gem and put it in the coin pocket of his Levi's.

"Think it's the real thing?"

"Damm if I know. We'll take it by Zuckerman's when we get time."

A group of Chinese men in front of the store grew quiet as the lawmen carried Fong's body through the doorway. TJ and Sketch laid the body in the buckboard with Fong's stiff arm pointing up to heaven as if calling for help. TJ turned the body so that the arm lay flat and Sketch covered it with the bedspread.

As soon as they were underway, TJ asked, "All right, what's your thinkin,' Sketch?"

"Well, seems simple enough. Fong woke up and surprised a big Chinee thievin' him. The sneak used Fong's own knife on him. Put up a good fight for a little guy, poor fella. Now, Fong had him a gun, could be a different story." Sketch grinned at TJ.

"Un-huh." TJ stared up Jefferson Street and listened to the hollow clump of the mare's hooves on the planked street.

"Somethin' botherin' you, Boss?"

"Yeah. Couple things. That opium for one. How come the killer didn't take it?"

"Well, Fong gets to screamin' his head off, so the killer gets scared, gets to thinkin' someone is gonna hear Fong, so he grabs the money 'cause it's easy to carry and hightails it. Only reason to leave them tins behind, seems like."

"What about breakin' into the store? Killer had to break a window in the front door, rummage around lookin' for the money drawer, break the glass in the case to get that knife, and God knows what else. How come Fong didn't come downstairs to see who's makin' all that racket? He's killed upstairs. Why?"

"Maybe he's a heavy sleeper, like me."

"Well, but we found him in room three, not his bedroom. Something woke him and he went into that room. Why?"

Instead of answering, Sketch spat a brown stream of tobacco juice into the street and slapped the reins on the rump of the mare.

At first, TJ's thoughts had been the same as Sketch's—a burglary gone sour. He'd kept from Sketch the way Wing, the headman, had treated him and now he had an idea of how the crime looked to someone who came at it fresh. It's how Wing wants me to see it, too, he thought. The headman had treated him to a high-priced cigar and asked him to look into a Chinee crime as if it were an ordinary request. If a Chinee killed Fong, as TJ suspected, Wing and his boys had a better chance of tracking him down than he did. Wing was using him but he had no idea why.

When they got to the morgue at St. Mary's, they found TJ's friend and the town coroner, Doc Hinkel, had come and gone. TJ filled in the time of delivery, name, race, age, and occupation of the deceased and then initialed the form.

He turned to Sketch. "Let's grab a bite at Sirpia's. We'll talk things over while we eat."

"Damm, Boss, almost forgot. This fella and his daughter is waitin' for us back at the office. Told him I couldn't say how long we'd be. But he says they'd wait."

"What fella? How come you're just now tellin' me?" He put his leg on the step and hoisted himself on to the buckboard.

"Well, this here murder pushed everythin' else outta my head."

"Is it important?"

"Seems so. They's upset, particular the girl." Sketch picked up the reins.

"Shit. Way this day's goin,' it's trouble. Guess lunch will have to wait."

3

Sunday, April 4

A girl in her teens sat on the bench beside the door of the sheriff's office while a man in his early forties paced back and forth. The man broke off pacing and walked up to meet the lawmen.

"You in charge?" he asked TJ.

"Yes sir." TJ studied him. The thin mustache, pince-nez glasses, and the worn, three piece blue suit said he worked inside, an office manager or bookkeeper maybe. The freckle-faced girl twisted a hanky in her hands and kept her eyes on the floor.

"She hasn't returned...we looked all over...can't find her..." the man said as he squeezed his hands together.

"Why don't we go into my office? Sketch, see if you can round up another chair." TJ followed father and daughter into the office, and sat down behind his desk. He took out a cigar, an El Gusto, but didn't light it.

Sketch dragged in a chair then busied himself getting a fire going in the potbelly stove. The man sat down and rocked back and forth while the girl sat on the edge of her chair.

"Sketch will have coffee in a minute."

"Please...no. I mean there's no time...I mean..." the man shook his head in frustration.

TJ reached over his desk and extended his hand. "Sheriff TJ Stone. I've seen you around town but..."

"Yes. Sorry. Hermanson. Olney Hermanson. We live out past Uppertown." He shook TJ's hand, relieved to get something cleared up.

"Sketch, why don't you take the buckboard back while I talk to these folks?"

Sketch nodded and left.

"Now then, how can I help?"

"We have...had...a guest staying over. But she hasn't come back. She's gone missing." He stared at TJ, eyes pleading, as if the sheriff could read his mind and answer the questions tormenting him. "She planned to be back at our house in time for Sunday service. At least, that's what my daughter here told us." Hermanson nodded towards the girl. "We only just learned of this…this plot the girls hatched up this morning." Hermanson's face flushed. He turned in his chair and looked at his daughter. "Your mother is beside herself…how could you…? Her folks! What in God's name will we tell the Thurgoods? I don't know what possessed you…I just…"

TJ held up his hand, stopping the father. Hermanson folded his arms across his chest and looked above TJ's head where a photograph of President Grover Cleveland stared at the world with the entitled look of a man in charge. The girl's chest heaved and tears spilled down her cheeks. She swiped her eyes with the back of her hands, which only increased her frustration. She cried without stint.

TJ looked at the ceiling and waited for a break between sobs and then said, "And your name is…?"

"Annika."

"Annika. Pretty name. Now, go on and cry all you want, Annika, we're in no hurry." He waited for her to catch her breath again and then asked, "Why don't you start by tellin' me everything that happened on…when was it?" He lifted a pencil out of the coffee cup with the broken handle, took out his notebook, and turned to a fresh page. He smiled and leaned back in his swivel chair, all the time in the world to listen.

Annika wiped her eyes and blew her nose. "Saturday. Yesterday morning. That's when it all started." Her words came out between breaths.

"All right, Annika, you doing fine. Now what started on Saturday morning?"

"I'm getting married in June. I asked Janey to come and stay over so we could plan my wedding. Janey is my best friend…she's ever so clever…knows the latest fashions… the right way to do just any old thing."

He held up his pencil. "And Janey's last name is?"

"Thurgood. Janey and me, we went to grammar school together, first two years at McClure too. Her dad lost the store three years ago in the big fire. They moved to Portland." She blew her nose again.

"About Saturday morning?" he asked.

"That's when Janey told me about…about the meeting. 'It's ever so important,' she said. At first I said no, I wouldn't do it. But she's so willful when her mind is set." She twisted one end of the hanky around a finger.

"What did she ask you to do?"

"To fib for her."

"Why?"

"So she could meet this man. She just had to, she said."

"His name?"

"She never said."

"And why was she meetin' this man?"

"I don't know," she said in a soft voice.

"She asked you to lie for her and didn't tell you why?"

"No," she whispered.

"I'm sorry. I didn't hear that."

"No! She never told me a thing about him. Not one thing!" She folded her arms under her chest and shoved her chin out.

"Let's back up a bit, Annika. Just what did you and Janey tell your folks?"

Annika glanced at her father who kept his eyes on Grover Cleveland. "Well, it was all Janey's idea—I only did it 'cause she's my best friend. We go to Scandinavian Lutheran, over on the county road near Abernathy. Janey promised she'd be back in time for church. I never for a minute thought she wouldn't come. I didn't, Dad. Honest." She looked at her father and her eyes welled with tears.

"All right, I believe you, Annika. Now, what exactly did you tell your folks?"

"I told them Janey wanted to visit the Niemis. Niemis and Thurgoods are old friends. So I'd said I'd drive Janey there in our buggy. When I came back without her, I told Mom that the Niemis asked her to stay over, you know, so they could have a proper visit. I said Mr. Niemi was to drive Janey to our house next morning in time for church." She sighed and glanced at her father before continuing. "Well, it's true what I said about Janey being back in time for service. I didn't really know who would drive her back. I didn't think to ask—I just thought it'd be her fella, the one she met. There. I've told you everything." She crossed her arms under her chest and leaned back in her chair.

"You or the Missus didn't question any of this Mr. Hermanson?"

"No, Sheriff, why should we?" Hermanson shoved his chin out and crossed his arms over his chest just like his daughter. "Annika never did anything like this before...I just...no, we never dreamed..." he waved an arm in the air and shook his head.

TJ wrote down what Annika said and then asked, "Where did you take Janey?"

"The post office. She asked me not to wait around so I didn't. I never did see her meet any man. Honest." She fixed TJ with a defiant look.

"What time did you get to the post office?"

"About four, maybe a little after."

"All right, we're almost done. Tell me what Janey looks like."

She sat up and her face softened. "Well, she's eighteen same as me but she's tall and has thick blond hair. Wears it up, most times anyway. And she has the bluest eyes."

"You recall what she wore?"

"'Course I do. See, Janey's mom is a seamstress, makes all her outfits. This one's a seaside costume. Wool dress, cobalt blue. The pleats fall from the waist and have red cotton trim. Her Russian leather belt is fiery red, and matches her walking boots. She took her favorite straw bonnet, red with parrot and ostrich feathers. Wore her suede gloves, the red ones, of course. What else? Oh yes, her red parasol, one with the pink ribbons tied around the handle." She sighed and looked at TJ. "Oh Sheriff, Janey should be on stage. Every boy at McClure was in love with her." Her lips parted in a smile and the face of the snub-nosed girl brightened. She became, if not pretty, at least pleasing to look upon.

"You want to add anything, Mr. Hermanson?"

"Well, Jane is a lovely girl, no doubt about it, and tall, maybe 5' 7." She is buxom and small-waisted…but, and I'm sorry to have to say this, Sheriff, she's a terrible flirt. The way she carries on can only lead to trouble, I'm afraid. Why, even with older gentlemen she…well, I won't say more. Then there's that foolishness with the theater and wanting to be an actress. Not healthy, the way those people live, not moral either." Hermanson's eyes burned into his daughter's.

TJ read back to them what he'd written. "A beautiful girl, about eighteen, tall, with a full figure, blond hair and blue eyes. She wore a blue and red dress with a red straw hat and carried a red parasol. Uh-huh. Should be plenty of folks take note of a girl like that." He stood up.

Annika leaned forward, hands clutching the arms of her chair. "She's coming back. She has to." Her eyes teared up again.

TJ looked up at the school clock on the wall at the back of the office. "Let's see, it's only a little past two o'clock. Still early. Lots of reasons why she might be late. Probably be on your doorstep before supper."

Hermanson got to his feet. "I've got friends in town. We can round up a search party."

"No, not right now, Mr. Hermanson, but thanks. My deputies and I will get a search goin' first thing. By the way, are you stayin' in town?"

"Yes. We'll be at the Niemis." Hermanson wrote down the address and gave it to him.

TJ glanced at the address and then said, "You'll hear from me in two hours time—sooner if I have news."

Hermanson nodded.

TJ put his arm around Hermanson's shoulders and whispered in his ear as they stepped into the hallway, "Best not to worry Jane's folks for the time being. Maybe no need for it."

Five minutes after they left, Sketch came in. "What'd they want?"

"That young lady's friend is missin,' last seen Saturday afternoon."

"You want me to round up volunteers?

TJ picked up his cigar and lit it. "Nope. You, me, and a few city boys can sniff around for a while. If she doesn't turn up in a few hours, we'll call in volunteers. But let's get Big Jim."

"He's gone up to Spokane for two weeks. Got time off for his Mom's funeral. Remember?"

"Ah shit. I forgot." He put his hat on and squared it off. "Grab your hat, Sketch. We got work to do and we're runnin' out of day."

At the city police station, TJ and the Sergeant on duty decided that TJ and his deputies would take everything east of Main Street and the city police everything west. They agreed to stop by the hotels, livery stables and boarding houses first and if she wasn't found by Monday, they'd get volunteers to search the woods and trails south of town including those that led down to Young's Bay.

Both TJ and the sergeant skirted around another possibility. Some girls found their way to sporting houses like the one run by TJ's friend Boss Bessie. TJ didn't expect Jane to turn up in a brothel—she had people in town that cared for her—but if they didn't find her tonight, they'd search Swilltown's forty or so sporting houses tomorrow.

By 9:00 o'clock that night they still had nothing, no sightings of Jane Thurgood since the one at the post office. TJ made a final check with the city police desk but they hadn't turned up anything. He and Sketch sat at the counter of Sirpia's cafe with what turned out to be their dinner that night, coffee and a slice of blackberry pie.

"We covered all the decent places, Boss. She's as good lookin' as Hermanson says, somebody shoulda seen her."

"Yeah. It bothers me, too."

"Bet she run off with her fella."

"If she did that, she'd leave a note for Annika."

"Seems like. Why else she missin' then?"

"Only reasons I can think of are ones I'd don't like."

He and Sketch parted and on the walk back to his boardinghouse, he reflected on the cussedness of how bad things piled up. He had a murder, a missing girl, and a fishermen's strike on his hands. Plus, he was short a deputy. It seemed to him that several days had passed since Wing called him and broke up his chess game with Doc. *Damm, that was just this morning.*

4

Monday, April 5

TJ got the fire started and then opened the hall window part way so that if Plato, his lop-eared tom, decided to show up he'd have a way in. The diamond Sketch found under Fong had turned out to be real so he sealed it in an envelope and stuck it in the office safe, a National so old the tracery around the handle had worn off. He sat down, lit an El Gusto, and made a list of places to search. Before he finished, Olney Hermanson poked his head in the doorway.

"Saw your light, Sheriff. Any news?" The circles under his eyes told TJ he hadn't slept last night.

"Still nothin.' Sorry."

"I've got six men at my house ready to help. What can we do?"

"I'm just plannin' the day. Come in and have a seat."

Hermanson sat down, his right leg jerked up and down; a piston in an engine going full out. Neither the city police nor TJ's team had enough men to do a thorough search of the hills above town. He told Hermanson the territory he wanted searched and then added, "Now, if anyone finds her body..."

Hermanson opened his mouth to speak but TJ put his hand up stopping him.

"Listen, I'm not sayin' she's dead, it's still early, but I got to think of the possibles, understand?" He looked at Hermanson hard.

"Yes, I suppose so."

"So in case you or your men come across her body, don't move it nor touch a thing near it. Next, get word to me or another lawman on the double."

"Yes, of course, Sheriff. But is this really necessary, at this stage of things I mean?"

TJ nodded.

"Sheriff, I suppose I should tell you. After you came by last night with no word of Jane, I sent a telegram to the Thurgoods. I made something up, said she might have eloped. If it'd been my daughter I'd want to know that she was missing right away."

"That's all right. I aimed to telegram them this mornin' anyway."

Hermanson rose. "What if you find her? How will I know?"

"Search headquarters is the city police desk. Send a man back there every two hours to check in and let them know where you are." He took a few puffs on his cigar. "And make damm sure your men keep in sight of each other. I don't want another search on my hands."

Hermanson nodded and left.

TJ's crew of Sketch and two volunteers searched the brothels and dance halls in the east side of town while the city police did the same on the west side. He stopped by the Paradiso and told Boss Bessie what Jane looked like.

"A girl looks like you say, why, news of her woulda gone up and down the waterfront faster than you could turn around." Bessie chuckled and shook her head. "She ain't here and she ain't in any sporting house in town either. Betcha five bucks on that, honey."

One o'clock and still no news. With the knot in his stomach growing by the minute, TJ stopped in the last of the seaman's boardinghouses on Water Street. When he told two old salts what she looked like and how she dressed, they looked at him wide-eyed in disbelief. When they realized he was serious, they broke out laughing. Wouldn't find a common whore in a dump like this, they said, let alone a girl like the one he described. He left the seaman's boardinghouse with his guts telling him something his head didn't want to hear.

A city policeman ran up and told him Jane's folks had arrived from Portland and waited for him at his office. When TJ ran for sheriff two years ago, no one had warned him that delivering bad news was part of his job. He dreaded telling a woman that the river had taken her husband or, worse, that he'd been murdered. But he corrected himself. He never used the word murdered, at least at first. The word dead was pain enough, already more than pain enough.

The owner of Big City cigars stood in his doorway and proclaimed it a fine day as TJ passed but TJ didn't respond and continued to walk slowly with his eyes down as if going to a funeral. He thought to delay his arrival and give himself time to come up with a comforting phrase or two. He'd tell them it's only been a day and a half, that there were still places to search. But these phrases sounded bleak to him and didn't promise to be of much comfort to parents consumed with anxiety. By the time he reached the courthouse steps, he still hadn't found any words or phrases that might give hope to a worried parent.

A couple sat with their backs to the stove, staring at a large, well-dressed man as he paced the floor of the sheriff's office. The man walked up and grabbed TJ's hand.

"Good afternoon, Sheriff. I'm Paul Purcell, Portland Police Commissioner, and these are Jane's parents, Thomas and Martha Thurgood." Purcell's smile showed a mouthful of healthy teeth framed by a mutton chop beard. He held his hand chest high and pushed TJ's hand down and back as they shook hands. The office smelled of lime cologne rather than of stale cigar, its usual odor, and it surprised TJ to discover that it came from Purcell, not Martha Thurgood.

Thomas Thurgood's suit coat showed the crease marks of last's night sleep in the economy class of a steamer. The wispy long hairs that looked like they usually covered his bald spot stuck out at an odd angle from the left side of his head. Mrs. Thurgood dressed in plain dark clothes and wore no bustle. She sat with her bonnet in her lap and offered him a weary smile in response to his greeting.

"You've found her—our Jane. Yes?" Her voice trembled.

"No ma'am, I'm sorry to say we haven't." Every possible evil to her daughter must have played itself over and over in her mind during the six-hour trip down the Columbia. TJ hated that he couldn't give her a scrap of good news. "You folks been to the city police? Could be…"

Purcell waved his hand, interrupting him. "We just came from there, Sheriff. They've nothing to report."

Mrs. Thurgood bit her lip and stifled a cry. "O dear God, Thomas where is she? Why doesn't anyone know anything?"

"They're doing all they can, Martha. I'm sure…"

"All they can? What good is that? All they can. I want answers. I want my girl."

"Martha please, this isn't the time…"

"Don't you shush me, Thomas Averill. I didn't want her to go without a companion—those steamers are full of riffraff—but no, you gave in. Like always. Oh, I know better—why didn't I insist?" She put a hand over her mouth, lowered her head, and sobbed.

Mr. Thurgood looked at his hands. Purcell turned around and stared at the school clock on the back wall. Mrs. Thurgood's sobbing and the tick of the clock were the only sounds in the crowded office for a time.

Purcell rested his hand on Thurgood's shoulder. "Thomas, why don't you take Martha back to the Niemis. I need to talk to Sheriff Stone. I'll come by shortly and tell you what I've learned."

TJ gave Purcell a hard stare. The man didn't have the right to order people around in his office but since the Thurgoods were not up to answering questions, he let it pass.

"Whatever you think best, Mr. Purcell," Thomas said. He reached for his wife's hand but she snatched it away and stood up without his help. The Thurgoods hurried out without a goodbye.

If TJ limited his gaze to Purcell's face he'd say the man looked like a teacher, maybe a professor, with his wide forehead, intense gaze, and thick brown hair that stuck out around large ears. Undersized oval glasses heightened his studious look. But his body, about six feet and 220 pounds, looked powerful and belonged to a man who earned his pay with his back rather than his mind. His clothes, however, belonged neither to professor nor dockhand but to a dandy. A brown suit with black stripes made the yellow rose in his buttonhole and his yellow tie stand out like sunflowers in a field of mud. On top of the showboat clothes, he carried a walking stick with a silver handle. TJ had seen adverts for walking sticks in a fancy catalog but never thought a sane man would let himself be seen in public with one. Astoria's mayor, Foster Dailey, played the dandy too but no one took much notice of Dailey. In contrast to Dailey, Purcell's presence filled TJ's office and said listen to me.

"So Mr. Purcell what's your interest in Jane Thurgood?"

"She works for my law firm in Portland. When Jane's father gave me the news, I decided to come along and offer my services. Seemed the least I could do." He pulled a chair towards him and sat down.

"Uh-huh. How long she work for you?"

"Oh, it must be close to three months now. But why do you ask?"

"Did she talk to you about personal things?"

"What are you getting at, Sheriff?"

"Did she have a fella, you know, someone she walked out with?"

"Oh, I see. Well, she's a beautiful girl and I'm sure she had a wagon full of admirers." He tapped his palm with his walking stick. "But wait just a minute. I do remember her mentioning a young man she seemed keen on...let's see...no, I can't come up with his name. Sorry." He paused to wipe his brow with a monogrammed handkerchief. "But let's get back to the search, Sheriff. The sergeant at the police station told us next to nothing. What have you learned?"

"Well, her friend, Annika, left Jane at the post office around four o'clock Saturday to meet some man. We don't know where she went or the man's name or what he looks like or, come to think of it, whether she even met him."

"Hmm...and just where have you looked?"

"The usual—hotels, the two steamship offices, and the livery stables. We've still got half the sportin' houses in Swilltown to check but so far no luck. She's gone up in smoke just like the girl in a magic show."

"I see. You haven't discovered much then, have you?" Purcell pushed his glasses up on his nose and grinned.

"Could be that's all there is to discover—for now." TJ looked hard at the man. "If you want to help, we can always use another pair of eyes."

"Of course, I'd be happy to assist any way I can. However, as I told you, I'm Police Commissioner and have some experience in making things happen. No offense, Stone, but you've just admitted that in, what's it been now...thirty some hours...you haven't learned one new thing." He pushed his chair back and stood up. "And now you've got your men traipsing through saloons and brothels." He shook his head slowly from side to side. "Good God, Stone. In spite of her youth, Jane understands the ways of the world. She'd never set foot in one of those places. Never. You and the chief need more than another pair of eyes—you need someone who knows Jane Thurgood. And it wouldn't hurt if he had some imagination as well."

TJ leaned back in his swivel chair. "And you're that someone?"

"I know the chief. Mike Connelly has his good points but I'm afraid imagination isn't one of them."

"Imagination? How's that come into play?"

Purcell laughed. "Humor me a minute, Sheriff. Let's start with things that don't require imagination. You've searched the docks and wharves along the waterfront, yes?"

TJ nodded.

"And covered the ground and hills from Smith's Point to Tongue Point and over to Young's Bay?"

"It's gettin' done."

"That takes care of the obvious. How about Chinatown?"

"Chinatown? Why in hell would she go there? Nothing but gamblin' dives, stores, and washhouses in Chinatown." TJ cocked his head and studied Purcell.

"Oh, she wouldn't. Not on her own, that is. But suppose that while walking through Chinatown, a Chinee grabbed her and dragged her into his den? It's been known to happen. And the Thurgood girl is white, young and beautiful—an irresistible temptation to a Celestial. Why, she could be in some dive right now, suffering repeated outrages at the hands of a fiend or, God forbid, a gang of them. Did you consider that possibility?"

"Can't say I have."

"You're telling me things like that don't happen here?"

"Look here, Purcell, I don't know what goes on in Portland but in this town, the only calls I get about Chinatown are for disturbin' the peace. Some Chinee celebratin' with firecrackers and drums wakes his white neighbor, happens regular on Chinee New Year...well, hold on just a minute...last Saturday night, a Chinee grocer got himself robbed and murdered. But that is way out of ordinary. In fact, it's the only time I've had such a call. So if some fool is snatchin' white women off the street I'd hear about it damm quick."

"I'm relieved to hear that. However, the murder you just mentioned contradicts your claim of a harmless Chinatown, Stone. It seems only prudent that you search every Oriental pesthole in town and put to rest any suspicions that she is being held in one." He studied TJ over the top of his glasses.

TJ waited a second or two before he said, "I got things need doin,' Purcell. If you still feel like helpin' out, you might see if the chief is ready for a dose of your imagination."

Purcell grinned. "Point taken, Sheriff. I'll be off for now but I'll drop by later. I'll have another idea or two for you by then."

"Yeah, expect you will."

Purcell put on his beaver skin top hat, tilted it just so, and then touched the handle of his walking stick to the brim in farewell. After he left, TJ lit an El Gusto to cover the lime smell that lingered in the office and thought about mister police commissioner.

Doc says you got to look at the board through the other fella's eyes. Why is Purcell steerin' me to Chinatown? What's he after? Suppose he steals our thunder and finds the Thurgood girl while I'm off on a wild goose chase? It'd show me up—the chief too. And he'd be the hero. Hold on. Isn't that cannery big shot, Jameson, runnin' against Purcell for senator? Yeah, read about it last week. By God, Purcell came down here just to shit in Jameson's back yard.

He didn't like Jameson much, Purcell even less. If he had a say in it, he wouldn't vote for either one but, of course, it wasn't up to him. The politicians down in Salem, a fair percentage of whom could be bought, had the only say so.

He left a note for Sketch, closed the office, and set off for the three Chinese brothels in town. He didn't expect to find the girl in Chinatown but he didn't want Purcell claiming he didn't do a thorough job.

5

TJ lifted his bedroom curtain and could see nothing but the outline of the massive cedar across the street through the fog. Even a light fog brought on twinges of his closed in feeling and this fog looked as if it would last the day. He shuddered at a familiar memory. Three years ago, he and Tug were floating a drift on an ebb tide. Sometime after midnight, a fog rolled in—what seasoned fishermen called a mudflat fog—thick and cold and impossible to see more than a few feet. A sneaker wave broke over them, capsizing the *Lucy Ann*. The boat rolled over him and when he lifted his head he bumped into something solid. Choking on the ice-cold water he swallowed, he yelled and thrashed around to no effect. His hands and feet were numb with cold by the time he found the gunnels, pushed under them, and kicked to the surface. He clutched a piece of rigging and pulled himself up onto the hull and only then thought of Tug. The big Swede couldn't swim. TJ could have swum around the boat to look for him—at least once. But his hands had tightened their grip on the gunels at the thought of leaving his safe island. Within minutes, other fishermen rescued TJ and pulled his net in along with Tug's body, legs tangled in the net. Other gillnetters said such things happen, said Tug died doing what he loved. But the words didn't help, didn't lessen his guilt.

Didn't hear him yell or call my name ...and couldn't hear much anyway what with the waves hitting the hull... He jerked reflexively and shivered as he relived the moment. *Christ! You're doing it again, TJ. Stop! It over and done with.*

He didn't fish the river anymore, didn't need to worry about fog swallowing up neighboring boats, lights, landmarks, or men. But logic didn't alter what he felt. The bad memories—being trapped under the *Lucy Ann*, not searching for Tug, and Dad locking him up in the coal cellar—rolled in with the fog. The guilt over Tug and the fear of being trapped in close quarters were as much a part of him now as the way he talked.

And the fog matched how he felt about Fong's murder: unable to see clearly which facts were important, which trivial. Last night just after they called off the search for the girl, he'd stopped off at Doc's house and asked about Fong's autopsy. Doc said he'd found bits of food in Fong's stomach, which meant that the grocer had been killed between four and six hours after he ate. According to Kao, Fong ate dinner around eight so that meant he died sometime between midnight and two Sunday morning. So far, so good. Then Doc spoiled things by telling him that the knife wounds probably didn't kill Fong—they weren't deep enough. Rather a blow behind the right ear with something heavy tore his scalp and fractured his skull. The blow probably knocked the grocer out and maybe killed him. But if one blow killed him how did his blood get on the bedpost, the bedspread, and the walls of the room? And if he died right away, why bother stabbing him? The more he learned the less sense it made.

He turned his thoughts to Jane Thurgood and admitted he had no idea where to look for her. The search of Chinese brothels had turned up nothing just as he expected. Wing didn't bat an eye when TJ asked to search his brothel. Mama Joy, the brothel overseer, escorted him through the girls' rooms as well as the dragon room where Chinaboys smoked opium.

The volunteers still searched the backside of Coxcomb hill and the waterfront around Young's Bay. Stump covered and overrun with salal, the hill wasn't a likely place to take a body; too much work to carry it up there. Still he insisted on having it searched.

Chief Connelly's men searched the west side of town but TJ didn't know how much they put into the search. Connelly had his own ideas of law enforcement and his men followed Connelly's lead like well-bred hounds. City police looked over the person needing help before deciding how much to give. Friends or those who paid, as the owners of saloons and sporting houses did, had reliable service. The less worthy were given little more than show help. So last night he decided to search the west side again. But the fog killed that plan.

After breakfast, he took his usual route down Concomly Street through Swilltown. Fog hid the trash and the grime giving the streets and buildings a soft, ghost-like look, the only thing fog was good for. At the intersection of Concomly and Polk, men's voices, charged with energy, reached him from the waterfront. It couldn't be a street fight this early on a weekday morning. Curious, he turned down Polk towards the voices and Kinney's Cannery. The silhouettes of men, some milling, some in groups of two or three, came into view as he grew close. A few men warmed themselves around an open fire while others nailed signs to sticks. He caught sight of Frank Manusco, the fishermen union boss, and called out. Frank left the group by the fire but stopped short when he recognized TJ.

"TJ. What the hell you doin' here?" He put his hands on his hips.

"What's goin' on, Frank?"

"Shit. Don't tell me you ain't heard."

TJ took a step closer. "Heard what?"

Frank studied TJ's face for a second then spit a stream of juice beside him. "A bunch of scabs come in from Portland this mornin.' Headed straight for Jameson's, the shitface."

"Wha...?" He must have heard wrong. "Scabs? Can't be. I know Jameson thinks he owns the town but that doesn't sound like him."

"Goddammit TJ, me and that mooncalf Sonny were walkin' a line in front of Jameson's. We faced them scabs down, stopped them too, by God." He turned and looked over his shoulder to the men at the fire. "Sheriff here says he don't believe Jameson hired them scabs," Frank yelled to the group, "says it don't sound like him."

One of the men guffawed and yelled back, "Tell him to look in the steamer office. It's full of Jameson's scabs headed back where they come from."

Frank turned back to TJ. "But that ain't the worst of it."

"Shit, what else?"

"They's Chinee. Ever last one of them. Jameson's a son of a bitch, sure, but nobody thought he'd take it this far. I sure as hell didn't." Frank leaned over and spit again.

The union boss was no teller of stories, TJ knew, but what he said couldn't be right. To call in scabs at this stage of the walkout struck TJ as a call to war—the dumbest thing an owner could do. And Chinese scabs to boot.

"You know for sure Jameson's behind this?"

"Why else they show up at his place? Besides the scab Chinaboss showed me a contract, had one of them red seals on it, ya know, official and all." Frank turned to go back to the fire but TJ grabbed his shoulder.

"Listen, Frank, this sounds wrong as hell—Jameson isn't stupid. He knows bringin' in Chinee scabs would be puttin' a match to gunpowder. Give me a chance to straighten this out."

Frank pulled his arm free. "One thing for sure, TJ. The next bunch of Chinee scabs come along ain't goin' back on no steamer," Frank said this in a voice loud enough to be heard by the group at the fire. They, in turn, nodded and grunted approval. Frank joined the group and TJ followed him to the fire. The men assembling signs left off and gathered around the fire as well. The eyes of some twenty men were on TJ and on more than one face, he saw the set mouth and furrowed brow of anger.

"I need you to hear me out." He looked directly at the hard faces. "I just heard about the Chinee scabs. Now, if Jameson is behind this he won't be welcome in town. But I'm goin' over to his place now, see if I can't get to the bottom of this. Until then, I don't want any of you tryin' to settle things on your own. I'll jail any man that breaks the law—any man. That's a promise."

A stocky, leather-faced man at the back said, "You gonna keep scabs outta here, Sheriff?"

"Tell you what. I'll talk to the steamship manager. Any Chinee comes in on a steamer stays on it 'til one of my deputies clears him. If he's a scab, he's goin' back where he came from. And that's a promise too."

"You do that, Sheriff. But we're stayin' put—just in case," the man said.

"In case? In case of what?"

"In case our Chinaboys gets ideas. Could be they take to the river to fish while we're on strike."

TJ knew that no one around that fire, including the speaker, believed what the man said. But truth didn't matter when fear ruled. TJ had to put the fear behind those words to rest.

"Listen, the only Chinaboy tried fishin' the river didn't last but a week. We all know what happened to him. But that's the past. Nowadays, any Chinaboy in town more than an hour knows enough to stay off the river."

Frank spoke up, "Maybe so, TJ, maybe so. But we ain't takin' chances. We puttin' more men on our line." The other men nodded agreement.

While Tacoma and Seattle had kicked the Chinese out of town, Astoria wasn't even talking about expelling them. So TJ didn't put much stock in the town losing its Chinaboys. But now it could happen. If Jameson ordered in scabs, it meant a long, bitter strike. A long strike meant the Knights of Labor boys mixing in. He nodded to the men around the fire, walked back up Polk Street to Squemoqua, and then headed east towards Jameson's Cannery.

The fog had thickened and that along with the feeling that he was losing control of things, made him quicken his pace. Within minutes he felt a pressure squeezing his chest; the fog turned into a living thing, stealing air meant for him. His heart raced and he forced himself to slow down, to take deep breaths. It's only fog, he told himself. I'm on land not the river. Besides it'll burn off soon. But nothing he told himself stilled the churning in his guts.

6

Tuesday, April 6

Jameson's Cannery was past Scow Bay, a good mile away, and though the fog had thinned, the tightness in TJ's chest hadn't lessened. He decided to stop for a cup of coffee at Sirpia's bakery to let his insides settle. But on the way to Sirpia's, he saw a light coming from the corner office of the courthouse, his office. Surprised, he took the steps of the courthouse two at a time and hurried down the hall. TJ prided himself on being first to work so it shocked him to see Sketch sweeping the floor and the potbelly already going. Sketch had a flexible sense of time; eight o'clock meant anywhere from five to twenty minutes after.

"Mornin,' Boss."

"Mornin,' Sketch. What happened—town run out of whiskey?" TJ hung his hat up.

"Nope. Met a girl. Libby's her name." Sketch stopped sweeping. "I...um...truth is me and her went to Sunday service." Sketch grinned and shrugged his shoulders.

"Be dammed." TJ looked at his deputy as if seeing him for the first time.

"Yep. She's temperance. Says I wanna be with her, I can't drink. Not even beer. Firm 'bout that, she is. Yessir."

"That's fine, Sketch, just fine. Guess church can't hurt a person." He didn't think Sketch's conversion would last and his voice carried the doubt.

Plato, TJ's big tom, opened his eyes when TJ came in but didn't budge from his seat in the in-basket. TJ plopped down in his swivel chair, picked up the orange tabby, and settled him on his lap.

Sketch dumped his sweepings into the trash bin and closed the door.

"Leave it open," TJ's voice was sharp.

"Heat's not up yet."

"When the office is open, the door stays open. It's first time you're here before me so you don't know."

"But Boss, why…?" His brow furrowed.

"Sketch, you don't need to know the why of it—let's just call it one of my rules."

In a small room such as his office, a closed door triggered TJ's affliction. As a compromise to his fellow workers, he put a stopper in his half-open office door when he wanted privacy.

TJ leaned back, swiveled from side to side, and stroked Plato's back. In a minute, he felt the tension in his chest ease. He realized he'd been hunching his shoulders since he'd left the strikers and shifted them up and down then back and forth. He retrieved his leather cigar case from his inside coat pocket and took out an El Gusto. He picked up his cigar cutter from a chipped cup, ran his thumb down the cherry wood handle, and thought of Lucy Ann. She'd given him the cutter on their first anniversary and he'd kept it in his office to soothe him when he felt troubled or tense, as he did this morning. He started to clip the end of the cigar but paused, remembered Jameson, and put the cigar back in its case.

"You hear about the Chinee scabs showin' up at Jameson's?"

"Yep. Boss, it don't make no sense, what Jameson done."

"I know, Sketch, but could be he didn't hire them. I'm goin' over there to find out what's what." TJ put Plato back in the in-basket and stood up.

"Well, you oughta talk to them union boys while you're at it. That union boss, Frank Manusco, came in just after I opened up, could hardly talk, he was so fired up. Mad at Jameson 'cause he brung them scabs in and mad at us 'cause we didn't stop 'em. Says if the law can't keep Chinee scabs out of town, the union will. Theys got a meet set—Liberty Hall, noon."

"Shit. Trouble is comin' at us like pigs at feedin' time. You hear anything on our missin' girl?"

"Nope. Want me to check with city police?"

"All right. But get back quick. I want you here in case the volunteers find something. I'll be back from Jameson's in an hour, maybe sooner." TJ grabbed his hat and strode out the doorway.

A row of barrels blocked the entrance to Jameson's Cannery and a dozen men walked a path in front of the barrels. They carried signs that read, "Go home John," and "White fishermen only." Just behind the entrance gate, a guard sat on a box cradling a rifle. TJ greeted the men in the line then went up to the gate.

"I need to see Jameson."

"Who's askin'?"

TJ opened his coat, showed his star.

The guard kept his eyes on the strikers as he let TJ in. TJ walked past bare worktables, empty fish carts, an unmoving conveyer belt, and climbed the stairs to the loft and Jameson's office.

Ambrose Jameson, Purcell's Republican rival for Oregon's senate seat, was a stocky 5' 8" but had the features and carriage of a statesman: a Roman nose; fleshy lips; and a head of thick, wavy gray hair. His always-visible tiepin featured a solid gold bucking bronc with the jaws opened around a two-carat diamond. Purcell's reputation was that of a man that could sweet talk the sour out of any deal and a man you didn't cross.

"Ah, Sheriff Stone. I was just about to pay you a visit. You heard?" Jameson said.

"The Chinee scabs?"

"Just what I needed, shit."

"You sayin' you didn't hire them?"

Jameson's mouth dropped open. "You think I...? Jesus Christ, Stone, you leave your brains home today?" He shook his head. "If I wanted to ruin my business, I couldn't think of a faster way to do it. Chinee scabs. My God..."

"So who? And why?"

"That bastard Kephardt and his Knights of Labor boys. Who else? But proving it is another thing. They probably hired some flunky to pose as my foreman and he struck a deal with a labor contractor in Portland who doesn't know us. A dollar to a nickel says you'll never find the son of a bitch who hired them. The headman, poor devil, showed up at my gate expecting a job and got Frank Manusco's fists instead."

"Well, right now we got a bigger worry. Strikers have called a meetin' at Liberty hall—you're about to be lynched. So you need to talk to them, tell them you didn't hire the scabs. They're ..."

"Fishermen know me, Stone, know I wouldn't hire Chinee to fish."

TJ put his hands on Jameson's desk and leaned forward. "Fishermen are mad as hell and not thinking straight. What they know is that you're a boss and they haven't forgotten that Union Pacific bosses brought Chinee miners in to break the strike at Rock Springs. You've got to convince them the white-fishermen-only rule is firm or the strike will get nasty. If that happens the Knights will be on us in a minute and spittin' fire."

Jameson held up his hand. "If they're as mad as you say, they'll hoot me down, won't hear a thing I say."

"I'll talk to them first. I used to be a gillnetter, a cannery foreman too. They know me. Once they calm down, they'll give you a fair listen to. I'll talk for two minutes and then call you. But stay out of sight until then."

"I could make things worse—could be a mess, Stone, a god-awful mess."

"It's already a mess. I'll talk to the union boss, Manusco, ask him for five minutes."

"Manusco is a hothead and finds something wrong with the way I say hello. What makes you think he'll listen to reason?"

"Frank is a hothead but he's fair, wants what's best for fishermen. He'll listen to me. Be at the side entrance, Liberty Hall, 11:45 sharp."

"All right, if they let me speak, I'll convince them...well, all but that jackass, Manusco." Jameson paused, took up a half-smoked double corona from his marble ashtray, lit it, then looked up at TJ who remained standing at the edge of Jameson's desk. "Sit down, for God's sake. I got something else to say."

TJ pulled a chair up to the desk and sat down.

Jameson pulled open a desk drawer and took out a bottle of twelve-year-old Cahill's. "Whiskey?" He poured a tumbler half full and slid it across to TJ.

"I don't take liquor."

"Is that a fact? Bet the saloon owners love you." Jameson chuckled.

"Was some hard feelin' early on. They know my ways now."

Jameson leaned back and sipped the glass of whiskey he'd poured TJ. "You've been a lawman for how long now, Stone?" He cocked his head and looked at TJ.

"Little over two years. Why?"

"You haven't had to put down a riot, one with outside muscle, have you?" Jameson jabbed his cigar at him.

TJ folded his arms across his chest.

"Thought not. I got word that Kephardt has come to Portland and partnered up with Purcell. Kephardt and the Knights of Labor are looking to run every Chinee out of the country. He's trying to scare folks into thinking no white man's job is safe. It's why I know he's behind this scab business." He studied his cigar ash.

"Why are you goin' on about Kephardt? Thought you said we can't prove anything."

"I'm going on about him because he's a worry, Stone. His Knights swooped down on Jacobs' wool mill in the middle of the goddamm night, rounded up his Chinaboys, and shipped them to Portland. They shut Jacobs' mill down."

"I read about it. But I can't be thinkin' about troubles in Portland. Got my hands full here."

Jameson made a fist and hammered the arm of his chair with it. "I'm not losing my Chinaboys, Stone." Jameson jammed the cigar in his mouth, stood up, and looked out the front window into the loft at stacks of empty fish boxes.

"Well, if real trouble comes, a riot say, we'll call in the state militia or the Army. You won't lose your Chinaboys."

Jameson stopped pacing in mid-stride. "The militia? Ha. The goddamm Emmett guard is full of Irish and they won't protect the Chinee against white men. And I'm not calling in the goddamm Army, like they did up north. If I can't control my own backyard, I might as well retire." He bit down hard on his cigar, cursed, and spit a piece of it into the tin pot that served as a spittoon. "I hear things, maybe only rumors—I don't know—but word is that some Chinee in town are buying guns, stocking up on ammo. We've got two thousand Chinee hereabouts, Stone. If it came to a shooting war...Christ!" Jameson shook his head from side to side as if overwhelmed by the thought.

"A shootin' war? Seems to me you're tryin' to look down a cliff that's still miles ahead."

"Maybe. But we're not going to let things get to that cliff, are we?"

"We? What's 'we' mean?"

Jameson turned sideways in his chair. "You said you were a fisherman and a cannery man, so you know John Chinaman first hand, right?"

"Wouldn't say that. All I know is they're hard workers, don't drink on the job, and keep to themselves."

"Yes, yes. Common knowledge. But you worked next to them. Must know more than that," Jameson said.

"Know a few cuss words," TJ smiled.

"You don't drink, Stone, so you don't spend time in saloons, don't know the owners."

"What of it?" TJ's jaw muscles tightened.

"No need to get your dander up." Jameson held up both hands. "Chief Connelly and his brother ran the Portside for a time. He knows the saloon owners, the ins and outs of the business. So I asked him to be our eyes and ears among the owners, let us know if they smell trouble. You know fishermen and," he smiled, "the Chinee."

"Told you. Don't know any Chinee. Not personal. Still don't see what you're drivin' at."

"I heard you put a stop to some white boys sporting with a Chinee, a peddler wasn't it?"

"How the hell you hear that?"

"Oh, I have ways." Jameson smiled wide enough to show a gold molar.

"Well, was nothin' special in what I did."

"Like hell. Don't know a policeman in Astoria or Portland would have stopped those boys from having some fun." Jameson pointed his cigar at TJ. "But the point is that by now all of Chinatown knows what you did. You've got John's trust now."

"Still don't see where you're going."

"I'd like you to be our man with the Chinee, our liaison, so to speak. Talk to their headmen, let me and the chief know what's going on."

TJ didn't say anything for a time and Jameson took this as assent to his proposition.

"Good, it's settled then." Jameson rubbed his hands together.

TJ locked eyes with Jameson. "Hold on. I already said I know next to nothin' about the Chinee. Don't understand their lingo, wouldn't know what they're thinkin.'"

Jameson waved his hand and smiled. "Doesn't matter. The headmen speak passable English. Meet with them, show yourself around Chinatown. Wouldn't hurt to take a meal in one of their restaurants from time to time. It'll steady them." He flicked the cigar ash on the floor with his little finger.

TJ's words were flat, allowed no argument. "Don't get me wrong—I'm for keepin' the peace—but I got my hands full keepin' peace between you and the strikers, not to mention Finns and Swedes. Don't have time to be some damm liaison."

"How about taking it on until the strike is settled?"

TJ didn't say anything for a few seconds and looked out at the river through the grime-streaked back window. "I'll think on it."

"Fair enough." Jameson inclined his head towards TJ. "Sheriff, the owners' association is prepared to offer you a little something, you know, to cover additional duties. Only right." Jameson tossed an envelope on the desk. "A small advance on your expenses."

"Keep it. I don't need bribes to do my job." He pushed the envelope back.

"Suit yourself." Jameson put the envelope in his pocket. "I'll see you at Liberty Hall."

"The side entrance, 11:45. Be on time."

Jameson waved his hand in dismissal.

7

TJ's footsteps echoed as he walked across the ballroom floor of Liberty Hall. It'd been four years since he and his new bride Lucy Ann had danced here. After her death, he'd lost all desire to dance and hadn't been inside since. He glanced up at the hall's huge chandelier, imported from San Francisco, and once again marveled at its size and beauty. On the ballroom wall, painted scenes showed nymphs, satyrs and cherubs frolicking in summer fields among strange, imaginary flowers and vegetation.

TJ climbed the steps to the stage, retreated to the wings, and within ten minutes plain-dressing, rough-talking fishermen started filing in. Soon the hum of excited talk and the racket of folding chairs being slammed into place told him that both the ballroom and balcony would be full. Jameson stood in the wings off by himself going over notes while Frank Manusco, the union boss, sat on an apple box, cracking his knuckles. Manusco wore clothes like those of the men filling the hall: knit cap; plaid shirt over a wool undershirt; wide suspenders; rubber boots; and a fishing knife in a sheaf at his side.

Although TJ did not dwell overmuch on how he dressed, what he wore for his job had evolved so that the way he dressed now felt right. Like most fishermen, he wore Levis and boots but unlike them, he wore a suit coat, vest, white shirt, and, for today's meeting, a string tie. Now, as he looked back and forth between Jameson, in his three-piece suit, and Manusco, in his work clothes, he realized that his clothes set him apart from both men. Conscious of being a lawman, an outsider, he realized that his allegiance could never be tied to either worker or boss. He looked at the gillnetters talking and joking and understood for the first time what it meant to be unattached. He felt alone—more so than at any time since taking this job.

Manusco looked at his watch and announced, "It's time, gents." He came up to TJ and said in a low voice, "By the way, that Purcell fella wants to say a few words. Says he can help us find out if Jameson hired them scabs. I gave the chief a minute to introduce him and Purcell five."

TJ didn't mind the chief speaking since keeping the peace was a lawman's job but he didn't want Purcell meddling. "Dammit, Frank, I haven't heard Purcell say a good word about the Chinee. If he talks against them, nobody will pay any mind to Jameson."

"Well, he says he's for unions and says he knows Chinee ways. Can't hurt to hear what he's got to say. Anyway, I gave the chief and him the same time I gave you and Jameson. Only fair. Anybody goes overtime, I'm cuttin' off." He looked over at Jameson and said, "You got five minutes, Jameson."

Jameson regarded Manusco with a cold stare. "Yeah, yeah."

TJ followed Manusco onto the stage and then sat down in one of three folding chairs at the side of the stage. Manusco stood only 5' 6" but had a strong sense of self. He strode to the podium with his broad shoulders back, his head up, and assumed an air of command. The union boss looked out, nodding and pointing to men he knew, while men cheered and applauded. He raised his hand and the audience hushed.

"Can you hear me in back?" he asked in a husky gravel voice.

Arms waved from the back that they could.

"Things is changed since I called this meet. Sheriff Stone asked if Ambrose Jameson could talk to us. I'm mighty keen on hearin' how them Chinee scabs ended up on his doorstep this mornin.' So I said he could."

At the mention of Jameson's name, the audience booed and hissed. Manusco opened his arms wide and shrugged. "How the hell could this happen? Ain't that what you been askin' yourselves?"

Lots of shouting and yelling.

"Yeah, it's how I feel too." Manusco waved his hand up and down and the audience quieted. "Well, I warned Sheriff Stone. Said fishermen wanted to see Mr. Jameson gutted, cleaned, and hung up for show like that other bottom feeder, Mr. Sturgeon."

Laughter, whistles, and cheers.

Manusco cupped his hand next to his mouth and leaned forward. "And I'm only repeatin' what the easy goin' fellas said."

More laughter and cheers.

"But Sheriff Stone says what happened this mornin' ain't how it looks. Sheriff used to be a gillnetter so I'm willin' to hear him out. Nobody never called the union unfair, am I right?"

Scattered applause and a few, "That's right."

Manusco looked to Chief Connelly who sat in the front row. "Now, Chief Connelly introduced me to Mr. Paul Purcell a while ago. Seems Mr. Purcell is Police Commissioner in Portland and knows a thing or two about the Chinee. Says he can help us get to the bottom of this scab business. So I'm givin' him five minutes same as Mr. Jameson. Like I said, a union man is a fair man."

Shouts of approval, applause.

Manusco nodded to Connelly. "Come on up, Chief." Manusco moved across the stage to the steps that led into the audience and waited for the chief. The chief's 260-pound bulk made climbing the six stairs difficult and by the time he crossed the stage to the podium, he was breathing hard. The chief never buttoned his coat, the top of his shirt, nor tightened the knot of his tie and looked as if he slept in his clothes. He stood at the podium unsure of what to do with his hands and, after an awkward moment, solved the dilemma by plunging them into his pockets. His pants now sagged around the tops of his shoes.

"Afternoon, boys. I won't waste time tellin' you somethin' you already know."

Groans and some "Get on with it" from the audience.

"Well, all I'm sayin' is them scabs comin' to town like they did is wrong, wrong as can be. Yessir. No two ways 'bout it. But we moved in on them soon as we got word they was causin' trouble and herded them back to the steamer office."

Cheering, yells of "Hang 'em" greeted his words.

"And don't worry none, boys. They're goin' back where they come from this afternoon. But now fer some good news. A good friend of mine, Commissioner Purcell, has come here from Portland to help us find that girl what's missin.' He heard 'bout the trouble over to Jameson's and, well, he's got something to say about that. Boys, how about givin' Commissioner Purcell a big Astoria welcome."

A smattering of applause followed.

Purcell climbed the stairs before the chief finished and crossed the stage to the podium with the confidence of a preacher with a fresh revelation from the Lord. Purcell wore a chocolate suit with a cream colored vest and a yellow rose in his lapel. His muttonchops framed his face and his slicked-down hair was parted exactly in the middle. *He's a dandy man*, TJ thought, *fishermen won't take him serious.*

"Thank you, Chief Connelly. Good afternoon, gentlemen. I happened to be in town on another matter, as the chief said, when I heard a most distressing report. Did a band of Chinee scabs show up at Jameson's Cannery this morning ready to take your place on the river?"

Purcell paused, turned, and looked to where Jameson waited in the wings. At the mention of Jameson's name, a few men hissed and one rose part way and shouted, "Goddamm traitor."

When the audience quieted, Purcell leaned towards the audience and looked slowly from left to right, without speaking. He softened his voice but it still carried to the back of the hall. "I fear what happened at Jameson's this morning will have the gravest consequences for your union, and for your city. Suppose word got out that canneries in Astoria looked to hire Chinee fishermen during a strike? It's not hard to imagine, is it? Working men all over the Northwest would feel betrayed. They'd say your union allowed cannery operators to run roughshod over decent white workingmen. They'd call your union weak, gutless." Purcell paused, walked from stage right to stage left, never taking his eyes off the audience. Heads turned and followed him as he crossed the stage.

"But if we can discover the man behind this scab business quickly, we'll keep the news from spreading and just might save the union's reputation. And gentlemen, as Police Commissioner I'm just the man to unmask the scoundrel. Further, I'll see that the villain gets the punishment he deserves." Purcell shot another look into the wings at Jameson. "That's a promise, gentlemen. And here's another promise. If I am chosen your next senator, I'll see to it that what happened at Jameson's Cannery will never happen again."

TJ noticed that men had stopped fidgeting and no longer whispered to their neighbors. Men at the back leaned forward so as not to miss a word. Purcell's deep, mellow voice, had authority, made what he said sound so right that to question it seemed mean spirited.

"Now, most of you don't know me so allow me to tell you what my friends and I are fighting for—the main reason I want to be your senator." Purcell stepped away from the podium and put his hands on his hips, pushing the tails of his coat away from his sides. "Gentlemen, I see danger ahead. There are thieves among us and more thieves on the way. The thieves I'm talking about steal jobs, jobs like yours, the jobs of true Americans." Purcell bent over part way and asked in a stage whisper. "Who are they, these thieves?" He stood up and rocked back on his heels. "The Chinee, that's who."

TJ swore at Purcell's mention of the Chinee. He started to get up but Manusco put a hand on his shoulder and pushed him back down.

"You'll get your chance," Manusco whispered.

Purcell came to the edge of the stage, extended his left arm out to the side, and pointed his index finger towards the Pacific Ocean. "They're no jobs over there." He raised his voice. "They're starving.

They're desperate. Their friends tell them, 'comee 'Merica, plenty jobee here."

Purcell's mimicry elicited laughs as well as curses from the audience.

"Well, they've been coming here for years now. In droves, they're coming. We passed a law in 1882. Supposed to keep John out. Do I have to tell you it isn't working? Of course not. You can see for yourselves it's not working." He paused again and came back to the podium. "John is going to keep coming to our shores until this country is full of Chinamen. In a few years, this land will be more Chinee than American. Is this what you want?"

Shouts of "Hell no" and "Kick John out," came from the audience.

"Well, some of us are tired of sitting back and doing nothing while the Chinee take over. With help from that fine organization, the Knights of Labor, we're taking the shops, the factories, and the streets of Portland away from the coolies and giving them back to the white workingmen of America. Make no mistake, gentlemen, the yellow peril is real. And this morning at Jameson's Cannery you got a taste of things to come if we don't act."

Men shouted, whistled, and clapped their approval. Purcell held up his hand and waited for the applause to die.

As TJ listened to Purcell raise the Chinese problem, he saw fear on the faces of some men, anger on the faces of others. Purcell had made fishermen more worried and angry than when they walked in to the hall. And why the campaign speech? The state legislature elected United States senators, not the ordinary Joe. TJ pulled out his pocket watch, saw that Purcell only had fifteen seconds left, and tapped Manusco on the shoulder.

Manusco stood up. "Time's about up, Mr. Purcell."

"All right. Gentlemen, I'll leave you with a promise I make to all workingmen. As your senator, I'll do all in my power to see that the heathens here go back to China and that the heathens over there stay there. Thank you and God bless the American workingman."

The audience stood and applauded and it took a full minute for Manusco to calm the audience enough to introduce TJ.

As TJ walked to the podium the hall grew quiet, too quiet. The silence of so many angry and fearful men filled the air with a tension as heavy as coal smoke. The air in the room, already stale, grew warmer by the minute. TJ looked out into a field of faces and felt sweat trickle down his sides. He had never spoken in a formal setting to so many men and his guts tightened. He looked for a smile, a friendly face, but didn't see one until he spotted Sketch leaning against a wall in the back of the room. TJ nodded at Sketch, took a deep breath, and began.

"Before I took this job, I use to be a gillnetter, like Frank said. So I know fishin' and know what the pay is. And I'd be walkin' that line with you now, if I was still a gillnetter."

Heads nodded and TJ heard murmurs of approval.

"Now, Mr. Purcell means well. But he's not a fisherman, doesn't know how we do things. Any of you recall last time we had trouble with the Chinee?" TJ waited and hearing no response, continued. "I started workin' the river at thirteen and can't recollect havin' trouble with them. Ever. I'm talkin' big trouble, like up in Tacoma and Seattle. You know why? It's 'cause inside workers and outside workers know their place, know better than to step across the line into the other fella's job." TJ paused to look at the audience from side to side. "Now, supposin' we chased Chinamen out of town like they did up North. Think hard on that for a minute." TJ paused, took another deep breath. "It's a damm fool notion, is what it is. And every one of you knows it. If we lost our Chinaboys, we'd have no one to can this season. Some inside jobs like tinsmithin' takes years to learn. You don't replace a tinsmith overnight. So those inside jobs will go beggin' this season, the next, and maybe the season after. Boys, it's simple. If Chinaboys go, fishermen lose, Chinee lose, owners lose, and the town loses." TJ waved for Jameson to come out, which he did.

TJ made a point of looking at Jameson. "I asked Mr. Jameson straight out did he hire those scabs. He said only a fool would do that. Now, you might call Mr. Jameson a lot of things…" TJ had to wait for the shouts of "Son of bitch" and "Traitor" to stop. "But I never heard anybody call him a fool. No sir." TJ paused, rocked back on his heels, and then straightened to his 6' 4" height. "One last thing before I sit down. I believe some sharper put those scabs on Jameson's doorstep to stir up trouble. I don't know who's behind this trickery yet but I'll run him down. And when I do, he'll get a lesson or two in the meanin' of sorry—and that's my promise. Thanks for hearin' me out."

The applause started two or three seconds after TJ finished and grew to a respectable level by the time he sat down.

Jameson stepped up to the podium with his coat unbuttoned showing off his horseshoe-shaped diamond stickpin. The tiepin said to TJ and to every fisherman there that Jameson, like Purcell, belonged to the world of money and to the hated class of bosses. Men hissed and catcalled as he stood at the podium. Jameson looked at his notes the minute or so it took the hall to quiet.

Jameson cleared his throat and then said, "I want to thank Frank Manusco for giving me a chance to talk to you face to face. Boys, I've been a cannery man in Astoria for close to sixteen years now. I make my living from the river, same as you, and my first year on the job I learned a few rules for getting along. One such rule is that a Chinee does inside work—he doesn't fish the river. It's a rule we live by and it's a good one. It's fair." Jameson paused and poured himself a glass of water from a pitcher on the podium.

Jameson sipped water then continued. "Boys, the long and short of it is—I didn't hire those Chinee scabs. It's something I wouldn't do, something I'll never do."

From somewhere near the middle of the hall, a man shouted something.

Jameson paused and called out, "Didn't hear that. What'd you say?"

The man stood up and said, "Is that a promise?"

"A promise? Well, why not? I promise never to hire a Chinee to fish for me. And what's more, I hereby declare a hundred dollar reward for the man who brings me the name of the bastard who sicced those scabs on me."

From the side of the stage, Manusco hollered, "Can we get that in writin'?"

The room erupted in laughter; men poked their buddies in the ribs and the tension in the hall collapsed.

Jameson smiled, turned to Frank, and said, "Anything to keep you happy, Frank. All right, I'll put it in writing."

More laughter.

Manusco came up to the podium, looked Jameson up and down as if sizing him up for a suit and then turned to the audience. "Well, you're askin' us to believe you when you say you didn't hire them scabs. How about you believe us when we tell you fishermen can't make it on four cents a pound? We need five cents."

The hall erupted in shouting and cheering and shouts of 'You tell him Frankie.'

The front row stood and clapped and, within seconds, every man in the hall stood and clapped. Manusco clapped too but then slowed the rhythm to a deliberate beat. The audience picked up the beat and a few men stamped their boots to the beat, others followed, and soon everyone stamped and clapped to a steady, uniform rhythm. The sound of two hundred men clapping and stamping in unison grew to a roar loud enough to carry outside to people on Lafayette Street.

Fishermen were smiling and gleeful as they clapped and stamped, all traces of fear and anger gone. A minute passed, according to TJ's watch, during which the volume didn't change. When the volume started to fade, Manusco walked to the edge of the stage and slowly raised his arms, palms up. The volume rose with his hands and increased above the earlier level. The floor of the stage shook under TJ's feet.

After a few seconds, Manusco, grinning from ear to ear, let his hands drift downward like balloons losing air. The noise subsided as his hands sank. When his hands touched his sides, the clapping and stamping stopped. No one spoke, no one shuffled, fidgeted, or coughed, the sudden silence as powerful, as arresting, as the roar of seconds ago. After what seemed to TJ a full minute, Manusco said, "Well, we're waitin' on your answer, Mr. Jameson."

Jameson had been outmaneuvered by the union boss and knew it. Everyone knew it. Jameson stared at Manusco and said, "I can't give you an answer now, Frank. But you know that. I'm going to an owners' meeting this afternoon. If the strikers behave, just maybe you and I will have something to talk about." Jameson slowed as he walked by TJ and said through clenched teeth, "You didn't tell me Purcell was going to talk, Stone. I won't forget this."

Manusco came over to TJ as Jameson left. "Sheriff, we're gonna keep on meetin' for a time; the boys and me need to talk things over. You don't need to stay."

TJ nodded and then hurried out of the hall hoping to catch Jameson and explain that he had no idea Purcell would speak. But Jameson had disappeared so TJ waited out front for Sketch. As the two lawmen headed back to the office, TJ asked, "You think they believed Jameson?"

"Well, he stood up like a man, told us to our face he didn't hire no scabs. Men like that. Trouble is that Purcell fella believes different, made out like Jameson is lyin.' So I can't say how it'll play out. Only thing I know for sure—Purcell hates Chinamen." Sketch bit off a chew from his plug and then pulled up short. "Boss, somethin' else botherin' me."

"What's that?"

"Well, it don't seem right, what happened to them Chinee. I mean they was lied to. Purcell had no call to blame them."

"No, he didn't. But Purcell wants us to think Chinamen are the enemy, not just those poor devils this mornin.' He's sayin' whoever hired them, hired the enemy. And by lookin' to the wings like he did, he made out Jameson hired the enemy, without actually sayin' it. He's a slick bastard, Sketch, damm slick."

Sketch had no more questions and TJ fell back to thinking about why Purcell came to town in the first place. Purcell said he wanted to help find Jane Thurgood. But now he was offering to track down the man behind the scab business. This last offer wasn't believable since all who heard Purcell could see he thought Jameson hired them. TJ was no longer sure why Purcell had come to Astoria.

8

Wednesday, April 7

It'd been four days since the Thurgood girl went missing—four days and still no news of her. TJ left the breakfast table of his boardinghouse before his second cup of coffee to avoid questions from his tablemates, questions he had no answers to. He paused on the front porch and looked out towards the Columbia. To the north, specks of sunlight danced on a smooth patch of the river just beyond Elmore's Cannery. To the east, a tugboat nudged a four-masted schooner away from the docks of the Clatsop Sawmill. Still further east and across the river on the Washington side, a trail of smoke pinpointed the Knappton Mills, a good seven miles away. With only a light breeze from the southwest, the day promised to be fair.

The strike had been settled yesterday afternoon, the union and cannery owners agreeing to four and a half cents a pound. TJ had stood with an excited crowd and watched the butterfly fleet head off to their drift sites two hours later. Most days he didn't miss the life of a fisherman but today his heart beat a little faster as he took in the river and recalled setting out with Tug on a fair day.

He sighed and looked at his watch—a little past 7:30. The butchering line at Astoria's canneries had been in place for an hour and a half. Several loads of cans had been filled, cooked, tested for leaks, re-sealed, and re-cooked.

He looked west and noticed a bank of clouds with a dark underbelly stretching across the horizon. He'd been premature in predicting a fair day. Even as he studied the cloudbank, the wind shifted and a blast of cold air hit his face. He turned up the collar of his slicker, climbed down the twenty steps to Columbia Street, and began his daily stroll—showing the colors, he called it—through the part of town known as McClure's Astoria.

He stayed on Concomly Street, which took him through the heart of Swilltown, a sad place on weekday mornings. The owner of the Merry Widow, liquor downstairs and sporting girls upstairs, painted the front of the building white with red trim only last week but no singing, laughing, or hollering came out of it now to give it any spark. The Merry Widow looked sadder than the shoe repair shop and cigar store on either side of it, neither of which had ever seen a coat of paint. The east-west streets through this part of town, Concomly, Chenamus, and Squemoqua, were named after Chinook chiefs but as he walked past the empty saloons and quiet whorehouses, he didn't think it much of an honor to have a street in Swilltown named after you.

He reached the courthouse before Sketch and found a boy of about ten sitting on the bench outside his office.

"Mornin,' son. What can I do for you?"

The boy stood up. "Mr. Jameson, over to the cannery, says you're to come right over, sir."

TJ had neither time nor inclination to listen to Jameson harangue him about Purcell being allowed to speak yesterday. "We're real busy now, son. How about tomorrow afternoon?"

"He said you might say that. Said to tell you it's important and, beg pardon Sheriff, to get your ass over there."

TJ smiled. "Well, guess I'll better go then."

TJ had to maneuver thorough an aisle created by pallets of empty cans to reach Jameson's glass-fronted office on the loft. Empties rattled and clanked on the conveyer belt as they traveled to the filling tables below. But at least the loft wasn't as noisy as the ground floor where butchers, slimers, fillers, and tank men had to shout to be heard over the din of machines.

Jameson sat at his desk in shirtsleeves, tie loose, silver hair ruffled. Beads of sweat dotted his forehead in spite of the cool office. He wiped his broad face with a handkerchief and glared at TJ.

"Stone. What kept you? Never mind. Sit down. I've got something to show you." He reached below his desk and handed TJ a small basket that held something wrapped in newspaper.

"Go on, open it." Jameson said.

TJ unwrapped part of the newspaper and saw what at first glance looked like a claw. He lifted the paper and saw a pair of human hands, their skin puffy and pale gray. He noted the pink flesh around the wrist where the hand had been severed. The idea of what he held hit him. He let go of the newspaper and put the basket on the desk. "Christ! What kind of stunt is this?" He sank back in his chair, fighting a rising sick feeling.

"If it's a stunt, as you say, it's a damm sorry one." Jameson pointed to the basket. "Go on, take a good look. They've got to be a woman's—too delicate for a man's."

He reached in with thumb and forefinger and lifted out a right hand. The little finger stuck up at a sharp angle from the other fingers, broken probably, and the nail had been torn off. The nails on the other fingers were long and manicured but unpainted. He turned the hand over and felt the palm. No hard work done by this hand. The base of each finger showed a dark bruise next to a thin, pale line. The base of the thumb wasn't bruised. He put the hand down and picked up the left hand and noted the same bruising at the base of each finger but not at the thumb. The pale line could be marks left by rings. But he didn't recall any woman who wore a ring on every finger. The hairs on the back of his neck stiffened as he wondered if the hands belonged to the Thurgood girl. *Slow down. Why the hell would someone cut off her hands and leave them in a cannery?*

"Where'd you get these? Where's the body? Goddamm it, Jameson, what's goin' on?" He put the hand back in the basket, covered it with the newspaper, and slid the basket across the desk.

"We found them this morning. Way I heard it, a tank man noticed some Chinee words painted on test tank number one just after he came to work. When he spotted the hands at the bottom of the tank, he had a fit, screaming and carrying on like the devil had him by the pigtail. Ran back to the Chinahouse without so much as a by your leave." Jameson stroked his beard. "Chinaboss says it's some kind of omen, a god is displeased, some rot like that. Anyway, I've lost my tank man for the rest of the goddamm day—maybe longer." Jameson waited for him to say something but he didn't. Jameson continued, "We've turned the place upside down. Didn't find a damm thing—no body, no clothes—nothing."

"How long you search?"

"An hour. That's all I could spare. But I had every man on it and we covered everything—even searched my office. But sniff around all you want, maybe we missed something." Jameson smoothed back his hair and again waited for TJ to speak.

"You any idea who the woman is?" TJ asked. A routine question but it provoked unexpected anger.

"What? How in hell would I know?" He flushed and his nostrils flared. "You're not thinking, Stone. She is probably some whore they filled with booze and then killed."

"They? So you're sayin' there's more than one killer?

"No...maybe...shit, how the hell do I know?"

"All right, let's skip that for now. But I wonder why they or he didn't dump her body in the tank. How come just the hands?"

Jameson cocked his head and tapped his palm with the pencil. "Am I supposed to have an answer to that? Christ almighty, Stone, you like playing the fool?"

"Just speculatin' out loud. No reason to rile yourself."

"Riled? I'm not riled. Not a bit. Just because…"

"You take a close look at her nails? They're well cared for, like a lady's."

"What's your point? Sporting girls go to beauty shops."

"Guess that's true but her nails weren't painted like the sporting girls I know."

" All right but so what? Dammit. Maybe she worked in an office, had a manicure every week."

"You sayin' she's an office girl?" He liked treating Jameson as a suspect. Somebody gets that angry over an innocent question and you got to ask why. Besides a little humbling would do the man good.

"Why are you asking me? Shit. For the last time, I don't know her, have no idea who she is or what she did. Use your head, man." Jameson squeezed the pencil he held with both hands.

"Uh-huh." He nodded at the basket. "Think the hands belong to our missing girl?"

Jameson looked out the glass wall of his office and watched a worker pulling a cart full of empties.

TJ knew that trick, looking off to give yourself time to come up with an answer. When Jameson looked at him, TJ asked, "You heard about the Thurgood girl—missing since last weekend?"

Jameson's face stiffened at the mention of the girl's name. "Of course. Whole town is talking about it. But why do you think the hands are hers? What reason…" he swallowed and his eyes searched TJ's face. "Oh, I see. More speculating, right?"

TJ took out his notebook and scribbled away. After a few seconds Jameson cursed under his breath and TJ heard him. "Something you want to say?" TJ asked without looking up from his notes.

"Goddammit, Stone, stop wasting my time. Do your job. Tell me what you think." Jameson broke the pencil he held in two and tossed the halves on his desk.

"What I think about what?"

"Who's trying to ruin me? And why?"

He gave Jameson his full attention. "Ruin you? Now, why do you say that?"

Jameson stood up and paced the office. "You know what'd happen to my cannery if word got out we found human body parts in one of our tanks?" He scowled and his voice boomed, "Who'd buy our salmon? Buy! What am I saying?! We couldn't give it away." He placed his fingers on the globe in the corner and gave it a spin.

"How about the Salvation Army?" TJ covered his mouth to hide a smile.

Jameson didn't take the bait. "The Salvation Army? Bullshit. They wouldn't take them either…be no one…no country…" He stopped the spinning globe, returned to his desk, and lifted an Upmann double corona out of a cedar-lined cigar box. "It wouldn't matter what we said, that it wasn't our fault, that we'd been honey-fuggled. Who'd believe us?" He rubbed his eyes.

TJ thought about Mac, the editor of The Star, whose dislike of Chinese came from a hate so deep it bore no connection to reason. As if he read TJ's thoughts, Jameson started in on the press.

"And the newspapers—Christ! Just last month, one jackass editor called Chinaboys nothing but filthy, opium-smoking, long-nailed, scum. Said any food packed by them is poisoned and he'd be dammed if he'd ever eat canned salmon." Jameson shook his head from side to side. "If a bastard like that got word of these hands, my cannery is finished. You take my point?" He thrust his chin forward, fleshy lips clamped tight around his cigar, a bulldog on attack.

"Yep." In spite of Jameson talking to him as if he were one of his hires, he felt a twinge of sympathy.

"It's the goddamm union, that's who's behind this. They didn't count on us settling as soon as we did, especially after that scab business. Maybe Manusco thought we needed another push and his boys used those hands to threaten me. Well, if it's a fight they want, they've got one." Jameson struck a match on the sole of his boot and lit his cigar.

"Now slow down, Jameson. You don't know who put those hands in there. Don't be lookin' to shoot your neighbor's dog just 'cause some of your chickens are missin.'" He leaned back and cocked his head to the side. "Besides the message on your tank is Chinee. Why would a union man write in Chinee if he wants to send you a message?"

"Ha! You forget those Chinee scabs sent from Portland? The Knights are using a Chinaman to get at me—trying to make me lose faith in my Chinaboys and stop me from hiring them. Christ, be a feather in their cap if they pulled that off. There's no end to their tricks, the bastards."

TJ pointed a finger at Jameson's chest. "Listen close, Jameson. I want you to sit on this for a few days. Give me a chance to look around. I've got a murder and a missing girl to think about but I'll get on this case as soon as I can." He thought of the hard feelings that would follow if the cannery owners reneged on the new contract. A move like that would lead to a long strike and, this time, the Knights could make the pot of anti-Chinee hate boil over without half trying.

Jameson rocked back and forth in his chair. "Soon as you can? What's that mean? I got to settle this quick, before word gets out."

"I know. How about three days? The other canneries don't need to know about the hands. Likewise the papers. Tell your Chinaboys, your foremen, and anybody else in the know to keep the lid on. I'll do the same with my deputies."

Jameson took the cigar out of his mouth and sat up. "You think that'll work?"

"It's worth tryin.' But I need a hundred per cent cooperation from you and your crew—no keepin' things from me, understand?"

Jameson nodded.

TJ folded the newspaper around the hands and picked up the basket with both hands as if it held a live animal.

"My foreman, Brady, is downstairs. He'll fill you in on the details." Jameson stabbed the air with his cigar. "And when you get the sons of bitches, Stone, by God, let me know. I want a piece of them."

"It doesn't work like that. Not with me. You'll find out who they are when I got them locked up, not before." His eyes locked on to Jameson's until the cannery boss looked away.

9

The din on the first floor of Jameson's Cannery reminded TJ why he quit working as a foreman. Cans banged and clanked as they came down the conveyer belt, loaded carts bumped over slatted floorboards, and furnaces roared as they kept the giant pressure cookers at the temperature necessary to cook salmon. TJ caught up with the foreman, Brady, as he worked on a gang knife that had jammed.

"Aw, fer Christ's sake, not another stoppage. We're behind as it is. Can't ya come back after work?" Brady regarded TJ with disgust.

TJ put his mouth close to the foreman's ear. "I need to see that tank."

Brady, short but with a wrestler's upper body and arms, wasn't accustomed to back talk. He squared his body to TJ's and didn't say anything for a second but then shrugged and motioned TJ to follow him.

At the center of a far wall, a test tank of hot water stood on either side of a huge pressure cooker. As they approached the first tank, a worker hoisted a pallet of filled cans out with a block and tackle, swiveled it over the side, and then lowered it onto a cart. Brady pointed to four Chinese characters in black paint on the wall of the first tank. Whoever painted it used a coarse brush and wrote quickly as the paint had run from the bottom of the characters.

"Bastard used our paint and brush, too," Brady said.

TJ pointed to a room and Brady nodded. They crossed the wet floor to where a half-dozen workers sat at a long table soldering tops on the filled cans. They could talk here without shouting.

"You know what those words mean?"

"Nope—Chinaboss couldn't read 'em. Chung, that China doc, has a store next to Liberty Hall. Ya know him?"

"I know the store."

"Well, he writes letters for our Chinaboys. He'll read it for ya."

"I'll bring him in. Make sure those words stay up there 'til he sees them. Now let's go over things from the beginnin.'"

Brady told him when the hands were found and where his men searched for a body but then started to complain about time lost. "By God, we've had enough damm stoppages for one day. This is the third one and it ain't even lunch time." Brady took a pouch of tobacco from the pocket of his overalls and stuffed a fistful in his mouth. "Can't hardly wait to see what foolery is next."

"What caused the second stoppage?"

"Caught one of our butchers with a China knife, a goddamm dagger more like. Chinaboss thinks the boy stole it. Why?"

"Someone cut up a grocer in Chinatown Sunday and stole a knife. I'd need to question that boy."

"Now?"

"Yes, now."

"Shit, Sheriff, I got a cannery to run."

"Brady, those hands didn't have a single ring on them. But the marks on the fingers say the woman wore rings, lots of them. Maybe you helped yourself to them. Guess I'll have to take you and that Chinaboy back to my office—do a real thorough study of what happened." TJ's eyes bored into Brady's.

Brady flushed. "I pulled the hands outta that vat—wasn't a finger had a ring—not a one." Brady shook his head, defeated. "All right, Sheriff, all right. Lum, the Chinaboss, will point Hop Li out. But keep it short, will ya? We lost enough damm time for one day."

TJ found the Chinaboss checking a temperature gauge on one of the pressure cookers. After the man understood what TJ wanted, he pointed to a worker at the front of a butchering line furthest from him. TJ stood a moment watching the butcher work.

A shaft of sunlight from a window high above the cannery floor fell on the shirtless butcher and his table. His chest and arms were wet with sweat and his muscles wiggled under his skin like trapped eels. TJ couldn't tell where the arms and hands of the butcher ended and the twitching, shiny, body on the cutting table began. A knife blade flashed here, there, but the butcher's hands were a blur; lift, cut, turn, cut, twist, cut, cut, and shove. From the time the pitcher slapped a Spring Chinook on the table to when the butcher slid the gutted halves to the slimer took just 45 seconds. Only at the peak of the run when the June hogs came in did the pace of butchering slow, had to slow, for these giants of up to five feet and seventy pounds.

He walked over to the table but the butcher continued to cut, glancing up to acknowledge TJ only after he'd tossed the head of a fish into a bucket of salt water and scooted the fin, tail and guts into a chute that led to the river below.

"Hop Li?"

"Yes. Me Chen Hop Li. What you want?" He wiped his hands on a towel and averted his gaze when he noticed the star on TJ's shirt.

"Chinaboss said you found a knife this morning. That true?" He studied the man in front of him. Early twenties, strong face with high cheekbones, and big for a Chinaman, maybe 5' 7," with good shoulders on him. Hop Li had no queue; only a small knot of hair at the neck held in place with rubber band.

"Yes. True. Knife no belong me. Warrior knife, that one." He pointed to a rack. "Find there, with other knife." He spoke with a firm voice though he continued to avoid TJ's gaze.

"Did you steal that knife?" TJ found that a surprise attack, a strong opening Doc called it, confused some suspects and they blurted out a confession. Most times he liked a creep up style; lulling a man into thinking he was safe, before hitting him with a tough question. He couldn't say why he chose one style over the other, only that as he talked to a suspect he got a feel for what might work.

"NO! Chen Hop Li no steal. No thief, Chen family." He put his shoulders back and his eyes flashed in anger.

"Easy now. I've got to ask questions. Find out what's true, what isn't. Understand?"

Hop Li nodded but still didn't look at him.

"Where is this knife now?"

"Chinaboss take."

"You know how those hands got in that tank?"

"Eh? Hands? No. Only what Chinaboss say."

"What'd he say?"

"Hands belong woman, maybe 'merican woman. Sweet Sunday Lady only 'merican woman I know." Hop Li shot him a glance then looked back to his table.

"Sweet…who?"

"Missy Taylor. She come cannery Sunday, teach Jesus religion. Teach English, Chinese also."

"So, you can read and write Chinee?"

"Yes. Some word."

"You know what the Chinee words on the tank mean?"

"One finish, one hundred also finish."

"That doesn't mean a thing to me."

Hop Li shrugged.

TJ wrote down what Hop Li said then asked, "About this Missy Taylor, your teacher. Know anyone who'd want to kill her?"

Hop Li frowned and looked at him for the first time. "Aiii...you think hand belong Missy Taylor?" He paused, mouth slightly open, and then shook his head. "Wah! No true. She bring biscuit, honey, sometime steam bun, all same like home. After Jesus lesson, everybody eat. Very fine lady. Why somebody kill Missy Taylor, hnnnn? No, hand not belong Missy Taylor."

"All right. That's easy enough to check."

The Chinaboss had watched them and now came up to TJ. "Maybe I help," Lum said.

"No, I'm not finished. And I need a place we can talk without shoutin.' Understand?" TJ said. "How about we go upstairs? I'll have him back here in fifteen minutes."

The Chinaboss frowned and glared at Hop Li as if he had asked for the time off.

"Ten minute," the Chinaboss said without looking at TJ. The Chinaboss stepped in front of Hop Li and picked up a knife then nodded to the fish pitcher to take Hop Li's place.

As he reached the second floor loft, TJ spotted two straight back chairs, a small table that served as a desk, and several fish boxes crammed with tools and machine parts in a corner—Brady's office. Brady looked up and swore as he watched TJ and Hop Li approach. "You're takin' him off the line?"

"Yep. And I'd like to talk to him alone. His English is passable."

"Suit yourself."

TJ dragged two fish boxes about fifteen feet away from Brady, sat down on one, and motioned for Hop Li to sit on the other. He glanced down and noted the large rubber boots Hop Li wore and made a note to check Hop Li's foot size later.

TJ took out his notepad and pencil. "You ever see that knife before this mornin'?

Hop Li shook his head but then hesitated. "Maybe. Wah Fong have knife all same like that one."

"Wah Fong's knife is missing. Could be the one you found is his."

Hop Li shrugged.

"You buy groceries, tools at Wah Fong's?"

"Sometime."

"So you saw that dagger at his store, right?"

"Yes. But no steal knife. Already say, no thief Chen family. Why you all time say I steal?"

"Well, someone stole it and maybe brought it here. You and Fong get along, did you?"

"What mean, get along?"

"Did you and Fong ever argue, fight, get angry at each other?"

"Eh? Maybe Wah Fong sometime yell, lose face. But we no fight. Wah Fong old man."

"So what did you do to make him angry?"

"Hah? Nothing. Wah Fong make self angry." He frowned at TJ.

"All right. Let's forget any fighting for now. What did you do last Saturday and Sunday?"

"Saturday after dinner, wash shirt, pant. Then play fan-tan. Go bed. Sunday morning, go Fatt Luk house. Eat breakfast. Then go Sweet Sunday Lady…sorry…Missy Taylor. Have Jesus lesson. English lesson also. Afternoon, fly kite Fatt Luk make."

TJ took down what Hop Li said.

"What time did you leave your Chinahouse Sunday?"

"Early. Still dark when leave."

"Where does this Fatt Luk live?"

"Live on hill…Young river side…not this one." He jerked his thumb at a South window.

"I see. So you didn't go through Chinatown."

"Yes, go Chinatown."

TJ stopped writing and looked at Hop Li. "That's out of your way. Why'd you go there?"

"Have tea, Tsai Soo cart. Always talk Tsai Soo Sunday, before go Fatt Luk."

"Un-huh. And where is this teacart? What streets?"

Hop Li shrugged his shoulders. "Soo cart, all time in Chinatown. Street is…Chan…nay…"

"Chenamus."

"Yes, that one. Other street, maybe Main Street."

"That's easy to check. Now, did anyone see you there? Someone besides Soo?"

Hop Li's face stiffened. "Why you say this? You think Tsai Soo lie?"

TJ looked into hard, defiant eyes. "I didn't say he lied, Hop Li. But I got to find out for myself what's true, what isn't. Now, I'm askin' you again. Did someone other than Soo see you in Chinatown Sunday mornin'?"

"Yes. Sea captain come Soo cart, drink tea. We talk."

"A sea captain? How come…shit…never mind. Tell me about him." TJ chewed on his mustache and turned a page in his notebook.

Hop Li described the sea captain as an older man, taller than Hop Li but not as tall as TJ with a full beard and a deep voice. He wore a hat with a shiny bill and braids, an officer's hat, TJ guessed. Hop Li couldn't see the rest of the captain's clothes as the man wore a slicker. The captain told Hop Li he had to take the place of another captain who was sick. He sailed for San Francisco in a few hours and wouldn't return for a month. Hop Li paused and glanced over his shoulder towards the stairway.

"All right, what's the captain's name? The name of his ship?" TJ tapped his pencil on his book.

"He no say." He looked towards the stairs. "Must go. Stay too long time, Chinaboss say Hop Li lazy dog, cut pay."

"Be finished soon. Anything else you remember?"

"Name of captain friend, John Malmo."

TJ frowned. "How come you know his name?"

"Sea captain pay two dollar fifty cent, keep box for John Malmo. I read name on box." Hop Li looked up for an instant. "Already say, I read English word. Chinese, also." His tight-lipped face held a challenge.

TJ said nothing for a second or two and wondered what he did or said that called out the stubborn in Hop Li. Maybe Hop Li was still angry for having to give up Fong's dagger.

"I believe you, Hop Li. You read the words on that tank."

He leaned in and made sure he met Hop Li's eyes. "Hop Li, did you write the message on that tank?"

Hop Li frowned and his mouth opened slightly. "You think I write?" He shook his head and frowned. "Wah! If I write that word, Missy Taylor say Hop Li stupid like ox, learn nothing. That bad writing." Using his index finger, he wrote some characters with a quick, fluid motion in the palm of his hand. "See? This way, right way."

TJ couldn't follow Hop Li's movements and didn't understand the significance of what he did. He made a note to ask the Taylor woman about it.

"All right if you didn't write the words, do you know who did?"

"No."

"Uh-huh. Let's go back to the box the captain gave you. What'd it look like?"

Hop Li pointed to the box he sat on. "Fish box, like this one. Tie with rope. Box not heavy."

"What's in it?"

He shrugged. "Not know. Sea captain say not open. I make promise, so keep promise."

"Do you still have the box?"

"No. Fatt Luk have box."

"When is this John Malmo comin' back to pick up the box?"

"Five, six day."

TJ stopped writing and thought. "That could be tomorrow or day after. How is this Malmo supposed to find you?"

"Come cannery, ask for Hop Li. Pay one dollar, take box."

"I need to know what's in that box now. Does Fatt Luk work here?"

"No. Fatt Luk first job, Jameson Cannery, like me. But have bad luck. Fish oil burn face, eye." He ran his finger across his right eye and down his cheek. "Eye no good, so wear patch." Hop Li covered his right eye with a cupped hand. "Fatt Luk garbage man now, work Chinatown, Astor Street. Everybody know Fatt Luk."

"Yeah, I've seen him around."

The Chinaboss came up the stairs. "Chinaboy work now."

"Thanks, Hop Li." TJ closed his notebook and both men stood up.

TJ motioned the Chinaboss closer. "I'd like to see that knife. Someone broke into a store and stole a knife Sunday. Could be the one we're looking for."

"Ah...yes. Knife. Maybe tonight, after work, you come. Yes?"

"No, goddamm it. Now. Let's go."

TJ followed the chinaboss out of the cannery and across a bridge built from railroad ties and pilings. Along both sides of the bridge, hundreds of fathoms of net hung on drying racks and the odor of the copper sulphate solution used to treat the nets, saturated the air. The bridge ended at a gravel path, which led to a raised piece of ground and Jameson's chinahouse. Constructed of planks arranged in a vertical pattern, the chinahouse looked like nothing more than a large barn. Chickens scratching in the yard and the fenced garden along the east side heightened the building's barn-like appearance. But the stovepipe at either end of the roof, the worn screen door, and the work shirts dangling from clotheslines revealed its true function as home to over ninety Chinaboys. As he followed the Chinaboss on a walkway of boards laid down over the muddy yard, he wondered how so many men could live so close together for so long in peace.

The Chinaboss slid a pile of rags from under his bedroll, opened the rags, and exposed a pearl-handled dagger with a guard and an eight-inch, doubled-edged blade that glistened with oil. A tiger in pale jade flew through the air on one side of the handle. Two Chinese jade characters were embedded on the other side.

TJ pointed to the characters. "What does it say?"

The Chinaboss traced a character with his finger, smiled, and then shook his head.

"You know anybody who could read this?"

"Dr. Chung read China word. Sweet Sunday Lady also. You know lady?"

"No, but I'm about to."

10

The odor of ether and other chemicals gave TJ a queasy stomach as he walked down the main hall of St. Mary's hospital. The hospital smell always bothered him but he hadn't felt this sense of dread for over a year and it surprised him. Images of the time he carried Lucy Ann down this hall flashed through his head. He had never felt more afraid, more helpless than the moment when the orderlies rolled her away and out of sight. He and the midwife had wrapped Lucy Ann in a blanket and when a nun tried to take the blood-soaked blanket from him, he wouldn't give it up. To give it up would be to give her up, the logic of panic told him, and he clutched it to him as if it were life itself.

After three days and nights, a gray-faced doctor put a hand on TJ's shoulder and said, "She didn't make it. Childbed fever. I'm sorry, son."

He'd sat there, not believing what he'd been told, and stared at the doctor in confusion. The doctor sat down and had to repeat what he'd said three times before TJ nodded and turned away. A nun came up to him then, said she'd clean the blanket, see that he got it back. He shook her off, hugged it tighter, and carried it with him when he went into her room to sit beside the bed. After an hour, that same nun came back. This time he let her take it.

His chest ached and a twinge of that same helplessness feeling passed through him as he recalled his vigil in the hospital. He sighed and forced himself to think about the present as he walked down the steps to the coroner's office.

At thirty-six, Doc Hinkel was the youngest physician in town and the coroner for Clatsop County. He claimed his olive skin and curly black hair came from his Greek mother, his love of learning from his German father, also a physician. Doc's thick glasses, thin face, and hawk nose gave him a predatory look, like an eagle eyeing a salmon in a river.

Doc didn't look up from making an entry in his log and pointed to the chessboard on its customary stand. They were replaying the 1873 match in Vienna in which Steinitz defeated his long time rival, Anderssen. Doc continued writing and announced, "Anderssen moved bishop to king two. Steinitz to move."

"Can't think about chess today, Doc," TJ said as he laid the basket on top of Doc's log. He lowered his big frame onto the only comfortable seat in the office, a stained, green sofa with a sagging mid-section that touched the floor.

"What's this? Lunch?" Doc rubbed his hands together.

"Not hardly. But you're welcome to take a look." TJ put on his poker face.

Doc pulled the basket towards him, lifted the newspaper and looked inside. "What the hell...?" His head jerked backwards. His eyes, huge behind his glasses, bore into TJ's.

"Kinda puts you off your feed, eh?" TJ said.

"You might say that. Christ! It's the last thing I'd expect to see in a basket." He took a deep breath and let it out with a whoosh. "Well, let's stop playing games. Whose are they? Where'd you get them?"

"A Chinaboy pulled them out of a test tank at Jameson's Cannery early this mornin.' All I know is that the hands are a woman's with long fingernails."

"A cannery? What the hell they doing in a cannery? And where's the rest of her?"

"Whoa, slow down, Doc. I don't know any more than what I just told you. And, before I forget, you can't tell a soul where we found these. Jameson's afraid The Star will find out and crucify him."

"Not a word shall pass these lips."

Doc got up and went over to a glass cabinet. "Now then, how about we take a close look." He spread a towel out on a cart beside his desk and then picked up a hand with a forceps and laid it on the towel palm side up. Both stared at the hand without speaking for a few seconds. Doc turned the hand over and studied the fingernails. He prodded and tugged the little finger, which stuck up at a right angle to the other fingers. "Hmm... fifth metacarpophalangeal broken."

"Shit, Doc. In English."

"Right pinkie broken at the first knuckle."

He took the other hand out and examined it. After a minute, he straightened up. "See that mark, a light band with dark, puffy skin on either side?" He touched the base of the index finger. "Here? And here?" He pointed to the third and fourth fingers. "The skin puffs up around those marks. Blood flows to the extremities, the feet and hands, except where it's restricted. Looks like every finger but the thumb had a band like that."

"Looked to me like ring marks. "

"That's a good bet. Hold on…" He reached over to his desk and took a magnifying glass out of jar holding pencils and a letter opener. He bent over the hand and examined the broken little finger. "Skin is torn at the base of this finger, one of the others, too. Take a look." He handed the glass to TJ.

"Yeah, I see. So what's it mean?"

"Could be somebody cut the rings off and tore the skin while doing it but that's just a guess." He put the magnifying glass back in the jar and sat on the edge of his desk.

TJ made a note of what Doc told him, then said, "Well, while I'm out looking for a body, you can earn your keep by seein' what else you can discover about those hands."

"Ha! When you stop stumbling around and find that missing girl you can holler about others not earning their keep. Until then I'd keep a humble silence if that's something you're capable of."

"Here's something else for you to puzzle over." TJ took the rag bundle from his pocket, removed the rag, and laid the dagger on the desk.

Doc bent down for a close look, turned the knife over with his forceps so that the tiger was visible, and whistled. "Just full of surprises today, aren't we? This is exquisite. Where did you find it?"

"The Chinaboss took it from a butcher at Jameson's. Chinaboss thinks he stole it. The butcher says he found it when he came to work."

"Busy place today, Jameson's." Doc gave him his thin-lipped smile. "This blade has been cleaned and oiled. Still want me to look at it?"

"A quick look. I need to show it to Fong's helper."

Doc put the knife down on the cart and got out his magnifying glass. He bent close to the knife, looking at the junction of blade and guard.

"Don't see any blood or hair." He wrapped the knife in the rag and gave it to TJ. "You think the butcher murdered Fong?"

"I'm not leanin' that way. Would you kill a man, steal his knife, and then show the knife to your friends the next day? It doesn't play out, Doc."

"You're thinking like a white man, a Westerner. You don't know what's going on in that Chinaboy's head. He could be avenging an insult to his honor. Maybe he showed off that knife to prove he's an honorable man."

"Christ, Doc. If he's guilty, he'll hang. You sayin' his life doesn't mean that much to him?"

"His honor may be more important than his life." Doc smiled, and then waved his hand. "But that's just a conjecture, my friend, I could be wrong."

"Yeah, I know you could. Damm your hide."

Doc clasped his hands behind his head. "You have any idea where the body is?"

"Nope. Jameson's men went over his cannery from top to bottom and didn't find anything. I'll go back and do another search but my guess is that it's a wide open hunt." TJ stretched and yawned. "Now, you thought any on why I found Fong's blood all over that room if he died right away?"

"I said he probably died in minutes, not right away. Could be he staggered around for a time." Doc paused and tapped the tips of his fingers together. "Of course, if he were alive after the killer stabbed him, I think he'd crawl over to the window and yell for help. But in that case, you wouldn't have found blood where you did."

"Shit, Doc, it isn't in you to give a straight answer, is it? All right, let's say Fong died quick when the killer hit him over the head like you said the first time. Why'd the killer have to stab him?"

"I can tell you the whats, maybe the hows, the whys are your business." He rose and emptied the remains of his cup in the sink. "Now, all this speculating has got me hungry as a wolf. Let's eat." Doc took off his white coat and put on his red sweater with the frayed cuffs.

"Lost my appetite carryin' those hands. You go on. I've got to see a fella about this knife."

Doc nodded and hurried out.

TJ walked out the double doors of the hospital and stood on the front steps for a minute, pulling the salt air into his lungs and chasing the hospital stink away. He looked out on the river and over to Tongue Point then up at the clouds floating overhead and, for an instant, felt the pull of the river and the life of a fisherman. He took a step and the dagger in his pocket bumped against his thigh. *Nope*, he assured himself, *I'm doing what I'm supposed to be doing.*

11

Thursday, April 8

Kao's shack was sandwiched between a shoe repair shop and a Chinese washhouse one floor below street level near the corner of Chenamus and Cass Streets. TJ breathed through his mouth because of the stink of fish offal and other garbage in the tidewater below. He knocked twice and called out but received no answer. But as he turned to leave, the door opened a crack and a soft voice said something in Cantonese.

"Kao, it's me, Sheriff Stone."

Kao grunted in recognition but didn't open the door further.

TJ held the dagger in front of the opening. "Is this Fong's knife?"

The door opened a little and Kao glanced at the knife.

"Aii-ee…yes. Fong knife!" He stepped back. "No kill Fong!" he hissed and slammed the door shut.

"No, don't believe you did," TJ said to the closed door. TJ climbed the stairs back to Cass Street and thought over what he'd discovered. The killer stabbed Fong with the grocer's dagger and if Hop Li was telling the truth, the killer carried it a mile and a half to leave it at Hop Li's worktable. Why? It occurred to TJ that the person who killed Fong and the one who cut off the woman's hands might be the same person. He needed a place to think and headed for Sirpia's bakery.

TJ waved to Sirpia as he entered and took a booth in the rear. He ordered the special and then thought about the hands in that test tank. Another cannery owner wasn't behind this stunt since the publicity would hurt all owners, not just Jameson. It sounded more like some bullheaded fool bent on revenge. So if the killer wanted revenge, he had to make sure the paper got the story otherwise it did no damage. He hoped to hell the story didn't get out but if it did he'd get the name of the person who gave it to The Star.

He came back to Jameson's theory that the Knights were behind the trouble at Jameson's Cannery. They could have sent those scabs from Portland since they provoked trouble whenever it suited them. But the dagger, the hands, and the Chinee writing on that tank didn't strike TJ as their style; it left too much to chance. If no one reported the hands to the paper, Jameson wouldn't be hurt. The Knights operated like a bull, not a snake. No, Jameson's theory didn't prove out.

Halfway through his meal Sirpia stopped at his table with a coffee pot but instead of re-filling his cup she leaned against the opposite booth and asked, "Any word on that missing girl?"

"Nope." He went back to his pork chops and mashed potatoes.

"Lord, it's got to be hard on her folks, waitin' around like this."

"Uh-huh," he said with his mouth full.

"You any idea at all where that girl is?"

"Nope," he said, still not looking at her.

"Honestly, TJ. I might as well be talkin' to a fence post. You don't know any more than my mailman." She put a hand on her generous hip.

TJ found his tongue, "I got lots on my mind right now, Sirpia, but we're lookin' hard for her."

"Well, maybe you're not lookin' in the right places."

"We covered the town, the hills, the waterfront—where else we supposed to look?"

"You search Chinatown?"

"Chinatown? Now, who you been talkin' to?"

"Why that nice policeman from Portland, that's who. He came in with the chief yesterday, talked to me like I had a right to know what's goin' on—not like some I know. Anyway, when he found out I lived here since forever he asked me all about Astoria. That Mr. Purcell is polite, a real gentleman."

"He ask you about Chinatown?"

"Matter of fact he did. Wanted to know if Chinee opium users caused trouble and could a lady walk through Chinatown after dark. Things like that."

"What you tell him?"

"Told him I didn't know of any problems—not in Chinatown proper. Swilltown and saloons, now, that's a whole 'nother kettle of fish. Anyways, he got me to thinkin,' TJ. Just 'cause there's never been trouble in Chinatown, don't mean there won't be."

"We searched all the Chinee brothels and gambling joints, two days ago. Didn't find a thing."

"Well, maybe they hid her, put her in…"

"Maybe nothin.' She's not there. Now, how about a refill before the coffee in that pot gets cold.

She filled his cup. "Well, I pray to heaven you're right." She turned around to leave but then stopped. "Oh my, here's our Sonny boy back already. He's looking for you, by the way. Want me to keep him away?"

He gave up on any more thinking time. "No, that's all right, send him over."

Sonny spotted him and shouted, "Tee Jaaay!"

Over forty and mentally slow, Sonny was given the Swilltown paper route because decent folk didn't want their boys exposed to Swilltown's vices. After delivering his papers, Sonny made the rounds of the firehouse, the newspaper, and the sheriff's office, looking for errands to do. At least once a month at each of his stops, he announced it was his birthday and would hang around with the patience of a hound 'til one of the men in the firehouse or sheriff's office came up with a present: a pencil stub; an outdated wanted poster; or an old political badge. Sonny might be a bit slow, TJ told his deputies, but he damm sure wasn't stupid.

Sonny was dressed in clean overalls and a patched blue work shirt buttoned to the top. His knit hat didn't quite hide the bowl haircut given by his Uncle Leo. On the bib of his overalls and surrounded by a half dozen political badges, Sonny wore a toy deputy sheriff's badge TJ had given him on one of his birthdays. His overalls were wet from the knee down and he squished as he walked across the floor. He slid into TJ's booth.

"Got a secret," he said and wiped his nose with his sleeve.

Sirpia came back with a slice of pulla for Sonny.

"Let me know if he gets to be a bother. He'll hang around 'til the sun goes down if you let him."

"Sonny knows a lawman has work to do, don't you Sonny?"

Sonny had a mouth full of pulla and nodded.

After she left, TJ said, "You gonna tell me your secret?"

"Maybe yes, maybe no."

"I'm real busy today, Sonny, don't have time to waste."

"Didn't tell nobody. Not even him."

"Who?"

"Uncle Leo. He whips me for tellin' stories. Not gonna tell him."

"Did I ever whip you?"

"Nope. You never did."

"Well then, tell me your secret, Sonny."

"Gotta promise not to tell."

"All right, I promise."

Sonny leaned across the table and whispered, "I found her."

"Found who?"

"The princess."

Sonny's words jolted TJ fully present. "Sonny, are you tellin' a story? Tell me true like a good deputy."

"No-oo. Can't lie to TJ." He frowned and shook his head violently. "I'm good deputy."

"All right, I believe you. Where'd you find this princess?"

"Under my house."

"What's she doin' under your house?"

"Just floatin.' She's dead."

"What'd she look like?"

"Gold hair like in my picture book. Didn't have no hands. Fish ate 'em."

"Did you take her out of the river?"

"Nope. She's too heavy."

TJ got up and put his hat on. "C'mon, Sonny, let's go see your princess. You're gonna be my deputy today."

Sonny wiped his mouth with his sleeve and scooted out of the booth. He waved to anyone who caught his eye as he walked behind TJ.

TJ wondered how they'd missed her but then told himself not to jump the gun. Drunks including an occasional sporting girl fell into the river every so often so it didn't have to be the Thurgood girl. But he had to check it out fast. If news of a woman floater got out, Jane's folks would come running to Sonny's place and they'd be put through hell even if it weren't her. And if it were Jane, he wanted to get her to St. Mary's fast so Doc could clean her up before her folks saw her.

12

T J stuck his head in the office doorway. "Let's go, Sketch."
Sketch didn't ask where or why, just grabbed his hat, locked the
door, and followed his boss and Sonny down the hall. Sketch
drove the buckboard south down Cass to Seventh Street, then turned
east on Arch and followed Pine across town. After the hard climb to
Uppertown, Sketch stopped to let the horses blow. After the horses
rested, Sketch drove at a steady clip until they neared the Hemlock
Tannery on Abernathy Road. The acrid stink made their eyes water and
Sketch slapped the reins hard, pushing the team to a quick pace. Sketch
breathed through his mouth while TJ covered his nose with a bandana
until they had left the tannery a quarter mile behind. They followed
Bonneville Road north past Badollet's Cannery and out over the river
for one hundred yards before turning east again. In ten minutes, they
pulled up to the remains of the Star of the Pacific Cannery.

What fire hadn't taken, scavengers had, and all that remained of
the Star of the Pacific were the dock flooring, a rail line stripped of its
rails, and an understructure of rotting pilings and cross beams. The fire
had spared the former cannery office, a three-room shack perched at the
end of the cannery about a hundred yards off shore. The rail line ran
from the shore to the cannery and served as the bridge to Sonny and
Uncle Leo's home.

Sketch tied up the team and TJ slung a coil of rope over his
shoulder then nodded to Sonny that they were ready. They followed
him on a narrow path of planking beside the rail line, stepping over the
occasional missing plank. As they approached the shack, TJ looked for
smoke coming from the stovepipe, lights, or any signs of Uncle Leo but
saw none. The fewer people who knew about the floater the better.

When they reached the shack, TJ looked upriver and spotted the
chimney of the Scandia Packing Company at a distance of a quarter

mile. To the west he saw nothing but river as the outcropping hid Badollet's Cannery. But whichever way he turned, he couldn't seem to escape the biting wind. He shuddered and recalled that river cold always felt colder than town cold. A harsh place to live, Sonny's place, and lonesome. Sonny's uncle drank most of what he earned from odd jobs and the two of them lived as exiles in a shack under constant assault by wind, rain, and cold.

A railing of two-by-fours ran around the perimeter of the shack and several pairs of bib overalls and long johns hung on a line that ran from the railing to a nearby piling. TJ stared at the river below through an opening created by a missing plank and guessed they were about twenty feet above water. Waves slapped the pilings underneath, churning garbage and cannery waste into a brown scum on the water's surface. TJ wondered how Sonny and his uncle could live here day after day with the stench.

"Where we headed, Sonny?" Sketch asked.

"My fishin' spot. It's a secret." Sonny swung his leg over the railing, onto the rung of a ladder, and disappeared underneath his shack. Sketch followed, then TJ. Sonny sat with his knees scrunched up to his chin on a platform made of twelve foot planks placed side by side and supported by cross beams. Sketch crawled over and sat next to Sonny while TJ stayed on the ladder. Sonny aimed a finger at a spot across from him, somewhere near the middle of the forty-foot wide jumble of pilings and timbers that supported the flooring. In the dim light, TJ followed where Sonny pointed and saw what looked like a log. But then a wave lifted and turned the object part way and he glimpsed a torso and face. Another, larger wave turned the face even further towards them. Long hair, the color of straw, billowed up around the gray face like the tentacles of a sea creature. With each wave, the body moved up and down, occasionally bumping against the piling.

"Is it her?" Sketch asked.

"Can't tell from here," TJ said.

He had to get down there to keep the body from banging against that piling. He saw no clear way down through the maze of timbers and cross beams and asked Sonny, "How'd you get down there?"

"There." Sonny pointed to a cross beam that led across other timbers to the piling against which the body bumped. TJ saw the way and climbed to where Sonny and Sketch sat, took off his hat, coat, and gun belt and handed them to Sketch. He put the coil of rope over his shoulders and climbed onto the first crossbeam, straddled the beam with his legs and scooted himself across. The pilings were about a foot in diameter and when he came to one, he put his arms around it, reached out with one leg, and shifted his weight to the next crossbeam. In this fashion, he reached the piling he wanted, wrapped his arms and legs around it, and lowered himself to within a few feet of the body.

He found himself hoping it wasn't the Thurgood girl and asked himself why he felt protective of a woman he'd never met. The head of the young woman tilted at a severe angle from the torso and he suspected her neck was broken. She wore a black, silk nightgown with an embroidered bird of some kind stitched over the heart and her full breasts moved freely under the gown. The clothes were not those Jane wore when last seen and the thought crossed his mind that the floater might be a sporting girl. He reached down, caught an arm, and lifted. As he pulled the arm out of the water, he saw what he hoped not to—a stump instead of a hand. He dropped the arm as if stung and clung to the piling.

Should have expected it, he told himself, *didn't Sonny tell me the hands were missing?* The floater matched the description of the Thurgood girl: young, tall, full-figured and beautiful, which he could see in spite of the bruises on her face and neck. He'd have to bring her folks in to make sure but he no longer harbored any doubts—the floater was Jane Thurgood. The sense of being dirty welled up in him just as it had with the hands he carried to St. Mary's. He swore, reached down, and slapped the water with his open hand.

13

Thursday, April 8

Under an overcast sky which TJ believed would bring rain later, they delivered the body to the back entrance of St. Mary's. Sketch took the buckboard back to Sherman and Ward's livery while TJ wheeled the body into the cooling room where Doc performed autopsies. TJ found Doc in his office, bent over a microscope. In a few minutes, Doc looked up and said, "So? What news, lawman?"

"We pulled a floater out from under a cannery, the one that burned down."

"Is she our missing girl?"

"Expect so. But the clothes are wrong. Only thing our floater is wearin' is a silk nightgown with a bird, a peacock maybe, over the heart. The Thurgood girl was all gussied up when Annika dropped her off."

"Well, that means nothing. Unlike some men I know, women change their clothes from time to time."

"All right, I'll give you that. But where the hell did her clothes go? You think somebody ran off with them?" TJ took out an El Gusto, bit off the end, and stuck it in his mouth.

"Any man capable of murder is capable of doing any fool thing. Now, anything else I need to know?"

"Yeah. Her hands are missin'—cut off."

"So, it's the cannery woman." Doc rubbed a hand across his forehead. "In God's name, why? I just don't understand…who in their right mind would do such a thing?"

TJ stared at the anatomy chart of the human eye that hung on the wall behind Doc's desk and didn't say anything. Some questions didn't have an answer.

"Give me a few minutes." Doc stood up." There's coffee in that pot, probably cold, but it's strong."

In five minutes, Doc came back from the cool room and confirmed that the hands were the floater's.

"I'll bring her folks in." TJ went over to the sink and rinsed out his coffee cup. "Dammit, Doc, do they hafta see everything? Can you cover her up so they see only her head and face?"

"Sooner or later they'll find out, TJ. What's the difference when?"

"Later is better. Their girl's dead, Doc. Murdered. They have to take that in. That's more than enough hurt for one time."

TJ stood by the door, watching Doc make an entry in his log. "Doc, how can you do this year in year out?"

"Do what?"

"Get used to people's pain. People come in here and you got to show them a body, a body that's cut-up, mangled, burned, or God-knows-what and you wait while they look at it, recognize it, understand, yeah, it's theirs, then stand by while they think on how long dead is. Christ, Doc, how do you get used to it?"

Doc looked at his friend without speaking for a few seconds. "Who says I get used to it?"

"Can you fix her up right away? I want the bastard who did this tomorrow if not sooner." TJ rose from the sofa.

"First things first. Bring in one of the Thurgoods to identify the body, then I can get to work." Doc rinsed his cup in the sink and said as much to himself as to TJ, "A man who'd do this ...well, there's something wrong with him, wrong with his mind."

"Can't argue with you," TJ said and waited for his friend to add some insight, some bit of wisdom that might help him understand the killer's motives but Doc didn't speak.

The ship's clock next to the door rang eight bells and both turned to look at it. "Four o'clock, my friend. If you're set on catching that killer tomorrow, you better get a move on."

TJ left St. Mary's under a dark sky that matched his mood. He recalled that Mrs. Thurgood had little confidence in her husband's judgment with respect to their daughter. She'd insist on coming to identify the body and, once there, insist on seeing the entire body. She wouldn't keep quiet after she discovered the killer had cut off her hands and then it wouldn't be long before The Star got the whole story. TJ couldn't let it get to that point. He'd make sure to bring Jane's father, and only him, to identify the body.

At the office, he told Sketch to hold off giving out any news until Thomas Thurgood had a look at the floater. He grabbed his slicker off the clothes peg and headed for the Niemi home where the Thurgoods were staying. Two blocks out of the office, a soft rain started to fall and he congratulated himself on getting something right that day. He lifted the collar of his slicker, picked up his pace, and thought over what he'd learned.

The killer used Fong's dagger to cut up the grocer and then left it at the Chinaboy's worktable. The hands in the vat belonged to the floater and they'd soon know for sure if the floater were Jane Thurgood. But after that he had nothing but questions. If the killer wanted money and valuables, why not keep the dagger? And why go to all the trouble of taking the dagger to the cannery, a distance of one and a half miles? And did the murder of the girl have anything to do with Fong's murder? The dagger seemed to connect the two killings but dammed if he could see where that led or what it meant. Maybe the Chinaboy Hop Li killed Fong out of revenge, like Doc said, but why kill Jane Thurgood?

Ever since he'd talked to Kao he had a strange feeling that he was playing in a game of some kind, a game with rules he didn't understand and against opponents he didn't know. He couldn't say why he felt as he did and he sure as hell wouldn't tell anybody about it, especially Doc. But all the way to the Niemi's house, the feeling stayed with him.

14

Friday, April 9

That night TJ felt trapped in a dream where he had to get someplace in a hurry but little things, not being able to open his safe, searching for but not finding his notes, and finding his way out of a building that seemed familiar but wasn't frustrated him. As he shaved, he wondered why his night had to be as plagued with obstacles as his day. He dressed, went downstairs to the kitchen, and grunted at his landlady, Helga. She glanced up from stirring a skillet of scrambled eggs. "Well, good morning to you too, Sunshine. Bad night?"

"Coffee ready?"

She jerked her head at the row of cups and mugs hanging under a cupboard shelf. He filled a mug from the tall pot on the stove and breathed in the life-giving aroma of Helga's coffee. On the *Lucy Ann*, he and Tug had relied on her coffee to keep them awake on many a cold night as they waited for salmon to move upriver.

"Ah-hh, just what I need."

"What you need is a wife. Slow you down, show you how to live. You'll be all used up by time you're forty, way you drivin' yourself."

"I don't take advice with my mornin' coffee, Helga."

"Is that so? Well, what time of day do you take it?" She poked her spoon at him and he jumped back, smiling.

She smiled too. "Go on, get out of here before I burn breakfast."

He went into the dining room and a short, powerfully built Greek, a dockhand new to Astoria, looked up from the morning paper.

"Ah hah! Mister Sheriff." His face lit up.

"Mornin.'" TJ regarded the Greek with the bristly mustache and stubble of whiskers with surprise. The man hadn't said two words to him in the month he'd been here.

"Girl missing, is same girl in river?" the man asked. The other eight men at the harvest table stopped talking and looked at TJ.

TJ stared at the man a second before managing to say, "What?"

"In paper. See." The man passed the paper to him.

Woman found in river, the headline said in The Star.

"Shit," TJ muttered. Bad news first thing in the morning stung him. He wasn't all the way into his skin, as he had often reminded Lucy Ann, who loved mornings. He started to get mad at Sonny then realized that Leo, Sonny's uncle, would be an expert in worming information out of his nephew. Uncle Leo had come on them loading the floater's body into the buckboard. TJ might have taken the man into his confidence, asked him not to say anything for a few days. But Uncle Leo, drunk and surly, cursed them and walked off after he found out there was no reward for finding the body. He realized it wouldn't have mattered what he said; Uncle Leo couldn't be trusted. His insides burned but to the men seated around the table he showed only his official face, calm and stern. He pulled out a chair, sat down, and read the story.

"*Earlier this week, The Star reported on the murder of a Celestial, Wah Fong, and the disappearance of Miss Jane Thurgood, a visitor from Portland. Yesterday, we learned that the body of a young woman was taken out of the river near an abandoned cannery. Sheriff TJ Stone allowed that the unfortunate woman may have been a sporting girl with a belly full of gin and had tumbled into the river. We learned from Mr. Sonny Wellborn that the woman wore a long black nightgown and no undergarments which facts support Sheriff Stone's conjecture about the victim's profession. Now accidents like this are not unknown to befall Astoria's girls of the line but it seems to us passing strange that we hosted a murder, a disappearance, and drowning by misadventure in the same week. That is considerable over the quota, even for Astoria. No arrests have been made as yet but Chief Connelly assured us that every effort is being made…*"

"Breakfast! No reading while we're eating. You know my rules, TJ," Helga said as she set a dishpan size bowl of scrambled eggs in the center of the table. A girl followed with a bowl of sausages in one hand and a plate of biscuits in the other. He gave himself over to the hot food. Two helpings of eggs and sausage along with four biscuits and raspberry jam went down before he wiped his mouth and pushed back from the table.

On the front porch, he finished reading the story in The Star. The paper didn't come right out and say it but readers would assume that the floater was Jane Thurgood. At least, the missing hands were not mentioned. As he descended the steps to the street, he watched a Chinaman in the neighbor's back yard turn soil for a spring garden. The Chinaman made him think of Kao and this, in turn, gave direction to his morning.

At the office, he told Sketch that Thomas Thurgood had identified the body as his daughter. "Doc showed him only her face so what happened to her hands is still a secret and I aim to keep it." TJ sat down at his desk and asked, "You see the paper this mornin'?"

"Nope."

"Daines has the story on our floater, even down to what I told Sonny's uncle."

"Jesus, Boss, how'd Daines get it so fast? Who the hell...ah shit...Uncle Leo. Guess he wasn't near drunk as I thought. Damm."

"Guess not. But what's done is done." TJ paused to light a cigar, leaned back in his chair, and said, "Sketch, we've been fumblin' around in the dark too long. I want you to go over to the Niemi place and talk to Annika. I'm fair certain she knows more than she's told us. So be patient and do lots of listenin.' Remind her, if she needs remindin,' that her friend is dead so there's no need to keep secrets. She's afraid of sayin' things in front of her folks, so talk to her alone, maybe in the parlor."

"Where you goin,' Boss?"

"Kao hardly opened the door last time I talked to him. He's scared and it's time we find out why. Doc said he'd finish the autopsy before lunch so I'll meet you there at noon. We'll be gone by the time the Thurgoods come to pick up their daughter."

TJ didn't find Kao in his shack or at Fong's. A young Chinaman now ran Fong's store and spoke enough English to tell TJ that Kao had not come by since the murder. TJ looked for Kao in Wing's Clouds of Heaven, the Kop Piu lottery office, and a couple of other Chinese dives before giving up. He stopped off at Sirpia's for coffee and stewed over the time wasted hunting Kao. He grumbled aloud about not having Big Jim, his mountain man deputy, here but the big man wasn't due back from Spokane for days. He hoped Doc or Sketch had news that would redeem the day.

15

A pale-faced Sketch sat on the green sofa with his legs splayed out, staring at the human skull on Doc's desk as if in a trance, and only nodded in response to TJ's greeting. Doc came in from the cool room, greeted TJ, and then rinsed out the coffee pot.

"What'd you do to my deputy, Doc?"

"I showed him the Thurgood body, hands and all, and told him what I've discovered. Haven't had time to pretty her up yet. Guess it got to him." Doc busied himself making coffee. "You fellows spend more time here than your place. Ought to charge you for coffee."

"Well, if weren't for our visits, you'd be lonely as a lizard in the desert. Ought to charge you for entertainment. What say, Sketch?"

Instead of responding, Sketch got to his feet and said, "Doc, I need a toilet."

"Use the sink in the cool room—but clean up after you."

Sketch hurried out without another word.

TJ waited until the sound of Sketch's retching subsided then took out his notepad and asked, "All right, Doc, what'd you find out we don't already know?"

"I don't know. What do you know?"

"Christ, Doc, don't start. How'd she die? Stabbed to death, drowned, what?"

"Neither, I'm fairly sure." Doc folded his hands behind his head, eyes twinkling.

"Wha...?" TJ's mouth stayed open.

"Not much water in her lungs and as for the knife wounds, it's hard to say. They weren't that deep but, if left untended, she would have bled to death."

"Then what the hell killed her?"

"Did you see her head and neck?" Doc leaned back in his chair.

"Yeah. Neck broken?"

"Right. Skull fractured as well. All that and the bruising around her face meant the killer choked her and beat the hell out of her before he threw her in the river."

"Anything else?"

"Well, she was pregnant."

"Christ! You sure?"

Doc looked at him over his glasses without speaking, adopting what TJ had come to know as Doc's not-encouraging-foolish-questions pose.

"All right, all right. How long?"

"I'd say 10 to 12 weeks."

TJ considered how this news changed things. An unmarried woman gets with child and no one wants to know about it, especially the father. And if that father is already married, he might kill the woman to keep her quiet. But then he thought of the hands and his excitement at Doc's news died. He saw no reason for the killer, father or no, to cut off her hands.

"Anything else you keepin' from me, Doc?"

"Well, I didn't find any food in her stomach so couldn't use food to estimate time of death. And this time of year river water is cold, 38° or less, and that would slow decomposition. But she had some bloating so my best guess, and it's only a guess, is that she's been in the river about three days. That any help?"

"Not much."

"Well, here's something definite. That gown she wore is Chinese."

"How the hell you know that?"

"Well, for one thing, the label says made in China. For another, that bird on her dress isn't a peacock, it's a phoenix. That yellow-orange ball the bird is looking at is fire or the sun, and in Chinese mythology the phoenix is born from fire or the sun.

"You a China expert now, Doc?"

"No. That's straight from Dr. Chung, an educated man. You could learn a thing or two from him, you know."

"Shit. You didn't bring him over here, did you?"

"Of course not. What'd you take me for? After seeing the label I went to his store. As soon as I described the bird and ball, he knew it was a phoenix. The phoenix stands for beauty, warmth, summer, the harvest, good things like that."

TJ took notes and then asked, "You don't have enough to do—you're takin' on my job?"

"Well, competition never hurt anybody. Now, here's some more detective work I saved you. Her gown smelled of opium, faint, but definitely present."

"Opium? Ah hell, Doc, that doesn't sound like our girl." TJ shook his head, puzzled, but a second later he smiled. "But hold on. What if she happened to be in a room with someone..."?

"Ah, very good. Now you're thinking like a detective, not jumping in bed with the first conclusion that sashays up to you. There's no way to know for sure how that smoke got on that gown. Now, you know all I know. I'll send my report over to the DA's office in a day or two."

"Doc, tell me one thing." TJ ran his hand over his mustache. "Was she alive when the killer cut off her hands?"

"Can't say for sure. I didn't see any ligature marks around her ankles—couldn't tell one way or the other from what's left of her wrists. It's hard to know what goes on in the mind of a madman but it'd be easier to do if she's dead." He rose and went over to the stove and filled three cups with hot coffee. "I'm used to seeing all kinds of accidents, mangled bodies, gore, but this is so...so goddamm deliberate. Can't imagine a reason for it either. Any suspects?"

"No strong ones. Fella she planned to meet is a possible. Her best friend says she knew him but, hell, we don't even know she made it to that meeting." TJ slipped his notebook in his pocket and stood up. Sketch came out of the cool room, face still pale but without the pained expression he'd worn earlier.

"How you feelin'?," TJ asked.

"Some better. Don't believe I'm cut out for lookin' on bodies, Boss."

"Don't think any of us are, Sketch. Sit down for a spell." He nodded towards the cool room. "All right if I go in there, Doc?"

"Why? You hate the stink of carbolic acid and it's strong now." Doc regarded his friend with raised eyebrows.

"Can't say for sure, Doc, but I'd like to."

In the last few days TJ had come to know Jane Thurgood and, though he didn't think of her a friend, she had become more than a corpse. He opened the heavy door to the cool room and went inside. The strong acid stink didn't mask the stench of decaying flesh and he breathed through his mouth. He lifted a corner of the sheet that covered the body. The surgical incision across the forehead, the bruised and mottled color of the skin, and the blisters on her face destroyed the beauty he'd seen earlier. He swallowed twice and let the sheet fall back.

Doc came up behind him. "One day, life ahead of her, the next, it's over. Not more than seventeen, eighteen. A shame."

Neither said anything for a time but then Doc coughed and said, "I've got errands to run. But you boys finish your coffee. We'll talk after the Thurgoods pick up their daughter."

TJ followed Doc out of the cool room, slid a stool up to his deputy, and sat down facing him. "Some things you ought to know, Sketch. Jane's hands were pulled from a test tank at Jameson's. I figure they were dropped in that tank sometime during the strike when canneries were empty. The killer left a message in Chinee on that tank but I haven't made sense of it yet."

Sketch frowned. "Boss, none of that makes a lick of sense. Why'd a Chinee cut off that girl's hands and dump 'em in a tank? It's a damm fool thing to do, seems to me."

"It seems so to me, too. But listen careful now. As of today, we're sitting on a keg of dynamite. You can't breathe a word about how she lost her hands, or that they were found at Jameson's Cannery, not a word. You hear me?" TJ put his face close to Sketch's and waited 'til Sketch looked up and nodded.

"Boss, what about Sonny? He seen the body, knows them hands is missin.' Shit, there's Uncle Leo, too. He came on us while we was loadin' her in the buckboard, kept pesterin' us with questions. He was corned close to staggerin' but could be he'll recall some of what you said."

"I only told him the floater might be a sporting girl. I didn't say anything about her hands being cut off. As for Sonny, well, he thought fish ate them. But I'll ask him not to say anything about her hands for another week. It'll cost us a double scoop of chocolate ice cream, but he'll keep quiet." TJ paused and leaned back on his stool. "The other problem is Daines. I don't expect him to find out about the hands but if he comes nosin' around, send him to me." TJ stood up, stretched, and asked, "How'd your meet with Annika go?"

"Middlin' fair. She acted kinda starchy at first. But I just listened, like you said, and she mellowed considerable." He turned a page in his notes. "Let's see, she did 'fess up to not tellin' ever thing she knowed. Seems that fella Jane set off to meet has got him a wife—was why they was sneakin' round. Guess he's rich too, well-off is how she put it."

"Good man, Sketch. What else?"

"Well, this here didn't make no sense but wrote it down anyways." He flipped a page in his notes. "Here it is. Seems Jane said her fella is a real topper—gonna read about him in the paper sometime soon she tells Annika. What's that mean, Boss?"

"Don't know. She say where this topper lives?"

"Nope. That's all I got. Seems like somethin' else is botherin' her but her dad come in then and tells me to git, so I did."

"You did fine, Sketch, just fine."

TJ told Sketch Hop Li's story of being hired by a sea captain to keep a box for the captain's friend and asked him what he thought.

"That Chinaboy's story smells 'bout like my feet at bedtime. All we gotta do is find his friend, that there garbage man. Bet he ain't got a box. The Chinaboy is lyin,' boss."

"Well, let's find out. Find the garbage man, go out to his place and bring him back along with any sealed fish boxes you find. Bring anything else that looks like it doesn't belong."

"Don't belong? Like what?"

"A gun, knife, woman's clothes."

Sketch nodded then said, "We got three Chinee garbage men in town. Which one we lookin' for?"

"He wears an eye patch. Goes by the name of Fatt Luk."

"I seen him around." He put his hat on then paused at the door. "Where you goin'?"

"I'm goin' after Kao. I'll be back by three o'clock and then we'll see what Fatt Luk has to say."

16

T J knocked on the door of Kao's shack and got no answer. He banged on the door and shouted Kao's name a number of times. Still no answer and he grew uneasy. He didn't have a warrant and had no justification for getting one. One good shove and he'd be in. No one would know he broke in and even if anyone saw him, no one would give a damm—it's only a Chink house, he told himself.

But he stopped that line of thinking. In his campaign for sheriff, he'd promised to be fair, take no bribes, and follow the law. If he had to break the law to get things done why be a lawman?

Just then a laundryman came out of the washhouse next door, emptied a tub of dirty water into the river, and looked him up and down before going back inside. TJ walked over to the washhouse but no one spoke English. One man indicated by signs that Kao had stuck his face in the door and waved to them that morning. TJ asked where Kao went in a variety of ways but couldn't get a sensible answer. Finally, the oldest of the three workers mimed smoking a pipe and then laying his head down. Even if he found Kao, he'd be lost in a fog of opium. He swore under his breath and climbed the stairs back to Chenamus Street. Before he'd taken a dozen steps, a woman's voice hailed him.

He turned around and met Annika dressed in mourning clothes: a black dress with a short cape, a full bustle, a black velvet bonnet with no flowers, and a cream colored parasol trimmed with black velvet. Her veil didn't hide her wet cheeks.

"Annika. I'm real sorry about Janey."

"I wanted to see you, Sheriff. I...oh, I'm not sure what to do. Please, can we go to your office? I need to talk."

Sketch could be back with Fatt Luk any time and TJ wanted to salvage something of the day. "Well, we're busy now, Annika. How about later tonight, after supper?"

She lifted her head. "It's important…I mean it could be. And we're leaving for Portland this afternoon for Janey's funeral. I won't be back for three days."

"Important? All right, then. My office it is." He offered her his arm and as they walked down Chenamus Street he asked after the Thurgoods and her folks. Though she answered politely, she was distant.

Patience. She'll tell you what's troubling her in time.

TJ turned the 'Back in 1 Hour' sign around, pulled the office door half closed, and stuck the doorstop in—his 'do not disturb' sign. He wanted Annika to feel like a guest, not a suspect, and dragged the straight-backed chair beside his desk. He stirred the ashes in the potbelly, put a log in, and found the coffee pot about half full. "Coffee be hot in no time."

"No thank you. I can't stay long." She sat down on the edge of the chair and folded her hands in her lap. "You ever wish you could undo something, Sheriff Stone?"

"Probably. But can't recall anything right now. Are you blamin' yourself for what happened to Janey?"

She looked at him without speaking. Tears fell down her cheeks.

"Listen, you didn't know where she went or who she planned to meet. You had no way of knowin' she was walkin' into trouble, did you?" He smiled.

"No, but I lied to my folks, Sheriff Stone…I lied. If I hadn't, oh, I wish I'd stood up to her, told her no, just this once. Why didn't I?" She lowered her head and sighed. "She'd still be alive if I had."

TJ leaned forward. "Now, you can't undo what's done. You believed you were helpin' a friend and that's what friends are supposed to do. Can't fault you on that." He took an El Gusto out of his leather cigar case, put it in his mouth, but didn't light it. "But is this what you came to talk about?"

"No sir."

He waited for her to say more and when she didn't he said, "You said you had something important to tell me, right?"

"Yes…well, it could be. Oh, Sheriff Stone, I'm not sure it's right…what I'm doing…I mean coming here." She chewed on her lower lip and fought back tears.

"You do something wrong, break the law?"

"No. Nothin' like that. It's more like breakin' a promise." She pulled a handkerchief out, reached under her veil and wiped her eyes.

"Well, you're right about not wantin' to break a promise. You give your word to somebody and they've got to count on it. Of course, there's times you have to break a promise, special circumstances. Now, did you make a promise to Janey?"

"Yes." She lowered her head and whispered, "It's her diary. She left it with me last Saturday just before we left the house, made me promise not to read it or show it to anyone. We signed our names on the inside—in blood."

"Janey's dead now, Annika, and anything you do or don't do can't hurt her. Did you read her diary, that why you're upset?"

"No. I didn't. I wouldn't."

"Well then, what's wrong? What's got you so worried?"

"Her secrets are in there. She said if any of them got out, why, it'd be the ruination of some people. She never said who or why but I know her. It's true."

TJ's thoughts started to fly. Jane might have named the father of her baby in the diary. "You want to keep Janey's secrets, is that it?"

"Yes, well, I did. I wrapped up the diary to give to her folks. But then I didn't. I couldn't. What if there's something in there that helps find that dreadful man who murdered her? It could, you know. But see, I don't know it will, not for sure." She stood up and paced back and forth in front of his desk. "Janey said she'd be ever so mortified if her Mom read it. I know Janey's dead, Sheriff Stone, but I can't tell her secrets to all creation for no reason. I promised. Oh, I want to do what's right. What should I do?"

"Tell you what, Annika. Suppose the only people to see Jane's diary are the ones that need to see it, me and maybe one or two others. If there's nothing in there that bears on her murder, I'll give it back and that's an end to it. But even if it turns out something important is in there, I'll do my best to keep her secrets out of the paper."

"Is that a promise?"

"Yep. It's a promise."

She stood up and took a deep breath. "I hope I'm doing right."

From her purse, she took out a package wrapped in brown paper and tied with a ribbon and handed it to him. "I couldn't find the key so I guess you'll have to break the lock."

"You're doin' right, Annika, and I'm much in your debt." TJ stood up and escorted her to the door. "If I have time, I'll come by the dock, see you off. What time you leave?"

"We leave at 3:30 on the steamer, Telephone." She extended her hand and he shook it.

After she left, he sat down and tore the wrapping off what turned out to be an expensive diary with a green, leather-bound cover and fitted with a brass lock. He looked at the initials on the cover and something wasn't right. The gold initials on the bottom right corner were LL not JT as they should have been. Could Annika have given him her own diary? But that wasn't right either since her initials were AH.

He pulled Tug's fish knife out of his boot, put the tip of the blade in the lock, twisted, pushed, and the lock snapped open. Jane wrote in a large, neat hand, with flourishes. The entries were dated but sometimes a week or more went by without an entry. He turned to the last page, a blank, except for the girls' dark brown signatures. He flipped to the last two pages of writing and read the top entry.

Thursday, April 1

April Fool's Day. But Lillie has no time for fools. Papa gave in—finally. Mama didn't like it but won't fight Papa over it. Astoria plan all set—hurray! A excited to have Lillie visit & talk wedding plans. Wait 'til she hears Lillie's plans! Secrets! Like old times.

N after me again—like an animal in heat. Told him he needs more imagination. Lillie let him kiss her today before putting him off. As a lover, he's no B but he's gaga about her & she can manage him.

The entries for the next three days were a shopping trip, plans for one of her sisters' birthday party, and the party itself. The last two entries were more revealing.

Friday, April 9

Busy day! Mama sent jams & bread along for the Hermansons—cautioned me against leaving the ladies' compartment for any reason. All the way to Astoria—imagine! Lillie goes where she pleases. Mama is a dear but such a slave. Always tired. She and Papa never go dancing or to theater. Lillie could never lead such a life—she won't.

Hush-hush meeting with a labor man from Seattle this am. Ugliest brute ever. Mailed B's report today. Will quit working for him once N & Lillie married. Haven't told B about us yet. Maybe Monday—after all settled.

Saturday, April 10—Astoria

House still asleep. Lillie can't. Too much on her mind. Lillie gives him her news tonite at a secret hideaway—delicious! He's getting a bargain & he knows it. His wife is a terrible drudge—so old, poor thing. Does he appreciate Lillie? He will, tho.

Told A Lillie's plans [not everything, silly] after breakfast! She is a love but can't keep a secret for a minute. Lillie made her cross her heart & swear in blood! She's scared but Lillie knows her—she'll do it!

He re-read the final entry with a growing sense of annoyance. He guessed that the initial A stood for Annika but that didn't help much. He had to go back several pages before either B or N showed up again.

Sunday, March 28

Sent off B's report today. Been ages since Lillie and he talked—heart to heart. Lillie misses him ~~but won't come~~ *& hasn't given up on him.*

Decided yesterday. N's yacht is smaller than B's but it's a yacht all the same. Met him in the park during lunch hour Friday. Gave him a dose of Lillie's tonic & it was a 'sin to Moses' the way he carried on—promised anything if she'd come to his hotel later. People started to notice so Lillie made him behave. He is Lillie's when she wants him.

Just you wait & see! When Lillie is Mrs. N & safe, B will come running. But if we become 'friends' again it will be on Lillie's terms—not his! She's learned her lesson—Lillie won't be a slave to any man!!

Somewhere in the middle of the diary he found an entry about R, a boyfriend.

Friday, March 5

Another slow afternoon. Bored to bitterness but then the Old Witch sent Lillie to druggist for her tonic. Had time so went by the store & visited. Found R in storeroom & teased him out of countenance. Made him promise to come by today & wouldn't leave 'til he kissed her. His face turned beet red but he obeyed. Lillie is shameless! Fun!!

Two weeks later the last entry about R appeared.

Sunday, March 21.

R came by & went to church with family. Afterwards Lillie & R went on picnic with Miss CC & Mr. GT. Sunshine most of day & we sang songs for an hour or so. Lillie brought peach pie. Miss C her famous roast chicken & apples. Stuffed ourselves! R tongue-tied when GT talked politics. R ~~is~~ *was fun but he's only a boy—really. And Sin of Sins—he's turned serious! Jealous, too. Ugh! Lillie gave him the mitten today. It's over! R went into the worst sulk—rude to GT too. Spoiled Lillie's day.*

There were no references to N in the rest of the diary and the only other references to B had to do with the weekly reports. TJ put his feet up on his desk and re-read the entries on the last page again. N is married and the man she wants to marry. He could be the mystery man she set out to meet that Saturday night but N lived in Portland, not Astoria. She did not mention N or B in the April 10th entry, only 'him.'

B had been her lover and maybe she planned to meet him that Saturday because she was annoyed with him. Maybe B found out about N, grew jealous, and killed her.

R had become serious and jealous but then she didn't write any more about him after she told him they were finished.

What else had he learned? She worked for B, sent him reports about once a week, but had decided to quit whatever she did after she married N. What did she do for B? And why did she write like that— always Lillie, never Jane or I? Jane or Lillie was telling him what he needed to know, he suspected, if he could only decipher it. Schemer, gold digger, and two-timer, all described Miss Jane Thurgood. *But by God she was a damm interesting woman.*

He pocketed the diary, lit his cigar, and thought of girls growing up together, the dreams and secrets they shared. Annika would know the names behind the initials in Jane's diary.

17

TJ scanned the fifty or sixty people at the Oregon Railway & Navigation Company dock and looked over the carriages, buggies, and the Occident Hotel omnibus, but didn't see the Hermansons or the Thurgoods. The sternwheeler, Telephone, docked, more buggies pulled into the waiting area, and just when he decided he had the time wrong, a barouche pulled into the loading area. Paul Purcell and Olney Hermanson climbed out and helped Mrs. Thurgood, Mrs. Hermanson and Annika down. The women were veiled and dressed in black. The men, except for Purcell, wore dark blue suits. Purcell wore a gray suit, wine-colored vest, paisley tie, and a pink rose in his buttonhole. A black armband was his only concession to custom.

TJ removed his hat, went over to the group, and offered condolences to the Thurgoods. Thomas Thurgood looked smaller to TJ and, in spite of having shaved and combed his hair, he had the blank stare of a man who hadn't slept for days. Martha Thurgood didn't take her eyes off the ground when TJ spoke. TJ left the group and walked over to where Annika and Purcell were talking.

"Annika, I need to speak to you," TJ said.

Before she answered, Purcell shoved his walking stick in front of her skirt. "For God's sake, Stone, this is not the time for your infernal questions. These people are in mourning."

"It's all right Mr. Purcell. I don't mind," Annika said.

Purcell pulled his walking stick away but didn't move from her side. "Well, go ahead, Sheriff, ask away—I won't interfere. And I must admit to some curiosity as to the progress of your investigation."

TJ ignored him. "Let's go over here where it's quiet." He led Annika to a spot some distance from the others. "It's about Janey's diary. I know you'd like to keep what's in there private."

"I appreciate that, Sheriff."

"I know you didn't read her diary, Annika, but you and Janey talked like best friends do, didn't you?"

In spite of her veil, he saw her lips turn up in a hint of smile before turning down again. "Well, 'course we did. We wrote letters after she moved to Portland but, well, that's not the same, is it?"

"Janey only used initials in her diary. I need the names that go with the initials for her men friends."

"Men friends? You mean her admirers, Sheriff?"

"That's right."

"I just know she has bushels of admirers in Portland." She paused and then frowned. "Did you show her diary to her Mom?"

"No, and I won't. When this business is over, I'll give it back to you, let you decide what to do with it."

"I truly appreciate that." She looked back towards town.

"This first initial is R. She went out with this fella for a time but about a month ago she got tired of him and broke it off."

Annika smiled and nodded. "Oh, that's Russell—forget his last name—works for Janey's father. Too young for her, she told me—oh, and fierce jealous, too. She hated it when men got that way, you know, wantin' her all to themselves. She is so…so sophisticated, Sheriff, I wish you'd known her. She is…I mean was… different from other girls."

"I'm finding that out. Now, how about a fella with the initial N?"

She thought for a moment then shook her head. "No. Can't think who that is."

"How about the initial B?"

She shook her head. "Don't know him either." She looked down and sighed. "I still can't believe she's gone—I miss her so. She coulda been famous, Sheriff, a famous actress, a somebody—I'm as certain of that as my name." Annika glanced past TJ's shoulder. "Dad is wavin' at me, wants me back. You have any more initials?"

"No, that's all I have. If I have more questions, I'll come by when you get back." He offered his hand and she took it. "You're a true friend to Janey, Annika. I'm sorry as can be about what happened."

Fresh tears spilled down her cheeks as she said in a shaky voice, "You're kind, Sheriff Stone, thanks again for keepin' her diary private."

No sooner did Annika leave than Purcell ambled over. "So, did you learn anything from Annika, Stone?"

"Not much."

"Annika is a sweet girl, sweet but a bit addle-brained. I wouldn't rely overmuch on what she tells you." Purcell lifted his beaver hat and wiped his forehead with his monogrammed handkerchief.

"She's goin' through hell right now, Purcell. Feels she's to blame for her best friend gettin' killed. It's not surprisin' she seems addled at times."

"Well, perhaps I am being too hard on her." He drew a figure eight in the dirt with his walking stick. "See here, Stone, there's something I feel duty bound to tell you. I trust you'll take what I'm about to say in the spirit in which it's offered, that is, as a bit of advice from an experienced lawman."

TJ had no idea what Purcell meant and didn't say anything.

"The Thurgoods are not at all pleased with how you've conducted yourself with respect to their daughter. It's not rational, of course, but Mrs. Thurgood blames you for that story in the paper."

TJ took a step back to get away from the smell of Purcell's lime cologne. "Blames me? For what?"

"About what you said or rather implied about their daughter."

"Not followin' you, Purcell."

"Your speculation about the woman you pulled from the river. Well-intentioned on your part, I'm sure, but Jane's parents were mortified, Mrs. Thurgood especially so."

"Why?"

"Well, think about what you told the paper. A sporting girl who fell into the river after a drinking bout. Good God, man. People I've talked to in town, most of them anyway, assumed that Jane was that sporting girl. The misunderstanding will be cleared up, eventually, but the damage has been done. The Thurgoods feel you've left a stain on their daughter's reputation and their good name."

"I said what I did to protect them. Didn't want…"

"Oh, I'm sure your intentions were noble, Stone, however, I'm afraid what you said offended them deeply and can't be dismissed so lightly. I believe you owe them an apology. However, if I were you, I'd wait until a more propitious moment to offer it, when their souls are not encumbered by grief."

TJ studied Purcell, looking for any sign of pretense but didn't see any.

The whistle of the steamer let loose a long blast, the gangway lowered, and the crowd, including the Thurgood party, headed for it. Halfway up the gangway, Annika turned and waved to TJ then disappeared into the crowd. Purcell stood next to TJ and watched the tide of people surge toward the steamer.

"Aren't you goin' with them?" TJ asked.

"Of course. I'm seeing to the funeral arrangements but the steamer won't leave for another ten minutes. But now a little more advice, one professional to another, about dealing with the public. You gave out false information in an effort to hide a disagreeable truth—a novice's mistake, which…."

"What's done is done, Purcell. No need to harp on it."

"I'm not harping on it. I'll just tell you what I tell my detectives. Don't give out information, true or false, about a crime to anyone who doesn't need to know. If you do, it'll come back to bite you. You're new, still green, but you'll learn." He chuckled and looked over at people moving up the gangway.

TJ's chest burned in anger at his last remark. The mayor, the chief, even Jameson never tired of reminding TJ of his beginner status, especially when their wishes clashed with his. But as far as he knew, he hadn't made any mistakes, not big ones anyway. So what if Jane's mother soured on him? He saw his job as catching Jane and Fong's killer, nothing else. He didn't need Purcell's advice but he held his tongue.

"I have a proposition for you, Stone, and I hope you won't take this the wrong way."

"More of that imagination of yours?" TJ folded his arms across his chest.

"Well, not imagination so much as using every resource at your disposal. I'm in a position to help you and perhaps restore you to the Thurgoods' good graces." Purcell smiled and tilted his head back as he looked at TJ over his glasses. "In Portland, we have men in the department, detectives, who specialize in crimes of murder. Now, much as I'd like to, I can't afford to send them here. But I can give them the facts of the crime to review and see what they make of it. You'd be surprised what a good detective can discover in a short time. I've already talked to Chief Connelly about my idea. He welcomes the help. What do you say?" Purcell drew a line in the dirt with his walking stick.

TJ didn't like Purcell, didn't like his political scheming, or his high opinion of himself. But as a police commissioner, Purcell probably knew a lot more about investigating a murder than he did.

"Guess it can't hurt," TJ said.

"Capital! Now then, the coroner told me that although you took Jane from the river, she didn't drown. How was she killed?" Purcell took out a pencil and a leather-bound notebook from his inside coat pocket.

"Well, she'd been stabbed in her chest and belly but Doc Hinkel thinks she took a beatin' and that killed her, rather than the stabbin.' Killer broke her neck too."

"But the killer stabbed her, you say. Have you found the knife?"

"Can't say for sure. Somebody murdered that Chinee grocer last weekend and used the grocer's dagger to cut him up. That same dagger showed up at a cannery. Could be the one used on the Thurgood girl."

"Any suspects yet?"

"A Chinaboy at Jameson's Cannery had the dagger the day after the strike. Could be he killed Fong but I don't see him killin' the girl. They didn't travel the same roads, if you know what I mean."

"No, of course they didn't. You know, Olney Hermanson told me that Jane ran off to meet some man. What have you discovered about him?"

"Not much. Jane told Annika just enough to carry out her plan."

"That's unfortunate." Purcell made a note then said, "Now, something else I wanted to know—what is it? Oh yes, the clothes. The paper said she wore a nightgown when found. But according to Mrs. Hermanson, Jane left the house dressed to the nines. What happened to her clothes?"

"We're lookin' for them."

"She might have been asleep or getting ready for bed when murdered. Do you know where she was killed?"

"Nope, but we're workin' on it."

"Well, that's not much for my boys to go on." He tapped his pencil on the notepad. "Now, is there anything, anything at all, you can add to what you've told me?" Purcell smiled but only with his lips, his eyes remained hard.

TJ didn't speak up right away and decided against telling Purcell about the diary since he'd promised Annika he'd show it to two or three local people and only if necessary. He hadn't mentioned Jane's pregnancy and figured Purcell's detectives should know that.

"Well, she was with child."

Purcell stopped doodling in the dirt with his stick and looked up sharply. "Eh? What did you say?"

"With child. Doc says maybe 10-12 weeks."

"Is he sure?"

"I've known Doc for some time now. Being careful is a religion with him."

"Well, that is news." Purcell turned away from TJ and stared down at the river.

Another long howl from the steamer's whistle interrupted Purcell and neither spoke during the noise. Purcell continued to stare at the river, brow furrowed in concentration, until the whistle stopped. Purcell faced TJ and said, "This changes things."

"How so?"

"Don't you see? We now have a motive. The father of the baby, an unprincipled rogue no doubt, murders Jane in order to save himself from scandal. By God, it makes sense, perfect sense. What do you think?"

"It's possible. From what I've learned, Jane Thurgood had plenty of men friends. Come to think of it, Purcell, you saw her every day, you must have known she wasn't shy around men. You sure you don't know any fella she was walkin' out with?"

"I've already told you, Stone. I knew about the boy who worked for her father but that's all."

"She broke up with him some time back. Any lawyers beside yourself work in your office?"

"Just one. Lyle Whittaker. But why do you ask?"

"'Cause some man she knew in Portland, a fella she trusted, is most likely the father. Where she worked is the first place to look, seems to me. Now, tell me about this Whittaker fella. Is he married? Does he fancy himself a ladies' man?"

"Dammit, Stone. I don't know a thing about Jane's personal life, as I've already said. You don't listen well, do you?"

"Oh, I reckon I listen as well as the next fella." TJ knew he had touched a nerve. Purcell's words were hurried, his voice sharp, and a frown had replaced the easy smile for an instant.

"I'm askin' about Whittaker," TJ continued, his voice slow and measured.

"Now, listen here, Stone. I trust Lyle...been with me five years...good lawyer... honorable... no, what you're suggesting is out of the question. Just because his family has money and he likes to entertain, people talk." Purcell turned his back to TJ.

"Maybe the talk has some truth to it. Tell me about this talk."

"That's no business of yours, Stone." Purcell turned around to answer but still didn't look at TJ. Another blast from the steamer shattered the air before either could speak again.

"It's time you got on board. I'd still need to know about Whittaker. You could write me about him or I could come see you. What's your preference?"

"I'm busy now...perhaps...yes I think it best if I write to you about Lyle. Well, I'm off." Purcell offered his hand and, this time, TJ squeezed it hard and pushed it back towards Purcell's chest. The muscles in Purcell's face tightened but he said nothing. As he headed for the steamer, Purcell twirled his walking stick at his side.

TJ watched Purcell board and thought about why the man irked him so much. Purcell appeared sincere in his offer of help but the man was fighting Jameson for power and that U.S. senate seat. Men hungry for power, TJ knew, didn't spend much energy or time on things that didn't bring power. Sure, Jane Thurgood worked for Purcell and, yes, he knew the family but Purcell had spent three days helping the Thurgood family and the city police. Three days away from a busy life in Portland. That didn't fit with how TJ saw the man. So TJ asked himself how helping solve this one murder furthered Purcell's ambition of becoming a senator. It bothered him that he couldn't come up with an answer.

18

It was after ten o'clock when Sketch ushered Fatt Luk into the office. Within seconds the odor of sweat, manure and rotten meat filled the room.

"Sorry for takin' so long, Boss. Fatt Luk lives way to hell and gone on the other side of the hill." Sketch carried an ordinary wood fish box under his arm and set it down on top of TJ's desk. When full, the box from the Columbia River Packing Company held forty-eight, one-pound tins of Chinook salmon.

Fatt Luk bowed and smiled at TJ. An eye patch covered his right eye and a pencil thin stripe of white skin, a burn scar, ran from just above his right eyebrow down his cheek as far as his mouth. Leather pieces covered the knees of his trousers. Another piece of leather, cut like a short vest, covered his shoulders. The top of the leather vest shone with years of rubbing from a shoulder pole.

TJ took out an El Gusto, clipped the end, and then lit it. Fatt Luk's eyes followed TJ's every movement as he went through the ritual of lighting his cigar. He offered a cigar to Fatt Luk who took it and stuck it in his shirt pocket.

"Smoke later," he said and smiled, revealing a missing bottom tooth.

"You speak English. Good." TJ cursed under his breath. He'd remembered Sung Gee, the boy translator. He'd forgotten all about him in his rush to question Annika.

"Yes. Sweet Sunday Lady teach." Fatt Luk grinned.

"Heard about her. Wants to turn all Chinaboys into Christians. Guess if your learnin' English, she's doin' some good. You're here, Fatt Luk, to answer questions about Hop Li. Hop Li says he's a friend of yours, that true?"

"Yes. Hop Li good friend."

"Guess you know he's in trouble?"

"Eh? Hop Li no want trouble."

"Well, he's got it." He looked hard into the garbage man's good eye. "Sit down," he said and pointed to the straight-backed chair in the middle of the room.

Fatt Luk sat down and looked from TJ to Sketch, smiling the whole time, as if TJ had just invited him to cake and coffee.

"You know someone murdered Wah Fong, yes?"

Fatt Luk nodded.

"Well, when we catch Fong's killer, he'll hang." TJ ran his finger across his throat. "And any fella that helps the killer is goin' to prison. You understand?

"No like prison." Fatt Luk's smile disappeared and he sat up.

"Good. Now, you can help Hop Li by answerin' my questions without keepin' anything back. Understand?"

"Yes. No tell lie, eh?"

"Right. Let's start with last Sunday." TJ pointed to the box. "Hop Li says he gave you that box to keep. For a sea captain. Is that right? "

"Yes. Hop Li have good luck."

"What's in the box?"

"Not know. I say Hop Li, we open box. Maybe money, jewel in box. We rich. Hop Li say no. I say, so take little…" he made a small space between thumb and forefinger, "maybe sea captain no see." He shook his finger in the air. "Hop Li laugh, say no. Make promise, keep promise. Hop Li good friend but all time…" he shook his head looking for a word then made a fist and pushed it into the palm of his hand.

"Stubborn, like a mule?" TJ made mule ears by putting a finger on either side of his head.

Fatt Luk smiled. "Yes, that one."

TJ looked to Sketch. "Let's see what's so valuable."

The box had been nailed shut and wrapped in heavy twine. An address, printed over the label, read: *Capt. John Malmo, Astoria, Ore.* TJ pulled Tug's knife out of his boot, cut the twine, and pried the lid open. TJ jerked back as the lid came up. "Stinks! Open the window, Sketch." He pointed to the tiny barred window in the back wall.

"It's already open far as it'll go."

Fatt Luk and Sketch bent over TJ and all three peered into the box. A bundle of loosely wrapped butcher paper, stained at one end, filled the box. TJ shook the bundle onto the floor and unwound the paper 'til a layer came off. After he peeled off two more layers, a sky blue cloth, rolled up in a tight ball, fell to the floor. TJ shook out the cloth and a long Chinese robe with wide sleeves appeared. A brown stain covered the front of the robe from neck to waist. The robe had been rolled up when wet and the cloth had stuck to itself. When TJ pulled the fabric apart a pair of embroidered slippers and a silk skullcap, black with a red button and tassel, fell to the floor. Stains discolored the toes of both slippers as well. TJ coughed and stood up. "Let's go out to the hall where there's fresh air."

Several tall windows lined the south hallway and photographs of prior judges and city fathers, looking stern, graced the wall opposite the windows.

Sketch pulled a chair underneath a window and opened it. TJ laid the robe over the chair and then placed the slippers and skullcap on the floor.

"You ever see this robe, these slippers before?" TJ asked Fatt Luk.

Fatt Luk shook his head, reached down, and fingered the hem of the gown.

"China robe. Beautiful. Now, all same garbage." He ran his hand over his shaved forehead and down his queue. "Why sea captain keep stinky robe, hnnnn?"

Sketch laughed and TJ smiled.

Somewhere near the front of the hall a woman shouted. All three looked up to see Daines dodge around the courthouse receptionist, a gray haired, heavy-set woman.

"How do, boys. Whatcha got there?" Daines called out and came to a halt about twenty feet away.

"I'm sorry, Sheriff, he just wouldn't stop," the red-faced receptionist said while trying to catch her breath.

TJ stepped in front of the chair, blocking Daines' view of the clothes. "We're in the middle of somethin' here, Daines, you'll hafta leave." TJ put his hands on his hips.

"You're puttin' me off again, Sheriff. You gotta talk to me sometime. Why not now?"

"Because we're busy. That's why."

"You're always sayin' that. C'mon, Sheriff, Mac says I gotta get more on that floater or I'll be back in the pressroom." Daines stepped to one side and looked back and forth between the robe and Fatt Luk. "Whatcha doin' with them Chinee clothes? Did a Chinee kill her?"

"We don't know one way or t'other."

"Sheriff, the whole town is talkin,' wonderin' what you're up to. There's a lot goin' on and you ain't sayin' much." He stretched his neck to the side trying to see around TJ and then pointed to Fatt Luk. "That the killer?"

"Goddammit! That's it." He took a step towards Daines but Sketch reached out and grabbed his arm.

"Boss!" Sketch yelled.

TJ stopped, turned and looked at his deputy, and then back at Daines who had retreated a few steps. TJ took a deep breath and told himself to slow down, that he couldn't afford a row with the paper.

Daines stepped to one side for a better look at Fatt Luk and the clothes. TJ swore, moved out of Sketch's reach, and went for Daines. The reporter put his arms over his head and hollered, "I'm leavin,' I'm leavin.'"

"From now on, you get a say so from the lady up front before you come in or, by God, I'll drag your scrawny ass to the river and see how good you can swim. That clear?"

"Yes sir."

After Daines left, Sketch gathered up the clothes and TJ escorted Fatt Luk back into his office. Sketch closed the door halfway and put the stopper in.

TJ sat down behind his desk and relit his cigar. "Now, you say the robe, slippers, and hat are not yours, that right?"

"No belong me. Yes."

TJ thought it time to rattle him, see if he'd blurt out something he didn't want to.

"That robe looks like it'd fit Hop Li, Fatt Luk. Those are Hop Li's clothes, right?"

Fatt Luk yelped. "Hah? You think China robe belong Hop Li?" He laughed and looked over at Sketch who smiled back at him. TJ regarded Sketch with a cool eye and Sketch lowered his gaze.

"It's time to tell the truth, Fatt Luk," TJ said.

Fatt Luk spit in the direction of the clothes. "Wah! China robe for rich man, no Chinaboy."

"Maybe Hop Li's rich uncle gave that robe to him, eh?"

"No rich uncle Hop Li family. Family poor, always write, say send money."

"All right. We'll come back to the robe later." TJ pulled out his notebook and flipped through half a dozen pages.

"Hop Li says he got to your place early Sunday mornin.' That right?"

He shrugged. "No clock, Fatt Luk house. Sun just show face."

"You ate breakfast and then the two of you worked in your garden the rest of the day, right?" TJ threw in this question to see what Fatt Luk would say.

"Eh? Hop Li say this?" He shook his head and his eyes widened. "No true, Sheriff TJ. Hop Li butcher, no farmer, no like garden." He smiled. "So, Hop Li make joke, eh?"

"Well then, what did you do after breakfast?"

"Go town, see Sweet Sunday Lady. All time Sunday, all same. After lesson, fly dragon kite. I make kite. Then, eat House Ten Thousand Pleasure. Hop Li pay." He grinned and nodded at the fish box. "Also Hop Li pay me one dolla, so I keep box."

TJ took notes and then said, "Cannery work just started Tuesday. Where did Hop Li get the money to pay for that meal? And to pay you?" TJ fixed his eyes on the garbage man.

"Sea captain say keep box, no lookee. Pay Hop Li two dolla fifty cent."

"That's a lot of money just to store a box."

Fat Luk grinned and nodded. "Sea captain rich man. Maybe sea captain have more box. Pay Fatt Luk two dolla fifty cent also."

TJ smiled back. "That's good wages, for sure. All right, tell me about Wah Fong. What do you and Hop Li buy from him?"

"Buy shirt, pant, boot, cigar, lichee nut, pickle, candy, rice, maybe wine. All time, all same."

"How about opium? You and Hop Li smoke a few pipes at Fong's place, do you?"

"Sometime. If have money, buy tin, smoke my house. But no Hop Li. Promise father no opium. Hop Li keep promise."

"Wait. You sayin' Hop Li doesn't smoke opium?"

"Yes. No smoke." He shrugged

TJ noted this then asked, "How much money did you owe Fong?"

"Maybe three, four dolla."

"How about Hop Li? How much did he owe Fong?"

The garbage man sucked air in through his lips and teeth and then shrugged.

TJ leaned forward. "Hop Li and you are best friends. Best friends talk, tell each other things. You want to go to jail, Fatt Luk?" He waited and the garbage man shook his head, no. "All right then, how much did Hop Li owe Wah Fong?"

He sighed and shook his head from side to side. "Twenty-five dolla, maybe more."

"How come he owed so much?"

"This year, fire dragon year, not Hop Li lucky year, eh? *Fan gway* push all brother out Seattle. You know?"

"Yeah. But what's that got to do with Wah Fong and Hop Li?"

"Hop Li work winter, long time. But bad men no payee Chinamen. So Hop Li have three dollar when come Astoria. Only three dolla. Hop Li need money."

"But you still didn't answer my question, Fatt Luk. Twenty-five dollars is a lot of money to owe so early in the season. Why did Hop Li need so much money?"

For the first time in the interview, Fatt Luk looked uncomfortable. He twisted in his chair, ran his hand over his queue twice, and turned his head to look at Sketch with his good eye. Sketch glanced at TJ who nodded at him, and then Sketch looked back at Fatt Luk. "We're waitin' on your answer, Fatt Luk."

Fatt Luk sighed again. "Hop Li get letter. Elder brother write, family rice bowl empty. Send fifty dolla. Hurry. So Hop Li ask Wah Fong, fifty dolla. Wah Fong say too much, give twenty-five dolla." He paused and let his breath out in a long whoosh.

"So he owed Wah Fong twenty-five dollars but needed fifty." TJ tapped his pencil on his notebook. "Where'd he get the other twenty-five dollars? From Wing, the headman?"

"Wah! Wing big boss. Only give rich man money, no Chinaboy."

TJ took down what Fatt Luk said and closed his notebook. He took a long pull on his cigar, blew a smoke ring and watched it drift to the ceiling. "All right Fatt Luk, you're free to go."

"Fatt Luk no go jail?" He looked back and forth between TJ and Sketch.

"No, Fatt Luk. Not this time." TJ smiled. "But don't run off—I might need to talk to you again."

"Run off? What mean, run off?"

"It means stay close by. Don't go to another town or city."

"Wah! Fatt Luk go work, go home, go work, go home. All day, all same. Carry garbage, feed pig, feed chicken. No run off, hnnnn!"

"You've been a big help, Fatt Luk. Thanks."

After Fatt Luk left, TJ asked Sketch what he thought.

"Well, believe he told true, boss."

"What makes you say so?"

"Well, he thought we was goin' to jail him—he's too scared to lie"

"That's how I read him, too. What'd else you learn?"

"Well, big thing is that there twenty-five dollars. Hop Li needed money. If your folks is goin' without food and ask for help, why, what fella wouldn't help? Yep, had him a powerful reason to steal—can't fault him. And here's somethin just come to me. Once old Fong is dead, Hop Li don't hafta pay back the twenty-five he borrowed. So he's fifty dollars to the good."

"All right, I grant you Hop Li had a motive to steal. Anything else?"

"Them Chinee clothes don't help him none."

"But you heard Fatt Luk—they're a rich man's clothes, only somebody like Wing could afford them."

"So, don't mean Hop Li couldn't steal them."

"Why would he do that?"

"Maybe to throw us off his trail. And see, it works too. You're sayin' it's only a rich Chinee could wear them clothes and first name you come up with is Wing."

TJ laughed. "Good point, Sketch. All right, we'll check to see if the robe and slippers fit Hop Li." TJ looked up. The school clock read 12 o'clock. "You best get your lunch now, then relieve Lucky. I've got some thinking to do."

After Sketch left, TJ put the fish box with the clothes in the bottom of the safe. He sat at his desk and recalled what Doc told him about an autopsy. "You look for patterns," Doc said, "but you won't see them unless you put some order into the mess of facts in front of you."

TJ picked up a fresh pad of writing paper and wrote HOP LI MURDER FONG? at the top of a page and then made two columns. He wrote GUILTY over the left column, NOT GUILTY over the right.

GUILTY NOT GUILTY

GUILTY	NOT GUILTY
Found with Fong dagger.	Wouldn't know about box of clothes if he hadn't told us.
Admitted going by Fong's early Sunday am.	Sea captain story backed up by Fatt Luk.
Had a fish box of bloody Chinee clothes.	Alibi can be confirmed if Capt. Malmo comes for box.
Owed Fong twenty-five dollars—needed twenty-five more.	Didn't try to dodge questions.
Can read and write Chinee—maybe wrote words on that tank.	
Doesn't use opium & opium not taken from safe.	
Had money to buy fancy meal & pay Fatt Luk to store box.	

He looked over both lists and, though the guilty list was longer, he thought Hop Li's willingness to tell them about the box weighed in his favor. But did that one fact offset the facts in the guilty list?

He turned his thoughts to Jane's diary. He suspected that the diary held information bearing on her murder but it needed someone who knew a thing or two about women and romance. It also had to be someone he trusted. The only someone who fit that bill of particulars was Boss Bessie, the queen of Astoria's brothels.

19

The aroma of frying sausage wafted out of the darkened doorway of the Portside saloon and reminded him that he hadn't eaten that afternoon. But he told himself Bessie first, then eats. In three hours the Paradiso would be full of scream and holler and Bessie's mind would be on her business, not his.

Though Bessie's fresh time had passed, she could still arouse him whenever she put on her innocent look and softened those green eyes. She had worked the three-card Monte on the Northern Pacific and earned her stake in less than five years. Sitting in the lounge car on the Seattle to Missoula run, she'd shuffle a deck of cards, look lonely, and show just enough high-top shoe. Easy as eatin' pie, honey, she'd say with a wink.

Except for the barkeeper, a barmaid, and a couple of Bessie's girls playing cards at a back table, the first floor of the Paradiso was deserted. The barmaid shoved a coin into the nickelodeon as TJ came in and the tinny notes of Love's Old Sweet Song filled the room, casting a gloom over the almost empty room. A girl with a yellow bow in her hair rose and came out from behind the card table. She smiled, smoothed down her dress, and started for TJ. He waved her back down and then crossed the floor to the barkeeper who looked up from his paper and nodded at TJ.

"Bessie upstairs?" TJ asked.

"It's her dinner time." He went back to his newspaper.

"I need to talk to her."

"What about?"

"Business."

"It always is, Sheriff." He looked over the top of the paper and winked.

TJ didn't say anything but his eyes changed from friendly to hard.

"All right, Sheriff. Just a minute." The man nodded to the barmaid and she ran upstairs. In a minute she returned and paused on the bottom stair to curtsy. "You can go up now, Mister Sheriff," she said in a little girl voice.

TJ turned at the top of the stairs and through a partially open door spied a half-dozen women sitting at the kitchen table in their bathrobes. One of the women rose and shut the door as he passed. He continued on down a long hall with five small rooms on each side. A window opened on to the hallway from each room and when open, allowed a customer and girl to look each other over. When a girl had a customer or was out of the room, she closed the window and now, mealtime, all the windows were closed.

At the end of the hall, he turned into what Bessie called her chapel, a room large enough to seat all of her girls, the cook, and servants. When a visiting preacher couldn't be coaxed into conducting Sunday service, Bessie herself held forth with her clear, strong voice. She offered a heartfelt but rambling homily and then led the worshippers in robust hymn singing. Then with duty to God and girls done, she squired everyone downtown to Carmichaels for ice cream sodas.

TJ crossed to the far side of the chapel and twisted the handle on her doorbell.

"It's open," her voice boomed.

A cut glass vase with a dozen roses graced the entrance table of the parlor along with a silver card tray that held a pile of cards. He

pushed aside the beaded curtain into the dining room, and got a whiff of her scent, orange blossoms. Bessie wore an emerald green robe cut low enough to capture the attention of any male in a room full of attractive women. A row of tight curls shaped like the letter "C" decorated her forehead while the remainder of her long, red hair was piled on top of her head in a bun. A black pearl, the center stone of her necklace, rested in the valley created by her ample breasts. TJ's eyes found their way to the pearl and stayed there for a time.

"TJ! You devil. Where you been keepin' yourself?" She waved her fork at him and the dozen bracelets on her arm clacked and jingled.

"Sorry to bust in on your dinner." He took his hat off.

"Come over here, let's have a look at you."

He moved closer and smiled.

"Oh dear me. An undertaker's smile. You'll spoil your looks you go around like that, honey."

"Bessie, I need to talk."

"Talk? My, my, guess times is changed. Well, c'mon, sit yourself down." She patted the chair next to her then cut into a Porterhouse steak that spilled over the edge of her plate. She pushed a fork full of steak into her mouth, closed her eyes, and chewed.

"Umm...goddamm...that's sweet. Gives me religion, a steak like this. Finally got me a cook, little Chinaman, knows what medium rare is. Here, honey, taste." She stabbed a piece of steak, held it out, and he closed his mouth over the meat, tender and with a rich smoky flavor.

"Plenty here for both of us. Grab yourself a plate."

"Haven't got around to lunch yet so don't mind if I do." He took a plate from the sideboard, smiled, and slowly shook his head. "Be dammed. You did it again, Bessie. Sidetracked me before I got word one about why I'm here."

She threw up her arms and laughed, shoulders and breasts shaking, bracelets clacking until, out of breath, she grabbed her water glass and took a long drink.

"If I couldn't get a man's mind off his work, I'd be in the wrong business, honey." Her eyes held his and she smiled, a sly smile, promising much: excitement, mischief, pleasure, and a sharing of confidences. The sequins on her dress shimmered in the light from the overhead gas lamps, her sauciness as seductive as ever.

She put half her steak on his plate along with a pile of mashed potatoes and passed him the gravy bowl. "Oh, and have some of that pulla—supposed to go with mornin' coffee—but I like it with my steak."

"Before you get me sidetracked again, I'd like your opinion on a little problem."

She paused and returned the fork full of meat back to her plate. "Uh oh. Lawman says he's got a little problem, Bessie knows she's got a big one. Thought you promised you wasn't gonna take side pay?" She wiped her mouth and eyed him as if seeing a TJ she didn't know. Then she waved her hand in front of her face and laughed. "Oh, what the hell. You're the only lawman not on my charity list. Sure you won't settle for a little lovin' instead, sweet potato? Got me a new girl, Jenny. She's young, a real sweetie."

"Not lookin' for side money, Bessie, or lovin' either..." he smiled, "...well, not at the moment." He ran his hand over his mustache. "Guess you know what happened to the Thurgood girl so won't go over that. A friend of hers gave me her diary. I read it; some parts three, four times, but can't get to the bottom of it. She uses initials that don't connect to anybody close to her. And sometimes her writin' sounds made up, you know, like a story."

"You want me to look at it?"

"Yep. And Bessie..."

She waved her hand, interrupting him. "I know, I know. Don't blab. Don't worry, honeybun, there's two things I'm proud to say I do well and one of them is keepin' a secret."

"Thanks." He took the diary out of his coat pocket and set it down next to her plate. She dipped her hands in a bowl of water, wiped them, and then thumbed through the diary.

"Last entry is the day she went missing," he said.

She turned to that page and read, not saying anything for a time and then laid the diary on the sideboard. "Who's Lillie? Thought her name was Jane."

"It is. But she uses Lillie for some reason—see that's the puzzle—she uses pretend names and initials. I don't know if the initials stand for real people or not."

"A girl growin' up likes to pretend. I did—still do—and those pretend people, men most often, can be just the way you want—handsome, rich, full of secrets, and crazy for you. It's your story, honey, you write it any way you want." She tossed her head back, laughed, and then said, "She's a smart little thing and knows what she wants—I'll say that for her. Give me two days and I'll see what I can make of it."

"How about tomorrow?"

"In a rush are we? All right, tomorrow it is."

"I owe you, Bessie."

"Damm right you do. Now, that's settled, tell me about your social life. Any woman you're serious about?"

He shook his head, no, and smiled. "Too busy." He tugged on his mustache. "Now, if you got time, I'd like your opinion on another problem—concerns that Chinee grocer murdered last week."

"Why on earth you frettin' over him? Chinamen kill each other from time to time, I suppose, but what Chinamen do don't concern us. But that white girl, now that's different, she's decent folk."

"Well, I'm keepin' an eye on trouble in Chinatown so the Chinee murder falls to me. Won't take but a minute to go over what I've got."

"I see there's no stopping you. All right, honey, go ahead. I'll keep eatin' while you unload yourself, you don't mind." She glanced over at a grandfather clock next to the doorway. "But in fifteen minutes you got to haul your skinny ass out of here. I got to get myself dressed for the evenin.'"

She listened to him recite the evidence against Hop Li, nodding her head at intervals, twice stopping him to ask a question. When he finished she wiped her mouth and clucked her tongue.

"Don't see why you're in such a fuss. That Chinaboy is your killer."

He argued with her, told her about Hop Li not trying to hide the dagger and that his alibi about the sea captain might be true in spite of sounding far fetched. "Killer could be any number of men, a white man who saw the grocer as easy pickin's, for instance."

She pursed her lips. "You got somebody in mind?"

"Nope."

She cut a slice of chocolate cake with chocolate icing, put it on a plate and held it out to him.

He shook his head.

She set the cake in front of herself, took a bite, and then lifted her eyes to the ceiling. "Mmmm. Don't know what you're missin,' honey."

"So what do you think, Bessie?"

She dabbed at the corners of her mouth with a napkin. "Chinaboy is your only suspect and everybody's hollerin' for you to lock him up. Well, suppose you do just that. There's not a soul in town think you done wrong." Bessie stabbed another hunk of cake and lifted it to her mouth.

"Except the Chinaboy. What about the evidence pointin' the other way, to the sea captain?"

"Where is he, this sea captain?" She poured coffee for them. "Honey, I'll tell you something then Bessie's gonna shut her mouth. You tryin' to be everything—sheriff, judge, jury—and that's not what you're paid to do. You done your job—let others do theirs. And I'll tell you something else. I've known two men, white men by God, been hung on a helluva lot less than what you got on that Chinaboy."

"That doesn't...dammit...it doesn't take much to hang a man if folks have an itch to. I'm not proud of it, Bessie, but I helped round up those Swilltown boys after the '83 fire. If they hadn't fessed up and quick, we would have hung 'em. But I'm a lawman now—can't do things that way." He drank half his glass of water to ease his dry mouth.

She finished the last of her cake then put her elbows on the table and rested her chin on her hands. "Now, I told you a fib earlier, honey, promised to shut my mouth after I said my piece. Well, I got something else to say. You don't like what you hear, you go on, do what you want." She gave him a crooked smile. "Men incline that way anyhow."

"I'm listenin.'" He looked at the painting over the mantel. It showed a war party of Plains Indians attacking a fort. Bessie poured herself a shot of whiskey, took a sip, and then licked her lips.

"Honey, I hear things from my customers. The word goin' round is that the Chinaboy killed that grocer and the white girl too. Folks is takin' it hard. You got to arrest him." She silenced him with a wave of her hand. "No, no. Now you listen to me. Don't matter a damm whether he killed that girl or not. So keep your doubts to yourself and lock that boy up. It'll calm things, buy you time to chase down your mystery man—which appears you're set on doin.'"

"Bothers me, Bessie, to do that. Could be they hang him before I find out whether he did it or not."

"So don't arrest him then." She pushed her lips out in a well-practiced pout. "I've been wrong before."

"But you don't think so now?"

"No, I don't. But what I think don't matter, Mr. Lawman. It's all on you and..." she paused, looked at him with raised eyebrows, then reached out and rested her hand on his. "You know what I'm thinkin,' honey?"

"No, what?" He leaned forward.

"You came here 'cause you doubtin' yourself. It just came to me. You don't need Bessie's help figuring out who done what. You'll get there quick as anybody. But you don't want to jail that Chinaboy and you're lookin' to me to say you're right—now ain't that the truth?"

"The hell it is." He felt his face flush and jerked his hand away from hers.

"Un-huh. Honey, as new as you are, you're ten times the lawman of our last scalawag. On top of which you don't charge me a dime." She looked at him and chuckled. "Makes you as common as a virgin in Swilltown. No, I got no complaints 'bout how you're doin' your job. So do what you think best and to hell with me or the whole town. You're pig headed, just like me, and you can't say otherwise. Don't know why I even tried steerin' you to my way of thinkin.'" She drank the rest of her whiskey then turned away and gazed at a bay window, a large stained glass of a trellis overflowing with roses.

He no longer wanted his coffee and pushed the cup away. Neither said anything for an uncomfortable few seconds.

"Guess I should be goin.'" He slid his chair back and stood up.

"Guess you should. " She looked at him tight-mouthed but the next second her face softened and she smiled. "TJ honey, you're takin' this law business too serious."

"How so?"

"Worry lines are sproutin' up all over that good lookin' face of yours." She wrinkled her nose and stuck her tongue out at him.

He laughed. "Guess I oughta thank you."

"Damm right you oughta. And you're welcome. Come see me when you're not carryin' so much weight on those big shoulders of yours." She lifted the black pearl nestled in her cleavage and let it dangle from the end of her finger. "Need you a good time is what you need." She tossed her head back and laughed. "Wait. Got just the medicine." She got up from the table and brushed crumbs from the front of her dress with her napkin. The painting of the Plains Indians turned out to be hinged and she pulled it aside and exposed a safe. Opening the safe, she removed a sack, loosened the drawstring, and shook out a coin.

"Had these made last month. We're first class now. Here." She tossed the coin to him and he caught it. One side said, "Bessie's Paradiso," the other, "Good for One." He flipped the coin in the air, caught it, slapped it onto the back of his hand, and covered it. He peeked at the coin, looked up and grinned.

"Now don't be gettin' ideas, Mr. Lawman, that coin don't buy me. I'm retired. Well, 'cept for a nice old gentleman of means I see every Sunday afternoon and my Wednesday boy. He's a Greek with curly hair and brown eyes that cut right through me. Says he wants to marry me."

"Bessie! You? Married!?" TJ burst out laughing.

She put her hands on her hips. "Well, what's wrong with that? Plenty others, sporting girls like me, marry. You bet." She stepped close, chin out, challenging him. "Just last year a woman, worked out of Pendleton, married a miner and they moved on to Boise. Heard they started a family, too."

"Well, I don't know. People might not find it…um…seemly."

"People? That include you, TJ?"

He stopped laughing and moved closer to her. "No, Bessie, you know it doesn't. You're always seemly in my book." He ran his hand over his mouth. "You gonna take the Greek up on his offer?"

"Maybe. Someday." She shrugged.

He reached out, put his arm around her waist, and kissed her on the cheek. She frowned and her eyes darted back and forth across his face, then they softened, her smile blossomed, and she tilted her head to the side. "You can do better than that," she said and then kissed him on the lips. When he tried to pull her closer, she pushed him away with a smile. "No, honey, like I said before, I'm spoke for." She picked up a small bell and rang it. "Come by tomorrow and I'll let you in on Miss Jane's secrets. And no later than 1:30, honeypie, 'cause my Sunday gentleman is payin' a call at 2:00." She walked over to the beaded curtain and held the strands aside. "Now, get out of here and catch you some bad men."

20

Saturday evening, April 10

He walked out of the Paradiso into a soft mist but within minutes the mist turned into a hard rain. The wind picked up. Gusts pushed rain into his face and water trickled down his neck. He pulled his hat down, tightened the collar of his slicker, and went over what he still needed to know. The Chinese characters on the tank and dagger hadn't been translated and he still knew almost nothing about Hop Li. The Sweet Sunday Lady could help him on both counts.

He unlocked the door to Sherman & Ward's livery and looked over the buggies. The doctor's phaeton, though small, would keep the rain out with its covered top. By the time he hitched up a mare, put the top up, and drove the five blocks up the hill to the First Baptist Church, it was after seven o'clock.

A cherry tree in the tiny front yard of the pastor's house had surrendered its flowers to the wind and the walkway to the porch was an inch deep in cherry blossoms. After five rings, a young woman opened the door and pointed to the sign that posted the hours of business.

"I'm Sheriff Stone and I need to talk to Mrs. Taylor. It's important."

"Well, if it's an emergency…" she lifted the hurricane lamp to get a better look at him then opened the door just enough to let him in. She closed the door, lit a coal-oil lamp near the stairs, and turned to examine him.

"It's Mrs. Taylor I need to see," he said as he stood in the foyer, dripping water on the hardwood floor.

She looked down at the pool of water forming underneath his slicker and then pointed to a pew next to the office, the petitioner's bench. "Why don't you have a seat and I'll tell her you're here."

His eyes had adjusted to the dim light and he saw that the woman, mid-twenties, thin, and about 5' 9," looked at him with a puzzled expression. Dressed simply in a black skirt and white blouse with a cameo at the neck, she was fair, Scandinavian maybe, with an angular face and straight nose, some might even say a too-large nose. Her eyes bore into his and he felt a challenge in her steady gaze, as if no emergency could be worth disturbing the peace of the house on such a night. He wiped his feet on the mat, took off his hat, and made a point of stepping around the carpet runner, a red and orange Persian, as he made his way to the bench.

In three minutes, she came back, descending the stairs with the grace and confidence of a dancer. She stopped three stairs above the floor. "I'm afraid Mrs. Taylor is busy, Sheriff. I'm Emma Taylor, Henry's sister. Perhaps I can help?"

He stood up and ran his fingers around the brim of his hat before laying it down on the bench. "No, Miss. I need someone that speaks Chinee."

"Mrs. Taylor speaks neither Cantonese nor Mandarin. It must be me you're after."

"You? I thought you'd be…older…married…" He felt foolish and realized he assumed the pastor's wife and the Sweet Sunday Lady were one and the same. He pulled out the dagger, bundled in oil-soaked rags, and took a step towards her but tripped on the carpet runner. He dropped the dagger. "Damm. Oops…sorry for the language, Miss." He picked up the dagger, took the wrappings off, and advanced.

She backed up. "What on earth are you doing?"

He stopped and held the handle out so that the Chinese characters faced her. "Couldn't find a Chinaboy could read this, Miss. Everybody says you read Chinee, so here I am." The words rushed out of him as if he had to get them out before she asked him to leave.

"Sheriff, please. Why don't you sit down and start over?" She smiled, her cheeks flushed, and her eyes lit up in a teasing, mischievous look. He realized he wasn't making much sense and returned to the bench, flustered, and sat down on his hat. "Dammit. Oops…beg pardon, Miss."

She broke out laughing. "My, you <u>are</u> having a difficult time. Here, you better give me that before you hurt yourself." She came down the stairs and took the dagger out of his hands.

"It's beautifully made." She looked at the tiger then turned the handle over and studied the two characters. "*Baochou.* Oh, yes. I know what that means—only too well. Revenge. It's an ingrained part of the Chinese way of life, unfortunately." She handed the dagger back to him. "Is that all you needed, Sheriff?"

"Well, no, Miss, there's…" he ran his hand over his mustache looking for the right words, "…somebody wrote Chinee words on a cannery tank and I'm hopin' you'd take a look at them."

"I see. Actually, I don't see at all. I…" she paused and looked at him. "There's more to this than you're telling me, isn't there?" Her eyes probed his face. "Yes. I thought so."

"I have a buggy outside, Miss. I know its late…" he swallowed "…but we could be down and back in thirty minutes, maybe less."

"Down where, Sheriff?"

"Jameson's Cannery."

"Now? Tonight?" She glanced over her shoulder at a sudden scratching outside the door. The wind had picked up and a branch of the cherry tree scraped against one of the shutters. "I'm sure it can wait until morning, Sheriff."

He allowed his eyes to lock onto hers before he said, "No, Miss, it can't."

"It's that urgent?" She studied his face a second and then said, "It's about the murder of that young woman, isn't it?"

"Well, yes, it could be." He felt as if he were back in school reciting a lesson.

"You look cold, Sheriff. Why don't you come upstairs for some hot coffee while I change? And you can tell my brother why you're abducting me." The corners of her lips turned up in a smile.

He didn't know how to respond to her last remark and felt his face warm. "You're right…I guess I best tell Reverend Taylor."

"Well, come along then. Henry is protective of me—more so than I need or want—so you'll have to convince him of the necessity of our trip. I'll just get my cloak and boots." She smiled again and her face lit up. "An adventure. How exciting!"

He told Reverend Taylor that the writing on the tank had something to do with the murders of Wah Fong and maybe Jane Thurgood and that he needed to catch the killer quickly. Reverend Taylor nodded, pleased to be taken into TJ's confidence, and gave permission for his sister to accompany him.

Outside, the wind flipped the branches of the cherry tree up and down. In the fierce wind her umbrella would be useless. He held his hat over her head as they dashed to the buggy. The pounding rain on the buggy roof made conversation difficult and neither tried to speak as he drove east through the outskirts of town. In the snug interior, he smelled her rose perfume, faint but pleasant, and since their shoulders brushed together whenever the phaeton hit a bump or dipped into a pothole he was keenly aware of her presence. He hadn't been this close to an attractive, decent woman since Lucy Ann, and, for reasons he didn't understand, felt uncomfortable.

The night crew at Jameson's Cannery were hosing down the floorboards, scrubbing the butcher's tables, cleaning the gang knives, and oiling machinery. Emma and TJ waited by the entrance until the foreman, an old fellow, spotted them. The foreman approached, glanced at Emma, and then took off his cap.

"Good evenin,' Ma'am." His leathered face registered no surprise, no puzzlement, at the appearance of a properly dressed woman in his cannery at night.

"Good evening, Sir," she said.

"We need to look at that tank with the Chinee writing on it," TJ said.

The foreman escorted them to the cooking area and pointed out the tank with the writing. Emma walked over and stared at the characters for three or four seconds then turned around and pronounced, "One finished and a hundred also finished." She looked at TJ. "That's the literal translation. It means that with the main trouble settled, all troubles have been settled—death is, perhaps, the best example. When someone dies all debts are canceled, that's how it would be used." She paused and frowned. "But why anyone would put that up there? Did something happen here?"

Hop Li had translated the words as Miss Taylor had and now he knew what they meant but he was still disappointed. He wanted the words to mean more, to expose a secret that would explain why someone murdered a young woman. What troubles settled? How did Jane Thurgood's death settle them? And why cut off her hands? The message is Chinese and so meant for a Chinaman but he saw no Chinese connection to the Thurgood girl. But then he remembered the Chinese nightgown she wore when found and that the gown smelled of opium, so a Chinese connection was possible.

"Is that all it says?"

"Sheriff, please. That's all it says. But if you doubt me, why don't you ask someone else?"

"Well, I aim to have Dr. Chung look at it, Miss."

"I think you'll find we agree."

"I'm countin' on that."

"Well and good. Now then, Sheriff, is that all you wanted?"

"Understand you teach Chinaboys on Sundays. You know Hop Li?"

She had turned back to study the writing and whirled around at his question. "Why do you ask about Chen Hop Li? Surely, Sheriff, you don't suspect him of any crime?"

"All I can say, Miss, is that I need to know about him, everything you can tell me."

"There are several Chen's at this cannery, you know. Perhaps you have the wrong one?"

"It's the right one, Miss."

"I see. So, he is a suspect." She pulled her cloak around her and pursed her lips. "Sheriff, I'm afraid I don't understand. Hop Li a suspect! If you only knew him…no…it's preposterous."

"People can surprise you, Miss, especially when they're desperate."

"Desperate? Why on earth would he be desperate?"

"Money. Needin' it and not havin' it can make a man desperate. Now, about Hop Li."

"You suspect him of stealing, is that it? I wish you would tell me what you suspect him of." She waited for him to speak but he said nothing. "I'm at a loss, Sheriff Stone, a complete loss."

"You teach him. Why don't you start with that?"

"Very well. Hop Li is one of the best students I've taught either here or back home—in China I mean. He's intelligent, yes, but it's his love of learning that makes him exceptional. He wanted to become a *sheng-yüan*, a government scholar, like his elder brother whom he worships. Of course, that's out of the question now that he's here. But he hasn't given up—do you know he is constructing his own English-Chinese dictionary?"

"That's a good start, Miss. How about other things, like what he'd do if he needed money, has he got a temper, does he hold a grudge, things like that."

"I would trust him with my life, Sheriff, if that's what you're asking. And something else which may help you understand his character." She paused and took a deep breath. "Unlike my dear brother, I am a realist. In our Canton Mission, I understood very early that most of our congregation were rice Christians…you know the term?"

"I get your drift."

"Hop Li is no rice Christian…no…," she spoke with passion, words poured out of her like water rushing over a falls, "…he questions everything. Why do we have only one God? Does God get lonely in heaven? What officials run the Christian heaven? And so on."

He chuckled.

"Yes, I know. Silly questions. But do you know, Sheriff, my other students never ask a single question about Christianity, let alone an original one." She paused, flushed, and lowered her voice, perhaps remembering that she had no need to shout. "What I mean to say, Sheriff, is this—not only is Hop Li a scholar but he has the makings of a true Christian. Do you see why it is absolutely ludicrous to regard him as a suspect?" Her tone carried the exasperation of a parent for a child who needs one explanation too many of the obvious.

"What you told me helps, Miss, but you didn't answer my questions."

She turned and walked a few feet away. Her hands shook as she pushed the hood of her cloak off her head. "I'm feeling…it's suddenly quite warm in here…and it's getting late. I would like to leave." Her eyes pleaded with him. "I don't know what else to say."

"What kind of man is he, Miss, I mean other than he asks questions and is leanin' towards Jesus?"

"You are the most persistent man." She chewed on her lower lip and scowled at him.

"Yep." He kept his eyes on hers.

After a second, she shook her head and laughed. "There's no getting around you, is there?"

"Nope."

"Very well. Hop Li is strong-willed, I admit, and I've seen him angry on occasion. It's true he is big and strong—any Tong would be happy to have him—but I've never heard of him bullying others. That is not his nature."

"Does he gamble?"

"Good heavens, Sheriff, don't you know? Gambling is a way of life with the Chinese. Yes, he gambles but with him it's strictly social. He sends most of his pay home, you know, and if gambled seriously he couldn't do that."

"Does he use opium?"

"Unlike most of his fellows, he has not acquired that filthy vice. He even confided…," she paused and studied his face, "…but you must promise not to reveal what I'm about to tell you."

"Well, I can't promise, Miss, but if nobody else needs to know, I'll see it dies with me."

"I'll accept that as good enough." She looked down and slowly shook her head from side to side before speaking. "Hop Li's father trained his second son to take over the family fish business. Unfortunately, the second son became an addict and broke his father's heart. Before Hop Li left for San Francisco, his father made Hop Li promise never to touch that loathsome drug. As far as I know, he has kept his vow."

"That's of considerable help, Miss. Now, one last thing. Hop Li got a bit flinty when I asked him about debts of honor. He ever get mixed up in something like that?"

Miss Taylor flushed, turned her back on him, and finally said, "Sheriff, I'm afraid I've said too much already. I...no, I'll say no more."

TJ cleared his throat. "It isn't always easy to tell the truth about a friend, Miss, especially at a time like this. But sometimes a fact which points to a suspect at the start ends up clearing him."

She turned around and looked into his eyes so long he grew uncomfortable. "I feel I can trust you, Sheriff, but, please, I ask that you suspend judgment until you hear me out. You need to understand why he behaved as he did." Her eyes searched his for reassurance.

"Well, I don't claim to know Chinee ways so I'll hold off judgin' him—leastways, I'll try."

She nodded. "Good. Well then, it all started that terrible night the Chinese were expelled from Seattle."

"I know about the roundup, Miss."

"Hop Li was staying at his cousin's laundry when a gang of brutes broke in and ordered them to leave. Hop Li's cousin has a wife and baby. Just imagine what those poor people went through!"

He nodded.

"I know him so I wasn't surprised by what he did. He attacked the leader but was overpowered by his henchmen. They beat him and cut off his queue." She looked at him as if waiting for him to say something.

TJ didn't know what to say so held his tongue.

"Yes, I know. Losing his queue doesn't seem like such a loss, does it? Not to our eyes. But a Chinese man's queue is a sign he obeys the laws and customs of his country, of the emperor. If he returned home now, without his queue, he would be executed for treason."

"That's not right—he didn't cut it off."

"That is of no consequence, Sheriff."

"It seems over harsh."

She folded her arms over her chest and looked at the ground. When she looked up, her eyes were moist. "He vowed to avenge the insult to his honor."

"What's that mean exactly, Miss, avenge the insult?"

"It means that he will hunt down the leader and... punish him."

"You mean he aims to kill him?"

"I...I don't know." She sighed, exasperated. "I've told you more than I should. Are you satisfied?"

"Yes and thank you." He had trouble concealing his excitement at hearing how Hop Li lost his queue. Emma Taylor confirmed what Fatt Luk said earlier and answered a question nagging TJ from the first: why the killer took the money but left the opium. Hop Li had vowed never to use opium and wouldn't touch the stuff. And since he needed twenty-five dollars, that's all he took. The story about the queue also told him that Hop Li held a grudge. Hop Li took the cash because he needed it to send home but revenge could have been a motive too.

"It's time we got back." He put his hand under her elbow.

The wind had died down and the heavy rain had turned into a light drizzle. He helped her into the buggy and after he climbed in and took the reins, she turned to him and said, "I trust I haven't misjudged you, Sheriff. You haven't closed your mind about Hop Li, have you?"

"No, Miss, I haven't. One or two things still bother me about Fong's murder. And as for the murder of the girl, well, there's too much I don't know."

"Surely, he is not a suspect in that murder, Sheriff?"

"I didn't say he was. He told me that the Sweet Sunday Lady, that's what they call you, is the only American woman he knows. Seems hard to credit—he's sure to run into other white woman on occasion."

He felt her shoulders tense before she spoke. "I don't find that hard to believe at all. Young men come here to work and that means from sunrise to sunset, six days a week. Their few hours of leisure are given over to gambling and smoking opium, at least for most. And, do you know, Sheriff, I cannot recall Hop Li missing one of my Sunday classes—ever. No, it's out of the question. Where would he find the time to meet a white woman?"

He didn't have an answer so said nothing. The rain had stopped and the only sound was the soothing clop of the mare's hooves on the planked road. As she remained silent, he guessed that their physical closeness had brought out her...what?...she certainly wasn't shy...maybe her modesty. But that proved wrong as well since after another minute, she said, "Something is bothering me, Sheriff, but it...well, it probably means nothing."

"No, Miss, let's hear it. Like I said, you can't tell what might be important." He pulled on the reins and slowed the mare.

"Well, the writing on that tank was not written by an educated Chinese."

"Pardon?"

"The characters looked as if they were written by a child or perhaps one of my students." She added quickly, "I am not saying one of my students wrote that, you understand, that is just how it looks."

"How can you tell?" He turned and looked at her.

"Goodness, that's easy. Remember when you were learning your ABC's? How large, shaky, and uneven your letters were?"

He laughed. "Yeah. I see what you mean. Makin' a "3" look different than an "e" took me a helluva long time."

From the play of light on her face by the buggy lamp, he saw the trace of a smile on her lips.

They turned down Olney Street, two blocks from her home, and he asked a question that had been puzzling him, "You mind my askin' how come you speak Chinee so good?"

"Not at all, Sheriff. My parents are missionaries in the Baptist Mission in Canton, China. I was born there and grew up speaking Cantonese, English, and some Mandarin. Up until two years ago, I taught in our mission school. My parents are there still." She paused and pulled her cloak around her. "It's strange...it's seems childish to admit this but...well, I find I grow more homesick with each letter I get from them. I didn't expect...well, it is so different here, isn't it? My life here seems so pale by comparison, so—oh, I am sorry, Sheriff—I mustn't impose my feelings on you." She turned away and looked out the buggy window.

"How come you left if you miss it so much?"

She hesitated then said, "Oh, it wasn't my decision. I experienced some...some difficulties of a personal nature and...well, let's just say my parents thought it time I serve a mission here. They meant well but...oh, it's a long story. I mustn't burden you with it. Another time perhaps." After a pause, she said, "But now I have a question for you."

"I thought you might. Well, I was born in Omaha, Nebraska but my folks brought my sister and me out here when I was three. So Astoria is home."

"That's not what I planned to ask. Henry tells me you do not drink liquor. Is that true?"

"It is."

"I see. How is that we have not seen you at our temperance meetings?"

She had surprised him with the question and he blurted out, "Last thing I need is another damm meetin.'" He slapped the mare's rump too hard and she started trotting. What the hell business was it of hers what he did? He knew a non-believer like himself going through the day minding his own business gave church people an itch, one not satisfied until they grabbed the non-believer by the collar and pushed him to his knees. She's probably one of those suffragettes, too, he thought. He slowed the horse to a walk.

"Surely there's more to it than that, Sheriff? One finds time for what's important, at least, that's been my experience."

"I'm sure you do, Miss, find time I mean. And you're right 'bout there being more to it. But I guess that story will have to wait, too. We're here." He pulled up in front of the pastor's house, jumped out, and tied the mare to the ring in the curb. He went around the buggy to help her out but she had already jumped down. She paused on the porch and turned to him.

"Sheriff, I didn't mean to pry when I questioned your reasons for not attending our meetings. It's just that we have so few men in our group. One of strong character like yourself...I mean...your presence would add a..." she shook her head and smiled, "...dear me...I'm doing it again. Forgive me, Sheriff. I do apologize."

"Apology accepted."

"I'm glad I could help with the translation and, please, if you need my help again I'll be happy to give it."

"Miss Taylor, I know it wasn't easy for you tell me about Hop Li. And it's sportin' of you to come out in the storm. I'm much in your debt. Thanks."

She held out her gloved hand. He took it and held on to it for longer than proper but she made no effort to withdraw it.

That night he took out his notebook and looked over the guilty vs. not guilty list he'd constructed earlier. He wrote "willing to kill Kephardt for cutting off queue" to the guilty column. To the not guilty column, he added "Miss Taylor gives good character reference."

He crawled into bed but couldn't sleep and found himself comparing Jane Thurgood to Emma Taylor. They were both attractive women but they couldn't be further apart in character, one willing to do anything to become an actress, the other willing to do anything to convert Chinamen. Still Emma Taylor, like Jane Thurgood, was full of contradictions. Emma Taylor came out with him at night without a chaperone, wasn't shy like a decent woman should be with a strange man, questioned him as easily as he questioned her, and offered strong opinions freely—all of which he was not accustomed to in a young woman but found, to his surprise, that he liked.

She's church people, he reminded himself. Forget her. But her smile and blue eyes kept him from sleep longer than anything else had this week.

21

Doc Hinkel leaned over the chessboard, a tiger about to pounce, and took TJ's bishop with his knight. "Check," he said and grinned. It was just after breakfast Sunday morning and the two friends sat next to the window on the second floor of Helga's boardinghouse in what she called the social room. A group of Finns played cards at a table in the middle of the room and ended each round with loud talk or a shout of triumph.

"You have to do that?" TJ glared at Doc.

"What's that?"

"Grin like a monkey after every move. You haven't won yet."

"I don't see much hope for you, my friend."

"Yeah, well, that's your opinion."

TJ leaned back in his chair, his long legs stuck out to the side, while Doc sat hunched over the table, his hawk nose inches from the board. The hand-carved chess pieces in Doc's set had defects: a pawn might be taller or fatter than its fellows, the white rooks were missing the felt on their base, and the black bishop had scars from doing battle with Doc's dachshund. But neither man would think of using any other set in their Sunday game.

"Your move." Doc looked at TJ from underneath his thick eyebrows.

"Know that. I'm thinkin.'"

TJ started to move his king but then pulled back.

"Un-huh. Not bad. But it'd only delay the inevitable," Doc said.

One of the Finns in the card game yelped in glee. Doc glowered at the fellow. TJ continued to study the board and when a minute passed without TJ moving, Doc re-lit his pipe and asked, "You plan to move before lunch?"

"Yeah. Yeah." TJ put a finger on his queen with the idea of taking the hated knight but then moved his king.

Doc looked over TJ's shoulder in irritation as somebody stomped up the stairs on the run. "You've got company."

Sketch paused at the top of the stairs to catch his breath, and then came over to TJ. "Boss, I know it's your day off but ya gotta come."

"What happened?"

"Daines come in, all dandied up and full of hisself, says he's got something we hafta see."

"Well, what is it?"

"Wouldn't show me. Says you gotta see it. And all the time he's struttin' 'round askin' questions like a banty rooster. He's waitin' on us back to the office."

TJ looked at his deputy. "I'm givin' Doc a good fight now, Sketch. Plus I've got to talk to Bessie later, after lunch. Can't it wait 'til tomorrow? "

"Asked him that. Says whether ya talk to him or not, he's gotta write this here story today. Could be it's nothin' but a bluff, Boss. Bet he's sniffin' around just to see what we got."

TJ suspected the reporter might have stumbled onto news TJ didn't want out. He stood up and stretched. "Shit, Doc, looks like I better go. But stay put and don't move a thing. I'll be back in a half hour."

Doc knocked the ashes out of his pipe and stuck it in his chest pocket. "Looks like mate for me in five, maybe six. Let's call it a day, shall we?"

"Like hell. Give me an hour. If I'm not back by then, we'll call it a draw." TJ stood up and took a last look at the board.

"Not on your life. You're on the rocks, my friend, and if you're not back in an hour it's a win for me. Now, let's see, I believe that makes ten, or is it eleven, in a row. I thought Sketch ought to know that." Doc grinned.

"It's only nine. Don't play poker with Doc, Sketch. He tends to count in his favor." TJ put on his coat and hat and said to Doc, "One hour."

Daines stood with his back to the potbelly and grinned as the lawmen came into the office. He wore a tie and a clean white shirt, though the shirt was a size too large around the neck. The unruly lock of hair that usually hung over his left eye had been tamed by a comb and pomade. But instead of making him look older, as he probably intended, the slicked back hair and oversized shirt made him look younger.

As TJ hung up his slicker and hat, Daines pulled up a chair to TJ's desk and sat down without waiting to be invited. "Got somethin' to show you boys," he said and searched his coat pockets.

TJ smiled at Daines' appearance and some of the antagonism he usually felt toward the boy dissolved. "It better be good to call me in on my day off. "

"It is, Sheriff." He pulled an envelope out of his coat pocket. "Mac found this here note in our mail box this mornin.' Says I was to show it to you after Mr. Jameson seen it."

TJ took the envelope from Daines. The envelope, addressed to EDITR, had neither return address nor stamp. He took out a sheet of ruled paper and unfolded it. The letters were printed in pencil with a large hand.

dear editr—

you lef sumthin out on that girl what was murded. they found her hands at jamesuns in a tank of hot watr. somebody cut em off & throwd them in ther. that aint all. they caght a china boy with a daggr. bet he knowd how them hands got in ther. sumthin ain't right over ther. you best find out what befor the pigtails kil agin.

a frind

TJ read it twice to make sure he understood it and then cursed. He'd been waiting for a note like this because he thought it would reveal the killer's identity but after reading it, he didn't see how it could. "Who else has seen this?" he asked and handed the note to Sketch.

"Just Jameson, Mac and me. And the chief. Now you fellas," he paused then added, "oh yeah, I told Brady what it said but didn't show him the note."

TJ cursed again when he learned that the chief had seen it. The chief knew where and when they'd found Jane's body, that her hands were missing, and that she was pregnant. But he didn't know her hands were found at Jameson's or that one of Jameson's butchers had Fong's dagger. The chief would give the new information to the district attorney and then Hop Li would hang for sure.

TJ put the envelope and note in the safe. "This note is evidence, Daines. I need to hang on to it."

"Don't matter none. Mac made a copy."

"Why'd ya hafta show Jameson the damm note?" Sketch moved close to Daines.

Daines looked up at Sketch, shifted his eyes right and left, and then said, "Mac thought it could be some damm fool playin' a joke so I hadda check it out. That foreman, Brady, cussed to beat the devil when I told him about it, said he knew them hands wouldn't stay no secret.

He fessed up to takin' them outta that tank but claims they wasn't no rings on her fingers and anybody says different is a damm liar."

"What else did Brady say?" TJ asked.

"Well, he said some Chinee wrote somethin' on that tank—yeah, and they caught a Chinaboy butcher flashin' a fancy Chinee dagger. So guess you got your killer, leastways, one of them." Daines took out his notebook and a pencil. "By the way, what is that Chinaboy's name? Brady or Jameson wouldn't say."

"You'll find out if you need to," TJ said.

"I'm writin' up this story soon's I leave here. I'd gotta have his name."

"You ain't listenin.' He already said no." Sketch clenched his fists.

Daines looked down at his notebook and didn't respond. No one spoke. Daines' right leg jerked up and down and he tapped his pencil on his notebook.

TJ broke the silence. "Did Jameson have any idea who wrote the note?"

Daines shook his head. "He didn't say if he did." Daines leaned back from Sketch's close scrutiny and grinned, remembering something. "Boy oh boy, but you shoulda seen him after he read it—steam comin' outta him like a kettle on a hot stove." He chuckled. "'Cussed me from here to Chicago, then throws me out. But it don't matter a nickel—just proved Mac right. See, Jameson blowin' up like he done is as good as God's word that everthin' in that note is gospel." Daines' grin froze when he looked into TJ's face.

"You stop to think what it'll do to Jameson when you put that story in the paper?"

"Ain't people got a right to know what's true, Sheriff?"

"And supposin' men lose their jobs 'cause of yer damm story. Don't that bother ya none?" Sketch said, so close to Daines that his coat brushed against the reporter.

Daines didn't respond and once again the only sound came from the tick of the clock. This time, Daines broke the silence. "That one-eyed Chinee in cahoots with the butcher?"

TJ pointed a finger at Daines. "He's not a suspect and don't you say he is."

"Well, how come you was questionin' him then?"

TJ paused to think what he should say. Daines hadn't talked to Hop Li yet so didn't know that Hop Li hid the box of blood-stained clothes at Fatt Luk's shack. If word got out about the box a fair trial would be impossible.

"He had some information about the crime."

"What kind of information?"

"I can't say. We're still investigatin' and don't want information to get out that might help the killer."

"So, you sayin' the butcher didn't murder that girl?"

"I didn't say that. Don't go puttin' words in my mouth."

"Chief Connelly says that butcher is guilty as sin. Says the Chinaboy and anybody what helped him is gonna hang."

"The chief's entitled to his opinion."

Daines turned a page in his notebook. "Sheriff, the chief told me a lot more about this here murder in five minutes than you ever did. Seems like you're still keepin things from me." Daines raised his hand to brush a non-existent strand of hair from his eyes. "Mac says if a madman is goin' around killin' women and cuttin' their hands off, people oughta know about it. Says maybe it's time the chief took over. What you got to say to that?"

"I say it's my case and I'll go about it how I think best. Before I arrest a man, I like to have some evidence says he's guilty."

"Yeah, sure. But everybody knows that butcher done it. So whatcha waitin' on?"

"I haven't found a reason for the Chinaboy to kill that girl. So you're wrong, Daines. I don't know the butcher killed her. Sketch doesn't know that either, do you, Sketch?"

Sketch hesitated but then said, "Nope, can't say as I do."

Daines looked down at his notes and turned a few pages. "Mac wants to know somethin' else…had to do with them scabs comin' here…yeah, here it is." He read for a bit and then said, "Seems a whole passel of things goin' on at Jameson's lately. Mac says it sounds like heathen monkey business, some kind of ritual. Either that or Jameson's Chinaboys got themselves mixed up in a Tong war. Which is it, Sheriff?"

"Aw for Christsake, Daines. Mac is lookin' to find sunlight by diggin' a hole in the cellar. Listen to me careful now. This is not about Chinee religion; it's not a Tong war; it's not even a fight between Ah Joe and Ah Jim. Last week somebody murdered a Chinee grocer and somebody murdered a white girl and we're huntin' for their killer or killers. That's all it is." TJ pointed a finger at Daines. "You tell Mac if he likes makin' things up, he oughta get out of the news business, start writin' adventure stories."

"Well, it'll just make him mad if I tell him that. By the way, what's the writin' on that tank say?

"It's information I don't want out. Not yet, anyway."

"How come?"

Before TJ could say anything, Sketch shouted, "'Cause he says so, goddammit." Sketch moved closer to Daines.

Daines turned in his chair, eyed Sketch, and then turned back to TJ. His right leg jerked up and down again and both eyes blinked at a fast pace.

"Relax, Daines. Sketch has got a temper but I can harness it—most days. Anyway, he hasn't hit anybody for...how long's it been, Sketch?" TJ looked at his deputy for an answer.

Sketch frowned before he caught on then grinned, looked down as if trying to remember, and finally said, "Hell, it's been a week at least."

Daines shoved his notebook in his pocket and almost tipped his chair over in his haste to get up. "Well, guess that's all. Oh, almost forgot. Jameson wants to see you, Sheriff."

"Now? It's Sunday. Did he say why?"

"Nope, just to come over on the double." Daines hurried out.

TJ waited until he couldn't hear Daines' footsteps and then said, "When that story comes out Monday men will be lookin' to tear Hop Li apart. If he didn't kill the girl, we best find out who did before then."

"What we doin' first?"

"I'm goin' over to Jameson's. I want you to track down Kao."

"Want me to bring him in?"

TJ started to say yes then had an idea. "You and Kao haven't met, have you?"

"Nope. What you gettin' at, boss?"

"Somebody has scared him into silence. You could follow him without makin' him suspicious."

"What's he look like?"

"He's a skinny fella, fifty plus, not much over five foot, has a gimpy walk. Should be easy to follow." TJ wrote directions to Kao's place and handed them to his deputy. "Wait close by and follow him when he leaves, see what he's up to. If his door is locked, go over to Wing's. Kao could be upstairs, doped up. If he is, come back here."

"Well, what if he ain't doped up and he meets somebody. What then?"

"Find out all you can but be back here before dinner."

After Sketch left, TJ thought about what they'd learned. The note came from somebody in town rather than from Portland, the grammar and expressions told him the writer wasn't Chinese, and the writer knew more facts than those reported in the paper. So the writer could be the killer. He thought of all the people who knew more than what had been reported: the Chinaboss and Chinaboys, Brady and the other foremen, office workers and their families. If he eliminated the

Chinaboys, there were still several white workers or members of their family who could have written it.

But it didn't make sense for a cannery worker to write the note. The bad publicity might close the cannery and both white and Chinese workers would lose their job. The note had to come from an uneducated non-Chinee, someone who didn't work for Jameson, he concluded. But if that were true, it didn't answer the question of how the writer came by the information.

22

Sunday, April 11

A skeleton crew was replacing one of the conveyor belts when TJ entered the first floor of cannery. A man paused in his work when he noticed TJ and pointed upstairs with his wrench. TJ took the stairs two at a time to the loft and Jameson's office.

Jameson shook his head slowly from side to side as TJ came in. "Goddammit, Stone. Thought I could trust you."

"Well, howdy to you too. Why don't you start at the beginnin'?"

"Are you saying you don't know?"

"Know what? I had a visit from Daines, if that's what you're askin.' And before you start hollerin,' I didn't see the damm note 'til a half hour ago."

"Goddammit to hell. My cannery's finished. I'm ruined."

"How'd Daines get Brady to talk?"

"The little asswipe told him the note was old news, that he just came by to fill in some details." Jameson ran his hand through his hair. "Brady confirmed every goddamm thing—shit."

TJ had no words to comfort Jameson. The headlines would be huge and the scandal could last weeks. TJ asked himself who stood to gain if Jameson or his cannery were destroyed and came up with two possibilities: The Knights of Labor and Paul Purcell.

Jameson took out a bottle of Cahill's whiskey and two tumblers from a bottom drawer of his desk.

"None for me," TJ said and sat down on a high stool.

"Oh, that's right. I forgot. Your old man must be a preacher."

"Well, he taught by example—what not to do—so guess you could call him a preacher." TJ took out his notebook and a pencil. "But back to business. Who's mad at you, Jameson?"

"You think I haven't thought about that? Manusco and his union boys wouldn't do this—cost a lot of jobs if we closed. The Knights are shits—it could be their handiwork." He drained his tumbler and poured himself another.

"You find out what those Chinee words mean?" TJ asked.

"Yeah. One score settled, all scores are settled, something like that. But doesn't mean a damm thing to me. What do you make of it?"

"Sounds like somebody is paying you back for something you did. You fire a Chinee recently?"

"The hiring and firing is up to Lum, the Chinaboss. But he hasn't fired a Chinaboy in three years."

"Well, first you had the scabs, then Jane Thurgood's hands, then your butcher had Fong's dagger, and now the leak to the paper. Somebody is mad at you, somebody with purpose and know how. Who hates your guts?"

Jameson looked at him then said, "Dammit. I told you—other than the Knights, I don't have any idea."

"How about Purcell? You're lockin' horns with him over that senator's job. And he went after you the other day at Liberty Hall. Sounds to me like he's tryin' to scare you off." TJ offered Purcell up as the villain to see what Jameson would do. Some facts, such as Jane's murder and cutting off of her hands, didn't point to Purcell, but others, the Chinee scabs and the anonymous note, did. TJ realized that if he saw the link, Jameson would too.

"Goddammit, Stone, I...that's not how it is," Jameson said before gulping down his whiskey. He wiped his mouth and pointed his forefinger finger at TJ. "You don't understand." His mouth went slack and he ran his tongue over his lips. The pleading eyes and the tilt of his head gave him the look of a bum asking for a handout.

TJ had never seen the cannery boss look so exposed, so helpless, and sensed he'd been given a glimpse at a room in Jameson's soul that was locked. He waited, hoping Jameson would open the door to the room and expose the secret. But the cannery boss picked up a glass paperweight and stared at the etched rose inside.

TJ broke the silence. "What don't I understand?"

"All right...yes, Purcell's a bastard... dirty tricks his stock in trade...but I just can't see him killing his secretary and cutting off her hands just to get back at me. Besides, I haven't done anything to him, at least anything that warrants a payback like that."

"Well, that Chinee message says somebody is payin' you back. Seems to me Purcell would be mighty pleased by the mess you're in."

"Forget Purcell. He's not behind this."

"How do you know?"

"Goddammit, I just know. Forget him."

"There's something you're not tellin' me."

Jameson passed the paperweight from one hand to the next without looking at TJ. When he finally did look at TJ, his eyes had narrowed and his bulldog mask was back. "I've told you everything." The moment of seeing into the soul of another had passed. Jameson got up, went over to the grime-streaked window behind his desk, and looked outside or pretended to. You couldn't see much from that window, TJ knew, only a loading dock piled high with pallets. After a few seconds, Jameson sat down at his desk, flipped open the lid of his Upmann double coronas, and held the box out to TJ. The offer surprised TJ since Jameson had never offered him a cigar before. TJ took one, lit it, and inhaled deeply. A rich man's tobacco, dark and mellow, that tasted as good as…what?… a breakfast of bacon, eggs and fresh Columbian coffee after a cold night on the river is all he could think of. The day he jailed the killer or killers of Fong and Thurgood, he'd celebrate with one of these and to hell with how much it cost.

Jameson licked a few drops of whiskey from the edge of his glass. "I've been thinking… maybe… maybe we can take the edge off Mac's story." He wiped his mouth with the back of his hand.

"What's your idea?"

"We know Mac's slant on Chinamen. He'll say my Chinaboy killed the Thurgood girl, cut off her hands, and did god knows what else. We can't change that. But if we make an arrest today, it'll show we're on top of things, and just maybe the story won't get much play in Portland."

"Hold on just a minute. You're rushin' to put a noose round Hop Li's neck. There's no evidence says he knew Jane Thurgood or that they crossed paths. Why would he kill her?"

"How the hell would I know? Money probably."

"Well, he did need money but he took all he needed from Fong's safe, that is, assumin' he killed Fong."

"I don't care. I've got—the town has got to move on this, Stone."

"I'll get the killer or killers but it'll take a little time. Meanwhile, I'll ask Mac to hold off on the story for a few days."

"Hold off? Bullshit. Every chance he gets he rants against Chinamen like a down-South preacher rants against sin. Dammit, Stone, I can't pussyfoot around. Time's our enemy here. Time and Purcell." Jameson's fingers drummed the arm of his chair.

"Whoa. Thought you told me to forget Purcell?"

"Yes, yes. For the killing. But when the story comes out and we haven't arrested the Chinaboy, Purcell will be all over me. He'll make it look like I'm siding with the Chinee. Christ, the story is made for him. A Chinaboy murders and mutilates a white woman, which shows they're a degenerate race and can't ever become Americans. You heard him at Liberty Hall—champion of the white workingman, wants to kick John's ass back to China—all that bullshit. No, I need this over with, Stone. The sooner, the better."

TJ folded his arms across his chest. "If you're thinkin' of doin' something on your own—don't. I'll jail you same as anybody."

"I won't sit by and do nothing. If it costs me my butcher, so be it. I can't have the Portland papers running this story week after week. Are you listening, Stone?"

TJ hadn't been listening. Somebody, with the persistence of pit bull, had gone to great lengths to get Jameson. Other canneries, a political rival such as Purcell, and the Knights of Labor, all stood to gain if Jameson went under. But the message on the tank smacked of revenge, struck him as personal, and if his thinking were right, it meant that the killer knew Jameson and hated him, which left the Knights out as suspects. TJ couldn't prove it yet but he suspected that the killer or killers had targeted Jane Thurgood. He just didn't know why.

"Sorry, I was thinkin.'" TJ took a long pull on his cigar.

"I said the longer the story runs in Portland, the more damage to me. Do I have to write it down for you?"

"Nope." TJ felt the muscles in his neck tighten. It annoyed him when Jameson talked to him as if he were a hick sheriff.

"Good. We understand each other. You've questioned Hop Li, right?"

"Yeah. Plan to talk to him again shortly."

"What more is there to talk about? He had that dagger the morning we found the hands." Jameson picked up the glass paperweight put it on his stack of papers. "Arrest him now. Let's get this behind us." He swiveled from side to side, avoiding TJ's eyes.

"I'm not sure he's our man. We need to check on…"

"You're not listening, Stone." Jameson smiled with his mouth, showed all his teeth, but the frown betrayed anger. "I need an arrest and I need it today, before The Star comes out Monday."

"Even if he didn't do it?" TJ's guts churned.

"For Christsakes, Stone, what's wrong with you? We're talking about a goddamm Chinee."

TJ's jaw muscles worked but he said nothing. The look on Jameson's face told him that Jameson's ears were shut. TJ stubbed out his cigar in the brass ashtray with only a third smoked. He grabbed his hat and squared it down.

"Well?" Jameson said.

"Well, what? I'll make an arrest when I'm ready to, not before."

"If you don't arrest him, Connelly will."

"So let him."

Jameson stuck his lower jaw out. "You don't give a damm what happens to me or my cannery, do you?"

"Not true. And you know it." He resisted the temptation to slam the office door on his way out.

TJ leaned into a stiff blow off the river as he left the cannery and turned on to Water Street. In spite of hunching his shoulders and keeping his head down, icy needles of air found their way down his neck and back. He shivered and tried to forget the cold by giving some order to the facts bumping around in his head. He knew what Jameson wanted, what most reasonable people wanted, but he balked at the thought of using a man, even a Chinaman, as a…what…a sacrifice, like a pawn in chess.

Only a Chinee, Jameson said, ready to toss his butcher away like yesterday's paper. The words stuck in TJ's mind like a bone in his throat. *Only a Chinee. Makes it easy, doesn't it? Dammit, TJ, you're not playin' chess and Hop Li's not a pawn.*

On Squemoqua Street, he walked by Wild Bill's shooting gallery and realized there was no way he'd find enough new evidence to clear Hop Li by tomorrow. When he reached the corner of Benton and Squemoqua, he turned and walked over to the custom office square instead of going to his office. He sat down on a bench not yet ready to face Sketch. The bench sat next to a young cedar tree and far enough from the entrance so that anyone coming and going wouldn't feel the need to hello him. He shoved his hands into his coat pockets and tried to reason through the killings.

If Hop Li had been after money he'd take the opium and keep the dagger hidden until he could sell it somewhere safe. If he killed Fong out of revenge, why did he take the dagger? If a white man killed Jane to keep her from naming him as the father of her baby, why the skullduggery with the hands, the dagger, and the Chinee words? Why not bury her body and clothes where nobody would find them? And what about the bloodstained Chinee clothes? If the killer wore them wouldn't he bury them too rather than give them to Hop Li? And if the sea captain was the killer why was he wearing Chinee clothes?

His head swam with maybes and what if's, dead-ends all. He kept coming back to the same two conclusions: Hop Li was his only suspect for Fong's murder and no one would give a damn if he arrested him for both murders. He walked to his office as if heading to the funeral of a friend.

23

Sunday, April 11

Sketch returned to the office after 4:00 with no news of Kao. TJ and Sketch decided to eat dinner after they questioned Hop Li. They locked the office and drove straight to Jameson's Chinahouse. As the lawmen made their way up the loose plank walk to the door of the Chinahouse, the pungent smells of turnips, fried pork and spices made their mouths water.

TJ told the cook's boy they needed to talk to Hop Li and within five minutes Hop Li came out wearing a clean shirt, pants and sandals. He put on his slicker and pulled his slouch hat down so that it covered the back of his head. TJ told him they'd like to ask him some questions and had something to show him. Hop Li yelled a few words to the cook and then got in the buckboard without a word.

The courthouse had closed for the day when they got back so they went in through a side door. TJ asked Sketch to check all the courthouse doors to make sure they were locked. He didn't want Daines barging in on them as he did before.

"Sit down, Hop Li." He pointed to the chair in the middle of the room. TJ slid an El Gusto from his leather case and offered one to Hop Li.

Hop Li sat down but refused the cigar. TJ cut the tip of his cigar with his cutter, lit a match, and waited for the sulfur to burn off before touching the tip of the flame to the end of the cigar. He executed the ritual with deliberate, practiced moves, pausing between moves to glance at Hop Li. He took a long pull to make sure the end had an even burn then took his place behind his desk, leaned back and puffed leisurely. He wanted to give Hop Li time to wonder why he was here and time to worry what might happen to him.

Sketch came back into the room out of breath and announced. "All doors is locked, Boss." He dragged a chair from his desk and placed it besides TJ's so both men faced Hop Li.

"You know what we found in that box of yours?" TJ asked.

"Yes. Fatt Luk tell me. Stinky robe, slipper, hat."

"Right. Did anybody come around askin' for that sea captain's box?"

Hop Li shook his head, no.

"So you still say that a fella is comin' by for those clothes?" He picked up his cigar cutter and passed it from one hand to the other.

"Maybe. That man pay me two dolla fifty cent so I keep box."

"Why would someone pay you to keep those bloody clothes, Hop Li?" He continued to pass the cutter back and forth.

Hop Li shrugged his shoulders.

He put the cutter down and locked eyes with Hop Li. "Right. No one's comin' for that box. The man at the tea stand just happened to stop there. And he isn't a sea captain. Who is he and what did you two talk about?"

Hop Li glared at him before looking to the side. "Already say. Man say he sea captain. Ask me keep box. Say not open box."

TJ got up, moved around Sketch, and went to storage cabinet in the corner where he lifted the piece of burlap covering the fish box. He took out the pair of stained slippers and dropped them on the floor in front of Hop Li.

"Put those on," TJ said.

Hop Li glanced at the slippers. "Slipper no belong me."

TJ's eyes narrowed. "Do as I say."

Hop Li sighed and put the slippers on. They went on easily.

"How they feel?" TJ asked.

Hop Li shrugged.

TJ knelt down, squeezed the end of the slipper, and felt almost no space between the end of the big toe and the front. He slid his finger around to the heel and felt no space at all.

"Look's like a fit to me, Sketch. You take a look." Sketch got up from his chair and repeated TJ's movements.

"Yup. Tight as a baby's mouth on his mama's tit."

TJ studied Hop Li as Sketch tested the fit. If the Chinaboy was frightened, he hid it well.

"All right, take them off," TJ said.

Hop Li took off the slippers but then picked one up and traced the red and gold embroidered flower design on the toe with his finger. "This rich man slipper, no Chinaboy." He let the slipper fall to the floor next to its mate.

TJ went back to the table and lifted the soiled blue robe out of the fish box. He shook the foul smelling robe, allowing the creases to unfold, then came toward Hop Li. Hop Li knocked his chair over as he jumped up. "No! No wear stinky robe."

Sketch stationed himself between Hop Li and the door.

TJ shook his head. "You don't have to put this on. Just turn around." He took another step towards Hop Li but the Chinaboy didn't turn around.

"What you do?" Hop Li's eyes moved from Sketch to TJ.

"He's fixin' to bolt, Boss." Sketch moved to block the doorway.

"Doors are locked, remember? He's balky 'cause this looks about as invitin' as fish gurry." He motioned with his head. "Sketch, come here and turn around."

Sketch moved away from the door and turned his back to TJ. TJ held the top of the robe up to his deputy's shoulders. The robe came down a little below mid-calf on Sketch's six-foot frame and was too wide for his slim build. TJ turned to Hop Li. "That's all I'm gonna do."

Hop Li grunted and turned his back. TJ held the robe up to Hop Li's shoulders. The bottom of it fell to just above his ankle tops and the shoulder seams were right where they should be. TJ looked over his shoulder to his deputy. "How's it look?"

Sketch looked up and down and then from shoulder to shoulder. "Made for him, I'd say."

Sketch took the robe from TJ, picked up the slippers, and returned them to the fish box.

Hop Li sat back down on the edge of his chair; his body had stiffened and the skin around the corners of his eyes had tightened. TJ saw the stare of a caged tiger, a mixture of anger and defiance, that he saw the first time he questioned Hop Li.

He puffed his cigar a while then said, "We got to have some answers, Hop Li. The stains on those slippers and that robe are human blood. The killer wore those clothes the night he killed Fong." He paused, took a long drag of his cigar, and let the smoke float towards the ceiling. "Don't recall ever seeing a Chinaboy big as you and the clothes in that box fit you, snug, like they're yours. What you got to say for yourself?" He looked straight into Hop Li's eyes.

"Clothes no belong me. I never kill nobody." Hop Li jumped out of his chair and, for an instant, locked eyes with TJ.

"Sit down." TJ said and nodded to Sketch. Sketch moved behind Hop Li and rested his hand on Hop Li's shoulder. Hop Li ignored Sketch's hand, bent his knees slightly, and moved his arms away from his body. TJ sat up and slid his right hand along his belt until it rested on the handle of his Colt. Energy bristled from every man and the tension in the room felt like the air in the still before a storm.

Hop Li's eyes darted from the gun at TJ's hip to Sketch. For a long second, the three men didn't move. Then Hop Li let his breath out with a whoosh and his shoulders dropped. He sat down with his hands resting between his thighs. With the crisis over, TJ took his hand off his colt and leaned back in his chair.

"Now then, you already said you went by Fong's store Sunday. Maybe you left your Chinahouse Saturday night and went there. You took his knife, the money, and when Fong woke…"

"No. What you say, no happen. I sleep all night, leave Chinahouse in morning."

"Sketch talked to the cook, other men, at your Chinahouse. No one remembers you at breakfast Sunday morning."

"That day, fishermen strike, so no work. All Chinaboy sleep, when I leave."

"Well, we only got your word on that. Now, I think what really happened is you killed Fong and then took the cash from his safe. Could be that the white woman was staying at Fong's and heard him screaming. So you had to kill her too." TJ took a long pull on his cigar and looked hard at Hop Li. Hop Li sat with a straight back and his face closed.

TJ continued, "After that, you changed into your own clothes and put the robe and slippers in the fish box. You waited in the store 'til morning light, then walked the two blocks to meet your friend Soo." TJ flipped through his notebook. "Soo says you talked to a big white man …that part is right…but he didn't say the fellow was a sea captain, did he Sketch?"

"Nope." Sketch tilted his head and looked at Hop Li. "Tea man says you and the white fella jawed some, then you both left. Says you walked away with the box. But says he never seen the white fella with that box."

TJ pointed his cigar at Hop Li. "With the money you stole, you paid Fatt Luk to keep that box at his pig farm. That's clever, Hop Li. Don't know a soul who'd go near a pig farm unless he had a damm good reason." He paused to knock the ash off his cigar. "And as for that sea captain you're waitin' on? I asked at the maritime office. They have no listin' for a captain by name of John Malmo. The post office didn't have anyone listed by that name either." He stretched his legs and put one foot up on the lip of the wire wastebasket. "Your sea captain story is nothin' but a pack of lies, Hop Li."

Hop Li shook his head from side to side when TJ finished. "No. No lie. All this you say, no true. Sea captain give me gold coin, two dolla fifty cent coin."

"Did you mail any money back to your folks since last Sunday?" TJ asked and swiveled from side to side.

A frown crossed Hop Li's forehead and he stared at TJ. "Why ask this?"

"Never mind, dammit, just answer my question."

"Send money home, two day ago. Dr. Chung help write letter."

"All right. How much did you send?"

Hop Li folded his arms across his chest. "No true—what you think"

"How much, Hop Li?"

"Fifty dolla." Hop Li's eyes stayed on TJ's.

"But Fong only lent you twenty-five dollars. Where'd you get the other twenty-five?"

"Dr. Chung."

"Yeah, sure. Maybe Dr. Chung will lie for you, too."

"Dr. Chung never lie. Tsai Soo, Fatt Luk, also no lie. You think all Chinamen lie, eh? So, go hell." Hop Li squared his shoulders and looked over TJ's head.

"Watch your mouth. I've been tryin' to keep an open mind but you keep on like that and we're through talkin.'" He leaned forward and pointed a finger at Hop Li's chest. He rarely got backtalk from a suspect, never from a Chinaboy, and found himself getting angry. He picked up his cigar cutter and stroked the handle with his thumb. When he had calmed, he said, "It'll go easier on you if confess, Hop Li. So why don't…"

"Confess? What is confess?" Hop Li met TJ's gaze. TJ scooted his chair up close to his desk and spoke in a low voice.

"It means you tell us the bad things you did. How you killed Fong and the woman, why you cut her hands off…"

"NO! Never confess," Hop Li shouted. "All thing you say, all lie. Chen Hop Li never kill Wah Fong, woman. No kill nobody." He folded his arms across his chest again, eyes wide in defiance.

"Looks like this is all we gonna get, Sketch." He rose. "Chen Hop Li, stand up. I'm arresting you for the murders of Wah Fong and Jane Thurgood. Put your hands behind your back." He slid his hand along his belt, showing his holster and Colt. Hop Li looked from TJ's face to the gun and stood up. Sketch brought Hop Li's arms behind his back, cuffed him, and then stepped to one side.

"We're takin' you to the jail now. In a few days, you can tell your story to a jury." TJ said

"What is jury?"

"That's a group of men who don't know you and listen to your…"

"You not listen. Why other men listen?" The defiant look changed to hate.

TJ continued. "The men on the jury have to listen to your story, just as they have to listen to the law's story. Then…"

"Wah! Why anybody listen Chinaboy, eh? No people listen. For sure bet, Hop Li hang." He spit the words out and stared at Sketch who lowered his gaze. TJ cleared his throat but didn't speak. Hop Li turned and faced the door but kept his head up. TJ went over to his desk, looked at the school clock, and then wrote in his log:

Arrested the cannery worker, Chen Hop Li, for the murders of Wah Fong and Jane Thurgood and for the burglary of Wah Fong's grocery. Said crimes took place on or about April 3, 1886 at 251 S. Main St., Astoria, Ore. Date: Sunday, April 11, 1886, 6:15 pm.

24

Lucky, the jailer, looked out the jail door peephole and then opened it when he recognized Sketch.

"A Chinee? What's up, boys?" Lucky wore a logger's cutoffs patched with leather scraps and a flannel shirt that rarely saw a washtub. His wide suspenders, brogans, baldhead, and bulbous whiskey nose gave him a comical look. At 44, Lucky was TJ's oldest deputy and walked with a hitch in his right leg after he broke it. He'd fallen from the third floor window of Mrs. Riippa's boardinghouse while trying to keep Mars Ruusti, drunk and suicidal, from jumping. Rather than let Lucky go, TJ made him permanent jail keep and in the two years Lucky ran the jail, TJ found little to complain about.

"This here is Chen Hop Li," Sketch said. "We got him for murders of that Chinee grocer and the Thurgood girl."

"Don't say." Lucky eyed his new charge from top to bottom.

Hop Li's eyes traveled around the room, from the horseshoe sized key ring with its two dozen keys behind the jailer's desk, to the rack of night sticks and leg irons in the wire covered cabinet, to the heavy timbered iron-plated door that led to the cells. A dinner plate with a half eaten portion of meat loaf and mashed potatoes sat on top of a pile of papers on Lucky's desk.

"Big one, ain't he? Where ya want him?"

"Anyone in the cages?" TJ asked.

"Nope."

"Good."

Lucky walked around his desk and grabbed the key ring. TJ took the keys from him.

"Finish your dinner. We'll take him."

"Appreciate it, TJ."

TJ unlocked the door to the cells and they ushered Hop Li into the dimly lit corridor. They put Hop Li in the first of two cages, which were reserved for prisoners charged with a capital offense or facing execution. Each cage was built of strap steel one inch wide and a quarter inch thick. The straps were woven in a basket weave pattern but with space between the strips to let light in from the corridor, which allowed Lucky to check on a prisoner at a glance. A solid wall of heavy timber separated the two cages and prevented prisoners in one cage from seeing into the adjacent cage. Once inside the cell, Sketch removed Hop Li's handcuffs.

Hop Li rubbed his wrists and said, "Jail stink like hell."

"Yep. Can't deny that," TJ said and looked around the seven by nine foot cell seeing it, or trying to, through the eyes of his prisoner. The cot, metal frame with wood planks, was six feet long and no wider than three railroad ties set side by side. The cot attached to the wall by chains and could be raised and latched onto a hook embedded in the wall. A drop down shelf opposite the cot held a wooden bowl for washing. A water bucket with a wood dipper sat underneath the shelf. The privy, a bucket covered by a wood box with a hole, sat in the corner furthest from the cot.

"Why you put me in monkey cage?" Hop Li asked.

TJ scratched his chin and said, "Nothin' against you, Hop Li. It's just how we do things." TJ said to Sketch, "Round up his personals while I talk to him." TJ unhooked the cell's cot from the wall, sat down on one end, and invited Hop Li to sit on the other.

"One day next week we'll take you to a judge. Until then, you gotta stay here. Now…"

"Where blanket, soap?"

"Sketch is bringing them. Now, anything you want to tell me before I go? Maybe about Fatt Luk?"

"What tell? Fatt Luk good friend, hnnnn! No kill nobody. All same like me."

TJ rose and stretched. "All right. If that's the way you want it. Guess I'll be goin.'"

Hop Li jumped up. "Wait policeman! You know Dr. Chung?"

"What's he got to do with this?"

"We long-time friend. Please, you talk Dr. Chung. He say Hop Li no kill Wah Fong, woman."

TJ pointed his finger at the Chinaboy. "I'll talk to him but don't count on his help. You're in big trouble, Hop Li. The only one can help you is me—maybe."

Sketch came back with bedding, soap, towel, and comb and laid them on the cot.

TJ looked over Hop Li's supplies. "Looks like you got everything you need." He walked out of the cell. Sketch followed and pulled the door shut. The door struck the frame with a loud clang and the ringing echoed up and down the corridor. TJ put his mouth close to the iron grill. "You decide to talk, let Lucky know. Could help yourself by tellin' me everything."

Hop Li pulled his legs up on the cot and wrapped his arms around his knees. He stared at the floor and didn't answer. The light from the overhead lamp in the hall shone into his cell, creating squares and rectangles of light and dark, like a checkerboard, across the floor, cot, and body of the Chinaboy. It must have been an illusion, a trick of the checkerboard pattern, but it seemed to TJ that Hop Li's body had shrunk.

Back in the jail office, Sketch told Lucky about questioning Hop Li while TJ leaned against a wall.

"Ya shouda seen it, Lucky. The Boss cut through that boy's story easy as slicin' bread. Once he put them Chinee clothes on, he was finished, yup, so much fried fish after that. He knowed it too." He paused to take a breath, and then rushed on, "Wasn't no need for him to confess. No siree. We caught him up in a net just like ol' Chinook." Sketch grinned at Lucky. TJ kept his arms folded against his chest and watched a moth circle the ceiling lamp.

"Ain't that right, Boss? Sketch glanced at TJ for the first time.

"Maybe." TJ pushed away from the wall.

"Maybe?" Sketch paused and brushed the hair off his forehead.

Lucky shifted his chew of Ames' Best from one side of his jaw to the other and looked from Sketch to TJ. "Somehin' wrong, TJ?"

"We bought some time by jailing that Chinaboy. It'll keep the big shots happy and keep the paper off our backs, for a while. Supposin' our Chinaboy didn't kill Fong or the girl. Could be the real killer or killers gets to feelin' safe, might take to braggin' about how he used that Chinaboy. And if he starts talkin,' we'll hear about it."

Sketch stood in front of Lucky's desk, mouth open, forehead wrinkled. "Boss, thought we got our man."

"Think, Sketch. You ever wonder who wrote the note to Mac?"

"Damm…forgot about that."

"Or why the killer left that opium in Fong's safe?"

"Umm...thought it's cause our boy don't use it." Sketch scratched his cheek.

"Maybe. But opium is good as cash in Chinatown and Hop Li knows that. And what about that diamond we found under Fong— where'd it come from and why didn't the killer take it?"

"Guess I forgot about it, too."

"Yeah. Well, I haven't. Those facts are stickin' in my craw like a chicken bone." TJ grabbed his hat. "Anyway, I'm goin' over to The Star, let Mac know we arrested Hop Li. I'll ask him if he won't favor us for a change and keep from stirrin' folks up more than they need to be. Guess I better let the Chief know, too. After that, I'm goin' to Sirpia's for a slice of pie. Got things to think on."

"Boss, didn't ya have a meet with Bessie today?"

TJ stopped with his hand on the door handle. "Ah shit." He pulled out his pocket watch—6:45, more than five hours late. Bessie would be madder than a trussed up pig.

25

TJ had been nursing a cup of coffee at the *Paradiso* bar for a good ten minutes when the bouncer came downstairs and handed him a note. The note said Bessie didn't have time for *Time Wasters!* He smiled and wrote back saying he'd only take a few minutes of her time. He folded the note around the *Good for One* coin and handed it to bouncer. The man returned in five minutes and said he could go up.

Bessie opened the door to his knock but stood blocking the entrance looking him up and down as if he were a peddler. Her dark green robe was tied loosely at the waist, revealing her black undergarments. She had piled her lush red hair into a bun, as if in haste, and strands of it fell down to her shoulders.

"Hello, Bessie."

"Hello, yourself." She kept one hand on her hip and the other on the door.

"Well, you goin' to let me in."

"Don't know why I should. I got up early this mornin' just so I could finish that precious diary of yours. Thought you said you was in a hurry." Bessie made no move to step aside.

He felt his face warm and spoke fast, "I was...I mean I am. But things came up, things I couldn't put off. Sorry."

"You don't sound sorry."

"Damm it, Bessie, you want me get down on my knees?"

"Well, that'd be a start." She smiled and opened the door for him. He followed her into the parlor and through the beaded curtains into the dining room. The aroma of meat cooking crept in from the upstairs kitchen and he realized he was hungry. She brought the diary out and said, "For pity's sake, sit down. You want somethin' to eat? Ah Yee can fix you a ham and cheese in a minute." She picked up the silver bell next to her saucer.

"Nope, coffee is fine." He wanted answers more than he wanted food.

She poured him a cup and then traced the letters, L.L., on the cover of the diary with her fingernail. "These here initials is the secret, honey, the key to her life." She opened the diary and smoothed out the top of a dog-eared page. "This little girl knew what she wanted, no mistake. I read this diary a couple times, some parts three, four times, and believe I know her. Listen close now 'cause it's easy to get lost." She winked at him. "Now, she calls herself Lillie in here and had her heart set on being an actress—already a damm good one, if you ask me—anyway, the little vixen pretends she's Lillie Langtry. You know her?"

"Think so but what's she got to do with this?"

"Well, silly, if Jane pretends she's Lillie Langtry maybe she calls the men in her life by same names as the men in Lillie's life—you know who Lillie's prince is, don't you?"

"Her prince? Christ, what are you playin' at, Bessie?"

"You need educatin,' darlin.' Lillie Langtry is the mistress, leastways one of them, of Prince Albert." She looked at him and shook her head, exasperated. "The Prince of Wales, dearie."

"Is this goin' somewhere or you just funnin' me?"

"Patience, darlin,' patience. It's all tied up in her mind, see. Jane wanted to be just like her, like Lillie, so she does what Lillie did. Lillie called her Prince, Bertie, so you can bet your bottom dollar the B in Jane's diary stands for her man, Bertie." Bessie nodded her head as if she had solved a grand mystery.

"B for Bertie. Shit. Who the hell is Bertie?"

"Well, honey, that's your job—you can't expect me to do all your work for you. But I'll tell you this much. Jane's B is her lover and if he's anything like Lillie's Bertie he's rich and a somebody."

"So is Prince Albert, this Bertie, married?"

"Of course. To Princess Alexandria. And rumor is that she knows about Lillie's foolin' around with Bertie."

"How about the Langtry woman?"

"She's married too. But her man is a gem, a real gem, has a yacht and enough money to keep her in a big house with servants and all." She got a far away look in her eyes and didn't say anything for a time.

"Yeah? So?"

"Well, don't you see? When Lillie needs her husband he shows his face. Otherwise he stays away and keeps his mouth shut."

"Why does he put up with her runnin' around?"

"'Cause he's a doormat, that's why."

"What's his name? This doormat?"

"Ah ha. You're catching on, sweetie, you're askin' the right question now. Lillie's husband is Edward Langtry and Lillie calls him Ned." She opened the diary to a place marked by a torn piece of paper and pointed to the initial N. "See? Give you three guesses what the N stands for and first two don't count, honey."

"All right, Ned. But Jane wasn't married."

"No, darlin,' but she was fixin' to marry Ned first thing."

"Yeah, I see the connection. But dammit, Bessie, it all sounds like a so much pretendin'—a girl playin' with dolls."

"Oh, no honey. She says she's comin' to Astoria to meet up with N or Ned and isn't that just where you found her? No, sweetie, these men is real all right. More coffee?" He nodded and she filled their cups. She added three lumps of sugar in her cup and made a face as she sipped the now-cool coffee. "You know, it's too bad what happened to that girl. She had ambition, imagination too. A damm shame, really is."

"Did the Langtry woman have a child by this Bertie?"

"Yes. A little girl, Jeanne Marie, be about five now. Nobody's sure who the father is, 'cept well, we know it ain't her husband..." she chuckled "...everybody agrees on that. He's off sailing his yacht while she's cuddlin' the royal member. The Prince built her a house outside of London, their own love nest—ain't that somethin'?! Wish I had me a Prince. Damm." She threw her head back and laughed. She poured herself two fingers of port from a glass decanter, took a sip, and then ran her tongue around the rim of the glass. "You want somethin' besides coffee?"

"No thanks. How the hell you know all this Bessie?"

"I read, darlin,' I read. The society news in particular. You remember that New York theater what burned down the night before Lillie's play opened. Everything 'cept the marquee with her name on it gone—was in all the papers—you musta read about it. Anyway, after that you couldn't open a paper without seeing Lillie's name next to this or that Mr. Big. Heard she made over $100,000 that year. Think on that, honeypie, one year and you're set for life. Now you know why our Jane wanted to be an actress. Don't know but what I wouldn't have done the same thing if I knowed how rich you could get paradin' around with your clothes on. Ha!" She slapped the table with the flat of her hand. "She even has her own railroad car, calls it the *Lalee*. Traipsin' around these United States like a queen—has maids, cooks, and I don't know what all. Cost her new man a quarter of million dollars that car did. Now, tell me you never heard nothin' about her, about the Jersey Lillie." She lifted an eyebrow at him.

"Not much." He'd remembered a drawing of Lillie Langtry on an advert for face powder or maybe a box of soap but thought she was a singer. He shook his head and folded his arms across his chest. "Dammit, Bessie, my head's spinnin.' Tell me if I got it right. Jane pretends she's this Langtry woman and does all she can to be like her. This rich fella Bertie is her lover and I'm guessin' he's the one put her in a family way. If it comes out she's with child and has no husband she's done for, ruined. So she finds herself another fella, this Ned, who wants to marry her." He paused and tugged on his mustache. "But how come she doesn't just marry the first fella?"

"My guess is that Jane's Bertie is married and won't get a divorce. Ned is well off and somebody too but not as rich as Bertie."

"But Ned's got a wife too. She's got the same problem with him as she does with Bertie."

"No, honeypie, she don't. Look here, what she says about him." She turned to the last entries and handed the diary to him.

He read the page again and noted the entry that said Ned was gaga about her and that he was hers when she wanted him.

"Yeah, sounds like she can boss him." He closed the diary.

"She found her doormat…only something went wrong." Bessie stuck out her bottom lip.

"What?"

"Well, if that poor girl is ten to twelve weeks along she don't have time to waste. Could be she pushed Ned too hard."

"But is that reason enough to kill her and cut her up? Why didn't he just walk out?"

"Could be he found out about Bertie and went wild jealous. But that's just a guess. It's up to you to find out what's true."

The clock on the mantel chimed and the two cherubs on its top turned in a tight circle. "Oh, look at that. I'm fritterin' away the night talkin' to you. Get out of here now and let me get dressed. Here, give us a kiss before you run off." They got up from the table.

"Thanks, Bessie. You've been a big help, as usual." He took the diary and gave her a peck on the cheek.

"Oh, now ain't that sweet? You're sure you ain't got yourself a new woman?"

"Only woman I met recent is not for me."

"Who is she anyway?"

"She speaks Chinee and is just helpin' me out."

"She have a name, this helper?"

"Emma Taylor."

"Taylor? I know that name...now where...oh my, you don't mean that preacher's sister? The one tryin' to turn Chinaboys into Christians?"

"Dammit, Bessie, don't be makin' anything out of this." He felt his neck and face warm, "Like I said, she's been helpin' me out is all, same as you."

She put her hand up over her mouth and shook her head slowly from side to side. "Great God in heaven—a missionary. Are you sweet on her, honey?"

He felt his face warm again. "Wha...? Hell no." He pulled his hat down so she couldn't see his eyes and added, "can't be—only just met her."

"Uh-huh. Heard tell she's a pretty thing, too." She stood up and then tightened the belt around her waist. "A missionary. My oh my. She'll make a Christian out of you before she's done helpin' you, sweetcakes." She threw her head back and laughed.

He felt embarrassed and couldn't think of what to say. After she stopped laughing, she said, "Now, just cause you're...well...got other interests don't mean you hafta be a stranger. If you need to talk, just send me a note and I'll fit you in. Here, you might need this sometime, Cowboy." She winked and handed him back the coin that said, *Good for One*. She waved her hand, dismissing him, and the bracelets on her arm clacked in farewell. He heard her chuckling as he pushed the beaded curtain aside and went through the parlor.

Downstairs, a couple of fishermen stood at the bar nursing a beer. A waltz played on the nickelodeon and one of Bessie's girls struggled to keep the drunk she danced with from toppling over. TJ took all this in but as if in a dream. Again and again, he heard Bessie ask if he were sweet on Emma Taylor and each time he felt a flush of excitement at the question.

Dammit, stop. You don't have time for this...what...this mooning over a woman you hardly know.

He needed to make sense of his confused feelings and hurried to the restaurant of the Parker Hotel. He took a seat at the counter and ordered the daily special. He couldn't get the Langtry woman out of his head. Why would some fool spend a quarter of a million dollars on a woman so she could ride around in her own railroad car? He stayed in a fog of wonder at the things love makes a man do until his roast beef and mashed potatoes came. Then he gave himself over to eating and, for a time, set aside thoughts of the diary, the murders, tomorrow's headlines, and the foolishness of a man in love.

26

Monday, April 12

TJ got up early and went downstairs to the kitchen where he found Helga reading The Star.

"Mornin,' TJ. I see you locked up Jameson's Chinaboy. About time, too."

"Coffee ready?"

"Be a couple minutes." She nodded at the large kettle. "That poor girl! That boy ever say why he cut off her hands?"

"I don't know he did—not for sure. Could be he didn't kill her or the grocer."

"You don't say. Well, sure looks that way to me."

"Let me look at your paper a minute, will you?"

"It's all yours. It's time I get breakfast started anyway." She handed him the paper. "Why'd you arrest that boy if he didn't kill her?"

"I said I wasn't sure. And if he's guilty, I want him alive for the trial. So he's safer in jail than runnin' around town."

The headlines screamed the news in one-inch, boldface, letters.

Chinaboy Arrested for Murders!

Half way down the front page, he found a drawing of the purported murder scene. He stared in growing anger at the drawing, which showed a voluptuous young woman in a nightgown bound to the post of an opium bed. One strap of her nightgown hung loose, exposing her shoulder and part of her breast. A Chinaman with a long queue, his face inches from the woman, grinned as he held a dagger under the other strap of her nightgown. The woman looked up at the ceiling, wide-eyed with terror. The caption under the drawing read: *John enjoys his prize.*

TJ turned from the drawing and read from the beginning of the article.

Yesterday, Sheriff TJ Stone arrested the Chinaboy Chen Hop Li, a butcher at Jameson's cannery, for the murders of Wah Fong and Miss Jane Thurgood, an 18-year old woman visiting Astoria from Portland. Miss Thurgood was staying with the Olney Hermanson family in Uppertown when it was believed she was kidnapped by the Chinaboy and taken to his den, a room above Fong's grocery. We can only speculate on how he was able to restrict her movements so as to undress her and subject her to his inflamed desires. It's possible an accomplice helped the Chinaboy capture and tie the terrified young woman to his filthy bed. The possibility that Miss Thurgood was drugged can not be excluded as Police Chief Connelly informed us that her silk nightgown reeked of opium.

No one involved in the investigation was able to explain why the butcher cut off her hands after satisfying his evil passions. Her hands were found in one of Jameson's test tanks shortly after 6:00 am the morning after the fishermen's strike ended. An ominous message in Chinese on the wall of the tank declared that a "debt had been paid."

The exact nature of this debt has yet to be determined but Police Chief Connelly suggested that, "He sliced her hands off as a sacrifice to one of his gods." The Chief added, "It's a known fact that the heathens worship all kinds of crazy gods."

Sheriff Stone had no comment on why Miss Thurgood's hands were cut off and refused to speculate on the butcher's motives.

Perhaps we'll never know what went on in the deranged mind of the fiend. All we know for certain is that her mutilated body, clothed only in a silk nightgown, was found floating in the Columbia River underneath an abandoned cannery last Thursday, April 8th.

"Coffee's ready." Helga said and then nodded at the newspaper.

"It's interestin,' reading what Chinamen believe. You think he was offerin' up a sacrifice to his god, like it says." She handed him a cup of coffee.

TJ nodded thanks as he took the cup and then said, "You can't believe half of what's in here, Helga. And Connelly's no China expert."

"What about that other Chinaman? You think he's the killer then?"

TJ looked up, "What other Chinaman?"

"That garbage man. The paper says you looked at him hard."

TJ muttered a curse and shook his head in frustration. He continued reading and saw that Daines described the scene in the hall of the courthouse where he and Sketch questioned Fatt Luk. The implication left with the reader was that since the garbage man with the eye patch was a friend of Hop Li, he'd been Hop Li's accomplice.

TJ had read enough. He folded the paper and threw it on the counter. He poured his half-full cup of coffee down the sink and grabbed his slicker.

"You goin' out without breakfast?"

"Yep. Lost my appetite readin' that damm story."

He went out the back door to avoid the congratulations and the questions of his tablemates.

As he walked through Uniontown, a few men waved and called out, "Well done!" or "Good job, Sheriff!"

But the praise wasn't universal. Aleski, owner of the Finnish meat market, stopped him. "Why you put Chinaman in jail? Big waste of money!" He winked. "My friends and me, we take care of that one— for free. You bet!"

TJ shook his head and said, "We don't do things that way anymore, Aleski. The law says he gets a fair trial and I aim to make sure he gets one."

As he walked down the hall to his office, he heard Sketch talking to someone and wondered who was calling this early. But then he heard a guffaw and recognized Big Jim's voice.

TJ walked in on Big Jim sitting at Sketch's desk reading The Star while Sketch peered over the big man's shoulder.

"Mornin,' boys." He hung his hat on the stand by the door and sat down at his desk. "Didn't expect you for a few days yet, Jim. What happened?"

Mornin,' TJ. Nothin' was happenin'—that's the trouble. Got bored sitin' in parlors and drinkin' tea with old ladies, talkin' about nothin.' After a week, I just couldn't take no more talk of Christians, good works, and crops. I went to the city, got me a bottle and cozied up with a bad woman for three days. Got myself straightened out and come back here early to see what you fellas is up to." He grinned and held up the newspaper. "Accordin' to this, you two been busy." He frowned and shook his head from side to side. "Damm! I leave and things get interestin.' Sketch been fillin' me in. There gonna be trouble like up North?"

Big Jim had been a bare-knuckle fighter at carnivals and in the back lots of saloons and the thought of missing a fight was to him what missing a steak dinner was to other men. He and the touts who sponsored him had their share of run-ins with the law so the fact that he could now break bones with the blessing of the law pleased him no end.

TJ said, "Not if we keep a step or two ahead of troublemakers."

"That Chinaboy as nasty as paper makes out?

"Nope. And could be he's not our killer."

"Wha...? Why'd you arrest him then?

"'Cause with the paper screamin' he's an opium fiend just itchin' to get his hands on another white woman, I figure the only place he's safe is in jail." TJ picked the paper off Sketch's desk, folded it, and dumped it in the wastebasket. "You came back in the nick of time, Big Jim, 'cause we need a deputy stationed with Lucky in case some fools try to take care of Hop Li on their own."

"You got any bunch of fools in mind?" Big Jim asked.

"Well, when the Knights of Labor boys see that story, they'll be on us like flies on shit. So you and Sketch will have to keep a night watch and rotate shifts."

"Maybe they won't come, Boss," Sketch said.

"I'd like to believe that, Sketch, but that story is convincin.' If I didn't know better, I might side with the Knights after readin' what Mac wrote and lookin' at that drawin.'"

"But that there drawin' wasn't how it was, Boss. That nightgown didn't have no straps fer one thing. Fer another, Doc says she wasn't tied up."

"Doesn't matter, Sketch. People see that drawin' and it'll stick in their heads like a barnacle to a rock."

"So what we gonna do?" Big Jim asked.

"What we're paid to do. Our job. See if we can't find out who killed the grocer and the Thurgood girl and soon. Big Jim, go on over to the jail and set up a schedule with Lucky that covers the trouble times—from dinnertime to about two in the morning. Men are in saloons then, drinkin,' talkin' tough, and feelin' mean." He stood up and grabbed his hat.

"What you want me to do?" Sketch asked.

"Round up Kao. If you leave right away you'll probably find him to home." He put his hat on and squared it.

"Where you off to, Boss?"

"I'm goin' over to Wing's. We need that boy translator when we question Kao."

TJ picked up the translator, Sung Gee, and got back to the office ten minutes before Sketch ushered in a sullen-faced Kao. Sketch deposited Kao in the straight-backed chair with the hard seat. Suspects felt uncomfortable in that chair after five minutes no matter how they twisted or turned.

"Followed him to that Chinee medicine store," Sketch said.

"Who'd he talk to?"

"Just that Chinee Doc. Figgered I best grab him before he gets his mornin' pipe." Sketch edged towards the door. "Boss, if you don't need me, I'll go talk to Lucky and Big Jim about our night schedule."

TJ nodded and then lit a cigar in his slow, easy way, ignoring Kao and the boy for the time it took to get an even burn. Then he went over to the door, walked it halfway closed and shoved in the doorstop. Kao sat hunched in his chair and watched TJ out of the corner of his eye.

TJ sat back down. "It's early in the day to be ridin' the back of the dragon, Kao. What you runnin' away from?"

As Sung Gee translated, Kao flashed TJ a look and then lowered his head without answering.

"I can smell it, Kao. You're keepin' something from me. What is it?" He put his feet up on his desk.

Kao stared above TJ's head and didn't answer.

"Well, you can clam up if you want to. But if I find out what it is without your help, it'll go hard on you. You're interferin' with my investigation." He studied Kao and saw the old fellow flinch as the boy translated his last words. TJ continued, "And I will find out, Kao, sooner or later. Count on it." He took several puffs of cigar and waited for the boy to translate. "But I'm an understandin' man. If you did something wrong, say broke the law in a small way, and you tell me about it, why that'd could keep you out of prison."

"Kao hide nothing." Sung Gee translated. Kao's forceful tone didn't go with the catch in his voice. TJ smelled a lie.

"All right. Have it your way." TJ picked up his notebook and flipped through pages until he found the page he wanted, studied it for a time, then looked up and asked. "You hear about the woman we took out of the river Thursday?"

Kao nodded yes and his eyes swept over TJ's face before he lowered his gaze.

"Somebody stabbed her and cut off her hands. You know anything about that?"

Kao shook his head no and kept looking at his feet.

"I think you do." TJ was fishing. When your opponent retreats, you have to keep pressing, Doc said, even when you aren't sure of your next move. Your opponent wonders why he can't see what you were up to, starts to question his strategy, and blunders.

"Now, I'm not sayin' you killed her. Maybe you happened to see somethin' or hear somethin' you weren't supposed to." As the boy translated, TJ watched Kao and noticed the tightening of his upper body. "Of course, could be you did more than that. I'm guessin' the dead woman weighed 130 pounds or so. Take more than one man to carry a body that heavy to the river without being seen. I'm bettin' the killer had help. Is that it? You helped the killer?"

A puzzled look came over the translator's face. "Kao say, never kill nobody."

"That's not what I asked." TJ took his feet off his desk and sat up.

The boy translated and Kao said something back but the boy didn't translate it. TJ waited then told the boy to ask Kao again.

This time Kao shrugged his shoulders and pulled his folded hands against his belly. TJ noted the helplessness of the gesture and leaned forward. "Did you cut off her hands and put them in that tank at Jameson's Cannery?"

Kao frowned and waited a few seconds before answering, "No. Kao say, never see hand."

TJ's words shot out of him, "Never see? He says he never saw her hands?"

The boy turned to Kao, translated, and then said to TJ. "Yes. Kao never see woman hand."

"But that means he saw the dead woman without her hands. Is that what he's sayin'?" He heard the excitement in his voice and saw the boy and Kao shoot him a look. Slow down, he told himself, give Kao time to sweat. He picked up his cigar cutter and ran his thumb up and down the pearl handle and over his initials.

The boy translated then leaned in close to the older man's mouth as Kao spoke in a whisper. "Kao say, woman dead already, hand cut off. Not know who take hand."

Questions came to TJ fast now and he told himself not to fumble in his eagerness to question Kao. He forced himself to speak in an offhand manner. "All right, but you saw her body before the killer put her in the river, right?"

Kao nodded his head, yes, as the boy finished speaking.

"So you know who killed the woman. Who killed her?"

Kao shouted his answer and the boy spoke in a voice as loud, "Kao not know!" Sung Gee paused. Kao and the boy talked back and forth at a furious pace for a few seconds. The boy's voice shook when he translated.

"Kao say, not know who kill Master Fong, white lady. When Kao come room, Master Fong on floor, lady on bed. Both long time dead." Sung Gee turned to listen as Kao continued to speak and then made a slicing motion with his right hand across his left wrist. "Woman hand already cut off."

TJ inched his chair closer to his desk and leaned forward as far as he could. Kao lifted his eyes to TJ's face but then lowered them quickly as he encountered TJ's stare. "Now, we're gettin' somewhere. I need to hear his story from the beginnin'—and this time, by God, tell him to leave nothin' out." TJ took out his notepad and pencil and then nodded for Kao to begin.

Kao let out a sigh and repeated the story he'd told TJ the first time but added that he found Jane Thurgood lying on the bed, face up, and dressed in a Chinese gown. Her hands were cut off. He didn't see them but admitted that he didn't look for them. Kao saw no weapon but assumed that the killer used Fong's dagger to kill them because he noticed it missing from the case downstairs. Somebody had piled the woman's dress, underclothes, shoes, parasol, and carpetbag on the floor of the open closet.

TJ read the story back and Kao corrected two minor details. TJ noted the changes and read the story again. This time, Kao made no changes. "You're doing fine, Kao, just fine. Got a few more questions and then we're done. How did her body get into the river?"

Kao shook his head and said, "Not know."

"Did you take her clothes?"

Kao didn't wait for the boy to finish before he shouted, "No!"

"All right. But you know who did, don't you. Who took her clothes, Kao?"

After the boy translated, Kao hesitated and said, "Not know." Both Kao and Sung Gee avoided looking at TJ when they spoke.

"Un-huh. And you were doin' so good up to now. Guess I'll have to lock you up after all."

Kao paled and shouted at the boy. "Kao say, no go prison. Everything he say, true."

"No, it's not true. If he doesn't want to go to prison, he has to stop lyin.'" TJ paused and took a long pull on his cigar and let the smoke out in puffs.

Kao tugged on Sung Gee's sleeve and then spoke, "Kao forget one thing." They talked for a time then the boy said, "Opium smell strong, that room. So somebody smoke. Maybe Sheriff think master Fong smoke pipe, eh? No. Pipe for lady. So white lady smoke opium. Must be."

When TJ finished writing he said, "Good, Kao. I wondered about that myself." He paused then smiled. "But let's get back to the clothes. Kao said he saw the woman's clothes in the closet. So somebody took those clothes after he saw them and he wants me to believe he doesn't know who took them. Well, I don't believe him. Ask him about the clothes again, Sung Gee."

Kao scrunched down in the chair and shook his head after the boy translated. TJ waited but Kao sat with his hands clasped tightly over his belly and didn't speak.

"All right, Kao. Let's forget about the clothes for now. Let's go back to the time after you found Fong and the woman. You didn't know what to do so you went to Wing's to ask for help. That's what you told me before, right?"

"Kao say, Master Wing Ti-sen wise man, honorable man." Sung Gee translated.

"Shit—that isn't what I asked." TJ concentrated on smoking his cigar for a few seconds. After a moment, he said, "Ask him again, Sung Gee."

Kao leaned towards the boy as the two talked back and forth. "Wing Ti-sen headman. Kao always go headman for help," the boy translated. Kao looked at the half open door as the boy spoke.

"You're doing fine, Kao, Just fine." TJ went over to the water bucket, filled the dipper, took a sip, and then held the dipper out to Kao. Kao grabbed it and gulped the water down. As TJ walked back to his chair, he said, "You trust the head man, Kao and that's fine. Everybody needs somebody to go to when they're in trouble. Wing said that he would take care of everything. Isn't that right?" TJ spoke softly and nodded at Kao.

Kao lowered his eyes as Sung Gee translated and whispered a word, "Yes."

"Yes. And what did Wing say to tell me, Kao?"

"Master Wing say tell policeman about Fong, nothing about woman," Sung Gee said while avoiding TJ's eyes.

"So then Wing took the woman's body and her clothes. What did Wing do with them?

After listening to Sung Gee, Kao sighed, any trace of defiance absent from face or posture.

TJ pushed, "Sung Gee, tell him he is in trouble for not telling me what he knew before today. But I'll go easy on him if he tells me everything now, and that means everything. So ask him again what Wing did with her body and clothes."

Kao and the boy talked for a considerable time and, finally, the boy turned to TJ and said, "Master Wing tell Kao go home, wait. Kao obey. Then, Master Wing send message, tell Kao wait outside Fong store. So Kao wait. Sheriff TJ come, ask Kao question. That all Kao know."

TJ stared at Kao for a second before asking, "Kao never saw Wing or any of his men take the body or clothes?"

"No. Never see." The boy said and Kao shook his head no, for emphasis. TJ took down what Sung Gee said and read it back to both of them. Kao sighed and nodded.

"Good. What you told me will help us find the killer, Kao. You did the right thing by telling me."

Kao bent close to the boy and spoke in such a soft voice that the boy held his ear no more than an inch from Kao's lips. "You put Kao in jail?" Sung Gee translated.

"Not this time. But if I find out he's still keepin' things from me, I won't be so forgivin.' Kao will go to jail for sure. Tell him that." Kao sighed after Sung Gee translated. TJ blew a perfect smoke ring and all three watched it float to the ceiling.

After they left, TJ went over what he'd learned. Wing had pulled strings behind the scenes from the beginning. But why the masquerade? Could Wing be behind the murders? TJ saw no reason for Wing to kill the girl or the grocer. And if Wing had killed them why not hide both bodies?

TJ grew angry as he thought about Wing's deceit. The headman had gone to great lengths to keep TJ from finding out what in fact he just had—that Jane Thurgood and Wah Fong were murdered in the same room about the same time. TJ could make no sense of Wing's actions but the headman was no fool—there had to be a reason for what he did.

27

Monday, April 12

Wing sat at a back table in the Clouds of Heaven with five men dressed in the clothes of successful merchants: colored silk gown, brocaded vest, and silk skullcap. The merchants snacked on pickled salmon cheeks and salted peanuts.

"Welcome, Sheriff TJ. Fortune smiles on these dogs today. You like play?" Wing said.

"Wing, we have to talk…" TJ looked around, "…but not here."

"Ah yes. So upstair, my office." Wing motioned to a dealer who took Wing's place.

In the upstairs hall, TJ got a whiff of opium as he passed the first room and it struck him that the smell signaled a line or boundary he just crossed, as if he were entering a foreign country. He felt off-balance and unsure of how to proceed when questioning Wing. If TJ believed in magic, he'd suspect Wing of having a second, invisible self that observed TJ and whispered TJ's thoughts and intentions to Wing.

TJ remembered to bend his head as he stepped through the moon gate. The incense, jasmine today, filled the office and Wing's songbirds chirped in a three-tiered bamboo cage next to the altar.

"Please, sit down. You like cigar?" Wing said.

"No. Not today." TJ sat down and fought against the knot of anger building in his chest at Wing's deception. Wing made a show of adjusting his red vest and then slipped his hands in the sleeves of his green gown. Wing assumed his serene mask that said I have all the time in the world.

TJ decided to open with a strong attack. "Kao just confessed, Wing. Said he found Fong and the woman's body in the same room." He studied Wing's mask for signs he'd hit a nerve.

The trace of a smile crossed the fat lips. "Ah yes, Sheriff TJ, you find lady in river. That bad luck, very bad luck."

"Bad luck… shit, Wing, is that all you can say? Bad luck! For Christsakes…" He took a deep breath. "The city police, me, my deputies, and a dozen volunteers wasted four goddamm days lookin' for her. Who you coverin' up for? I want the truth—no more lies."

Wing held up his hand. "Forgive please, Sheriff TJ. Yes, yes, understand. It is fault of Wing…this business with unfortunate lady. I…"

TJ bolted halfway out of his chair. "Are you sayin' you had Fong and the woman killed?"

"No, no. Wah Fong and 'merican woman not killed by me, not killed by any Han brother. Of this, I am certain."

"But you know who did ?" TJ sank back into his chair.

"No, not know."

"Then what in hell are you sayin'?" TJ stared hard at the overdressed, overfed merchant.

Wing bowed. "Sheriff TJ, please. I answer all question, eh? In time, you know all Wing know. But much to tell. So, patience, please. We eat, then talk, yes?"

"Goddammit, no. I need answers and I need them now." He felt his face flush with anger.

Wing nodded and said, "Yes, yes. You busy man. Forgive, please. So talk first, then eat." He picked up a silver bell on his desk and rang it. A door slid open and the gray-haired servant appeared from behind the paneled screen next to the altar. Wing said a few words in rapid fire Cantonese. The servant bowed then left.

"Now, please. You have question?" Wing put his hands back in his sleeves.

"Kao came to you, scared, and you told him you'd take care of things, told him what to tell me, right?" TJ ran his hand over his mustache.

"Yes. True. Ah, Sheriff, most unfortunate, body found. Now, much trouble for Chinamen, hnnnn! I much afraid…" Wing's lips formed an O and he sighed.

"You admit to puttin' the woman's body in the river? Jesus, Wing, you're damm right you got trouble. You meddled in the law's business. All right, tell me everything from the time Kao walked in here last Sunday mornin' to today." TJ took out his pencil and notebook.

Wing shifted in his seat. "It is as Kao say. He find body of lady, body of Wah Fong in same room. We put dress, other woman thing, in bag. Bag in basement. Now, no reason hide clothes. So you give bag to family of woman, yes?"

"What'd you do with her body?"

"My friend, Wu Choy, have ice house. Keep body there." Wing took a silk fan out of his sleeve, snapped it open, and fanned his face in rapid, short strokes. "That night I tell men when tide high, row boat out from shore, away from pier, away from fish trap. Put body in river. Tide carry body to ocean. No one find, so no trouble for Chinamen." Wing sighed. "But sometime my men have cabbage in head, not think, hnnnn! Only Jade Emperor know what men do." Wing sighed again. "Bad luck, body catch piling. Very bad luck."

"Wing, did your men cut off her hands?."

"Wah! Why do such thing?" Wing raised his eyebrows and the corners of his mouth turned down for a second before the pleasant mask returned. "Hand cut off when Kao find body. My men look but not find hand." He sat back in his chair.

"Did one of your men take Fong's knife?" TJ cocked his head at Wing.

"Knife belong Fong family. If my man steal, I cut off ear, feed ear to my pig, hah!" Wing rested his elbows on the arms of his lacquered mahogany chair. Wing's pose in the horseshoe-shaped chair spread his body, made him look large and in command. He wagged a stubby finger at TJ. "So, why ask what happen knife? You find next day, Jameson Cannery." Wing allowed the corners of his lips to turn up.

"Damm. How the hell…"

"It strange, yes? Thief steal knife but leave. Why leave knife, eh? Thief stupid?" Wing put his fingertips together and studied him.

"Strange? Yeah, it's damm strange. Guess you already heard…" TJ swore at himself under his breath. He almost let out where they found the hands.

"Yes, Sheriff TJ?" Wing pushed his glasses back up his nose.

"Never mind. Just talking to myself."

"Talk to self sometime good idea. Self not sleep when you talk, eh? Hee, hee." Wing's upper body shook though his laugh was little more than a whisper.

Behind the screen, a man coughed. Wing lifted his hand, palm down, and made a scratching motion. The servant carried in a tray with a purple teapot, food, and two blue porcelain saucers and cups.

When the servant left, Wing filled both cups and then slid a saucer and cup across to TJ.

"White Mountain tea, best tea," he said and lifted his cup with both hands, inhaling the aroma before sipping. "When I drink tea, I back home, in garden of father." Wing sipped with his eyes closed before slowly lowering his cup.

TJ took a sip, put his cup down, and said, "All right, let's get back to my questions."

Wing pushed the plate of food across the desk to TJ. "Rice cookie? Pickle date?"

"Wing, seems like every time I come here, we got to eat before we talk. I don't have time to waste."

"Sometime drink tea, waste time, best way. No hurry, no mistake, eh?" Wing set his cup down and turned the bowl so that the dragon in the bowl's design faced him.

"Mistake? What you tryin' to say, Wing?"

Wing waved his hand in front of his face as if brushing a fly away. "I answer all question. But one question most important, hnnnn! Why China council make plan for woman body—this, number one question—this, Sheriff TJ need understand."

In time, TJ decided that Wing would tell him all he knew. "How'd you get her body out of the room? I didn't see but one set of footprints besides Kao's."

Wing told him that his men wrapped the woman's body in a blanket, tied it, and lowered it through the window to a wagon in the alley below. They kept her body in the icehouse until after midnight when his men carted it to the river, rowed it out a ways, and then dumped it.

"Were the large footprints from one of your men?"

"Not belong men. Not belong me." He slid his foot out from behind the desk and TJ noted the small size of the slipper. Wing held up his first finger. "Also tell men, not step in blood."

TJ filled two pages in his notebook then said, "Tell me about Chen Hop Li."

"Good butcher, make top pay." The warm room brought beads of sweat to Wing's forehead and he fanned his face. "You think Chen Hop Li killer? Ha! I make bet, Sheriff TJ." He waved the fan in a wide arc. "Ten to one odd for you—killer not Chen Hop Li, not any Chinaman."

"Why you say that?"

"Opium not taken. Number one man count tin—maybe two hundred dolla' opium in safe. Also killer not keep Fong knife. Why?"

"Maybe he didn't know it was valuable."

"Fong knife worth much money. All Chinaboy know this." Wing stopped fanning himself and said, "Also, if Chinese try pawn knife, I know name in one hour."

TJ wondered why a Chinese killer who knew the knife could be traced back to him wouldn't dump it. But Hop Li hadn't dumped the knife so was either damm stupid or damm smart to show the knife around. This line of thinking was old ground and TJ stopped himself.

"Wing, would Hop Li kill Wah Fong to settle a grudge?"

"Grudge? What mean, grudge?"

"When someone hurts you so bad you can't rest 'til you pay him back, you know, like a debt of honor."

A furrow appeared between Wing's eyebrows for an instant. "You think bad blood Wah Fong, Chen Hop Li?" He paused, considering, then said, "I know nothing of this."

"How about if Hop Li needed money?"

"Hop Li hard worker—good bet. Can borrow from me, from Wah Fong, from Wah Toy also. Anytime."

TJ added this information then put his notebook in his pocket.

"You not ask about hand Yung Po find?" Wing studied TJ's face.

"Yung Po?"

"Yes. Find lady hand in water, Jameson Cannery."

"Shit." TJ sighed.

A smile crossed Wing's lips. "Yung Po have much fear. Ask priest what omen mean. Soon I know all Yung Po tell priest."

TJ shook his head. "Goddammit. Is there a Chinaboy in town doesn't know about those hands?" His squeezed the bridge of his nose between thumb and forefinger.

"I tell all Chinaboss. Say nothing to any white boss, any white people about hand."

"Well, that's one good thing you did, Wing. Will they do what you say?

"Worker lose job, maybe lose life, if paper tell story of hand. So white people not hear of hand from Chinaboy." Wing paused, bent down and pulled a small red lacquer chest from under his desk. The front of the chest had a brass hasp in the shape of a large butterfly and the drawer pulls were caterpillars. Wing settled the chest on his lap then turned his back to TJ. After a few seconds, Wing turned around and placed the chest on the desk with one of its drawers open. Wing lifted an enameled pillbox out of the drawer and handed it to TJ.

"What's this?"

"Open, please."

TJ lifted the lid of the pillbox and took out a piece of rice paper folded into quarters. He put the paper on the table, unfolded it, and stared at two gems, one wine-red, the other a pale, mottled green. A ruby and emerald. He picked up the ruby. Its facets sparkled even in the dim light of the overhead lantern. A flag went up in his head and he felt as if he'd been kicked in the stomach.

"Shit, Wing. You bribin' me now?" He looked at the fat merchant and his jaw muscles clenched.

The tiny smile appeared at the corners of Wing's mouth "No, Sheriff TJ, no bribe."

TJ laid the stones in the rice paper and pushed the paper back to Wing.

"Why'd you show these then?"

Wing pulled a lavender-scented cloth from his sleeve and wiped beads of sweat from his forehead. "Sheriff TJ, Wing very sorry. Old Kao think he clever, like monkey. Jewel small, so Kao think, keep for self. No one know, hnnnh! Two day ago, Kao pawn jewel, Wah Toy shop. Wah Toy old friend, bring jewel here, tell what Kao do." Wing leaned his head to one side then the other. "I talk Kao—that worm not try trick again." Wing pushed the gems back to him. "So now, you keep. Maybe help find man kill Fong, woman."

TJ had been too quick to judge. Wing could have kept the jewels and no one would have known, except Kao and the pawnbroker. Need to learn patience, he reminded himself. "Well, thanks, Wing. Don't know if these will help but..." he paused and sat up straight. "Where did Kao find these?"

"Find under bunk. Kao clean room after Sheriff TJ take Fong body."

"But these could have been dropped anytime, by anybody."

"Not so. I ask Kao same thing. Wah Fong tell Kao clean all room very good. Rich man come next day. Kao clean room Friday after dinner. So jewel in room after Friday, eh? Must be." Wing smiled and pushed his glasses up with his index finger. "Jewel not belong Chinaboy, eh?"

"Nope." TJ chewed on his mustache. "Kao tell you who rented the room that weekend?"

"No. Kao say boss very happy. Rich man rent all room for two day."

"But we looked at Fong's ledger. No guests signed up that weekend."

Wing sipped his tea. "Ah, Sheriff TJ. Sometime white people pay so name not go in book." He chuckled and the folds around his eyes creased.

"Yeah, guess that's right, too." TJ leaned towards Wing. "Kao said he didn't see the people who rented the room. You believe him?"

Wing paused. "Not know. That dogface lie easy." He made a hissing sound between his teeth.

TJ took out his notebook and added some notes. When he finished, he looked up and asked, "Anything else, Wing?"

"Maybe now Sheriff TJ listen, why Wing hide woman body."

"All right, but I'd appreciate it if you'd get to where you goin' quick."

"Yes, yes. So..." Wing looked over his head for a second then said, "...this bad luck year for Chinese."

TJ frowned. "Bad luck year? What you gettin' at Wing?"

A hardness came into Wing's eyes. "Those Knight like hungry tiger. Push Chinamen out Tacoma, out Seattle. You know all this. But tiger still hungry. Come Oregon City, push Chinamen from mill. Mill close. Tiger come Albina, push woodcutter out. All woodcutter job gone. So how Chinamen eat, eh? So far, Chinamen lucky in Oregon—no one die."

"What's that got to do with the murders?" TJ drummed his fingers on the arm of his chair.

"So, Sheriff TJ think someone kill white woman in Wah Fong store, no matter? White people not have anger like bear when poke with stick?" Wing lifted his body out of chair halfway and folded one leg under him, adding three inches to his seated height. He looked straight across into TJ's eyes. "Paper already say Chinamen bad." He raised a stubby index finger. "So if paper say white lady kill in Chinatown, hand cut off. White people say must be Chinaman, yes? People read in paper, so must be true." Wing lifted his thin eyebrows. "Hate all same like train—once start, hard stop."

"Yeah, all right. But when I lock up the killer, things will calm down."

Wing bowed. "Sheriff TJ, you honorable man, much skill. China council wish much success." Wing ran his hand down the dozen or so long strands of his beard "But maybe take long time catch killer. Big gamble. Best thing, woman not found Chinatown, eh? Then, no trouble for Chinamen."

"I see why you tried to hide her body—but, dammit Wing—you broke our law, you and your council, you muddied things and gave the killer time to cover his tracks. You and every man jack who helped you could go to prison." TJ shook his head in anger and frustration.

"You worry for Wing, Sheriff TJ?" Wing smiled and bowed. "Many thank you. But you not understand China ways...so...how...?" He pushed his chair back, stood up, walked into the center of the room and looked around. "Sheriff TJ, you one time fisherman, yes?"

"Yeah. Where's this goin' Wing?" He sighed. Wing didn't seem a bit concerned that he might go to prison. What the hell made him tick?

Wing searched from corner to corner before letting out a soft "hah!" He darted over to the banner that hung down the back wall of his altar and cut two pieces of twine from the tassel with his penknife.

"So, from family shrine. Yes! Very good." Wing strode back to his chair, sat down, and pushed his glasses up. He tied the two pieces of twine together in the middle with a square knot and then spread the knotted twine on the table in the shape of an X.

"What knot catch, eh?" He asked.

TJ stared at the knot, at Wing, then frowned.

"Just so." Wing inclined his head. "Question stupid. Knot catch no fish, catch nothing. But if tie knot, add line, tie knot, add line." He tied an imaginary line at each of the four ends. "So, soon net hundred fathom this way..." he stretched his arms from side to side, "...thirty fathom this way." He turned his arms to the vertical. Wing picked up two ends of the knotted twine and centered the knot over the bridge of his nose. "So now this knot help catch big fish, yes?"

"Wing, goddammit, I don't have all day. We have a net that catches fish. So what?"

"Wah! Maybe not so good, Wing talk. Forgive, please. So Wing headman, all same like cork at top, pull net up. Headman also all same like lead at bottom, pull net down. Cork, lead make net tight, all same like wall, catch fish. Chinaboy is knot. Cork, lead, knot—all necessary. Headman help Chinaboy find job, feed when no job, lend money, bury when die. Later, dig up, clean bone, send home so can sleep with ancestor." He lifted himself part way out of his chair and folded his other leg under him. "Keep trouble away from Han brother, also headman job. So, Sheriff TJ, you understand? Headman job, protect all brother. So best thing, woman body not found, Chinatown."

"I take your point, Wing." TJ closed his notebook. "I'm still angry at your playin' hide an' seek with that body. That's not how we do things." He put his hat on. "Now, I'm sayin' this only once. Don't try a stunt like that again. If you find out anything, you tell me, and tell me right away." He folded the rice paper around the jewels and stuffed the paper in the coin pocket of his Levis.

"Yes, tell Sheriff TJ first. Council make mistake—our way, your way, not same. Forgive, please." Wing bowed. He escorted TJ out of the office, down the stairs, and held the saloon door open for him. An angry east wind blew rain into their faces.

"Umbrella, Sheriff TJ?"

"No, I'm used to it." TJ pulled his hat down and his coat collar up.

"Sheriff TJ, you listen today. Ten thousand thank you. Listen, first step understand China way." He bowed from the waist.

"Just remember Wing, you hear any news, anything at all, you get word to me first thing. Understand?"

"Yes, understand. So maybe Sheriff TJ hear news, tell Wing, eh?"

"All right, it's a deal."

Wing bowed again and closed the door.

TJ bent his body into the wind and headed down Chenamus Street towards his office. At the corner, a violent gust almost ripped his hat off. He braced himself and leaned further into the wind. Underneath him, a log slammed against pilings and foam from the river spurted up through the cracks in the street planking. He pushed the wind and rain out of his head and thought of what he'd learned. If Wing told the truth, it meant that someone murdered two people in Fong's room last Saturday night or Sunday morning, cut off Jane Thurgood's hands, and took a small amount of cash. But if the motive were robbery why did the killer leave the jewels behind? And why put the dagger and Jane's hands in Jameson's Cannery? "The motive," he said out loud, "what the hell is the motive?"

28

The next morning at breakfast, TJ heard the doorbell ring followed by Helga's helper speaking to someone in the hall but since his chair faced the kitchen he didn't bother to turn around. Seconds later, the dozen men at table stopped eating and looked towards the front room. The sudden quiet made TJ look over his shoulder. Emma Taylor stood in the doorway of the dining room with her gloved hands clasped over her parasol. Her eyes swept over the faces of the gawking men until they came to rest on TJ. Over a simple green dress with a full bustle, she wore a form-fitting dark olive green twill coat with a high neck. An ostrich plume and a cluster of pink roses decorated her straw bonnet. Helga came out of the kitchen just then with a tray of hot biscuits and came to a full stop. Still holding the tray, she stared at the unfamiliar sight of a well-dressed, beautiful lady in her dining room.

TJ stood up too quickly, spilling some of his coffee. Helga finally lowered the tray of biscuits and followed TJ across the room. In the short time he'd known Emma Taylor, TJ expected surprises but barging into his boardinghouse without warning shocked him. No one, least of all a proper lady, did such things. He knew that by now the rough men behind him were winking and chuckling to each other, conjuring up reasons why TJ's lady friend had to see him as such an early hour. In a whisper, TJ introduced Helga to Emma and then asked if they could use the parlor. Helga's face lit up with a smile as she looked from TJ to Emma and back again. In the parlor, Helga took the dust cover off the settee and said she'd be back in a minute with coffee and hot biscuits. TJ glowered at Helga's back as she hurried out. He should have told Helga it was only business right off but then realized she wouldn't believe him. He had little influence over what went on in Helga's head or, for that matter, any woman's head and told himself to hell with it.

Emma sat down at one end of the settee as soon as Helga left. TJ sat at the other end, leaving a proper distance between them.

"You've arrested Hop Li." Her voice trembled but she did not avoid his eyes. "Why, oh why? It's so wrong, so—oh, I'm so upset I can't think straight." She squeezed the handkerchief in her hand into a ball.

"Now, hold on, Miss. There are things you don't know. We've found out…"

"Found out? What on earth is there to find out?"

"Well now, if you'll let me speak, I'll tell you."

Her body stiffened as if he'd slapped her.

"We tried some Chinee clothes on him, clothes the killer wore. They fit."

"Oh pshaw, Chinese clothes, my heavens, they must fit any number of Chinese men."

"No Miss, they wouldn't. Have you seen a Chinee bigger than Hop Li? I haven't."

She looked at him without speaking, red-faced and confused.

Suddenly, his annoyance at her coming to his boardinghouse left him. She wasn't arguing Hop Li' s case well and he felt sorry for her. "Those clothes would fall off any other Chinee. So the clothes, the other evidence, well, it all points to him."

"He didn't confess, I know that."

He frowned. "How do you know that?"

"Because I've just come from the jail. He told me he didn't kill anyone. I believe him."

Helga waltzed in with a tray of coffee and biscuits. "Hope I'm not interrupting anything." She beamed at Emma as if acknowledging a secret between them. They watched Helga in silence as she arranged the cups and saucers and silver napkin rings just so on the coffee table. Helga finished and stood stiffly, hands folded across her belly, and waited for someone to speak. Finally, TJ remembered to thank her and she backed out of the room, nodding to them once before pulling the French doors shut after her.

TJ filled their cups and held out the tray of biscuits but Emma shook her head. "No thanks—I can't." She rose and went over to the curtained bay window. "I'm not familiar with the American legal system. How much evidence does one require to make an arrest?"

"Well, I don't know as there's a simple answer. If it looks to me like a fella has committed a crime, I can arrest him. Of course, gettin' arrested is one thing, gettin' tried and convicted is another."

"Sheriff, please, don't patronize me. You know Hop Li won't get a fair trial. Will other Chinese, for instance, be allowed to sit on his jury?"

"Well, no, Miss, they can't. Chinee aren't citizens."

"Yes. And if a white man says he did something and Hop Li says he didn't. What then?"

TJ looked away and didn't answer.

"Oh, Sheriff, Hop Li is going to hang. You know that as well as I do."

"Now, hold on a minute. We don't know that for sure. Lots could happen…" he wanted to say more, to reassure her, but he couldn't. He asked himself if he'd arrested Hop Li solely on the evidence or to quiet talk that he wasn't up to the job, that the chief ought to take over? He didn't have an answer and it troubled him.

She frowned as she studied him then came back to the settee and sat down. Close enough this time so that he smelled her scent, soap with a touch of lilac. "Sheriff, Hop Li and I spoke in Cantonese this morning. He told me things, things he said he didn't tell you."

"What things? Why didn't he tell me?"

"You didn't use a translator, did you?"

"He speaks fair English. Didn't see the need."

"Ah, Sheriff, there's so much one can miss—you can't possibly know what or how Hop Li thinks." She lifted an eyebrow and stared at him, exasperated.

"How he thinks? I don't take your meanin,' Miss." TJ felt his face warm. He wasn't unfair, he told himself, he hadn't beaten a confession out of Hop Li as some would. Why didn't she keep to Sunday school and stop meddling?

"Don't take this personally, Sheriff. I expect any non-Chinese would have fared no better than you. Please, just hear me out, will you?"

"All right. I'll listen but I don't expect you'll change my thinkin.'"

"That's all I ask, that you listen." She opened her handbag and took out a piece of paper with small writing in a neat hand on both sides. She looked at her notes and said there are four things Hop Li told her that might be important. "Hop Li has a good ear for languages and said the man spoke not as a worker but as I do. In other words, the man is educated."

In spite of his resistance to her meddling, he found himself listening.

"And at one point the white man became angry. Wait…" she searched the page with her finger, "here, in Hop Li's words. 'He offered me a dollar to keep the box. He talked to me with words covered in honey and I agreed. I said I would store the box at Fatt Luk's house. But when I asked for another dollar for Fatt Luk, the white man exploded. Words flew out of his mouth covered in spit and he turned his back on me. It took some time for the white man to recover his tongue.'" She stopped and sipped her coffee.

As TJ listened to Hop Li's words, the sea captain came alive and he could see the white man raging at Hop Li. "Anything else, Miss?"

"Yes. I asked Hop Li to tell me everything they talked about. He remembered that the man asked him what he did and where he worked." Emma leveled her gaze at TJ. "That scoundrel knew to put the knife at Hop Li's work bench, Sheriff. Though why he cut off that poor girl's hands or put them in that vat is beyond me. You never told me about her hands, by the way." She cocked her head at him.

"Yeah, well, you didn't need to know that. Anything else?"

"Hop Li thinks the man is rich." She smiled as she looked at her notes. "He said the captain took a fistful of coins out of his pocket and handled them as if they were salted peanuts."

TJ started to say something but she held up her hand, stopping him. "Yes, yes, I know, this proves nothing. But the man did give him a two dollar and fifty cent gold piece, fifty cents above the price agreed to. Overly generous, I'd say, and leads me to think the man is either rich or desperate or both. What do you think?"

"Could be. Now, is that everything?"

"Yes, but we only talked for twenty minutes." She paused and took a deep breath. "Now, I have a favor to ask, Sheriff."

He shook his head. "Miss, like I already said, I..."

She held up a hand in protest. "It's not what you think. Hop Li would like his notebooks and writing materials. Is that allowed?"

"Don't see any harm in it." He went over what he learned. The man Hop Li called a sea captain was educated and quick to anger but those facts didn't help Hop Li much. Neither did the coins the man flashed—he knew men to carry a pocket full of coins just to show off. But he couldn't dismiss the man's questioning of Hop Li so easily. Why did the man want to know what Hop Li did and where he worked? Even more puzzling, why did he even stop on a Sunday morning to chat with a Chinee?

"When I take Hop Li his notebooks, I'll have another talk with him," Emma said and offered him a full smile for the first time.

He sipped his coffee, unsure of how to respond to her smile. He didn't want her to think he'd changed his mind about Hop Li because of her. She believed in Hop Li's innocence and wanted to help him. Nothing wrong in that, he decided, but he reminded himself that she was a missionary and would take over if given half a chance.

"Well, I thank you for the information, Miss Taylor. Could help at his trial."

"Thank you, Sheriff." She stood up and held out her gloved hand. "I should be getting back—I told Henry I was going for a short walk."

"I'll walk you back."

"That isn't necessary but thank you."

"But I'd like to anyway. We can talk more about Hop Li."

Two blocks into the walk, he heard the faint, tinny sound of band music. Emma stopped.

"Listen...yes, it's coming toward us. I expect it's a Temperance Society Wagon." Her eyes widened with excitement and she tugged on his arm. "Oh, do let's go and see it. Please." She held her arms out, lifted her head to the sky, and spun around in a circle, a young girl again. He knew that feeling and smiled as he remembered that magic time, once a year, when the circus bandwagon rumbled into town.

"Thought you had to get home."

"Oh, bother Henry," she said and, holding her parasol out in front of her for balance, she did a pirouette. She pirouetted again and then skipped down the sidewalk for half a block. He watched her as if in a dream and felt a rush of joy followed by a feeling of lightness and peace. He stood unable to move, mesmerized by the transformation of a proper missionary woman into a carefree girl. When he still didn't move, she looked over her shoulder, laughing, and called out, "stop dilly-dallying. We'll miss it if we don't hurry."

He broke out of his trance and came up to her. "You...um...do that often, Miss, dancin' and skippin' around in public?"

She looked at him a moment, laughed, and said, "Well, not as much as I would like. Our religion forbids dancing but I have never been able to accept that dancing, proper dancing, I mean, is sinful. God gave us music to enjoy, don't you agree, Sheriff?"

"I do. Before she died my Lucy Ann was teachin' me to dance. Learned to do a fair waltz and got to where I could polka without fallin' down. I've never thought dancin' sinful."

"My love of dance and, I suppose you might say, my wild nature, has tested the patience of my parents—I've caused them heartache, I know. And poor Henry doesn't know what to make of me. He's absolutely scandalized by what he calls my secret vice." She laughed softly. "So now I dance alone and, when outside, in places where no one can possibly see me. But at times when my heart is about to burst with joy, I simply can't hold back—I must dance." She blushed, looked at the ground, and didn't speak for a second or two. "Dear me, I don't know why I'm telling you all this. You must think me an utter fool."

"Don't think any such thing." He wanted to say more, to tell her that her free spirit pleased him and made him feel alive, feelings he hadn't experienced in years. But he didn't trust his feelings, didn't believe another woman could make him feel as he had with Lucy Ann.

"Do you still dance, Sheriff?" she asked while still looking at the ground.

"No. I've lost interest."

"Well, if your interest returns, I would be pleased to continue your lessons." She glanced up at him and smiled.

"Lessons? But your brother thinks dancin' is a sin, Miss. Won't he stop you?"

"Oh, he'll try, Sheriff, indeed he will. But let's cross that bridge when we come to it, shall we?"

29

Tuesday, April 13

The music was close and within minutes they came upon a wake-up wagon covered in red, white and blue bunting. The band consisted of six men who had the broad backs and muscular builds of draymen. The drummer, the shortest of the lot, wore a velvet green stovepipe hat that distinguished him from the horn players who wore straw hats. The only man TJ recognized was the driver, a boy who worked for Sherman and Ward's livery. TJ listened to the music for a time and thought there wasn't much you could say in its favor.

"They're loud enough," he yelled in Emma's ear.

"Terrible. They need lessons," she yelled back.

The wagon came abreast and the message on its side said: WHITE WORKERS UNITE—FIGHT CHINESE SLAVE LABOR. TJ grabbed a flyer from a boy running by.

America at the crossroads: Why the Chinese must go!

An informative talk given by: Marvin Kephardt of the Knights of Labor.

When: Today 3:00 pm,

Where: Turk's Tavern, corner of Concomly and Benton

Complimentaries: Beer and sausage

TJ stuck it in his pocket. "I better get you back." He put his hand under her elbow and escorted her through the crowd. After they'd walked a block Emma stopped and asked, "What's that man doing here?"

"What are you gettin' at, Miss?"

"The Knights of Labor man. He's not from around here, is he?"

"From Portland, I'd say."

"It's the worst possible time for an anti-Chinese speech. Hop Li will never receive a fair trial now. Never." She looked down and shook her head.

"Now hold on a minute, Miss. I arrested Hop Li Sunday afternoon—a day and a half ago. Those boys couldn't know about Hop Li yet. Has to be a coincidence."

"Coincidence? Do you really believe that, Sheriff?"

He knew a spy could have telegrammed Portland but why? Even if the word got out, it wasn't possible the Knights could organize a talk so soon. Then he remembered that the story about the scabs had been out for a week.

"Well, last week Chinee scabs showed up at Jameson's Cannery. Bet that's what brought those fellas here."

"I want to hear that talk."

"Miss? That's Turk's place. No. That's no place for a lady."

"Are you going?"

"Thought I would."

"Then I would be pleased to accompany you." She turned her blue eyes on him. "Henry can't object if you escort me." She smiled and put her arm through his.

Damm, he thought, *it sure is hard to say no to this woman.*

The afternoon promised to stay clear and warm so he took the buckboard when he picked Emma up. On Concomly Street, sporting girls leaned out the window or over the second floor balconies of saloons and called out to men passing by, flirting and taunting as if it were a Saturday night. It seemed the whole town knew about the talk.

The Knights had parked the wake-up wagon in front of Turk's saloon crosswise so that it gave the same angle of sight to anyone standing on Benton Street as it did to those on Concomly Street. A barrel of beer sat on a makeshift table next to the Turk's front door. A barkeeper took the jar or tin handed to him, filled it, and gave it back without looking up. On a patch of bare ground a few feet from the boardwalk, a boy fed wood into a fire underneath a grill. The pale-faced cook, a Saturday night regular in TJ's drunk tank, held a mug of beer in one hand while nudging sausages around on the grill. The lines of men and sporting girls waiting for a free sausage and beer ran down Concomly past Lafayette Street.

TJ parked the buckboard at the back of the crowd. A trumpet shrieked and heads turned to watch a barouche pull up. The trumpet man jumped down from his seat next to the driver and opened the carriage door. Turk stepped out waving his hat to the crowd followed by a young man in a dark, three-piece suit. A man with a scowling face exited last. A voice nearby said, "That's Marvin Kephardt," in the hushed tones men speak of the famous. A coarse black beard framed Kephardt's broad face. Powerfully built with wide shoulders, a deep chest, and long arms,

Kephardt's upper body did not go with the lower body's slim hips and short bowlegs. With his bandy-legged walk and large upper body, he looked like an ape making its way through a jungle.

When Kephardt came alongside the buckboard, TJ saw that his nose had been broken and was off-center. The corners of his mouth were turned down and the mouth along with a scar on his upper lip gave TJ the impression that the man had just swallowed bile.

"Not a face a child would take to," TJ volunteered.

"Nor a woman," she said.

TJ looked over the crowd and saw a handful of Clatsop Indians leaning against the wall next to the cook. As he continued to look around, he realized there were no Chinese faces among the sea of white faces.

A brougham pulled up behind the barouche. A hand pushed aside a curtain, flicked an ash off a cigar, and then retreated behind the curtain. Someone tugged on his coat sleeve. He looked down into Daines' face.

"Want a snort, Sheriff? Gonna be long afternoon." Daines shoved a hip flask at him.

"You're not old enough for liquor." TJ slapped the outstretched hand.

"No offense meant, Sheriff. Just tryin' to be friendly." Daines put the flask in his back pocket and grinned, the grin of a poker player who just laid down a winning hand. "Heard you arrested the butcher for killin' the woman. That true?" Daines whipped his notebook out of his back pocket.

TJ couldn't believe his ears. "Could be."

Daines's grin spread wider. "Well, fellas what oughta know say the Chinaboy did it, kilt 'em both. I tried to talk to that Chinaboy but Lucky said visiting hours was over." He found his pencil, ready to write. "Now, what's that boy's name?"

"Chen Hop Li." TJ had given Hop Li's name to the city police after the arrest so Daines could get the name from them if he didn't give it.

"Why'd he do it?"

"Don't know. I'm still investigatin.'"

"Still investigatin.' How come?"

"Dammit to hell, that's it." TJ reached down, grabbed Daines by his collar and lifted him a foot off the ground. "How come is 'cause I am. That's why."

In his anger, TJ had forgotten Emma and was surprised by a light touch on his forearm.

"Sheriff, he's only a boy. You mustn't hurt him."

Daines's skinny arms hung limply at his sides and his hands poked out of his sleeves a good six inches. He looked like a scarecrow in need of stuffing. TJ smiled at the image and let go of the squirming youth. Daines fell on his rear and dropped his notepad.

"Now git before I lock you up for violatin' liquor laws," TJ said.

Daines scrambled to his feet and walked off three or four paces before he turned around. "Don't matter none if ya talk to me—the chief tells me everythin' anyhow." He pointed towards the speaker's stand. "And when that Knight's fella hears what that Chinaboy done, there's gonna be Jesse to pay, by God."

TJ said to Emma, "I wasn't goin' to hit him even though he needs it."

"He was only doing his job. Why did he anger you so?"

"Oh, it's not him so much as the paper. The stories they write, well, some of them anyways, are full of lies. And you can't undo a lie once it gets in the paper. It leaves a stain that lasts." He reached in his pocket for a cigar then drew his hand back. He didn't know how Emma felt about smoking.

Emma's blue eyes got an intense look just as they did when she questioned him about Hop Li. "Was it about you, this untrue story?"

"No, not me, about my wife or rather her father—but I don't want to go into it. She's gone and so is he."

"I'm sorry, Sheriff. Words can indeed hurt more than blows."

Neither said anything for a while and Emma opened her parasol and looked over the crowd, which had doubled in size. Kephardt's young assistant, looking important in his three piece suit and pince-nez glasses, sat at a plank table in front of the wake up wagon and wrote in a ledger. Emma whispered to TJ that the stench of beer and cooking meat had made her light-headed. "It reminds me of a time when…well, of an unpleasant event back home"

"Want to leave?"

"No. We're staying."

He put an arm around her waist. She shifted closer to him and rested her head against his shoulder.

Marvin Kephardt climbed into the speaker's wagon followed by Turk. The two huddled a moment before Kephardt sat down. At 275 pounds and 6' 6," Turk cowed most men when one on one. But his tinny voice failed to gain the attention of the crowd, some of whom were already drunk. Turk fired his gun into the air and the crowd hushed. Kephardt rose, came forward as far as the side of wagon allowed, and looked over his audience for a second or two before speaking. But as soon as he uttered his first sentence, people hushed. His voice, a rich baritone, made people overlook the face from which the sound came. His words flowed into the ears of the crowd as easy and as welcome as a glass of cold water on a hot day. Though Kephardt didn't smile, his face radiated energy and passion and made the hard look of his face tolerable.

Kephardt thanked the workingmen of Astoria for letting him speak and then launched into the troubles for the worker if the rich capitalists continued to hire slave labor from China. Bosses, he said, didn't care a whit about how many decent, white workingmen they put out of work. He told of hard-working Americans he knew who could no longer feed their wives or children. In despair, some took to crime. It oughtn't to be that way, he said. Any crimes committed by such men should be laid at the door of the bosses.

"But it don't hafta be this way. We gotta push the bosses—yes, that's right, I'm sayin' we can change things, we can bargain for a better wage, a better life. But there's somethin' we gotta do first." Kephardt paused and reached over to take a drink of water before continuing. "Nothing is gonna change, not a damm thing, 'til the Mongolian coolie is gone from our shores. I'm asking you to help American workingmen today. I'm asking you to help yourselves. The bosses won't help you. No sir. Politicians, lawyers, and the well-fed folks will tell you to go easy, to let the laws work. When no one hires a Celestial, he'll go back to China, they say. Well, I've heard that gospel for four years now. There's just as many Celestials workin' in the country, in Astoria, as ever. The heathens are eatin' and you ain't. That sound fair to you? Is that what America stands for?"

The crowd responded with an explosion of no's and wild cheering. Emma pulled away from TJ and stared in front of her with her arms crossed over her chest. At times, TJ felt Kephardt was talking to him, counseling him as a friend might in a time of trouble.

"Well, not much new in what he says…" TJ said.

"But what?"

"But it sounds different when he says it."

"Yes. He talks as if he is confiding a secret, telling us something we are desperate to know. But it's rubbish, all rubbish."

Kephardt held up his arms and quieted the applause.

"Now, I'm askin' you to come down to our wagon. Right now, this minute. Add your name to the list of workingmen ready to fight for what's yours. Join the Knights of Labor and help us rid America of the job-thieves from Mongolia." He paused and people in the crowd looked around. No one moved toward the wagon. Kephardt lifted his arms again.

"Now, I know what you're thinkin.' How you gonna pay dues if you got no job, no money, right? And our fight does take money. Dues is a dollar a month...but!" he shouted the last word and then paused. He stretched up on his toes and pointed at the sky, "but you pay nothin,' not a damm dime, unless you're workin.' You got a job, you pay, you're out of work, you don't. Simple as that. Be better world if the bosses were fair as that, wouldn't it?"

Kephardt held his arms up to shush the crowd and waited. He leaned out over the wagon as if about to jump into the crowd. "Now, who'll be the first to sign up?"

Behind TJ, on the fringes of the crowd, a man shouted, "By God, I'll sign up. Let me through." A solidly built man in a checkered shirt, logger cutoffs and boots, waded through the crowd. Within seconds, a voice in another part of the crowd yelled, "I'll join. I need a job."

TJ saw a green stovepipe hat bobbing through the crowd like the dorsal fin of a shark. TJ had seen that hat before but where? Within five minutes, a line of men had formed in front of the table manned by Kephardt's assistant.

Kephardt bent down and spoke to his assistant then stood up and called for quiet.

"Brothers and Sisters, though it pains me to be the bearer of bad news, I feel it's my duty to tell you of a worrisome situation." A murmur rose from the crowd. "I read in your paper that the sheriff arrested one of the disciples of Confucius Monday for the murder and mutilation of a white woman."

A second of silence greeted Kephardt's words. People then turned to their neighbors and talked in excited tones. Kephardt shushed the crowd and then cupped his hand around his mouth, an actor conspiring with the audience. "That Chinaboy is gonna come before a judge next week and his lawyer is gonna ask for bail." Kephardt paused and spread his arms out and turned his head in a slow circle taking in the crowd from one side to the other. The audience quieted and then grew so still that TJ heard the breathing of his mare and the clink of metal as she shifted in the harness.

"Well, if I've learnt anythin' in this job..." Kephardt said and paused. People in the back craned their necks and pressed up against those in front of them, "if I've learnt one thing..." Kephardt repeated in a louder voice, "it's that the Chinee devil is sly. He knows how to get around our courts. You mark my words, citizens," his voice boomed, "some fancy pants lawyer, a traitor to his race, will come here from Portland. He'll talk his slick-talk and that Chinee fiend will walk out of that courtroom free as yonder sea gull." He extended his arm and pointed into sky over the river. Heads turned and watched a sea gull circle once then settle on the roof of Hustler's warehouse. "And that'll be the last you'll see of him." Kephardt shouted, face red with anger. "You call that justice?"

Shouts of "no!" and "hang him!" were hurled back at the speaker. Kephardt stretched his arms and held his hands palms up like a preacher at revival meeting. He allowed something like a smile to flit across his face. When the crowd hushed, he said, "Guess you all know what we done in Tacoma and Seattle. So, you know we're not just talk. That's all I'm gonna say right now. I'll be talkin' to you again—real soon." He sat down amid cheering, whistling, and shouting that went on for a minute.

Daines staggered out of the crowd and stopped a few yards from the buckboard. "That fella is the beatingnest talker I ever heard. Your butcher ain't gettin' off, Sheriff. No way in hell. No sir. Ya can't stop them Knights, can ya Sheriff? Can ya?"

TJ ignored him and before Daines could say more, a youth Daines' age pulled him away. TJ turned to Emma. "You feelin' better?"

"My stomach, yes, a little. But my heart aches. It's not Christian of me to harbor bad thoughts or say bad things, Sheriff, but Mr. Kephardt is a scoundrel. He talks as if the Chinese are plotting to steal all the jobs in America. What they want is a chance to work and live like anybody else—what is wrong with that? Oh, I'm afraid for Hop Li, Sheriff. Can't you stop that loathsome man?"

"Well, he's a worry, Miss, I grant you. I'll keep a close eye on him."

Kephardt's speech had sparked the crowd and TJ had to keep that spark from lighting a fire. He edged the mare through the crowd and pulled the buckboard to the side just in time for the brougham to pass. As it did, TJ caught a glimpse of Jameson with his collar pulled up. The high collar did not hide the savage look on his face.

"He worryin' about losin' his Chinaboys," TJ said more to himself than to Emma.

"Who?" she had not looked at the brougham.

"Jameson. He's a boss but he's not all bad."

"Oh, you're referring to Hop Li's boss. I shouldn't worry about him, Sheriff. No, Mr. Kephardt is the one with a soul burdened by hate. I must pray for him. I'll ask God to grant Mr. Kephardt a little compassion."

From what Kephardt and his Knights did up north, TJ knew that Kephardt and compassion were strangers and would stay that way. They drove in silence until they arrived at the parsonage. They paused on the front porch and both tried to speak at once. An awkward silence followed, during which they tried, without success, to avoid looking into each other's eyes. Finally, TJ said, "I appreciate you lettin' me know what Hop Li told you, Miss. Now, if you discover anything else, you could come by my boardinghouse...well, that isn't such a good idea...maybe I could come here, I mean, if that's all right with your brother...well, guess that's not a good idea either. Maybe if you just stopped in at the office?" He felt as flustered as when Mrs. Lattia had called on him to recite.

Emma smiled and her eyes softened. "Thank you. I will stop by if I learn anything." She waited a second and then added, "I'm afraid I haven't been good company since we left that wretched talk. I'm worried."

"What's botherin' you?"

"Well, it's just an uneasy feeling I have."

"You thinkin' about what happened up north?"

"Yes, I suppose I am."

"That won't happen here. I won't let it."

"I am not sure why but I believe you, Sheriff. And somehow, I just know you'll prove Hop Li innocent." She smiled and extended her gloved hand. He took it. She rose up on her toes and kissed him on the cheek. Then she turned and hurried into the house. He stood on the porch, unable to move, and for the second time that day he felt a rush of joy he hadn't felt since courting Lucy Ann.

30

Next morning he decided to find a quiet place where he could think through what he learned from Bessie. After leaving Uniontown, he found an empty bench next to the net drying racks of the Kinney Cannery. Two gillnetters sat on the wharf mending a net and, even from thirty yards away, he heard the rhythmic click of their needles. The soothing sound reminded him of how he used to watch his hands as they mended net, moving as if they had a mind of their own, one that needed no guidance from the head.

He soon found himself thinking of Jane Thurgood and the men in her life. She wanted to get back with her Bertie so, TJ felt sure, she still loved him. And her love for Bertie suggested that Bertie fathered her baby. *How the hell did she think she could get away with marrying one man while keeping on as the mistress of another? It's impossible to keep a secret like that.* But then he remembered that the Langtry woman didn't waste time on the rights and wrongs of sharing her bed— it didn't matter who that woman slept with or who knew about it so long as the fellow had money and power.

He turned his thoughts to Ned and saw him as a paunchy, middle-aged businessman who had lost his head over a beautiful young woman. Ned had enough money to give Jane the life of riches she pined for and didn't mind being her obedient puppy.

Bertie, unlike Ned, came across as a real cock of the walk. Bertie kept Jane as his mistress while using her to spy for him. *He's a cold-blooded bastard—she might have been caught—hell, maybe she was. Maybe that's why she was killed.* Jane wanted Bertie back but TJ had no idea if Bertie wanted her back. Maybe Bertie didn't care for her in the first place since he didn't mind asking her to spy. He wondered if Bertie used other women as he had Jane?

Jane worked for Purcell so she must have been spying on him. Why Purcell? The fellow who'd be most interested in how many legislators Purcell had in his pocket or what he paid them had to be…Jameson. *By God, that's it.* TJ stared at the river with unseeing eyes and felt a tingling at the back of his neck. *Jane sent reports about Purcell to Bertie so Jameson had to be Bertie. Yep.* Why hadn't he seen this before? Jameson acted like he barely knew Jane, pretending concern and worry only for his cannery. Jameson knew that if TJ made the connection between Jane and him, he'd be a suspect in the murders.

He stood up and stretched. Except for a patch of black clouds over Cape Disappointment, the sky was clear with a light breeze from the Southwest. Probably wouldn't rain. Good night to fish if the day kept on like this. He took Washington Street to Squemoqua and didn't slow down to gab with shopkeepers as he did most mornings. He stopped at his office and told Sketch what he'd suspected about Jameson and asked Sketch to take the three jewels to Zuckerman's to see what the jeweler could tell them.

Three blocks into his hike out to Jameson's, the first drops of rain fell and within five minutes, the drizzle turned into a hard rain. Water dripped off his hat and down his neck. Halfway to the cannery, the back of his shirt was soaked and by the time he reached the cannery, his mood had turned as foul as the weather. When the foreman told him that Jameson had left for Portland and wouldn't be back until tomorrow night, he cursed. He told the foreman he wanted Jameson in the sheriff's office as soon as he got back. No excuses.

On his way back, he stopped off at Sirpia's bakery for a pastry and coffee but she had sold out the first batch of baked goods and told him it'd be thirty minutes before another batch was ready. He refused coffee and stormed out, his mood darker than the sky. When he walked in on Sketch scolding Sonny, the paperboy, he exploded.

"What the hell's goin' on?"

Sketch threw his pencil down hard on the top of his desk. "Shit, it's no use boss. He's hopeless."

Sonny wore his bib overalls and long-sleeved shirt, buttoned up to the top. As always, his toy deputy's badge was the centerpiece of the dozen or so political badges pinned to his chest. Sonny had added an engineer's hat, Southern Pacific, to his uniform but it was too large and he had to tilt it back to see. He clutched a thin bamboo rod about a foot long in one hand and sat on his chair, knees to chin, as if waiting out a flood. His lips were squeezed shut and he fought back tears.

"Calm down, Sketch, and tell me what this is about?"

"He came in here blowin' that goddamm train whistle and sayin' he's got a secret. Says he's gotta talk to you. So I says come back later. But he hunkers down on that chair like an ol' horsefly. Been sittin' there for good fifteen minutes now. Won't tell me nothin.' He's gettin' worse, Boss, damm if he ain't."

TJ looked at Sonny's face and saw nothing but fear. "It's all right, Sonny, no one's gonna hurt you. C'mon now, let's hear your secret." TJ nodded encouragement.

Sonny looked back and forth between the two lawmen, shook his head defiantly, and wrapped his arms around his chest.

"It's all right, Sonny. Sketch won't tell, will you Sketch?"

"Ah shit…" Sketch rolled his eyes and sighed. "All right, Sonny, I promise. I won't tell nobody nothin.'"

Sonny wiped his nose, glared at Sketch, and shook his head again.

"Ah fer Christsakes, Boss, we're wastin' time—I found out 'bout them jewels and…"

TJ held up his hand, silencing Sketch, and then squatted down in front of Sonny. "What's wrong, Sonny?"

Sonny pointed his bamboo whistle at Sketch and said, "Not him."

TJ looked over his shoulder at Sketch. "He's skittish, Sketch. Go on over to the jail, see if Lucky needs anything but be back here in ten minutes.

"But what 'bout them jewels?"

"Later, Sketch, later." After his deputy left, TJ reached out and touched Sonny's shoulder. Sonny winced and pulled back.

"What is it, Sonny?"

"Red hit me."

"Who's Red?

"The boss."

"Boss? What's he boss of?"

"Dunno."

"You know Red? Ever see him around town?"

"Nope. Never did."

"Tell me why Red hit you."

"'Cause he's mad—that's why."

"You do somethin' wrong?"

"Nope. Not me. Fatt Luk. He's mad at Fatt Luk."

TJ rose from his squat, pulled a chair up to Sonny's and sat down facing him. He softened his voice and asked, "All right, Sonny, tell me why Red is mad at Fatt Luk?"

"Can't tell."

"Why not?"

"Red'll hit me again. See." He lowered the strap on his overalls, unbuttoned the top button of his shirt, and pushed the shirt off his right shoulder, exposing a red welt that covered the top half of his bicep.

TJ cursed under his breath. "Listen to me Sonny. I'll lock Red up if he hits you again, you hear? Now, it's all right. You're safe now. Tell me about Fatt Luk."

Sonny toyed with the whistle then held it out to TJ.

"Fatt Luk made it." He smiled and his face brightened before clouding over. "Fatt Luk in trouble."

"Why is Fatt Luk in trouble, Sonny?"

"He's bad."

"Why is Fatt Luk bad?"

"Fatt Luk kilt a woman. Red said so."

TJ thought about what Sonny said. If Red isn't local, it probably means he's one of Kephardt's Knights. TJ had no idea why the Knights were interested in Fatt Luk. Could the Knights have connected Fatt Luk to Hop Li and the murders? But how? Then he remembered Daines. The reporter saw TJ and Sketch questioning Fatt Luk in the hallway; saw the cannery box, the Chinee skullcap, the bloody robe and slippers. Daines had seen it all and must have spread the word that Fatt Luk and Hop Li were in it together.

"Listen to me, Sonny. Red is wrong. Fatt Luk didn't kill anyone." He leaned back in his chair and asked, "Now, go on, tell me the rest of your secret."

"They took Fatt Luk away."

"What? Jesus…where?" TJ shouted.

Sonny jerked and the fear returned to his face.

TJ lowered his voice. "Where'd they take Fatt Luk, Sonny?"

"Dunno." Sonny's eyes widened. He stared over TJ's head, reliving the encounter with the Knights. His lips moved making no sound for a time but then words came, loud and quick.

"Tie Fatt Luk up. Throw Fatt Luk in wagon. Go home, Sonny. No. Don't wanna. Go home, Sonny." Sonny's face flushed, his neck muscles tightened, and his breath came fast and shallow. "Don't hurt Sonny!" he shouted.

"Whoa Sonny, calm down." TJ put a hand on Sonny's good shoulder. "Take a deep breath. Here, watch. Do what I do." TJ inhaled and let his breath out slowly. Sonny watched, and then imitated. They repeated the action. TJ nodded and said, "All right, that's better. Slow and easy now. Tell me the rest of your secret."

"Sonny run away. Come here." He wiped his nose again and said, "That's all."

"Sonny, do you remember the name of the street? The street where you left Fatt Luk?"

Sonny screwed up his face, puffed out his cheeks but after a struggle, looked down and sighed.

"That's all right. Can you take me to the place where the men caught Fatt Luk."

Sonny's face lit up. "Yep. Sonny show you." He jumped out of his chair and shoved the bamboo whistle in the upper pocket of his overalls.

TJ unlocked the gun case and took the Remington 10 gauge, the Winchester .44 and a box of cartridges. He grabbed his hat and told Sonny to follow him. TJ ran out the door, through the hallway, and down the steps of the courthouse on to Benton Street. He slowed down once and glanced over his shoulder for Sonny who turned out to be right behind him.

At the jail, TJ handed Sketch the shotgun and said he'd explain on the way. With Sonny leading now, they ran down Jefferson Street past the Columbia Hotel and turned south when they reached Polk. Sonny ran at a surprisingly good clip, once even jumping a sleeping dog without losing stride. TJ stayed a step behind Sonny urging him on while Sketch, breathing hard, lagged ten yards.

As he approached the intersection of Seventh and Polk, TJ saw two women talking together on the front porch of the corner house. He came up to the house and saw Fatt Luk's shoulder pole, the overturned baskets, and spilled garbage in the ditch that ran alongside Seventh. The young woman handed the baby in her arms to the older woman and ran out to meet them, settling on TJ as the man to talk to.

"Oh, thank God, Sheriff, you've come. Oh, that poor man, I'm so afraid…" her words tumbled out and TJ had trouble understanding her.

"Slow down, Ma'am, just tell me where they took him."

"There, straight down this street." She pointed west toward Holloway's cabin behind which an old-growth Sitka stood in a patch of vacant land. The Sitka's double trunk and logging superstition had saved it from the axe and its thick lower branches were ideal for hanging a man.

"He…our garbage man I mean…only just left…I was feeding Jeremy and heard this awful racket…shouting and yelling. I came to the window… saw a wagon driving off… men walking along side…never did see Fatt Luk. I waited 'til they'd gone then came outside. That's when I noticed his things." She pointed to the shoulder pole. "There."

TJ's heart sank as he listened to her. "That's fine, Ma'am, fine. We'll talk later." He pointed at Sonny. "Sonny, I want you to stay here to protect these women."

"I'm a deputy, too," Sonny said and pointed to the badge on his chest.

The woman ignored Sonny and took a step towards TJ. "Here, he might have a need for this," she whispered and shoved a piece of black cloth into his hand. It was Fatt Luk's eye patch. One of its straps was missing.

TJ waved for Sketch to follow and then ran full out down the middle of the street, heart pounding more from fear than the running. For as far ahead as he could see, the street was empty. For a time this gave him hope and he skirted potholes and ditches as easy as a deer but when he passed the intersection of Seventh and Madison with still no sign of life, he felt the silence screaming at him–too late, too late.

Finally, breathing hard, eyes watering, he reached Spruce Street and turned south toward Holloway's vacant cabin. He stopped, bent over, and gulped air for a second. The rain hadn't let up and he wiped his eyes with his bandana so he could see. Spruce Street dead-ended two blocks ahead and turned into a trail that wound up the hill through salal and the stumps of huge fir, spruce and hemlock. In the distance he made out the forked trunk of the big Sitka, the hanging tree, but saw no men, no wagon, and heard nothing but rain hitting the dirt road.

31

Thunder rumbled in the distance and a howling wind lashed the bodies of the lawmen with rain. TJ put his head down, hugged the Winchester, and kept to the middle of the road. Every few steps he looked up but saw no one in the road or around Holloway's cabin. Holloway's lot and the acres behind it had been logged years ago and now only the largest of stumps showed their tops above the thicket of salal and wild blackberry. Holloway, a former blacksmith at the Astoria Iron Works, had moved to Oregon City and the cabin had remained empty since then. He waved for Sketch to cover him.

TJ kept out of the sight line of the door and front window and, in a crouch, made his way to the side of the cabin without a window. He called out Fatt Luk's name, waited, and pressed his ear against the planked wall. He heard nothing and motioned Sketch to a stump about twenty yards to the side of the house that had a clear view of the front porch. TJ waited for Sketch to get in position behind the trunk then bent down and crept onto the porch. He rapped on the door with the butt of his rifle and called out again. Nothing. He pushed against the rough wood door rattling the lock and waited. Again, nothing. When he lifted his head and peeked in the window, he saw a broken chair, a small table, and the wood stove without a fire. As his eyes adjusted to the dim light, he could see that the one room cabin was empty. TJ stood up, waved for Sketch to follow him, and moved back to the road.

Still a block ahead, the Sitka stood on a level patch of ground about thirty yards off to the side of the road. A winding footpath cut through the salal that led to the base of the seventy-foot tree. TJ kept his eyes on the road and willed himself not to look at the tree, like a child willing himself to pass a dark closet without looking in.

He reached the end of the street and turned toward the tree, allowing his gaze to travel up one of the scarred trunks and out to the lowest branch, hoping not to see what he did. The figure, so small and thin, seemed, for an instant, nothing more than a large broken branch but then the wind gusted and the figure turned in a slow, uneven circle, destroying the illusion. He made his way up the path and stood under Fatt Luk's body, trying to make sense of what he saw. Fatt Luk wore pants but no shirt. His hands were tied behind his back. He had been whipped with a knotted rope and the bloody skin of his back hung down in strips exposing muscle. The bloated face, a pulpy mass of skin and muscle, was not recognizable as Fatt Luk's, not recognizable as human. Loose skin and blood covered Fatt Luk's facial scar that had once terrified children and strangers. Fatt Luk's three-foot long queue had been cut off and the larger end jammed into his mouth. His queue, a badge of honor in life, had become an obscene thing, hanging out of his mouth like a snake he had tried to swallow in his death struggle. One of his sandals had fallen off and lay at TJ's feet. TJ picked it up and tried to slide it on the swollen foot but it wouldn't go on in spite of his stubborn attempts. The skin of TJ's hands turned pink from the rainwater washing blood off Fatt Luk's body. He shuddered at the sight and pulled his hand away. He wiped his hands on his pants and put the sandal in his coat pocket next to the eye patch.

"Godammit to hell," he said aloud. But the swear words sounded too weak—weren't dirty enough—to express what he felt. His arms and legs felt heavy and he put his head down, trying to still the waves of nausea passing through him. In a few seconds, the nausea eased but the taste of bile remained. He made his way over to the trunk of what had once been a massive hemlock and sat down on the wet ground. He pressed his back against the trunk, grateful for its support, closed his eyes, and put his head between his knees.

TJ heard a string of words and grunts that were incomprehensible at first but then turned into "Jesus, God" said over and over in a mechanical voice. Not long after this he heard Sketch retching and vomiting. In time, Sketch made his way over to the stump. His face was drained of color and his eyes still stared at something a man ought never have to see. TJ looked away and shut his eyes. Sketch slid to the ground next to him. After a few minutes of silence, TJ put a hand on Sketch's shoulder and asked, "How you feelin'?"

"Feelin' puny, Boss. I...never seen...nothin...'" Sketch shook his head, got to one knee, and wiped his dripping face with his bandanna. He stood up slowly, leaned over, and put his hands on his knees.

A loud squawk came from the Sitka and both men looked up to see a flock of crows bickering as they fought for space on a branch just above the body. A latecomer dived at those on the branch sending crows flying off. The crows circled and chased each other for a time before settling back down on the branch above the body.

"Goddammit, git away. Git, git, git, Goddammit," Sketch yelled and ran at the tree, waving his arms over his head. The crows ignored him. He bent down, picked up a rock, and threw it at the tree. The rock bounced off one of the Sitka's trunks. The crows screeched and shifted their position on the branch but didn't fly off.

TJ waited for Sketch to stop yelling. "C'mon back, Sketch. Leave the birds be."

Sketch made his way back to where TJ sat, tried to speak but couldn't. His face was flushed and he was breathing hard. He choked back tears and covered his eyes with his hand.

"Sit down, Sketch. Rest a spell."

Sketch sat down and leaned against the trunk. TJ waited a few minutes until Sketch's breathing slowed and then asked, "You feel up for work?"

"I reckon. What's first?"

"Go back to town and bring the buckboard. Be quick but don't run. I'll keep an eye on things here. Maybe we can get him out of here before the gawkers come."

Sketch picked up the shotgun and scooted down the path past the Sitka never once taking his eyes off the ground. When he turned and headed up the road, TJ shouted after him, "And if you run into Kephardt's boys, don't start anything. A dead deputy is no good to me. You hear?"

Sketch lifted his free hand and waved without turning around. TJ watched his deputy until he was out of sight then took an El Gusto and stuck it in his mouth. Even though he couldn't smoke in the rain, he hoped chewing the cigar might ease the wait. But the cigar smelled like floor sweepings and tasted bitter. He tossed it over his shoulder in disgust, shut his eyes, and tried not to think about Fatt Luk or how he died.

He shoved his hand in his coat pocket and felt the eye patch. What should he do with it? Be a shame to throw it away, someone could use it. But he realized that didn't make sense—how many men, blind in one eye, didn't already have an eye patch? Well, then, he ought to make sure Fatt Luk's next of kin got it. But then he sighed and shook his head. He couldn't imagine why his kin would want the eye patch.

After a long, cold and wet thirty minutes, he heard the buckboard bouncing towards him. He got up, made his way through the path, and waited in the road. Big Jim drove while Sketch rode shotgun. Big Jim brought the horse to a halt directly across from the

Sitka and stared, open mouthed, at the hanging man. By now the rain had cleansed the torso of blood but this only brought the loose skin and exposed muscle into stark relief. Big Jim finally turned his back on the body, lowered his head and slowly shook it in a wide arch from side to side while muttering, "Damm, damm, damm." In a moment, he turned around with a question on his face but then looked at TJ and didn't ask it.

TJ felt naked in front of the others, had nothing to say that would make them feel better. He wasn't sure why but he felt guilty and suspected they did too. It wasn't anything they did or didn't do. The guilt, he decided, came from being white and knowing that Fatt Luk had been lynched because he wasn't.

The mare, smelling blood and the fear in the men, laid her ears back, turned and looked back at Big Jim wide-eyed in fear. Big Jim tightened his grip on the reins and called out in a low voice, "Whoa, slooo, girl, who-o-oa, slooo now." The mare shook herself twice before quieting. TJ waited until the mare put her ears forward and then said in a soft voice, "All right, let's take him down."

Sketch untied the rope, payed it out, and let the body slide onto TJ's shoulder. TJ carried the body, so much lighter than he expected, back to the wagon. Sketch loosened the hangman's knot and lifted it over Fatt Luk's head. TJ lowered the body onto the floor of the buckboard while supporting Fatt Luk's head with his hand. Sketch hoisted himself into the back and yanked the queue hard several times before it came free from the jaws. He tucked the queue under Fatt Luk's belt then stared at the gaping mouth before trying to push the jaws shut. But the jaws were broken and stayed open. Sketch draped a heavy canvas over the body and TJ climbed into the shotgun seat, squared his hat, and nodded to Big Jim.

While the rain had turned into an on-again-off again dribble, the wind blew colder than any time that day. TJ's pants were soaked and though he wore his Levis over his boots, his socks had somehow got wet too. TJ didn't feel like talking to anyone, including his deputies, but the Chinese had a right to hear what happened from him, from the law, not from some drunk full of boast.

Big Jim turned down Jefferson Street, heading east, and when they reached Lafayette, TJ told him to stop.

"Ain't we goin' to Doc's?" Big Jim asked.

"We are, rather you are. I'm gettin' off here. And drop Sketch off at the jail," TJ said. "Sketch, I want you to stay with Lucky 'til I get someone to relieve you."

"Where you goin'?" Sketch asked.

"I need to tell Dr. Chung and Wing what happened before they hear it from somebody else." TJ nodded towards Fatt Luk's body. "So you're on your own, Big Jim. Doc will help you with the death report."

"Whadda I do after Doc?" Big Jim asked.

"Bring the papers back to the office. I'll sign them there."

"All right. But don't start nothin' without me, hear?"

TJ smiled. "I promise. If there's a war, it won't start without you. Now, go on, get movin.'"

TJ watched the buckboard pull away, straightened his shoulders, and headed down Lafayette Street to Dr. Chung's pharmacy.

32

Cold, wet, and bone-tired, TJ considered going to his boardinghouse for dry clothes and a rest before talking to Dr. Chung. But some things such as telling a man his friend had been hanged couldn't be put off. TJ forced himself to think about the investigation. If Hop Li had killed Fong and taken the money in the safe, he'd have the fifty dollars his folks asked for. Hop Li said he borrowed the twenty-five he needed from Dr. Chung but did he?

As he approached the pharmacy, he knew he couldn't question Dr. Chung while withholding the news of the lynching. Dr. Chung wrote the letters home for Astoria's Chinaboys and probably knew Fatt Luk well, might even be a close friend. And according to Emma, Dr. Chung was second only to Wing, the headman, in influence among Astoria's two thousand Chinese. If trouble broke out between the Knights of Labor and the Chinese, he'd need Dr. Chung as an ally. He'd tell Dr. Chung about Fatt Luk right away but would the man feel like answering questions? Hop Li's arraignment was tomorrow morning and TJ needed answers today.

Underneath the Chinese characters on the window, bright red letters said: *Dr. Chung Lap Him: Drug Store, Remedys & Medicins of All Kinds.* A bell tinkled when TJ opened the screen door and a spicy aroma from cooking food filled the room with a smell TJ didn't recognize. Dr. Chung sat behind a counter at the rear of the store listening to Mama Joy, the ill-tempered overseer of Wing's brothel.

Dr. Chung acknowledged TJ with a nod then turned back to Mama Joy, nodding and grunting in response to a stream of words spit at him in a shrill voice. TJ stayed well back from the counter, granting them privacy, and studied the doctor. Dr. Chung was around fifty, thin, and not much over five feet tall. The skin of his wide forehead was smooth except for a small birthmark in the shape of starfish above his right eye.

The gold-rimmed glasses, thin nose, and pursed lips gave him the serious look of a judge. A bushy mustache and thick beard, trimmed short, softened the serious look. TJ hadn't paid much attention to Dr. Chung when he'd come to the cannery to translate the writing on Jameson's tank. Soft-spoken and polite, Dr. Chung hadn't even asked why TJ wanted the words translated.

As TJ watched the doctor's long, slender fingers take the woman's pulse, first the left, then the right, and finally both at the same time, he saw how well the man fit his surroundings. TJ recalled Emma's story about Dr. Chung's healing powers and, ever the skeptic, had dismissed the story as hokum. But now he wondered if he'd been too quick to judge. Soon after Dr. Chung arrived in Astoria, the story goes, a panic-stricken white couple had sent for him after Western doctors failed to cure their son of blood poisoning. Dr. Chung stayed with the family for over a week, treating the boy with herbs and ointments. The boy recovered and now both Chinese and white, even from Portland, 75 miles away, sought him out. Emma had smiled as she recited Dr. Chung's invisibility principle: The color of my skin is not visible to a person with an illness.

Ten minutes passed and TJ thought about coming back later. He dismissed the thought even though his face felt flushed and his skin itched, the first signs of his affliction. To keep his mind off his body, he looked around the store. No larger than most stores in town, the pharmacy consisted of a long narrow room with the rear third split in two by a partition, creating a living space on one side and a storage area on the other. The sparse furnishings of the living quarters, a wide bunk bed, a plank table, a straight-backed chair, a calendar, and a pot-bellied stove, created an island of open space in spite of its small size.

In contrast to the living area, every bit of space in the remainder of the store appeared occupied. On either side of the center aisle, work clothes, tools, and sundries for the cannery worker overflowed shelves while sacks of rice, lentils, and beans crowded the floor. The counter held the tools of the pharmacist: a set of scales, a small and large mortar and pestle, and a row of blue and brown bottles held in place by a wood rack. Built-in shelves in the wall directly behind Dr. Chung held row upon row of drawers with a character or two inscribed on each drawer. The shelving extended from a foot off the floor to as high as the doctor could reach, perhaps seven feet. Emma had told him that Dr. Chung had enough herbs, bark, roots, fossils, sea horses, insects, horns, antlers, and organs both dried and in solution to make over 500 medicines. At the time, TJ thought she'd exaggerated but now, looking at that wall of drawers, he realized maybe she hadn't. Over Dr. Chung's head, strings of garlic, dried herbs, and the skins of rattlesnakes and other reptiles dangled from wires that ran from one side of the room to the other.

A wave of nausea passed over him and a line of sweat trickled down the side of his head. He took a deep breath but the stale air and strange odor only increased his nausea. He hadn't felt this bad since he'd been in Wing's saloon. Then, it had been too many men in too small a space that brought on his affliction. But why now? He puzzled over this until he recognized it was the same unsettled feeling he had as he walked the long, dark hall upstairs at Wing's. He didn't know the language, didn't know what to expect of the Chinese, and didn't know what they expected of him. He had that same unsettled feeling as a boy when his Dad walked in the house drunk on a Saturday night. The smallest thing, a look, a careless word, could send Dad into a rage and once enraged, the fists came out. After the beating, he was locked in the coal cellar. He spent many a night in the cellar trying to understand his Dad but never did learn the why of the rages. Only after his Dad left for good did he realize the truth: Dad didn't know the why of them either.

Mama Joy leaned across the counter and lowered her voice to a whisper. Dr. Chung nodded, said something, then rose and took a sprig of some plant from one drawer, a piece of root from another, and a scoop of white powder from a bottle on the counter. He cut and ground up the root and plant then mixed them in with the powder, sniffed, added a pinch more of powder, then weighed the mixture. He poured the mixture into an envelope and wrote something on the front. Then with the speed and ease of an eel chasing a fish he slid the balls of the abacus back and forth with his little finger. He bowed, said something, and Mama Joy slid a few coins across the counter. The old woman clutched the envelope to her chest and as she squeezed past TJ, she lifted her head and smiled, victorious in a competition only she understood. After she left, TJ wiped the sweat from his face and neck with his bandanna and stepped up to the counter.

Dr. Chung smiled and the wrinkles in his face seemed to smile as well. "Welcome, Sheriff TJ. Sorry you wait. That old woman need my ear more than medicine." His gaze traveled over TJ's face and body at a measured pace, the wide-set brown eyes so focused and intense that TJ grew uncomfortable. Dr. Chung nodded finally and said, "So, you not feel good? Come close. Put wrist here, please." He pointed to a small black pillow where he took pulses.

"Oh, no, sorry. Nothin' s wrong—with me I mean. But there's news." Sweat poured out of him, his mouth felt dry and his throat constricted. He glanced around for a place to sit. Dr. Chung, who hadn't stopped looking at him, finally grunted and said, "So, you not trust China medicine?"

"No, it's not that, it's just, well, I don't have time right now. But I'll take a cup of water if you have one." TJ continued to look around for something to sit on.

"Water sometime best medicine. Excuse please, one minute." Dr. Chung disappeared behind the curtain to his storage room and came back with a dipper of water in one hand and a stool in the other. He handed the dipper to TJ and set the stool down beside him. TJ drained the water in a few gulps and sat down.

"So, what is news?" Dr. Chung tucked his hands into the wide sleeves of his gray tunic.

TJ took off his hat and studied the brim. "This mornin' some men lynched a Chinee, a fella by name of Fatt Luk." He wiped his brow with his bandanna, now soaked.

"Lyn-ch-ed? Please, Sheriff, not understand."

"It means they hung him. Fatt Luk is dead." TJ still didn't look at him.

Dr. Chung sucked air in between his teeth then lowered his head. He sat down on his stool and covered his head with his hands. "Aii! No, no, no. Not Fatt Luk."

Stock words and phrases came to TJ but at the same time so did the memory of Lucy Ann's wake and how he felt when friends tried to comfort him. Their words were stupid, useless, and made him want to lash out at those who uttered them or break something. So he said nothing. Dr. Chung stared at the floor for a long minute then said, "Excuse, please." He got up and went into the storage room. TJ heard a muffled choking sound and then, minutes later, water splashing in a pan. In spite of wanting an answer to his question, TJ wondered if he should leave and come back. The knot in his stomach tightened and another wave of nausea shot through him. He swallowed repeatedly, closed his eyes, and thought of the river on a blue-sky afternoon as he and Tug set out to a drift site. It helped. In a few minutes Dr. Chung came out wiping his eyes with a towel and carrying a kettle.

"Sheriff, please, you stay five minute? White flower tea—best tea. Yes?" His voice shook and he fought back tears.

"Yeah, all right. And if you're up to it, I'd like to ask you something about Hop Li."

Dr. Chung shoved sticks of kindling in the stove, blew on the embers, and brought the flame to life. He put the kettle on the stovetop.

"So, who kill Fatt Luk?"

"Some men, outsiders. They thought he killed Wah Fong and the American lady."

"Fatt Luk? No. Not that one. Even his pig, Fatt Luk not like kill. Fatt Luk everybody friend. I know this."

"Well, I never thought he killed anyone and don't think most folks around here do either, except for that jackass who runs the paper. I can't say for sure who put the rope around Fatt Luk's neck, but I suspect the Knights are behind it."

"So, it start, eh? What we do now, Sheriff TJ?"

"What? I don't understand."

"Chinamen stay here, they die." Dr. Chung stood up as tall as his five feet would allow and narrowed his eyes in anger. "Why so hard understand?"

"That's not goin' to happen."

"How stop?"

"I've got all my deputies now and I'm bringin' in volunteers first thing. Won't be any more Chinee lynched on my watch."

Dr. Chung studied TJ's face. "Even Knight not kill Chinamen, maybe they put Chinamen on ship, send First City [San Francisco]. All same like Seattle, eh? Knight have many men. How you fight?"

"I'll do my dammedest—that's all I can promise."

The kettle whistled and Dr. Chung brought it over to the counter and set it on a square of smooth marble. From a nook on the shelf behind him he brought out a purple teapot and two small cups. He put three pinches of tea into the teapot, poured in water, replaced the lid and sat down.

"Headman of Knight come Astoria. All time say same thing: Chinamen must go! Chinamen must go! Why we must go? What we do wrong, eh? What Fatt Luk do wrong?" He paused a few seconds before continuing, "Answer not necessary, Sheriff TJ. Chinamen all time working too hard—that Chinaman mistake—only thing Chinaman do wrong." He lifted the lid of the teapot, sniffed the tea and nodded. He filled both cups, slid one cup across the counter to TJ, and then waited until TJ picked it up before lifting his own. Dr. Chung took a sip and then put his cup down.

"So, you know Fatt Luk, Sheriff TJ?"

"I knew him—one of the garbage men in town. Answered my questions when I brought him in without lyin.'"

"Yes, yes. Garbage man—raise pig, grow vegetable—only thing white people know. But Fatt Luk more than garbage man, eh? Have big heart. Sometime give poor 'merican family vegetable—you know this?"

"No, I didn't." TJ realized he knew almost nothing about Fatt Luk, a man he saw at least three times at week going on his garbage rounds. "Did he have a wife?"

"Yes. Wife stay China. So, who write, say Fatt Luk dead? How say, big mistake, bad men kill Fatt Luk?"

"Would you write to her Dr. Chung?"

"You not know China writing so must be Dr. Chung, eh? So how tell Fatt Luk family, son dead, tell wife, husband dead? Wah! Word no good." He sighed and sipped his tea. "So, I write letter."

"I appreciate you doing that, Dr. Chung."

"Fatt Luk everybody friend." Dr. Chung shook his head slowly from side to side. "Fatt Luk like tell joke, make people happy, make toy for children, for Sonny—that one people all time make joke on. You know?"

"Yep."

"Yes. Even Sonny, Fatt Luk friend. So, Fatt Luk more than garbage man, hnnnn!" Dr. Chung stood, slid his hand out of his sleeve and pointed over the door where a kite with six leaves hung. On the front leaf, a ferocious dragon in reds, blues and golds glowered at TJ. "Fatt Luk number one kite maker—make that one." He shook his head and sighed. "But now bad time in China, rice bowl empty. Nobody buy kite. So Fatt Luk come *Gum Shan*, work hard, go home rich man, honorable man. Now, Fatt Luk dream over."

They sipped their tea in silence and TJ thought about the unconnected events that led to Fatt Luk's death. Fatt Luk had come to Astoria to work in a cannery but an accident took his eye and scarred his face so he became a garbage man, a job shunned by other Chinese. If he'd gone somewhere else, say John Day in Eastern Oregon, he'd have been a miner, and maybe saved enough by now to go home to his wife. And if he'd been sick today and stayed in bed, he'd be alive. And if Hop Li weren't his friend, he'd be alive. TJ forced himself to stop. Playing with ifs could drown you in a sinkhole of misery fast.

"I'm real sorry about Fatt Luk, Dr. Chung." TJ stood up. "Why don't I come back later? We can talk about Hop Li then."

Dr. Chung didn't act as if he'd heard. In a soft voice, he asked, "You believe in spirit, Sheriff TJ?"

"Spirits? Um…no, can't say as I do."

"Spirit of Fatt Luk make trouble now."

This wasn't what TJ wanted to hear. He put his hat on and squared it down.

"Fatt Luk spirit maybe become *Gur*. You know *Gur*?"

TJ shook his head.

"*Gur* is ghost, not happy ghost. When good man die bad death spirit become *gur*. *Gur* have no place rest, no peace, so make trouble for living. We need pray, make plenty offering, so Fatt Luk spirit find peace. Only way help Fatt Luk now."

"Well, guess you know what's best." TJ turned to leave but Dr. Chung reached out and touched his arm.

"Wait, please. You have question, so ask question." He came around the counter and his eyes met TJ's. "You think Hop Li kill Wah Fong, 'merican lady?"

"Well, the facts point to him. But I'm still lookin' into things. Maybe he didn't kill them."

"Yes? So, I know Chen Hop Li five year. Good son—respect father, elder brother, all family. Work hard, send money home. Keep little for self. I know this. So, he never kill any people." Dr. Chung tapped his heart. "I know this here."

With the mention of money, TJ saw an opening. "Dr. Chung, how much money did Hop Li send home the last time he sent money?"

"This help Hop Li?"

"It could."

Dr. Chung bowed and went back into his storage room and came out with a ledger. He flipped through it and ran his finger down a column of entries. "Ah, yes. Tuesday. Write letter Tuesday." He closed the ledger and sighed. "Very bad time, Hop Li village. Elder brother write, say only one bowl rice each day, all people. Soon, all rice bowl empty. Please, send fifty dolla. Hop Li have twenty-five dolla. I lend ten dolla, so Hop Li send thirty-five dolla home." Dr. Chung studied TJ as he sipped his tea.

"But Hop Li said he sent fifty dollars home. Why would he lie about that, Dr. Chung?"

Dr. Chung nodded. "Yes. Yes. Family say send fifty dolla. Hop Li not send what family ask, have much shame. So he tell Sheriff TJ, send fifty dolla home. Understand?"

"I think so. A matter of honor, right?"

"Yes, honor." Dr. Chung raised an eyebrow and said, "So, this answer help Hop Li?"

"Yep, it does. Thanks, Dr. Chung." He shook Dr. Chung's hand and left.

Once outside, he took in three or four deep breaths of salt air. The rain had stopped and he walked down Lafayette Street until he reached the wharf and an empty slip. He leaned against the rail and looked across the river to the Washington side. Sea gulls appeared overhead as if by magic, squawking for handouts, and he watched one circle and land on the piling closest to him. He was just here, now, on the river, feeling the breeze on his face, smelling the salt air, and watching seagulls. After a time, the nausea in his stomach eased. He stretched and looked at his watch—almost 2:00 pm. He turned and headed up Lafayette to his office. Wing could wait. He needed to tell Silas Hoskins, the District Attorney, what Dr. Chung just told him.

33

Thursday, April 15

On his morning walk through Swilltown, TJ went over the day's tasks. Silas Hoskins proved more stubborn than TJ had anticipated and said the new evidence wasn't solid enough, that Hop Li could have kept the money he stole and still borrowed ten dollars from Dr. Chung. So the arraignment was going ahead as scheduled. TJ had a hunch that Kephardt and his Knights would gather outside the courthouse looking for a chance to raise hell. TJ saw Kephardt as a showman and expected him to wait until Hop Li appeared in front of a crowd before starting to rabble rouse. TJ decided to take Hop Li from the jail early and deny Kephardt the opportunity for mischief. With that problem solved, his thoughts turned to the murders and sensed something he'd forgotten to do or needed to find out but couldn't recall what. The mental itch nagged at him all the way to his office where he found Sketch had the potbelly going and coffee brewing.

"Mornin' Sketch. You're early again. You buckin' for my job?" TJ took two El Gustos out and offered one to his deputy.

Sketch grinned through a mouth full of tobacco and declined the cigar. "No sir. Didn't sleep but a couple winks last night so got up early. Kept seein' that little fella...up in that tree." Sketch frowned and looked down.

"I know, Sketch. Didn't sleep much myself. Couldn't eat much either," TJ said and then filled Sketch in on his talks with Dr. Chung, Wing, and Silas Hoskins. Wing already knew about Fatt Luk by the time TJ got to him and only wanted to know how TJ planned to stop more hangings. "Anyway, the arraignment is goin' ahead." He lit his cigar, leaned back in his swivel chair, and recalled that Sketch was somehow connected to what he couldn't recall. "Sketch, somethin's been pesterin' me, somethin' we need to do or find out about but damm if I can remember what. You any idea...?"

"Zuckerman and them jewels?"

"By God, that's it! Good man. What'd you find out?"

"Gimme a second, Boss." Sketch went over to the small table that served as his desk, picked up his drawing pad, and flipped through the pages. "Yep. Here 'tis. Zuckerman says them three jewels is real enough and come outta the same settin.' First, he says they fell outta a brooch, you know, them do-dads ladies wear."

TJ nodded.

"But then he comes up with 'nother idea. Says they might could come from a ring, a special ring rich folk give their sweethearts. That's what he calls it too—a sweetheart ring. I never seen one myself but then I ain't spent much time hobnobbin' with rich folk."

"Sweetheart ring? What's special about it?"

"Well, there's a secret to it. See, each of them jewels stands for a letter. If you set them down a certain way, why, they spell out a word."

"That doesn't make a bit of sense, Sketch. What word do our three jewels spell out?"

"Well, them three don't spell out nothin'—wasn't enough letters yet."

"I don't follow, Sketch. Maybe I best talk to Zuckerman."

"Hold on a minute, Boss. Lemme draw it out. It's a wonder when you see it." Sketch turned the page, wrote something, and then showed the page to TJ.

D ...Dimmun
E ...Emrul
A... ?
R ... Rubi

TJ studied the oversized letters and unique spelling, nodded, but then asked, "How come the A doesn't have a jewel next to it?"

"Well, 'cause we only had them three jewels. So Zuckerman had to guess the missin' one—has a funny name—am miss... somethin' like that. Anyways, it fit."

"Amethyst?"

"Sounds right." Sketch stood up. "So, what's it mean, Boss?"

TJ knew that if the jewels were from a ring, they could belong either to Jane or her killer. Since Annika said Jane only wore costume jewelry, a ring probably belonged to the killer. But then he asked himself why the killer didn't pick the jewels up, at least the two in plain sight. *Hold on*, he told himself, *he just killed two people and, from the*

*way the room looked, Jane put up a fight. So maybe he left in a hurry
and didn't notice the missing jewels 'til later.*

"Well, if those jewels come from a sweetheart ring and if the ring
belonged to the killer and if we find a man wearing a sweetheart ring
with three stones missing, we'll have the son of a bitch."

Sketch smiled and said, "We gettin' close, Boss?"

"Not enough to start celebratin.'" TJ took his feet off his desk and
sat up. "But enough theorizin'—we got things to do. You hear any
scuttlebutt on the Knights?"

"Nope. But Big Jim did. After he takes Fatt Luk's body to Doc's,
he stops off at the Portside for a beer. He hears talk 'bout a watch on
the courthouse today. Could be nothin' but bar talk, boss."

"All the same, we don't want any surprises." TJ stood up,
snapped the leather guard off his holster, and eased his peacemaker up
and down a few times.

"What's first, boss?"

"We're pickin' up Hop Li and stashin' him in the office. Then you
find Big Jim but don't bring him here. I want him out front of the
courthouse with the buckboard by 10:15. Tell him to keep out of sight
'til then. And he'll need the shotgun so take that along." TJ put his hat
on. "I'll stay with Hop Li 'til you get back then I'm goin' over to Chief
Connelly's, see if I can get some help."

"Connelly? He ain't gonna help, Boss. When I tell him about Fatt
Luk, he just laughs, says it's one less John to fool with."

"I know how he thinks. But if things get out of hand, a riot say,
one of his pals could get hurt. So I believe he'll help if only to keep his
friends safe."

"That don't cheer me up much."

TJ smiled. "I know but that's how it is. C'mon, let's get Hop Li."

They stood on the courthouse landing and let the heat from the sun
warm their faces. A southwest breeze blew the cannery stink away
from town and TJ pulled the clean air into his lungs with a long, deep
breath.

"Gonna be a fine day," Sketch said.

"Maybe," TJ said and looked up and down Benton Street.

A table constructed of planks and sawhorses sat outside Hakala's
harness shop, directly across the street from the courthouse. But the
absence of chairs and signs at the harness shop, the shoe repair shop
next door, and Finley's corner drug store told him that the Knights were
still getting organized.

Lucky brought Hop Li into the jail office with his hands cuffed
behind his back. Hop Li acknowledged no one and stared vacantly at

the front door, a door that led to freedom and a world in which he held a prized job—number one butcher in a large cannery.

"He don't look so good, Boss," Sketch said.

TJ looked closely at Hop Li, noted the rings under his eyes, and his lack of interest in where they were taking him. When TJ had questioned Hop Li at Jameson's and again at his office, the Chinaboy had been proud, even defiant. But the man facing him now showed no trace of defiance. Time in jail can make a man give up, TJ knew, but he had never known a man to change in so short a time.

Lucky handed TJ the sign-out log and said, "He's takin' water only. Ever since that China doc came by. Been off food three days now."

"How come you're not eatin,' Hop Li? Food no good?" TJ asked.

Without breaking his stare Hop Li said, "Not eat now."

"That's all I get outta him, 'not eat now.' Maybe he thinks we're poisonin' him?" Lucky shrugged.

They didn't pass anyone in the street as they walked Hop Li to the courthouse. Once inside the sheriff's office, Sketch put Hop Li in a chair as far from the door as possible. After Sketch left to get Big Jim, TJ unlocked Hop Li's handcuffs and re-cuffed them with his hands in front. "Be easier on you this way, Hop Li, 'cause we got a long wait." He sat down at his desk and picked up The Star but after five minutes looked up. "You want something? Coffee?"

Hop Li lifted his head and said, "Water."

TJ got the dipper, filled it from the water bucket, and handed it to him. Hop Li drank slowly and then nodded thanks as he handed the dipper back.

 TJ sat back down but didn't pick up the newspaper. He wanted to see if he could discover something that might help Hop Li if his case went to trial.

"Sorry about Fatt Luk," TJ said.

Hop Li looked up. "Sorry not help Fatt Luk. I ask Fatt Luk keep box, so he die. I make mistake—big goddamm mistake." Hop Li turned to the side and spit on the floor.

"You didn't kill Fatt Luk, Hop Li. You trusted that sea captain—that's the only mistake you made."

Hop Li eyed TJ closely before he looked down again.

"Dr. Chung said you only sent thirty-five dollars to your folks. He told me why you lied, and I'm inclined…"

Hop Li straightened and glared at him. "Hah? What Dr. Chung say?"

TJ didn't expect the sudden anger and paused before speaking. "Well, he just said you did what an honorable man does—protect the family name. Leastways, that's how I took it. No reason to take offense."

"Dr. Chung good friend but sometime talk too much."

Just then Sketch walked in and said he'd given Big Jim his instructions.

TJ nodded and said, "Anything goin' on outside?" He looked up at the school clock, which read 9:15.

"Not much. A few Chinee is down the block a ways and some white boys is up the other way. Everybody is sittin' around tryin' to look like furniture." Sketch nodded at Hop Li. "How's he been?"

"No trouble." TJ turned to Hop Li who maintained his statue-like stillness. "If you want something, Hop Li, coffee or water or to use the privy, just ask Sketch."

Hop Li shook his head in response.

"Sketch, you can close the door after I'm gone if you want. I won't be long with Connelly."

TJ put his hat on and walked out. Halfway down the hall, he heard the door slam shut and smiled at Sketch's caution. Big Jim was just the opposite of Sketch and charged every problem like the brawler he'd been before becoming deputy. But TJ was thankful for both men just because of their difference in temperament.

TJ paused on the courthouse landing to re-light his cigar and take in the street. A Knights' banner now hung down from the table in front of Hakala's shop. Kephardt's clerk sat at the table with a ledger in front of him while Kephardt squatted next to him. Five men sat on boxes or chairs in front of Finley's drug store. One of them, a stocky man with broad shoulders, sat with his chair tipped against the wall. His head of coarse red hair competed with the scowl on his face for being the most noticeable thing about him.

In the other direction, two Chinese sat on boxes outside the Pak Kop Piu lottery office playing dominos while another three stood watching the game. No one, white or Chinese, appeared to take any notice of him but he knew all had watched him leave the courthouse. Something about the man with the red hair poked TJ's memory and he turned back for another look. It took a second but then he noticed the green top hat in the man's lap. He recalled that same hat slicing through the crowd at Kephardt's speech. The fellow was the drummer on the Knights' music wagon and the others with him were Knights. TJ doubted they'd try to take Hop Li from him in daylight; still he congratulated himself on picking Hop Li up when he did. He pulled the brim of his hat down and came down the steps without a glance at the Knights' table. As he passed the drug store, the redhead leaned over the railing and spit into the street.

TJ told the chief he needed half-dozen men to control the crowd and to make sure no women or children got hurt. The chief, pleased that TJ was asking for help, said he'd see what he could do.

Back at the courthouse, TJ found Silas talking to a curly-haired, fat man whose wide smile and good teeth gave the appearance of a traveling drummer.

The fat man reached for TJ's hand. "George Mayhew, for the defense."

To his surprise, TJ found, that Mayhew didn't cup his hand or hold any part of it back as Jameson and other bosses did. Mayhew's open coat revealed a mountainous mid-section divided by a belt that would have circled TJ's waist twice. Mayhew wore a pink carnation in his buttonhole, the only relief from the yards of black worsted in his Prince Albert suit.

"Silas has praised you to the skies, Sheriff Stone."

"Call me TJ. How come Hop Li can afford a big city lawyer like you?"

"I'm not at liberty to divulge that. Let's just say that Hop Li has friends in Portland." Mayhew smiled and dimples appeared in his cheeks.

"Come by my office after lunch. There's a few things I'd like to say in Hop Li's favor," TJ said.

Mayhew's face lit up in a full smile and the dimples re-appeared, deeper this time. "Capital! You know, it's been my experience that some lawmen are, well, how shall I put it, not always so willing to help when my client is Chinese. I appreciate it, TJ, I truly do."

Silas spoke up, "We're early but let's go in. Where is Hop Li by the way?"

"Somewhere safe." TJ smiled and headed down the long hallway to his office.

34

The courthouse proceedings ended after twenty minutes with Hop Li bound over for trial. Mayhew won a minor victory as the judge allowed the defense an extra two weeks to go over the new evidence supplied by Dr. Chung. After the judge left, Emma turned to TJ and said in a strained whisper, "Such vile language, TJ! 'Mutilate,' 'depraved,' 'fiendish.' Really! If that district attorney is allowed to use such words to a jury, Hop Li will surely be convicted. Can't you do something?"

"Wish I could, Miss Taylor—lawyer talk bothers me too. But I don't have any say here."

"Oh, I'm so angry I can't think straight." She nodded towards Silas. "That man is determined to crucify Hop Li. He should be ashamed of himself!" Emma sat back in her chair, shoulders slumped, hands balled into fists. After a minute, she gathered her things, said a few words to Hop Li, and rushed out of the courtroom with only a nod to TJ.

TJ understood Emma's anger. The contrast between Silas' baby face and the nasty words coming out of his mouth made the crimes seem the worst ever committed. Mayhew said little, sitting there as if everything were going his way. He smiled at Silas, the judge, Hop Li, and once, he turned around to smile at the spectators. To TJ, the lawyers seemed like actors in a play, one they knew by heart, and one in which they played only to the judge and to each other.

TJ waited until Silas and Mayhew filed out and then he and Sketch escorted the handcuffed Hop Li out of the courtroom. When the lawmen appeared on the courthouse steps with Hop Li between them, shouts and catcalls burst from the fifty plus men on the sidewalk. Silas stood halfway down the steps while the redhead with the green hat hollered up from the middle of the crowd, "What's happenin,' when's the trial?"

Silas held up his hands for quiet. "Well, he's going to trial…but…"

"But? But what? When's the trial?" The man put his hands on his hips.

"It's been moved back two weeks."

"Moved back? What the hell for?"

Mayhew moved down next to Silas and waved his wide-brimmed hat for quiet. The big man's size commanded attention. "The delay means that the DA has a problem." Mayhew's fat face beamed confidence. "New evidence has turned up that weakens the DA's case." Mayhew tilted his head and looked at Silas in mock pity then, as swift as an actor, his face turned stern and, jowls shaking, said,"Gentlemen, I believe that if the case comes to trial—and that's a big if—the good people of Astoria will do the right thing and acquit my client. He's innocent of all charges."

"Like hell he is," Marvin Kephardt's deep voice roared. Eyes turned toward him as Kephardt pushed past the redhead and moved up to within six feet of the lawyers. Kephardt pointed a finger at Hop Li. "That there Chinee butchered a white woman." Kephardt's red-face and the scar on his upper lip made his sneer menacing, his anger contagious. The men closest to him backed off a step or two as he screamed, "And he's gonna hang!"

TJ looked over the crowd and sensed their growing itch to do something. He saw Big Jim sitting in the buckboard but the crowd stood between the steps and the buckboard.

Kephardt turned to the crowd. "This here city lawyer outfoxed the judge—just like I said was gonna happen." He jabbed his thumb over his shoulder at Mayhew who was no longer grinning. Kephardt filled his massive chest, threw his head back, and boomed his voice over the crowd. Passersby across the street stopped to listen. "The shyster tricks is just beginnin,' folks. Trial delayed for new evidence. Ha! Next thing, the shyster is gonna get that moon-eyed whelp clean off." He looked from one end of the crowd to the other. Three men crossed the street to join the crowd.

"Mark my words. The court is gonna set that pigtail free. Free to find hisself another white woman. Could be your daughter or your wife this time. He'll take her to his den, do things to her decent folk ain't fit to hear, then cut her up in some fiend ritual. Is this what folk here call justice?"

The spellbound crowd hollered, "No!"

Kephardt pointed a long finger at Hop Li. "You gonna let rat-eaters like that take over our country?" He hollered and spittle flew from his mouth.

"No!" The shout louder than before.

TJ looked around but didn't see any city police.

Just as the uneasy feeling in the pit of his stomach grew into a hard knot, he heard what sounded like gunshots coming from the rear of the crowd.

Sketch yelled, "Hey!"

As TJ turned toward his deputy, Hop Li broke free, and charged down the steps screaming in Cantonese. A split second later, TJ's head exploded in pain. He felt himself stumble and couldn't stop himself from falling. His shoulder hit the ground hard, more pain, then the front of his head slammed into something solid, another bolt of pain. Then he felt nothing.

The next thing he knew, he felt a hand under his head and a voice, far off, saying something. He tried to lift his head but pain stopped him. After a second, he opened his eyes and saw only confused, blurred images. Something wet and sticky, blood he guessed, dripped into his left eye. In the distance he heard a sound, a roaring, that rose and fell like waves at the ocean shore. The sounds and pain disoriented him—he didn't know where he was.

He opened his good eye and a fuzzy image of Silas's face appeared. Silas's concerned voice came through now. "TJ! C'mon, wake up! TJ! You hear me?" Silas wiped blood from TJ's eye with his handkerchief.

TJ jerked his head away.

"Dammit, don't move," Silas said.

TJ opened both eyes and separate images of Silas' face merged into one.

"Wha...happen?"

"Don't talk. Put your hand here. Keep pressure on that." Silas put TJ's hand on the handkerchief and took his hand away.

"Somebody clobbered you and..." a yell followed by shouts came from the street.

"Help me up," TJ said. The pain in his head had lessened. Silas put an arm around his waist and helped him stand. TJ looked at the empty steps above him and asked, "Where's Sketch?"

"Didn't see him. I heard a helluva commotion behind me. Before I could turn around, the Chinaboy ran past me screaming like a banshee. The crazy bastard plowed straight into Kephardt. He couldn't possibly escape—what the hell was he thinking?"

"Any city police around?"

"I saw one—but he's just standing by watching the fight."

"Goddammit. Run over to the police station, tell them one of their men is gonna die."

Silas eyebrows shot up. "How the hell you know that?"

"'Cause I'm about to shoot one of the bastards. Now, get goin.'"

Silas hesitated.

"I'll be all right in a minute. Go on, man, run," TJ said.

Silas ran down the steps and called over his shoulder for TJ to stay put.

TJ moved his shoulders, arms, wrists and hands one at a time. Nothing broken. He took a step and didn't feel light-headed. More shouts came from a circle of men in the street. The buckboard wasn't in front of the courtroom and Big Jim was nowhere in sight. The knot in his stomach tightened and he wondered what had happened to his deputies. He made his way down the steps and into the street but couldn't push through the circle of yelling, excited men. He drew his Colt and fired a shot in the air.

"Sheriff, goddammit, lemme through."

He shoved and pushed his way through the circle, smelling whiskey when a man turned and cursed him. He reached the open space and saw Kephardt circling Hop Li who was turning so as to keep Kephardt in front of him. Hop Li bled from his mouth and his right eye was swollen shut.

Kephardt faked a charge, then lunged. Hop Li pulled his fists apart as far as his handcuffs allowed and put his arms up. Kephardt slipped his arms under Hop Li's armpits, locked his wrists behind Hop Li's back, and squeezed.

"Heathen shit!" Kephardt bellowed and lifted Hop Li off the ground.

Air burst from Hop Li's lungs but the Chinaman somehow managed to drive his head up and into Kephardt's face. Kephardt's head snapped back and blood spurted from his nose. The big man howled in pain. Hop Li pulled free for an instant. Kephardt recovered and slammed his fist into Hop Li's chest. Hop Li hit the ground with the back of his head. Kephardt dived on him and grabbed his throat.

TJ fired another shot into the air and shouted, "Kephardt! Get off."

Kephardt ignored the warning and kept his grip on Hop Li whose face was turning red. TJ moved closer to the men, looking for a shot that would not hit Hop Li or a spectator. Just then Big Jim burst through the circle, yelling "KEE -YAAA," locked his arms around Kephardt's neck, and shoved his knee into Kephardt's back. Kephardt reached up with both hands for the arms around his neck. Released from Kephardt's chokehold, Hop Li fell back, gasping and coughing.

As Kephardt pulled against Big Jim's hold, his head moved close to the Chinaboy's. Hop Li drove his head up into Kephardt's chin. An oomph escaped from Kephardt and his body relaxed. Big Jim rolled Kephardt off Hop Li and plunked his 275 pounds on Kephardt.

"Behind you!" TJ yelled.

Big Jim twisted part way and put an arm up. The axe handle caught him in the forearm and he toppled off Kephardt, clutching his arm.

"Like that, big mouth? Here's another!" The redhead yelled and raised the axe handle. TJ slammed the butt of his Colt into the man's temple before he could strike. The man dropped the axe handle and sagged to his knees. TJ shoved the man on the ground face down and planted his boot on the man's back. With the help of much cursing, Big Jim pulled Kephardt's arms behind his back and snapped the cuffs on with his uninjured arm. Big Jim got off Kephardt, grinning from ear to ear. He glanced over at TJ and shouted, "Behind you!"

TJ turned and saw men inching forward, closing the circle around them. TJ straddled the man on the ground and fired his gun in the air. Men froze, eyes fixed on him in anger and frustration. What right did the sheriff have to spoil their fun? They wouldn't have it, their faces said. TJ glanced around for a City policeman but saw none.

"Get over here, Jim," TJ said without taking his eyes off the men facing him.

TJ handed his cuffs to his big deputy and said, "Cuff this one."

The man jerked his hand away when Big Jim reached for it. Big Jim grabbed a handful of the man's red hair and yanked. "Move again and I'll tear your goddamm head off. Savvy?"

The man grunted and lay still. Big Jim cuffed him, dragged the man over to Kephardt, and draped him over Kephardt's back. Big Jim stood up with his back to TJ, faced the circle of men, and drew his Remington Army .44. TJ turned so that his back touched his deputy's. When he felt TJ behind him, Big Jim reached down with his injured left hand and eased a Barns pistol out his boot. The Barns held only one .50 caliber ball but the pistol looked like a small cannon in his hand. Big Jim whispered over his shoulder, "Probably miss a cow at ten foot if I hadda shoot with this bad arm. But don't expect them boys want to find out. What now, TJ?"

"Stare 'em down," TJ said and straightened his shoulders. He slowly looked over the circle of faces for the man most likely to challenge him. He settled on one of Kephardt's men, a tall fellow with a crooked mustache who tilted his head and smirked at TJ. TJ slowed his breathing and willed himself not to blink. After what seemed like five minutes but was only a few seconds, the man blinked. TJ trained his eyes on the skinny man next to him. This man not only blinked but lowered his eyes.

TJ moved with the deliberation of a snake going after a mouse. Big Jim turned as TJ did and, in this way, each only had half the circle to cover. After the first three men, others looked away as soon as TJ's eyes met theirs. TJ took a deep breath and said, "All right, boys, show's over. Go on about your business. Let's go. Nothin' left to see."

With their leader gone, the crowd had no focus and men's anger cooled. A voice in the rear swore at TJ while men on either side of the Kephardt's man drifted away. TJ's eyes came back to Kephardt's man. The fellow looked at TJ for a second, spit once, and then walked off.

Silas ran up to TJ with two City policemen in tow. TJ pointed to Kephardt and the man under him. "Take those two to jail. We'll see to Hop Li."

As the policemen picked up Kephardt, he fixed TJ with a black look. "Ya arresting me? What for? The heathen bastard started it." Blood flowed from Kephardt's nose and over his lips; the scar on his upper lip was a white gash in a field of red.

"Inciting a riot is one, interfering with a prisoner is two." TJ walked up to Kephardt and put his face close to his. "That'll do for a start—I'll come up with more 'what for's' later."

"Goddamm your hide. You're arrestin' a white man for defendin' hisself against a yellow. That's wrong, Stone, wrong as hell. I ain't gonna forget it."

"Well, I hope to hell you don't," TJ said and went over to Big Jim who sat on the ground massaging his forearm.

"How's the arm?"

"Feels broke." He looked at TJ and grinned. "But it ain't near as broke as your face." Big Jim chuckled then laughed full out, shoulders and belly shaking.

TJ smiled, started to laugh, and then grimaced in pain. Silas came up to TJ, looked at his face for a full second, and then just shook his head. "Here, you dropped this." Silas handed him the handkerchief he'd given him earlier, now soaked with blood. "And for Christ sakes, sit down. These bullyboys are through causing trouble. After I see to them, I'll send a runner to fetch Doc."

Hop Li sat up, coughing and spitting, and tried to clear his mouth of blood and dirt. A plum-sized mound of flesh surrounded his closed eye.

TJ went up to him. "Any bones broken?"

Hop Li rolled his shoulders, then flexed his feet and winced. "Foot no good."

TJ and Big Jim eased him up. Big Jim took out his bandanna and wiped blood from Hop Li's nose and mouth.

"Where is Blackbeard?" Hop Li mumbled through swollen lips.

"Who?" TJ asked.

"The dog-face I fight." He nodded towards the group heading to the jail.

"He's goin' to jail—he's done fightin' for some time."

"I hurt him? He bleed?"

"He's bleeding plenty. You did all right for being cuffed. But now, maybe you'd like to tell me why you jumped him. You didn't stand a chance—you know that, don't you?"

"No matter. In Seattle, Blackbeard cut off queue. So promise ancestor, I fight him. All time in jail, I pray warrior god, Guan Di, send Blackbeard Astoria. Today Guan Di answer. So today, my chance."

"Jesus, lucky for us he was cuffed, Boss," Big Jim said.

"Why?"

"Well, without them cuffs, could be he kills Kephardt. And then folks would get to thinkin' that Kephardt was right, ya know, hang 'em or ship 'em out. Tryin' to keep a lid on things then be like tryin' to put out a barn fire by pissin' on it."

"Point taken, Jim." TJ glanced up and down both sides of the street and saw a half dozen old timers standing around the now deserted Knights' table. Some boys and a sprinkling of men sat on the courthouse steps, waiting for something to happen, another showdown maybe. But the Knights were gone, the crisis over for the time being. But then he remembered Sketch. "Jim, you see anybody jump Sketch?"

"Nope. I'm waitin' in the buckboard when Silas and that city lawyer come out. Next, I seen you and Sketch come out with the Chinaboy. But then some damm fool throws a string of firecrackers under the buckboard and spooks the team—they run off like they's racehorses—like to never settle 'em down. By the time I get back all hell is breakin' loose—can't see you, Sketch, or the Chinaboy. But then I hear a shot and seen you headin' into the crowd. I figgered it's time to join the fun."

"Can't recall ever being so glad to see that ugly mug of yours." TJ started to laugh but grimaced in pain. "But you never saw Sketch again?"

"Nope."

"I heard him shout just before I got hit. Guess somebody got to him. Damm."

Half dragging, half carrying Hop Li, the lawmen shuffled to the buckboard now parked in front of the Chinese lottery. When the lawmen and their prisoner had taken but a few steps, a voice cried out, "Chinee butcher." A second later, another voice screamed, "Hang the heathen!"

35

TJ woke up the next morning with an aching head and a stiff back. Purple bruises covered half his face and the bandage wrapped around his head left a stiff patch of hair sticking up. He looked in the mirror and saw something resembling an overripe pineapple. He washed, shaved and tried to hide the bandage by pulling his hat down but even resting his hat on his head hurt. He decided to go hatless until his wounds healed.

Yesterday, when Doc came to the courthouse to look after him, he said that one of the Knights' toughs had clobbered Sketch and pushed him off the landing. Sketch broke his right tibia just above the ankle in the fall. Two city police had carried Sketch a block to firehouse number two and then one ran to St. Mary's and brought Doc back. Sketch's leg would be in a cast for ten to twelve weeks.

"I'll tell you what I told Sketch," Doc said as he peered over his glasses. "Take three days off and do a lot of nothing the following week. And that's an order, my friend."

But TJ couldn't afford a day off—Hop Li went on trial in thirteen days.

After breakfast, he paused on the front porch of his boardinghouse to take in the day. The cool morning air brushed over his bare head and he shivered. Without his hat, he didn't feel fully dressed, felt exposed and vulnerable.

On his walk through Swilltown, he passed a man here and there who'd been part of the mob in the street yesterday but not a one looked him in the eye. But he'd proved himself—kept a mob from killing his prisoner and had jailed Kephardt. He'd shown one and all that Astoria didn't need vigilantes.

But the brawl had sidetracked the investigation and he needed to get back to it. He found Sketch on the porch of his boardinghouse, broken leg resting on a chair, a drawing pad in his lap.

"Mornin,' Sketch. How you feelin'?"

"Left wrist is achin' some, can't chew food proper, got an itch I can't scratch, and the goddamm cast makes walkin' a chore. Otherwise, can't complain."

TJ stepped onto the porch and Sketch whistled. "Damm, you look worse than me, Boss. How'd you get so banged up anyways?"

"Another time, Sketch. You recall any rings Jameson wears?"

"Nope." He put his drawing pad aside and asked, "You thinkin' Jameson is our killer?"

"Don't know yet. What I do know is that the bastard's been lyin' to us from day one." TJ handed Sketch an El Gusto. "I gave Big Jim the office 'til I get back. Can you take a spell at the jail and relieve Lucky?"

"Yep. As long as I don't hafta chase any bad men, I'll get by. Where you off to?"

I'm goin' over to Jameson's, see if I can't scare some truth out of the weasel."

TJ walked the mile and a half to Jameson's in a little over forty minutes. He reached the cannery at the start of the mid-morning tea break and waded through a crowd of Chinese workers, silent and sullen after their stint on the butchering line. Three workers passed him wearing oilskin aprons and cotton gloves, smeared with fish scales, blood, and mucous. In their rubber boots, they took the short, stiff-legged steps of slimers, the wettest and messiest job in the cannery.

He found Brady on the first floor and learned that Jameson had gone to the Occident Hotel for a haircut and breakfast. He'd worked himself into a righteous ill temper by the time he reached the Occident, a hotel he never liked. The thick, red carpet in the lobby wasn't made to be walked on, especially with muddy boots, and he felt like an intruder. He walked down the lobby past the Occident's saloon and noted the brass cuspidors polished to a soft, shiny glow. *It'd take a man mighty high on himself to spit in one. If I were a drinkin' man, I wouldn't step foot in that saloon—it isn't a place I could let go of the day.*

He paused at the entrance to the cavernous dining room and the headwaiter ran out from behind his stand and up to him. "Sheriff? What can I do for you?" His tone held a dose of surprise along with a helping of irritation.

"I'm looking for someone...ah, there he is." TJ pushed the headwaiter aside and weaved around several tables to Jameson's.

"Mornin,' Jameson." TJ pulled out a chair and sat down.

Jameson oozed vitality and success with his ruddy cheeks, just-trimmed silver hair and Van Dyke beard. In contrast, TJ presented an image of a man down on his luck with his bandage, bruised face, and tangle of uncombed hair. Jameson looked up from his paper and froze.

"Stone…what the hell…you look like shit! That fight at the courthouse must have been a doozie! You want breakfast? I'm having the cattleman's special—fruit bowl, pork chop, sausages, eggs, potatoes, biscuits and jam." He raised his hand for the waiter.

A waiter came over and TJ ordered coffee. "I've got some questions but go on and finish your breakfast."

As the cannery boss ate, TJ noticed a pinky ring on his right hand. The ring had a large diamond in the center of a gold band with a small diamond on either side. But he saw no other rings.

"Thought you had some questions," Jameson said as he cut into his pork chop.

"Sorry. My mind's wandering."

"Uh-huh. Kephardt do that?" He pointed his fork at TJ's head.

"One of his boys. But we jailed him."

"Congratulations. What about the rest of those pricks?"

"We jailed another fella, too."

"That bilge The Star wrote has already cost me an order, Stone. The Jameson label is poison for the rest of the season. I'll have to use another company's label just to keep my losses down. So I want every last one of those bastards jailed."

"That'd suit me fine." TJ waited for Jameson to swallow his food then said. "We got news on the murders."

Jameson ignored him. "Too bad about the Chinaboy—one of my best butchers, too. But if that boy is hung soon, the anti-Chinee crowd will settle down. Can't wait to put this behind me."

"There's a problem with your thinkin.' The Chinaboy isn't guilty."

Jameson's fork stopped in mid air and he frowned. "What the hell are you saying? I heard he tried to escape—he's guilty as sin."

"The facts say different."

"What facts? He had the dagger that killed the girl—at his work table, for Christsake."

"So he did. But now stop and think a minute. You're sayin' the Chinaboy is gonna wave that dagger around and show off the murder weapon? That sound smart to you? Hop Li's ornery as hell but he's not stupid."

"Dammit, Stone, what about the money? The paper said the day after the murders he bought a meal for himself and his sidekick—paid with a $2.50 gold piece. Payday at my cannery is two weeks away. Where'd he get that gold piece?"

TJ paused before he said, "Whoever killed Jane and Fong wasn't after money."

"How the hell you know that?

"By what the killer left behind. Fong had over two hundred dollars in opium in his safe. Any Chinee would take that."

"Maybe he didn't know what it was…maybe…"

"The killer also left three jewels behind. Had to be worth a hundred dollars, easy. Robbery wasn't the motive."

Jameson didn't speak and drank half the water in his glass. He set the glass down and looked up, his face pale. "So tell me, Stone, why was she killed?"

"Well, let's look at some other facts. The girl's hands end up in your cannery, that's one. Fong's dagger ends up with your Chinaboy, that's two. Those Chinese scabs showed up at your cannery—and only your cannery—that's three. Sounds to me like somebody has a score to settle with you, a somebody with clout, too. Any idea who?" TJ cocked an eyebrow at Jameson.

"Shit, it's all coincidence…wait a minute…what about that Chinee writing on my tank? That points to Chinee killer, it has to." Jameson smirked.

"Well, I don't know who wrote that but do you recall the meanin'?"

"No. But does it matter?"

"It matters. The writing means, death settles all debts. The meaning is clear whether it's in English or Chinee—revenge."

"So? Couldn't the Chinaboy be out for revenge?" Jameson crumpled up his napkin and threw it on his plate, still with a sizable portion of food on it.

"Who is Hop Li suppose to be gettin' even with? You? Why? Nope, makes no sense. I'd bet a month's pay he didn't kill anybody and didn't write that Chinee message either. See, everybody's got a way of doin' things, a style you could say, and all that sneakin' around and leavin' messages, well, it's not Hop Li's style." TJ paused and glanced at his empty cup. "This coffee's better than jailhouse—I'll have a refill, if you don't mind." He waved the waiter over and asked for more coffee for both of them.

TJ took out his cigar case and offered Jameson one of his El Gustos. Jameson absent-mindedly took the cigar and bit off the end. TJ lit Jameson's cigar then his own and watched the waiter refill their cups and place a marble ashtray in the center of the table.

"Well, if my Chinaboy didn't do it, who did? Let's stop playing games, Stone."

"How about you stop lyin'?" TJ blew a stream of smoke at the ceiling.

"Huh? You calling me a liar? Goddammit, that's it—I'm leaving." Jameson pushed his chair back.

TJ waited until Jameson stood before he said, "We can do this here or at my office. Your call."

Jameson slipped back into his chair. "I've told you everything I know."

"Uh-huh. Did you know Jane Thurgood kept a diary?"

Jameson picked up his water glass and took a sip. "How the hell am I suppose to know that? Besides, what's that got to do with anything?"

TJ's eyes hardened and he paused before he spoke, "Cause you're in there, Bertie. The Thurgood girl was spyin' for you, spyin' on Purcell."

Jameson's face blanched and he ran his hand through his hair. "A diary...shit...she kept a goddamm diary. Horseshit." He let his breath out in a long sigh. "I should have guessed—her and her goddamm play acting."

TJ watched a column of smoke drift over the table. "All right, let's hear it. I want the whole story." TJ took out his notebook and pencil.

"Listen Stone, I did some things...all right...I admit it...but I didn't kill the little minx. You've got to believe that."

"I don't have to believe a damm thing." TJ took notes and then said, "But keep talkin.'"

"All right, all right, I admit it. She worked for me, sent me a report every week on Purcell's doings. That bastard is full of tricks. He shipped bums up here from California to vote for him. Gave them a dollar, a shot of whiskey, and then sent them packing the next day. But Jane helped me stay a step ahead of him. I knew every politician he'd bought in Salem and what their price was."

"She your mistress?"

"That's none of your damm business, Stone."

"Like hell. She was with child. She tell you that?"

"Wha...no. I don't believe you. Anyway, it wasn't mine."

"Well, I'm bettin' that if you're the father, she'd ask you to do the right thing and marry her. That what she did?"

"I'm a married man, Stone. I told her I wouldn't marry her and she knew that from the start."

"But maybe she told you about the baby and said you were the father. Be nothin' but trouble for Jameson and company if Jane told, eh?" TJ winked at him. "Hell, The Star would feed on that for two weeks and the papers in Portland would keep it goin' for another two. Hiring your mistress to spy on the man you're runnin' against. Yep. That's a stack of sins to own up to, even for a politician. Seems to me Purcell would win in a walk. What's your take on it?"

"For the last time—she never said she was with child. I never suspected it for a minute."

TJ wrote in his notebook then turned to a fresh page. "Where were you Saturday night, the third of April?"

"Jesus, Stone, you're not listening—I didn't kill her! I'm telling the truth."

"Well, that'd be a change to the good. But I still need an answer to my question."

Jameson picked up his cigar but then put it back without smoking it. "The third, let's see, that'd be the first Saturday of the month, ah, yes, that'd be our poker night."

"Was the game at your house?"

"No. Ed Martin's place. He runs the St. Louis brewery."

"Where's he live, this Ed Martin?"

"Why? What do you want to bother him for?"

"I don't aim to bother him. I want to ask him if you were at the game. Now, what's his address?"

Jameson said nothing for a time, picked up the cigar, and once again put it back without smoking it. "All right, Stone, all right. But you've got to promise you won't breathe a word of this to anybody. Will you do that?"

"I'm not promisin' you a damm thing. Now, I got things to do. Let's hear it."

"I was with someone—a woman."

"A sporting girl? You're sayin' you were at a whorehouse the night of the murders?"

"Goddammit, no, that's not what I'm saying. This woman is...well...she's a decent woman...but...see...um...she's married and...hell, that's it. No more. That's all I'm saying on the subject." Jameson pressed his lips together and scowled.

"Let's see. First, you don't bother to tell me Jane is your mistress and that she spied for you, then you lie about being at a poker game, now you're askin' me to believe you were with a married woman the night of the murders. Sure." TJ closed an eye and puffed on his cigar. "I've got to know who she is, this married woman."

"No, I can't say. I...she'd be ruined...no...make of it what you will, Stone, but I won't name her."

TJ nodded, took more notes. "You diggin' yourself a deep hole, Jameson. I'll find out what's true sooner or later and if you're lyin,' I'll come down on you faster than a seal on a Chinook."

"Are we finished?" Jameson picked up the bill, pushed his chair back, and rose part way.

"No we're not. Sit down. Jane's dad said she liked jewelry. That true?"

Jameson sat down and spent some time re-lighting his cigar before answering. "Jewelry? My God, but she loved it—necklace, brooch, earrings, rings—didn't matter as long as it glittered. She play acted a role, Lillie Langtry the actress, and needed the jewelry as part of her costume. Even when we…well…when she undressed she kept her jewelry on, even that goddamm pearl necklace. And I had to play a part too. She called me Bertie for some reason I never knew. And I had to call her Lillie when we were alone. If I forgot, she'd get furious. I laughed and teased her the first time I forgot. She threw a tantrum and walked out on me. From then on, if I called her Jane instead of Lillie, I apologized right away. God, she could be infuriating. She loved acting the grand lady—ordering me around—and I liked it, at first, I won't deny that. Later, something changed, she became…I don't know…strange. She became less and less Jane and more and more the Langtry woman. I had to end it—the affair was getting dangerous."

"You ever give her jewelry, real jewels I mean?"

"Hell no. Why should I? She couldn't tell the difference between real and fake jewelry. No sense wasting good money, right?"

TJ finished writing and looked up, puzzled. "Did you pay her to spy?" He thought Jameson must have felt something for her but, as far as he could tell, Jameson treated her as one of his clerks.

"In the beginning I took her out to dinner and to the theater. But that wasn't wise so I stopped. I mailed her tickets to a play or a cheap trinket from then on. But as far as a regular pay, no, nothing like that."

TJ paused in his note taking. "I don't get it. Why'd she spy for you?" TJ folded his arms across his chest to keep from smacking Jameson in the mouth.

"She liked the intrigue, being in on things, just as I suppose the Langtry woman does. And I think she still liked me. She kept asking to see me after she started working for Purcell. But I'd learned my lesson. Sooner or later she'd cause a scandal. She'd be the talk of the town and glory in it. My God, but she craved attention! So I told her the affair was over. I'm close to beating Purcell—can't risk a scandal."

"Guess you were a mite late cutting her loose, eh?" TJ smiled. "She planned to marry a fella called Ned. You know who that is?"

"Ned? No. Could be anybody. Why'd she want to marry him?"

"All part of her plan to live like Lillie Langtry. Ned's rich, like yourself. So she marries him and keeps a rich lover on the side—that'd be you."

"Christ, what a schemer! But I was done with her, the romance part anyway. Jane married—I'll be dammed!"

TJ filled out another page and closed his notebook. But then something struck him. Jane was an asset to Jameson only as long as her spying remained secret. On the last page of her diary, Jane said she planned to quit spying for Jameson as soon as she married Ned. What if Jameson discovered her plans? If he did, he might kill her to keep her quiet.

But Purcell wasn't off the hook either. All the dirty tricks played on Jameson suggested someone had a score to settle. If Purcell discovered Jane's spying, he'd be looking to get back at Jameson and Jane. Killing her and ruining him would be sweet revenge. It was time to pay Purcell a visit.

36

Gusts of wind tossed bits of paper into the air as TJ and Sketch stepped off the Oregon's gangplank at the Stark Street dock in Portland. TJ pulled up the collar of his slicker and watched his deputy's stiff-legged walk and slow progress with concern.

"How far is it?" Sketch held on to his hat to keep the wind from taking it.

"About seven blocks."

"I'm slowin' ya down, Boss. How about we take a hack?"

"Can't, Sketch. The Commissioners thought I short-changed them by bringin' along a deputy with a bad leg so our allowance only covers one and a half men."

"How'd you sell 'em on half a man?" Sketch leaned into the wind.

"Told them I only needed your hands, not your legs. They grumped some but pungled up in the end."

They reached the Ainsworth bank building and the upstairs office of Purcell and Chambers before noon. The secretary, a narrow-faced, middle-aged woman, studied the two bandaged men and then slowly pulled her glasses down over her long nose.

"Yes—s—ss?" she said through tight lips.

The typewriter on the desk across from hers was covered and a dozen or so cards with black borders lay in a silver tray next to Jane Thurgood's nameplate.

"How do, Miss. I'm Sheriff Stone and this is my deputy. We're here to see Mr. Purcell." TJ took his hat off.

"Oh yes. We received your telegram, Sheriff, but I'm afraid Mr. Purcell isn't in. You didn't give us much notice." She put her hands in her lap and studied TJ. A wood banister separated the lawmen from the secretaries' space.

"How about the other fella, Mr. Chambers, he in?"

"Mr. Chambers keeps his own schedule—I don't expect him today." She pushed her glasses up and turned the platen in her typewriter. "If you wish, you may wait over there." She pointed to a skinny-legged settee that didn't look as if it'd support the weight of two children. A hat-stand with a rack of deer antlers for pegs stood against a back wall between the two secretarial stations. The hat-stand looked top heavy and TJ thought it'd topple over if it held more than three hats. The delicate settee, the antlered hat stand, and the Persian runner in front of the banister didn't go together, even to TJ's eyes. The rich furnishings were there, he suspected, to tell one and all that these boys knew how to win.

TJ leaned over the banister and looked at a photograph hanging on the wall above the secretary's desk. It showed two men dressed in top hats and tails shaking hands.

"That one on the left is Purcell—the other man Chambers?" He asked.

"Good heavens no." She shook her head and frowned. "That other gentleman is our former president, Chester Arthur."

TJ nodded and read the secretary's nameplate, Elizabeth L. Cramer. The woman in front of him struck him as efficient and organized like a lady in an advert for a secretarial school.

"You look like a person the bosses can trust, Miss Cramer. Keep a close eye on things, do you?" TJ smiled at her.

"It's Mrs. Cramer, Sheriff. Well, you have to, don't you? Some people who come to us...well...you can't imagine. We get all types in here..." Her eyes landed on Sketch who had an inch of thumb up his left nostril, "all types."

"What can you tell me about Miss Thurgood?"

"She wasn't here long, poor child. A pretty girl and capable, even if she didn't always...well, never mind." She played with a strand of hair that hung down from her upswept hair do.

"Yeah. Think I know what you mean. A few always have to do more than their share. But someone has to be responsible."

"You are so right about that, Sheriff. Jane...Miss Thurgood that is... was never late and I must say that out here, with me, she worked just fine. It's just that...well...she spent way too much time back there, in the offices. I spent less than half the time she did when I took dictation." Mrs. Cramer pushed her chair away from her desk and brushed lint from her black skirt. She looked over at the empty desk across from her. "She was new, I grant you, and perhaps didn't know better. Even so, it wasn't professional. Didn't look right, if you know what I mean." Her lips squeezed into a thin line.

"I do." He lowered his voice. "You think something went on back there." TJ nodded to one side then the other.

She lowered her voice to match TJ's. "Sometimes supervisors, well, they're men, aren't they? Some women in my position, in a secretarial position I mean, have had their trust betrayed. I know that for a fact, Sheriff."

"Either one…ever…with you?"

"Good heavens no! The idea!" Her cheeks reddened, she coughed and couldn't stop for a time. When she recovered she said, "I'd soon put such a scoundrel in his place. Make no mistake about that." She lowered her glasses, went over to the water cooler, and drank a cup of water. She returned to her chair, sat down, and adjusted her skirt.

"You are a true professional, Mrs. Cramer."

"Mind you, Sheriff, I've never had a problem with those gentlemen. Why there's a fresh flower on my desk every morning, all year long! No, I couldn't have two nicer gentlemen to work for." She pushed her glasses up again.

"To get back to Miss Thurgood. You ever ask her about the extra time she spent with them?"

"Well, I did broach the subject a few times. She said they just liked to talk, wanted somebody to listen to their ideas. She was intelligent, Sheriff, even if she was…well… overly ambitious."

"So then you don't think anything improper went on?"

"Well, no. I don't believe those gentlemen would encourage her attentions. I'm not saying she…but you know…they wouldn't stand for such shenanigans."

"You're a keen observer of human nature, Mrs. Cramer."

"Well, one has to be in this office, doesn't one?" She smiled at him and he smiled back.

As if by afterthought, he asked, "Maybe you can help us out in another matter. From what people tell us, Miss Thurgood loved jewelry. I wondered if she wore her jewelry at work."

"Oh, she wore gloves like a respectable woman to and from work but as soon as she came in she took them off and put all those rings on. I got after her that first day—said it gave the wrong impression for someone in her position to be putting on airs. I told Mr. Purcell about it but he just laughed, said as long as it didn't interfere with her work to let her wear them."

"Do you know what a sweetheart ring is Mrs. Cramer?"

"I do indeed. Mr. Purcell has one—he's quite proud of it and showed me how to read it. His ring spells out the word, DEAREST. Mrs. Purcell—her family is related to the Hill's you know—gave him that ring on their first anniversary. It's so romantic, don't you think?"

"Did Miss Thurgood wear one?"

"Oh, my gracious no! She wasn't married or engaged so she had no reason to wear one. Besides they're expensive and Miss Thurgood's taste ran to the…the more common accessories."

"Thanks, Mrs. Cramer. You notice details. I can see why Mr. Purcell puts so much trust in you." TJ had difficulty keeping the excitement out of his voice. Purcell couldn't dance around the sweetheart ring and its missing jewels. Jane didn't own a sweetheart ring and Jameson hadn't worn one when TJ questioned him. He paced back and forth along side the banister. Sketch's chin now rested on his chest.

By god, it can't be this easy, can it? Doc's always sayin' to count to ten after making a good move 'cause a fella gets so all-fired pleased with himself he can't see the snake sitting front of him. All right Doc, I'll try it. What's wrong with my thinking? He stopped pacing and sat down next to Sketch who hadn't moved. How many men wear a sweetheart ring? There's a lot of money in Portland, he realized, and there'd be four or five rich men's clubs full of men who could afford one. And so what if Purcell wears a sweetheart ring? Does it have to be the same one as the one in the crime? And if Purcell were the killer and the gems fell out of his ring, he'd notice it the next day. He wouldn't wear the ring but would he dump it? His wife would ask him why he wasn't wearing it. If Purcell were the killer, he'd get the jewels replaced and fast. He wouldn't go to his usual jeweler either. TJ wondered how many jewelry stores were in Portland. A dozen at least and no more than twenty. *That's better*, he told himself, *you're thinking now*.

"Any idea when Mr. Purcell is gettin' back?" he asked.

"Oh, I couldn't say. But you're welcome to wait for him." She smiled as if granting a favor.

37

Saturday, April 17

Paul Purcell breezed into the office as TJ finished his fourth issue of Leslie's Illustrated Weekly.

"Afternoon, gents," Purcell said and dropped his walking stick into an umbrella stand made from an elephant's foot. He looked like a carnival barker in his three-piece beige suit with dark brown stripes, cream colored tie, and red carnation boutonnière. After going through the banister gate, he tossed his derby at the hat rack and it caught on an antler. He bowed as if expecting applause. Purcell was an actor staging an entrance, filling the room with his clothes, antics, and presence.

"The meeting with the mayor and his crew lasted forever. What's first on the docket?"

"These two officers to see you…from Astoria. Remember?"

"Ah, yes. Sheriff Stone." Purcell reached his hand over the banister and TJ felt a large ring as they shook hands. As Purcell withdrew his hand, TJ looked down and saw a gold ring with the raised letters PP set in a black background of onyx on the first finger. On the fourth finger of his left hand he wore what looked like a sweetheart ring but from his quick glance, TJ couldn't tell if any jewels were missing.

Purcell's corner office featured eight high-backed chairs with velvet seats tucked around a heavy mahogany conference table. His desk stood at the far end of the room, its only furnishings a white marble pen set, a cedar humidor, and a brass ashtray. The wall on TJ's left was lined with shelves holding law books. The large windows on the opposite wall looked down on Oak Street. Purcell stood behind a high-backed swivel chair and pointed the lawmen to two ornate, delicate looking chairs in front of his desk. While the chairs were fit for a king's parlor, they were not made for comfort.

"I'm fixing a brandy. Looks to me as if you boys could use one," Purcell said.

"No. But thanks all the same," TJ said. TJ and Sketch exchanged glances then Sketch shook his head and said, "No thanks, Sir. I'm off liquor." Sketch fumbled in his coat pocket, pulled out a package of tobacco, and shoved a pinch in his mouth.

Purcell shrugged and turned to the liquor cabinet behind his desk. The liquor bottles inside the cabinet, an oak bookcase with leaded glass doors, were neatly arranged with the labels facing front. The decanter and wine glasses sparkled. TJ looked over the room at the shelves of law books, the dust-free surface of the conference table, and the framed photograph hanging on the wall behind the desk. This photograph, the only one in the office, showed a young Purcell with a prim-faced woman in a traditional studio portrait; Purcell sat while the woman stood to the side of him with her hand resting on his shoulder. To TJ, everything seemed too arranged, too neat; the office a stage rather than a workplace.

Purcell poured two fingers of brandy into a large glass. He held the glass under his nose, inhaled, and then raised his glass to them. "Hope the other boys in the fight look as bad as you two. To your health gentlemen." He sipped his brandy.

"The other boys are in jail where they belong." TJ's eyes locked onto Purcell's.

"Ah, well then, here's to law and order, Sheriff." He took another sip, walked back to his desk, and sat down. "Now then, what can I do for you?"

Hop Li's description of the sea captain had been of a large man with a full beard, no glasses, and wearing a slicker and beaked cap. Purcell came closer than Jameson to fitting that description and, in spite of some differences in beard and facial features between Purcell and Hop Li's sea captain, TJ wondered if Purcell might be the captain. TJ needed a likeness of Purcell to show to Hop Li but couldn't ask either Purcell or Mrs. Cramer for Purcell's photograph. So TJ had asked Sketch to draw Purcell's face while TJ questioned the man. It came down to Sketch and his skill in capturing a man's look with a few lines. But Sketch had to do it without Purcell's knowledge.

"We're tryin' to clear up a few things about the Thurgood murder," TJ said.

"Thought you arrested a Chinaboy—it was in all the papers."

"We did but the facts point otherwise—to a white man, most likely the fella Jane met the night she was murdered," TJ spoke slowly—he wanted Purcell to feel each word.

"I'm not sure how I can help you. By the way, why is your deputy taking notes?" Purcell's eyes narrowed.

"Oh, when there's two of us, it's easier if one takes notes while the other talks. You mind?"

Purcell took another sip and sat back. "So I'm a suspect, am I? Maybe I should get myself a lawyer, eh?" He smiled, lifted his glass to Sketch, and then said, "I've nothing to hide. Go ahead and take all the notes you want, Deputy."

TJ supposed that Purcell thought him, a country sheriff, in over his head, which suited TJ fine. TJ had watched Purcell's hand as he drank his brandy and noticed that no jewels were missing from what did turn out to be a sweetheart ring. He couldn't ask Purcell about his ring but didn't need to. TJ would find the jeweler who'd replaced the gems sooner or later. What else? Jameson hadn't known about the diary—maybe Purcell didn't either.

"Did Jane ever talk to you about Ambrose Jameson?"

Purcell put his brandy down and sat up. "Jameson? No, why should she? She knew he and I are running against each other. That's all. Why do you ask?"

"Well, 'cause she spied for him, sent him a report of your doings every week." TJ wanted to take notes but had dug a hole for himself by assigning the note taker job to Sketch. He hoped Sketch would remember the important points and maybe think to write them down.

Purcell's thumbs traced tight circles on the arms of his chair. "Spying on me—for that prick? Are you sure? What would possess her to do a thing like that?"

"Jameson 'fessed up, said they had an affair. From what I found out, I'd say she still loved him and would do whatever he asked. The rogue is old enough to be her father but guess she didn't mind."

"How do you know all this, Stone?"

"It's in her diary."

"Her WHAT?" He removed his oval glasses and leaned over his desk. The veins in his neck stuck out and his face grew pink. His bushy eyebrows, the dark mole on his cheek, his protruding lower jaw, all set off by his mutton chop beard gave him a menacing look.

"You heard right. A diary. She had a way with words, too. Makes for interestin' readin.'"

"Does it? Well, don't keep me in suspense. What does she say?" Purcell clutched the arms of his chair in what looked like a struggle to control his temper.

"The afternoon she went missin,' she set out to meet a fella, a fella she planned to tell she was with child. She expected him to divorce his wife and marry her. You find any of this interestin'?"

"Why should I? None of it has anything to do with me."

"Oh, I think it does. Both you and Jameson had reason to want Jane dead."

"Really? And what's my reason, if you don't mind letting me in on your thinking."

"Well, suppose you found out she was spyin' on you, giving Jameson an edge in the election, could be you killed her to put an end to her spyin.' Plus with the election comin' up you couldn't afford a scandal, so you had to make sure she didn't tell anyone what she knew." TJ cocked his head to one side and looked at Purcell. "That's the first reason."

"There's another? And what might that be?" Purcell's voice had steadied but his hands still squeezed the arms of his chair.

"Well, suppose, for argument's sake, you're the fella she met up with. And suppose she says the baby is yours and asks you to marry her. Maybe you tell her no dice. But Jane's a smart girl—always thinkin' ahead. So she says she knows things about you the newspapers would find interestin.' She'll tell all unless you marry her so you kill her and shut her mouth for good. That how it went?" TJ leaned back as far as the chair let him and crossed his legs at the ankles.

"It's all rubbish! Nothing but wild conjecture." Purcell pushed back his chair, rose, and went to his liquor cabinet. He added another finger of brandy to the portion in his glass, swirled the liquor around, sniffed, and then took a sip. He sat down, held his glass up, stared at the brandy, and smiled when he said, "You're not lacking imagination, Stone, I'll give you that." He shook his head from side to side. "But let's look at your thinking. First, you say she loved Jameson so doesn't it make sense that he is the father, not me? Second, I only just learned that Jane spied on me. How can this be a motive to kill her when I didn't know about it until now?" He looked up at the ceiling.

"I only got your word on that."

"Well, I guess you'll just have to accept my word as a gentleman." He smiled and took a sip of brandy. "And I didn't know she was expecting until you told me—on the dock in Astoria, five days after her murder. Now, if I didn't know about her spying or her pregnancy until after her murder, I had no motive to kill her. You agree?" He put his brandy down and folded his hands across his stomach.

"Can't say as I do. I got nothin' to back up your word." TJ wanted to reach across the desk, grab Purcell by the collar, and slap the smile off his face. He couldn't prove when Purcell knew of Jane's spying or pregnancy. Except for the outburst over the diary, the man seemed unruffled by TJ's questions. Why? What made the son of a bitch so cocky?

TJ decided on a different tack. "Let's talk about Jane's last week. Did she say why she wanted to go to Astoria?"

"She wanted to help with Annika's wedding plans."

"Did she happen to mention a fella named Ned before she left?"

"Ned? Ned who? I know several Ned's."

"Ned is all I got."

"Well, it doesn't matter. She never said anything about meeting Ned or any other boyfriend—at least to me." Purcell's smile was friendly.

"Maybe she said something to Mrs. Cramer?"

Purcell's eyes lit up and he chuckled. "Could be. But I don't believe those two shared confidences."

"When did she leave for Astoria?"

"She worked 'til noon that Friday, so she must have left that afternoon. Ask Mrs. Cramer if you really need to know." Purcell's face radiated good will.

"She say anything else about her plans Friday morning?" TJ asked.

"I didn't come in Friday so I didn't see her that day."

"Why didn't you come in?"

"I had business elsewhere." Purcell yawned.

"Where?"

"Tacoma. Railroad business. Didn't get back 'til Sunday night." Purcell swiveled from side to side in his chair.

"You happen to have your railroad ticket?"

"No, didn't keep it." He shook his head and smiled again. "Didn't know I'd need it."

"Can anybody vouch for you being in Tacoma?" TJ glanced at his deputy. Sketch stared over Purcell's head and idly twisted a pencil through his fingers.

"Stone, I hope you're looking at Jameson as hard as you're looking at me—I hate to think I'm the only one you're picking on." Purcell's smile froze and he held TJ's eyes for an instant before the confident lawyer face returned. But in that one instant, TJ felt hostility and challenge. That challenge told TJ he'd struck a nerve and the adrenaline flowed in him. He took a deep breath to steady his voice.

"I'm not partial—Jameson's got to account for his whereabouts, too. Now, can anybody vouch for you or not?"

"Oh, all right. Here, I'll make it easy for you." He opened a desk drawer and shuffled through a stack of business cards, pulled out one, and handed it to TJ. "Leyland Sundstrom. Good railroad man but all work. A dull weekend, I'm afraid."

TJ stuck the card in his vest pocket.

"Well, what's the verdict, Stone, am I off the hook?" Purcell beamed at both TJ and Sketch.

"For now," TJ said.

Purcell took a sip of brandy and then stood up. "Now, boys, I have some last minute fiddling to do on a talk and...say...would you two like to come? I'm speaking on the Chinese question tonight at the Elks club. You might learn a thing or two, Stone."

"Maybe another time," TJ said.

Sketch stood up suddenly and said, "Boss, me and some friends got to arguin' about that there Chinee question last week. They showed me up but good. Figger I could use some educatin.' Maybe we oughta go."

TJ couldn't remember a time when Sketch had shown the least interest in the Chinese question.

"Ah, there you see, Stone! Your deputy is a wise man. Besides the chicken dinner is on the house and I won't talk more than twenty minutes." Purcell smiled, any trace of hard feelings from TJ's questioning gone from his face and voice.

"Well, we got to eat sometime and could be we'll learn somethin.' All right, we'll take you up on the offer."

Purcell found two tickets in his top desk drawer and gave them to TJ. "All I ask is you listen with an open mind." Purcell offered his hand to shake, holding it high and close to his body. The two men locked hands and Purcell pushed down and away with energy, confident of victory. TJ held firm, didn't give an inch.

38

The steamboat A.B. Field left Portland before dawn in a steady rain but by the time the steamer rounded Tongue Point and blew for the landing, the rain had stopped and patches of blue sky showed around the clouds. Sketch sprawled on a bench, sound asleep, while TJ thought about Purcell's talk the night before. Purcell never shouted and stomped around as Kephardt had but the hate came through all the same. The Chinese could never assimilate, Purcell claimed, never become Americans. Purcell, a rich man, spoke to an audience of other rich men and yet no one but TJ laughed when Purcell claimed to be the 'champion of the workingman.' TJ didn't know if the audience believed the claptrap Purcell spewed but, whatever they believed, they cheered and applauded Purcell for three minutes when he finished.

TJ was glad he'd let Sketch talk him into going to the dinner. After they'd left Purcell's office, Sketch said that he had started to draw during the meeting but then worried that the movement of his hand, so different from the way a hand moves in writing, would attract Purcell's attention. So he took notes for the rest of the interview. TJ congratulated him for thinking like a lawman.

At the dinner, Sketch had drawn Purcell in various poses without fear of being detected. Sketch also drew the mayor, a wide-faced man with a long, pointy-tipped nose and full beard, and the president of the Elks Club who introduced Purcell. Sketch ended up with a dozen pages of busts of the three men. TJ picked up the pad of Sketch's drawings and flipped through them and, once again, admired his deputy's skill at capturing the look of a man.

TJ and Sketch went straight to the jail after the steamer docked in Astoria.

"Boss! Didn't expect ya back so soon. How'd things go?" Lucky kept his face turned to one side but the ruse didn't hide the whiskey on his breath.

"Things worked out all right. Any trouble from Kephardt?"

"Well, he needs him a room with thick walls or maybe a jailkeep who's deef. Damm near drove me crazy with his jabber."

"Un-huh. Is Hop Li takin' food now?"

"Well yeah, he's eatin' all right." Lucky scratched his nose and looked at the desk.

"But?" TJ hung his hat up on a peg.

"That there China doc visits ever day. The two of them git to movin' round like they's stuck in molasses, wavin' their arms over their head, stickin' one leg up in the air, and I don't know what all. Exercisin',' the China doc says, when I asks 'bout it. But it don't look like no exercisin' I ever seen." Lucky took a sip of coffee and wiped his mouth with the back of his hand.

"Sounds like there's no harm in it."

"One good thing—the Chinaboy ain't near ornery as was."

Sketch took the keys and opened the heavy timbered door into the cells. Hop Li sat on a stool, a writing brush in hand and his notebook in his lap as the lawmen approached.

"Ah, Sheriff TJ, Sketch. You have news?" He closed his notebook and laid the writing brush on a scrap of toweling. He rose and bowed.

Sketch unlocked the cell door and the lawmen stepped inside. "Mornin,' Hop Li. Move some of your things, will you? We've got something to show you." TJ said.

Hop Li emptied the ink stone into the privy and then wrapped his writing brush in the piece of towel and put it and the ink stone into his cigar box. He slipped a rubber band around the cigar box, slid it and his notebook under his bunk, and then tightened the blanket on his bunk.

Sketch tore a drawing of each man from his sketchpad and placed the drawings on the blanket with Purcell at one end.

"Sketch drew these men in Portland. Do you know any of them? TJ asked.

Hop Li leaned over his bunk and stared at the three faces. He hesitated over Purcell's drawing before moving on to the President of the Elks Club and then to the Mayor. He looked back and forth between the drawings for a time before straightening up.

"Maybe see this man—some place. Who is, please?" He pointed to the drawing of Purcell.

" I hoped you'd tell me," TJ said.

Hop Li looked back and forth between TJ and Sketch, apparently waiting for instructions.

"Take a good look, Hop Li," TJ finally said. In his mind, he already had the cuffs on Purcell and felt a stab of disappointment at Hop Li's failure to identify the man. *You've been lookin' too many moves ahead*, he told himself. As Doc warned him more than once, if you play with your head in the future all the time, the present would beat you.

Hop Li covered the lower half of Purcell's face with his hand and grunted. After a time he looked back at TJ and said, "This one, maybe see before. Not know other."

"Where, Hop Li? Where did you see this man?"

"Not know." Hop Li could see that his answer didn't satisfy TJ and his eyes darted back and forth between the lawmen before he lowered them. TJ pulled on the end of his mustache and tried not to let his disappointment show but it must have for when Hop Li looked up, he said, "Sorry, Sheriff TJ."

"Well, thanks anyway, Hop Li. That's all we came for." TJ turned to leave.

Sketch grabbed TJ's arm. "Hold on, boss, something ain't right."

"What? What's not right?"

"We forgot what Hop Li told us. These drawings' ain't how they oughta be."

"I don't follow, Sketch."

"Wait, I'll show ya." He sat down on Hop Li's stool and opened his sketchpad to a fresh page and copied the drawing of Purcell onto the new page. He drew the forehead, eyes, nose, and the muttonchops as before but then began filling in the beard covering up the mole on Purcell's cheek. Next, he left off the oval glasses, which softened Purcell's face. Without them, Purcell looked more like a tough foreman or indeed a ship's officer, someone at any rate used to command. Sketch had only started on the hat when Hop Li shouted, "ai—yee! Him! Yes. That one. That is sea captain!" Hop Li pointed at the drawing, his voice cracking with excitement.

"You sure, now? You weren't so sure a minute ago." TJ pointed to the huge round face of the mayor with the beard that reached halfway down his chest. "What about this fellow?"

Hop Li jerked his head furiously from side to side. "No. Not him. This one!" He reached in front of TJ, snatched the pad out of Sketch's hands, and held the drawing up. "This man give me box, Sheriff TJ. This man."

"Sometimes our mind plays tricks on us, Hop Li." TJ tapped his head with his finger.

"No! Mind not play trick, hnnnn! Hop Li see sea captain face all time—at night before sleep, at morning when wake. No. This face, I not forget, Sheriff TJ. Please, what is name?" Hop Li handed the sketchpad back to Sketch.

"Paul Purcell."

"Why Purcell give me box?"

"He gave you the box because it had those Chinese clothes inside. Everybody would think the clothes belonged to you. And he picked you because you're of a good size for a Chinaman."

Hop Li handed the drawings of the other men to Sketch and sat down on his bunk."Why Purcell kill Wah Fong, 'merican lady?"

"Don't know that yet. And it's gonna be hard to prove he killed them. He says he was in Tacoma on railroad business that Saturday and Sunday. A railroad official up there will vouch for him." TJ sat down next to Hop Li.

"Vouch? What mean, please?"

"It means that the other man says Purcell was in Tacoma, just like Purcell said."

"Wah! Men lie, Sheriff TJ." Hop Li pulled on the ragged strands of hair where his queue had been. "Purcell give me box, pay two dolla fifty cent." Hop Li sat up straight and slowly lifted his head so that he looked into TJ's eyes. "So, you think Hop Li say true?"

TJ looked away and chewed on his mustache.

"Yeah, I do. But…"

"Eh? You not sure. Why not sure, Sheriff TJ?"

"It's not that easy, Hop Li. I got to prove Purcell and his friend are lyin.'"

"Show this Tsai Soo." Hop Li picked up the drawing of Purcell. "So, Tsai Soo vouch Hop Li, hnnnh!"

TJ stood up, took a turn around the cell, and then halted in front of Hop Li.

"We'll show these drawings to Soo after we leave here. If he picks Purcell as the sea captain, that'll back up your story. And then we'll talk to the stable boys at the liveries. If Purcell came to town that weekend he rented a buggy and there's a good chance one of the boys will remember him. If so, we'll have the son of a bitch!" TJ slammed his fist into the palm of his hand. "Should know everything this afternoon, Hop Li. Tomorrow for sure."

"Then Hop Li free?" He got up from his bunk.

"Yep. Then Hop Li is free."

Hop Li bowed from the waist and said, "Ten thousand thank you Sketch, Sheriff TJ."

Out front in the jail office, TJ asked Sketch to make another drawing of Purcell like the corrected one. When Sketch finished TJ told him to find the tea man and to show him the three drawings with no coaching or hints, just as they had with Hop Li.

TJ walked out of the jail into the crisp afternoon air, as full of energy as when he felt the weight of a dozen June hogs in his net. He drew close to Sirpia's bakery and smelled fresh baked goods. The aroma brought to mind their kitchen in winter when Lucy Ann had tossed him a hot kolache just out of the oven. His mouth watered as he looked over the pastries in the bakery window. After he talked to the livery boys, he'd come back here for coffee and a pastry. It was Sunday and Sirpia always baked something special on Sundays. Maybe she'd made kolaches.

39

Sunday, April 18

The smells of horse, alfalfa, and manure in Sherman and Ward's Livery were good smells, smells a man could leave behind when he left work, unlike cannery stink, which crawled onto a man's clothes and into his skin. Cannery stink stayed with a worker all day until he scrubbed down and changed clothes. Flies buzzed around TJ's face and a huge draft horse turned his head and watched TJ as he walked to the rear. In the office, a stable boy of about fifteen told TJ that the boss, old man Jensen, wasn't due back for an hour.

TJ left and went to the second livery it town, the Astoria Freight and Passenger Line. They had only rented to locals that weekend. So he went across the street to the restaurant in O'Brien's Hotel and spent an hour reading The Star and The Oregonian while nursing several cups of coffee.

When TJ returned to Sherman and Ward's Livery, he found Jensen lugging a saddle and talking to himself.

"Good afternoon, Mr. Jensen."

Jensen paused, squinted at TJ for a second before acknowledging him and said, "Nothin' good about it."

"Oh, why's that?"

"'Cause everthin's fallin' on my shoulders today and they were hurtin' bad before the day started." Jensen let the saddle slide down his leg to the ground. "Guess you'll be wantin' the buckboard."

"Not today. I need to know if you rented a buggy to a fella from Portland—be on the third of April." TJ walked over and picked up the saddle. "Where you want this?"

"Over there." Jensen pointed to a rail with a row of saddles on it.

TJ carried the saddle to the other side of the stable, heaved it up onto the rail, and then returned to Jensen.

"You want a job?" Jensen spit a stream tobacco juice on the ground and slid a wad of straw over it with his boot.

"Got my hands full with the one I got. Now, about your records?"

"Sure. Let's take a look."

Jensen lifted a stained ledger off his desk then flipped pages until he found the one he wanted. "You got a name?"

"Purcell. Paul Purcell."

Jensen studied the page for a time and then shook his head. "Nope. No one by that name."

"Can I have a look?"

"Help yourself." Jensen handed him the ledger.

A Wm. Perkins from Portland rented a top buggy with curtains on Saturday, April third. "Did you rent the buggy to this Perkins?"

"Don't recall. Let's see that." Jensen took the ledger. "Nope. It were Slim rented it out."

"It's Slim I need then. Got somethin' to show him."

"Well, you're outta luck. Slim's gone, vamoosed. Been close on two week now. Luther, my other boy, is out too, with the ague or some such. And to top things off, I got a carriage to clean for a funeral tomorrow. Dammit to hell—Slim sure picked a helluva time to run off." He scratched the gray stubble on his chin.

"Is Slim a drinkin' man?"

"Well, not regular. Ever so often he runs off in the middle of a workday, gets liquored up, and hires himself a girl. He's gone a day, two at most. But this time, he never showed no signs."

"Signs? What signs?"

"Well, if he's fixin' to take some time to hisself, he'll come in mean, won't hello nobody. Then before the mornin' is out he'll pick a fight with me or Luther over nothin.' That's a sure sign he ain't comin' back that afternoon. But this time? Nothin.' Didn't think he'd skip off without leavin' word. No sir. I knowed Slim close on four year now, knowed him like he was my own. Can't think what got into him."

"You send somebody over to his place?"

"Yep, after he didn't show Thursday mornin,' I sent Luther around. But Slim wasn't to home."

"When did you see him last?"

"Well, let's see now." Jensen took a leather pouch from his back pocket and added a wad of tobacco to the chew in his mouth. "Yep. It were Tuesday evenin,' quittin' time. He didn't seem bothered or nothin,' just waved goodbye like always and left."

"Mr. Jensen, I think you best tell me all you can about Slim." TJ took out his notepad and pencil.

"You thinkin' somethin's happened to that boy?"

"Can't say. Man gets drunk, walks home late at night, misses a step, and falls into the river. Been known to happen."

Jensen shook his head in denial. "I know what your sayin,' Sheriff, but it don't seem likely. He drinks some, can't deny it. But not so's he's fallin' off bridges, less he's on one of his toots. But like I said, that ain't often."

"How about family? Maybe one of his kin is ailin' and his folks sent word for him to come home."

"He didn't have no kin, alive that is. Besides, if it'd been kinfolk trouble, he woulda told me."

"What's he do in his off time?"

"Well, he don't tell me much about his off time, leastways not anymore. I don't like him wastin' time and money on doggeries and bad women. And he knows what I think 'cause I give him Jesse ever time he runs out on me."

"Is he a gamblin' man?"

"Nope... well now, I take that back. Slim shoots pool over to Bailey's and Luther, my other boy, claims Slim is a crack shot. Slim makes him a few extry dollars ever week is what I hear. But maybe it ain't gamblin,' if he's that good."

"Anything else? Friends? A saloon or cafe he favors?"

"Well, Slim and Luther pal around some but Slim is private and don't talk much about his friends. Most days, he takes meals at the Riverside or that other place down the street, can't never remember the name."

"Shipmates," TJ said.

"Yeah. That's it."

"Any saloons he's partial to?"

"No, none that...wait...Friday nights after six he's off to Turk's for the special. It's a sucker play 'cause once the place is full, Turk doubles prices. You'd think Slim would catch on, him bein' a pool sharper and all, but no, he heads over there ever Friday, regular as sunset."

TJ took down the information and then asked, "What's Slim's real name?"

"Well, he don't want me to give it out. What you need it for anyway?"

"I'm goin' over to the telegraph office, see if Slim got any messages last week. Operator needs a last name to search the log."

"Messages? Now, who'd be sendin' him messages?" Jensen shooed a fly away from his face. "Never mind. Don't hafta think about it. He never got no messages—leastways, none I heard about."

"There's always a first time. I need his real name, Mr. Jensen."

"Well, guess if you need it, you need it. It's Ezra Whipple—but don't you go tellin' him it were me give it up."

"I won't and thanks, Mr. Jensen." TJ wrote the name in his notebook, "By the way, where's Slim live?"

"Has him a room above a barber shop. It's on Water Street coupla doors down from the Central Hotel. Barber's a old fella, name of Barney or Billy, somethin' like that."

"I'll find it."

"And if you catch up with Slim, you send his ass over here— pronto. Slim's a knothead but he's good with horses and a hard worker, most days anyway." Jensen turned and spit on the floor. "And I'm used to havin' him around." Jensen and TJ shook hands.

The freshly painted barber pole outside the barbershop told TJ which half of the skinny, two-story building belonged to the barber and which to his neighbor, a tailor. TJ pushed the screen door open and stepped inside. The aroma of after-shave cologne and soap greeted him and reminded him that he'd missed his last haircut appointment. The investigation was eating up too much time and he realized with a pang that he hadn't talked to Emma since he'd returned from Portland. After he talked to Slim, he'd give Emma his news.

"Mornin' sir." The barber stared at TJ's bandaged head and asked, "Shave?" He snapped a sheet in the air and invited TJ to sit in his chair with a wave of his hand.

"Mornin.' No, not right now. Maybe later. I'm looking for your renter. Official business." TJ put his hands on his hips and showed his badge.

"Renter? Well, I've got three. Which one you looking for?

"His name's Slim. Works over to Sherman & Ward's."

"Slim. Mr. Reliable—pays on time, never causes me a nickel's worth of trouble." He paused and looked towards the front. "Thing is, I ain't seen him in some time now." He brushed off the chair with a towel. "He in trouble, Sheriff?"

"I hope not. I need to see his room. You have a key?"

"Key? Sure thing." The barber walked to the rear of his shop and came back with a key. "Upstairs, number two."

"Thanks. I won't be long."

TJ climbed the stairs outside the barbershop and knocked on Slim's door. No answer. He knocked again, louder, but still heard nothing so he unlocked the door and went in. The room smelled of stale cigar smoke. He raised the shade over the one window and looked around. The blanket over the cot was stretched tight and the corners folded U.S. Army style. Two work shirts and a pair of work pants hung on hangers in the open closet. A pair of worn but well-shined brogans stood on the floor next to the bed and faced front with the laces tucked inside. He pulled open the three drawers of the bureau: underclothes, socks, a couple of clean sheets, some keys, a shoe horn, shoe polish, a roll of twine, and a cigar box. The cigar box held a dozen or so receipts, a packet of needles, a roll of black thread, buttons, and under the receipts, a faded photograph of a middle-aged woman in a black dress and white lace collar. The woman stood with one hand on her hip and scowled at the camera. Under the bed he found a clean chamber pot and an empty suitcase with one hinge missing.

TJ grew uneasy as he closed the suitcase. This room wasn't that of a man who'd left in a hurry or gone anywhere for that matter. The small knot in his stomach tightened as he looked over the tidy room. He had this same unease and tightness when he felt a heavy, not-giving-in pull on his net, which meant a snag. If the snag turned out to be a log half buried in bottom muck it would be hell to free and meant no fishing that night.

He tried to convince himself that Slim could be lying drunk in some floozy's bed but didn't succeed. Slim had been missing close to two weeks and an absence that long wasn't about a sporting girl or drink. He closed and locked the door, dropped the key off at the barber's, and hurried back to his office.

Even if the tea vendor backed up Hop Li's story, it wouldn't mean a damm thing. TJ needed Slim to testify that Purcell hired a buggy on the weekend of the murders because Slim's testimony contradicted Purcell's witness in Tacoma.

But maybe he was getting ahead of himself, creating problems where none existed as Doc had to remind him in re-plays of their games. Slim's disappearance might be a coincidence. He'd check on Slim's comings and goings first thing. But all the way to his office the snag feeling stayed with him.

40

TJ and his deputies traipsed all over town Monday but found no one who'd seen Slim in two weeks. The ticket clerks at the Oregon Rail & Navigation Company and the Ilwaco ferry office knew Slim but said he hadn't purchased a ticket. The boy at the Western Union office had found no messages for either an Ezra Whipple or a Slim. The barkeeps and the sporting girls who worked downstairs Fridays at Turk's said Slim hadn't been in for some time. Sailors, dockmen, loggers, and fishermen filled Turk's saloon on Friday nights for the ten cent special and TJ wondered how Turk's employees knew if Slim had been in or not. But a sporting girl named Angel knew Slim, said he was a good tipper, and that she always looked for him. She hadn't seen Slim the last two Fridays.

The manager at Bailey's pool parlor said Slim had played pool after dinnertime that Tuesday, two weeks ago, and left about ten with a young woman. The manager took her for a sporting girl but admitted he couldn't be sure because she didn't flirt or pay attention to any man but Slim. The manager added that he couldn't say for sure if they knew each other or were friends, as she seemed content to sit in the spectator's bench and cheer for him.

By late afternoon, TJ suspected that Purcell had Slim killed or else shanghaied. He sought out Bessie on the off chance she'd think of other possible reasons for his disappearance and managed to corral her long enough to ask about Slim. Bessie smiled and shook her head when TJ told her about the girl Slim left with.

"Sweetie, that girl tells me all I need to know. Crimps grabbed Slim five minutes after he left Bailey's. And if it's me makin' the arrangements, I don't use locals 'cause I don't want any of them knowin' what I'm up to. So even if you catch you a local and get him to talk, you don't learn a damm thing 'cause he don't know nothin.' See, if it's my crew, they come in Tuesday mornin,' take Slim that night, and are eatin' oysters on the trip back to Portland Wednesday mornin.' No, Honeypie, your witness is gone. Forget him."

TJ left disappointed even though he heard what he'd expected to hear. He took a back booth at Sirpia's, ordered coffee, and reflected on the highs and lows of the past two days. Maybe someday, when he had a few more years under his belt as a lawman, he'd learn not to let his emotions boil over at the thought of an imagined victory. Belief that he had a game won or had a man like Purcell trapped excited and pleased him, even if, as too often happened, he'd overlooked an obvious countermove by his opponent.

He finished his coffee and decided to talk Silas into releasing Hop Li. He and Silas went round and round for a time but eventually Silas admitted that the ten dollars Hop Li borrowed from Dr. Chung to send to his folks convinced him that Hop Li didn't rob Fong or kill anyone.

Back at the office, TJ found Plato curled up in Big Jim's lap, purring in concert with his snoring. Sketch sat with a sketchpad on his lap drawing the two sleepers.

TJ winked at Sketch and shouted, "Wake up, Jim. Time to start the day."

Big Jim awoke with a start and then gazed with red eyes at TJ. Finally, he stood up and rubbed his face with his hands. "What the hell time is it?" He looked from Sketch to TJ for information but both just grinned back at him. "Shit. Like to gimme heart attack, TJ." He stretched and then asked, "Well, ya find Slim?"

"Nope. Bessie's fair certain Portland crimps took him after he left Bailey's. So our witness is gone, boys. But at least Silas has come around to our way of thinkin' on Hop Li. I told him we oughta pick up Purcell but he says without Slim we don't have enough evidence. But we'll think on Purcell later."

TJ picked Plato off his chair, sat down, positioned the tom on his lap, and then thought about getting Hop Li out of jail. Hop Li's large size, his fight with Kephardt, and the newspaper accounts of the murders had made the Chinaboy's name and face easy to recognize. Within minutes of the first idler spotting him, news would be all over town that the fiend who butchered the Thurgood girl was out. They couldn't let anyone see Hop Li as he left jail. "We're turnin' Hop Li loose tonight, boys. Any ideas how to keep folks from spottin' us?

"We ain't et yet, TJ. I don't think so good on empty." Big Jim moved to the doorway.

TJ looked from one deputy to another and saw by the look of anticipation on Sketch's face that he agreed with Big Jim. Annoyed, TJ wondered why Big Jim couldn't put off the feedbag for an hour anyway. But in the next instant, he realized he'd pushed himself and his men hard in the last two days. His irritation at them owed as much to his own hunger as it did to his frustration over not finding Slim.

"Well, guess it's past supper time. All right, let's eat but I want us back here in a half hour."

They were in luck as Sirpia had made salt pork stew with raisin dumplings that day. All three had stew and finished with apple cobbler and cream, though Big Jim started his meal with a herring salad and ended with a second piece of cobbler. On the walk back to the office, TJ once again looked upon his deputies as allies and handed each man an El Gusto. TJ and Sketch lit their cigars while Big Jim put his in a shirt pocket and then stuffed a chew of Cloverleaf in his mouth. Both deputies pulled their chairs close to TJ's desk.

By the time they reached the office, TJ had a plan. "Big Jim, I want you to keep the office open, make folks think we're in here workin' late. Sketch, get the buckboard and meet me at the jail. Oh, and put a couple empty barrels in the back, a tarp, and a board heavy enough to keep the tarp down

Sketch's face twisted in puzzlement at the last request but he didn't question the order. "Anythin' else, Boss?"

"Yeah. If the stable boy asks what we're up to—but only if he does—tell him we're helpin' Doc move some things to the hospital."

TJ stepped outside to a clear sky with only a slight breeze. He looked up and saw the tip of a full moon over Uppertown and cursed the calm night. He needed a dark night with a hard rain and a stiff blow, a night in which every stray dog in town would be holed up. He wondered why the weather couldn't favor him once in a while.

At the jail, Lucky stared at TJ, mouth open, when TJ gave him the news about Hop Li. Finally, he found his tongue. "Lettin' him go? Shit, Boss, thought he done it, thought…"

TJ held up his hand. "Silas and I have been over it, Lucky, Hop Li isn't our man," TJ continued, "another thing—I want Kephardt and his boys to think Hop Li is still here, least for two-three days. Can you do that?"

Lucky slid the large key ring off its peg and then laid it down on his desk while he moved his chew from cheek to cheek. "Well now, let's see…yep. That ain't hard to do. Sure. See, I always hello every boy on my rounds, make sure they's still among the livin,' know what I mean?"

TJ nodded.

"Well, then, supposin' I just keep on helloin' that Chinaboy's cell at breakfast time, like always? Can even put a roll in his bed with a blanket over it, if you want. Then if a fella looks in that cage, why all he sees is somebody sleepin.' Ain't nobody gonna know he's gone."

"Hirin' you was smartest thing I ever did, Lucky."

Lucky grinned and reached for the key ring on his desk.

TJ held out his hand. "I'll take those. I need to chat with him before we go."

Lucky lifted a key. "This here is his."

"Take it off and let me have it. Less noise the better. Now, can you open the big door without rousin' the boys in there?"

Lucky gave TJ the cell key and then slid the longest key on the ring into the lock of the heavy timbered door. He turned the lock and TJ heard a soft click. Lucky opened the door, TJ stepped inside, and then Lucky closed the door without letting it latch.

The light from the two oil lamps cast long shadows in the corridor creating the familiar dreary and foreboding atmosphere while the fug of the cell block—shit, piss, mold, and foul air—stunk as bad as ever. A twinge of his closed-in feeling hit him after the big door shut. In the two years he'd been sheriff, getting through that first minute in the cellblock hadn't got any easier. He breathed through his mouth and allowed the tightness in his chest and guts to subside. While he waited, the thought crossed his mind that the inescapable stink of the place was a kind of torture, almost as bad as the loss of freedom. Just then a snore erupted from the wooden cell next to him and gave the lie to his conclusion. Maybe some men could get used to the stink and to being locked up, he admitted, but dammed if he could.

When his closed-in feeling lessened, he walked over to the cage, put a finger up to his lips, and waved Hop Li to him.

"Listen close, Hop Li. We're lettin' you go tonight—you're free," TJ whispered.

Hop Li's eyes opened wide and shouted, "Hah!"

TJ put his finger over his lips again and whispered, "No! No shoutin,' no noise. Understand?"

Hop Li nodded but continued to frown.

"Good. Now, go get your things and be quiet about it—quiet as a mouse."

Hop Li stared at him without moving as if he didn't understand.

"Go on, man, do it now," TJ hissed and waved him away from the bars.

Hop Li turned, knelt down in front of his bunk, and pulled out his notebook and the cigar box from under his bunk. He retrieved a medallion with a leather thong from under his pillow and hung it around his neck. Next, he pulled an undershirt from under his mattress, put his possessions in the middle of the undershirt, gathered it into a bundle, and knotted it. He pulled his slouch hat down tight and nodded that he was ready.

TJ unlocked the cell and opened the door slowly. Even so, the hinges squeaked, making an eerie, piercing sound that echoed through the length of the corridor. But the pattern of snores coming from the cell across from him hadn't changed. Anyone in the drunk tank could have seen Hop Li and TJ leave but the tank was empty this early on a Tuesday evening.

Sketch had parked the buckboard on Jefferson Street across from Captain Flavel's mansion and waited for TJ and Hop Li in the jail office.

"Anything goin' on at the Flavel house?" TJ asked.

"A light's on in the parlor is all. Street's empty."

Lucky handed Hop Li a paper bag and said, "Your belongin's."

Hop Li took his leather purse out of the bag. He opened the purse and looked inside.

"It's all there. Go on, count it," Lucky said.

Hop Li counted out two dollars and thirty-one cents, put the money in his purse, and stuffed the purse in his coat pocket. He bowed to Lucky and said, "Ten thousand thank you, Mr. Lucky."

Lucky cleared a space off his desk, set a receipt book down, and then held an inkpad out to Hop Li. "Press yer right thumb here, then press this here receipt right where I'm pointin' at."

"Give pen, please. I write name."

Lucky looked up in surprise.

TJ nodded at Lucky and the jailer handed a pen to the Chinaboy. Hop Li wrote his name first in Chinese then in English.

"I need to tell you a couple things, Hop Li," TJ said and put his hat on. "We'll make sure you get to your Chinahouse but from then on you're on your own. Understand?"

"Eh? Not worry about Hop Li, Sheriff TJ." He smiled at each man in turn.

"The Knights mean business, Hop Li. I don't want you endin' up like Fatt Luk."

Hop Li's eyes hardened. "Ah, yes. Understand. Hop Li not look for trouble."

"Good. So I'm thinkin' it'd be best if you find work elsewhere. There's got to be canneries across the river, say in Ilwaco or Megler, that could use a butcher."

Hop Li straightened his shoulders and shook his head vehemently. "No. Have job Jameson Cannery. Number one butcher." He glanced up and held TJ's eyes briefly before looking away.

"Well, it's your choice. But it'd be a good idea to lay low for a while. Can you do that?"

"What mean, 'lay low'?"

"It means stay out of town and keep to your Chinahouse when you're not workin.'"

"You want Hop Li stay in shell, like turtle, eh?" Hop Li smiled.

TJ smiled back. "That's exactly what I mean."

"Hop Li tiger, Sheriff TJ, no turtle."

TJ pulled his hat down. "Un-huh. Well, I warned you." TJ turned to Sketch. "See if anybody's walkin' around outside, will you?"

Sketch opened the door and stuck his head outside. "Nope. Ain't a soul about."

They filed out with Sketch leading, followed by Hop Li, then TJ.

As they came up to the wagon, Hop Li stopped to look up at the moon, now fully risen above the hills of Uppertown. TJ took his arm and tried to steer him into the buckboard but Hop Li pulled back. "Please, one minute." He inhaled deeply and looked out to the river. Hop Li sniffed the air with his eyes closed like a wild animal, smiling all the while. Watching him, TJ breathed deeply and smelled the tang of river mixed with the odor of beer from the distant St. Louis Brewery. Hop Li opened his eyes and took another deep breath. "Free air smell good, Sheriff TJ!"

Although Hop Li objected, TJ had him sit on the floor between the two barrels just behind him and Sketch. TJ stretched the tarp over the barrels then placed a board on top of the tarp. Any passerby who looked at the wagon would see two men driving some goods covered by a tarp.

They turned right at Lafayette Street, then right a block later and followed Squemoqua Street east. They rode without speaking; the only sounds the creak of the harness and the clop of the team's hooves. TJ felt that if they spoke, they'd call attention to themselves and an onlooker might suspect they were up to no good. He knew his thinking made no sense—they weren't doing anything wrong—so why did he feel this way? But in order to get Hop Li, a free man, out of town, they had to sneak him out. He hated skulking through his own town like a thief.

They passed the net drying racks of George Hume's cannery and came abreast of two Chinamen jabbering in loud voices. Hop Li apparently took the sound of his language as a signal to speak. "So Sheriff TJ, you put Purcell in jail?"

"No, not yet." TJ looked straight ahead as he spoke.

"Why not?"

"We lost our witness. We have no one to say Purcell was here the night of the murders."

"Eh? Hop Li see Purcell, also Tsai Soo. We be witness."

TJ didn't speak for a long time but finally said, "Only the word of that livery boy counts, Hop Li." TJ kept his eyes on the road ahead.

"Why this?"

" 'Cause he's white, that's why. It's the law." TJ leaned over the side and spit.

"Law no goddamm good!" Hop Li said.

TJ and Sketch looked at each other but didn't speak.

"Purcell rich man?" Hop Li asked.

"Yeah, he's rich. Why you ask?" TJ said over his shoulder.

"In China, rich man pay, so never go jail. All same 'merica, I think."

Sketch whooped and said, "Damm! Ya got that right, Hop Li."

TJ looked back over his shoulder. "Not this time, Hop Li. I'm gonna put that son of a bitch in jail. Don't care if he shits money."

TJ had enough talk of Purcell and said nothing more. He drove over the rough road, occasionally glancing up at the full moon. An image of Emma standing on the porch of the parsonage came to mind and he smiled. He decided to call on her after he'd jailed Purcell. He'd do it proper, too, letting that blatherskite brother of hers know his intentions were honorable. His heart quickened as he held on to her image and he slapped the horses' rumps too hard. The buckboard bolted forward a half a block before he got the team settled.

In ten minutes, they turned off Hemlock and down the long muddy drive that led to Jameson's Chinahouse. Smoke curled out of one of the chimneys in the long building and oil lamps lit up two groups of men in the yard. One group stood around the cook and his helper playing dominos while in the middle of the yard a barber shaved the forehead of the Chinaboss, Jim Lum. Five men squatted in a semi-circle behind the barber, smoked their long pipes, and waited their turn for a shave.

One man recognized the buckboard and shouted something, which two or three others repeated. Jim Lum waved the barber off, stood up, and made for the buckboard. Men inside the Chinahouse, roused by the commotion, came out and soon thirty or so men ambled towards the buckboard behind Jim Lum. TJ pulled up at the end of the plank walk that led to the Chinahouse.

"You're home, Hop Li," Sketch said and lifted the board and tarp off the barrels.

Hop Li stood up and yelped with joy when he saw the Chinaboss and his co-workers approaching. But at the sight of Hop Li, the men froze as if slapped in the face. As Hop Li looked at them, his body stiffened, and then he grunted. A silence descended on the men, a silence interrupted by the soft splash of a small wave as it broke on the inlet next to the Chinahouse.

"Everythin' all right?" TJ asked.

Instead of answering, Hop Li climbed over the side of the buckboard and grabbed his bundle from the seat. Still without speaking, Hop Li turned and faced Jim Lum and the others. The tension in the air, already heavy, increased to the point where TJ found himself clenching his fists. Something wasn't right but damm if he could figure out what.

Jim Lum's sullen face didn't change as he watched Hop Li come toward him. None of the other men came forward or greeted Hop Li.

"Well, stay out of trouble, Hop Li," TJ said.

No one, including Hop Li, gave any sign of having heard him. As TJ turned the buckboard, he heard Jim Lum say something to Hop Li. Hop Li replied and soon the two were talking loud and at the same time. Just before TJ turned back on Hemlock Street, he looked over his shoulder and saw that everyone but Hop Li and Jim Lum had gone inside. The two men stood face-to-face, apparently still arguing.

41

Tuesday, April 20

The next morning, TJ sat Big Jim and Sketch down, handed each a cigar, and lit one himself. He told them that Silas had a team of Pinkertons lined up to start questioning jewelers in Portland. Big Jim cocked his head to the side. "Why we got to wait on Pinkertons?"

"Silas's a stickler. Before he gives us a warrant, we've got to find the jeweler who fixed Purcell's ring."

"Well, it's your say so, TJ. But if it was up to me…" Big Jim blew a stream of smoke at the ceiling.

"Boss, who's goin' with you?" Sketch asked.

"Nobody. I want both of you here in case the Knights get frisky."

"Hell, them Knights ain't been a worry since we jailed Kephardt. Anyways, we can call on city police if trouble comes," Sketch said.

TJ took his cigar out of his mouth and pointed it at Sketch. "That's just what I don't want you to do." TJ took his boot off his desk and sat up. "You recall when Purcell came to town pretendin' to help us search for the Thurgood girl?"

Sketch nodded.

"I asked myself why he's spendin' so much time in Connelly's office and sniffed around some. Found out he and Connelly go way back. Now, a lot of things are startin' to make sense. Those Chinee scabs marched in here the day after the fishermen went on strike and they ended up at Jameson's Cannery. We got thirty-nine canneries hereabouts. How come those scabs were so choosy? A few days later Kephardt waltzes in here preachin' hellfire against Chinamen in general and Hop Li in particular. How come he knows about Hop Li so soon? Then our only white witness disappears before we can question him. Somebody in Portland knows a helluva lot about our business and way too soon. That somebody is Purcell. And another somebody in town makes sure Purcell knows what we ate for breakfast."

Sketch frowned. "You sayin' Connelly is spyin' on us for Purcell?"

"Yep. But I can't prove anything yet so don't repeat that, all right?"

Sketch nodded.

"Now, if Kephardt works for Purcell like I'm thinkin' and Purcell wants Kephardt out of jail, Connelly knows this. Once Connelly finds out two of us have run off to Portland he could sic the Knights on Lucky one night."

"Jesus..." Sketch muttered.

"Yeah. That's why I'm goin' to Portland by myself. I want one of you inside the jail with Lucky at all times. The other can run things from here." TJ fingered his cigar cutter and then said, "I'll be gone two, maybe three days. Now, if you smell trouble, Sketch, go ahead and deputize another half-dozen men from our list of reliables."

"A breakout... Jesus, boss, I don't know..." Sketch stood up and ran his hand through his hair.

"You'll do fine, Sketch." TJ nodded to Big Jim. "Besides you've got the big man here to help you."

"Won't nobody get into that jail 'less I want 'em to, Partner." He looked from Sketch to TJ and chuckled.

Sketch pushed his hair off his forehead again. "Boss, maybe we oughta go ahead, deputize them boys right now?"

TJ shook his head. "No. That'd tip off Connelly and he'd tell Purcell, give the bastard time to cook up a new alibi, maybe make a run for it. I need..."

A bang on the door with a cane or stick froze them and before anyone could speak, Emma marched into the room waving her parasol back and forth, clearing a path through the cigar smoke.

"I apologize for interrupting your meeting, gentlemen, but I must speak to you, Sheriff. It's urgent." Emma's lips were tight as she looked at each man in turn.

Big Jim stood up so quickly he knocked his chair over. He righted his chair and then pointed to it but she refused it with a shake of her head.

TJ turned to Sketch. "You and Big Jim go on over to the jail, work out a duty roster with Lucky."

Both deputies mumbled good day to Emma who acknowledged their departure with a nod. Emma wore a dark gray jacket buttoned down the middle over a simple olive green dress and a modest bustle. A small cluster of pink roses decorated her otherwise plain straw bonnet. In all, a proper costume for a young, unmarried woman going to town. But her appearance wasn't that of the confident woman TJ had come to expect. A strand of hair stuck out over one ear and her hands, usually still, fidgeted with the handle of her parasol and drew his attention. Her gloves were two different shades of green. The mismatched gloves told him he faced a troubled woman. When he glanced up, he noticed beads of sweat on her forehead.

"You want to go outside?" he asked.

"No. I must tell you about Hop Li. He came by the parsonage this morning. At first, I couldn't believe what he told me—it's so unfair. But I know the Chinese, you see, I should have expected something like this. But I was so thrilled at seeing him, at learning that you'd released him, that I couldn't think about anything else," her voice shook and the pitch rose as she talked. "Oh, I've been a fool, TJ, I wasted precious minutes wondering what to do—I should have come straight here after he left." She looked down, fighting back tears.

TJ waited for her to say more but she glanced up at him, confused and fragile, more so than he'd ever imagined she could be. "All right Emma. I want you to sit down, take a deep breath, and start at the beginnin.'"

She sat down on the edge of Big Jim's chair, closed her eyes, and didn't speak for a few seconds. When she did, her voice no longer shook. "That terrible fight in front of the courthouse frightened the Chinese. That's understandable but they blamed Hop Li for it, you see, and called him a bad luck man. Do you know what that means?"

"A man with a run of bad luck is all it means to me. But what's that...?"

"It's not like that. It's more serious. No Chinese wants to be around a bad luck man. They believe a bad spirit lives with such a man, that anyone associated with him will have bad luck."

"Well, but what happened to Hop Li could happen to anybody. Wasn't any of it his fault."

"Fault doesn't enter into it. When you consider the evidence, all that's happened to him, you can see why his friends think as they do."

"Evidence? Emma, talk plain. What do you mean?"

"Well, look at all Hop Li went through this year. First, he has that fight in Seattle where that brute cut off his queue. So now whenever his friends set eyes on him, they are reminded of his shame. Next, you arrest him for murder and throw him in jail, which added to his reputation as a bad luck man. And then Fatt Luk is lynched. Hop Li's best friend. Imagine! That was the final straw, the worst..." Emma paused to catch her breath before continuing, "...every day now, I hear how those ruffians, those so-called Knights, roam the waterfront looking for Chinamen to bully. Do you see why no Chinese wants to be seen with Hop Li?"

"So that's why he got the cold shoulder at his Chinahouse. Well, does he need some time off?"

"No. No one will work with him—he's lost his job. The Chinaboss paid him for his time and Mr. Jameson added ten dollars termination pay. After what Hop Li's been through, it's so unfair, TJ. I gave him a little money and asked him to kneel down with me and pray for guidance but he refused."

"Did he say what his plans were?"

"He told me he had a debt of honor to settle before he did anything else. I asked him about it but he wouldn't say more—he can be so vexing at times. I begged him to talk to Dr. Chung before he did anything rash. He said he would but... I don't know...I think his mind was made up before we talked."

"Did he mention a name in this matter of honor?"

"No. No one. And he made me promise not to tell a soul what he just told me. I promised I wouldn't tell but after he left I wasted a half-hour debating with myself about what to do. I'm afraid his heart is set on vengeance. Do you have any idea who has angered him so?"

"Maybe. What time did Hop Li leave your place?"

She looked up at the clock on the back wall. "About an hour and twenty minutes ago. He and Dr. Chung are good friends, perhaps he followed my advice...perhaps...oh, is it possible he's there still?"

"Why don't I go find out?" TJ stood and put his hat on.

Emma rose and faced him. "I'm going with you." She straightened her shoulders and compressed her lips into a tight circle.

"There's no need."

She looked into his eyes without speaking, her breathing steady, and seemed to grow taller with each moment. For an uncomfortable second, they regarded each other without a word before he broke the silence. "All right, all right. But if Hop Li isn't there, I want you to go on home without fussin' at me. I got some time this mornin' so I'll look around, see if I can't find him before he does any harm. But I'm searchin' by myself, Emma. Agreed?"

"Agreed," she said and offered him her arm.

42

Tuesday, April 20

An overcast sky and a cool April morning greeted Emma and TJ as they left the courthouse. As they walked, she told him about Hop Li's family, how much hope they placed in him, and how dutiful he'd been in carrying out his obligations. But he listened with only half an ear as he tried to work out who Hop Li was after. Kephardt was in jail so Hop Li couldn't get to him. When TJ left Lum and Hop Li arguing at the Chinahouse, he didn't think they were angry enough to fight but now he wasn't so sure. And what about Purcell? Hop Li knew that Purcell killed Fong and the girl and tried to make him look like the killer. If Hop Li were after Purcell, he'd head for Portland.

"Sheriff Stone, are you listening to me?" The furrows between her eyebrows betrayed irritation.

"Sorry. Thinkin' about other things. You were sayin'?"

"I was talking about Hop Li's life in China. But another time. Dr. Chung's pharmacy is just around the corner."

They stopped and stared at the sight of the pharmacy. Rough boards had been nailed over the large front window and shards of glass stuck up around the window frame.

"Oh, my heaven…I hope nothing has happened to him," Emma said and put her hand over her mouth. TJ opened the screen door and guided Emma into a dark interior lit by a single oil lamp above the counter. When the bells above his door tinkled, Dr. Chung put his cup down and squinted at them for some time before calling out, "Ah, Miss Taylor, Sheriff TJ. Welcome." He stood up and bowed.

A pungent odor from something cooking in Dr. Chung's kitchen along with the closeness and darkness of the store brought on TJ's closed in feeling. TJ breathed through his mouth and told himself they wouldn't stay long.

"Please, sit. Just make tea. Green tea with...ah...not know 'mercian word...in China we say *ju hua* flower. Best long life tea. From Fujan." He pointed Emma to his customer's stool but she remained standing.

"What happened to the window?" TJ asked.

Dr. Chung lifted a brick that sat on the counter. "Last night, some devil throw this." He pulled on a strand of his pointed beard. "I sleep there." He nodded to the alcove. "When window break, my heart leave body, fly up to roof." He looked at the ceiling and smiled. "Heart stay on roof long time." He shook his head slowly from side to side. "When wake up with fear—bad thing—spirit leave body. Maybe spirit not come back."

TJ took out his note pad and pencil. "Did you find a note?"

"Note not necessary."

"You know who threw the brick?"

"Yes. Those Knight. They all time come by, look in window, make ugly face. All time make trouble."

"Un-huh. Did you see the fella who threw the brick?"

"Go outside but see no one." He shrugged.

TJ closed his notepad. "Sorry."

"Knight hang Fatt Luk. Maybe next time, hang me. Why you not put Knight in jail?"

"Well, I'd like nothin' better, but I need evidence. If you or anybody saw who threw that brick, I could do somethin.'" He couldn't do much and the city police would do nothing. Connelly had made his position clear to TJ: every celestial in town should be rounded up and shipped off to China. The sooner the better.

"So, maybe Knight buy new window, Sheriff TJ?" Dr. Chung smiled politely but the look on his face demanded an answer.

"Well, I can't make them do that unless I know a Knight broke it. But I'll send a deputy to look in on you on his way to and from work for a week. I aim to catch the fella who murdered Wah Fong and the American woman soon. And when I do, I'm hopin' the Knights will skedaddle back to Portland and leave us alone."

"Most grateful, Sheriff TJ." He bowed slightly to TJ.

Emma turned to TJ. "Can we talk about Hop Li now?" She faced Dr. Chung. "We came here looking for him. If you know where he is, please tell us."

"You try help. Yes, yes. I know this. But, please, patience. Sit, drink tea."

Emma sat down and patted the top of a barrel next to her for TJ to do the same but he refused. She talked in Cantonese to Dr. Chung who

260 |R i c h a r d   B.   P o w e r s

smiled and answered in kind. As they talked Dr. Chung reached to the
shelf behind him and took down three small purple cups and saucers.
He filled the cups from a small teapot and handed cups to his visitors.

Emma took a sip of tea and then said to TJ, "Dr. Chung tells me
that Hop Li came by and that they had what he calls a heart talk. He
will tell us about it but wants to make sure…" she paused and smiled at
Dr. Chung "…that we listen with both ears."

"Just so." He returned her smile and again motioned for TJ to sit.

TJ's closed-in feeling had increased and the thought of sitting
down for a long talk increased his anxiety. He wanted answers, wanted
to get outside to open space, wanted fresh air. But he sat down.

Dr. Chung drank his tea with much slurping and smacking of lips,
while Emma drank hers without a sound. TJ finished his tea, set the cup
in the saucer, and pushed the saucer away from him. "All right, Dr.
Chung, about Hop Li."

Dr. Chung nodded. "Hop Li come here, yes, but he not self…" He
looked at Emma and broke into Cantonese.

She nodded and said, "Yes, yes. Understand." Emma looked at TJ
and said, "Dr. Chung used the expression, 'the seven cavities spurting
smoke.' It means…"

"Can guess what that means."

Emma nodded at Dr. Chung and he continued, "When always
hurry, hurry, like 'merican man, only trouble come. So, make Hop Li
sit, drink tea. Soon fire from Hop Li eye not so hot, eh? So now, maybe
he listen." He paused and offered more tea to Emma and TJ. Both
refused. He filled his cup and took a sip before continuing, "So I ask,
what you do, where you go? Go Portland, he say, bring honor back to
Chen name. Honor first, then find job."

"Has he already left for Portland?" TJ asked.

"Yes. First boat."

"Damm." TJ said and wondered how Hop Li had passed through
Astoria's waterfront to the steamer ticket office without being
recognized. His puzzlement must have shown for Dr. Chung smiled.
"How Hop Li walk in street, like tiger in desert, so nobody see, eh?"

"That crossed my mind."

"He wear work hat." Dr. Chung pointed to a stack of wide straw
hats stacked on a shelf of workmen's clothing. "He carry shoulder pole,
walk behind me. So, people see servant, not Hop Li. I buy ticket. We
go to bottom deck, only Chinese on bottom deck. So, no trouble." Dr.
Chung finished his tea and pushed his cup and saucer to the side. "But I
have worry. Big worry. I ask, you want kill *Ta siu yan*…" He looked to
Emma for help.

"Troublemaker," Emma said.

Dr. Chung bowed in thanks and continued, "Hop Li not answer but I know him, know here." Dr. Chung tapped his chest over his heart. "Old way best, I tell him. Priest know honorable way beat troublemaker. Talk to priest I say." Dr. Chung looked from TJ to Emma.

"Will Hop Li take your advice?" Emma asked.

Dr. Chung thought and then blew his breath out with a soft, whistling sound. "Not know. Hop Li wood person, warrior. Warrior act before talk. But also good son, obey father, elder brother. Maybe Hop Li listen. Maybe."

TJ had stopped listening after the words, kill troublemaker. Now he knew that Hop Li had set out to kill Purcell and if it came to a fight one on one, the Chinaboy would win. But even if Hop Li didn't kill Purcell, the outcome would be the same. Hop Li would hang. Suddenly, catching Purcell before Hop Li found him became urgent. TJ needed to find that jeweler in Portland and fast. "Did he tell you the name of the troublemaker?"

Dr. Chung pursed his lips in thought. "No. Not say name."

Emma leaned forward and touched Dr. Chung's arm. "Dr. Chung, why didn't you stop him? You might have said something. Oh, I fear for him—he has no friends there, no one to turn to, the police don't…"

Dr. Chung reached over and put his hand on hers, stopping her. "Eh? You think I not try stop? But Hop Li say, stay Astoria, Knight hang Hop Li. So go Portland, maybe police hang. But fight for honor necessary, so go Portland." Dr. Chung nodded north toward Washington territory. "Go across river, I say. Trouble not find you. But he say no. Family honor first."

As TJ listened to Dr. Chung, he felt as helpless as if he were drowning. He didn't know whether the feeling came from listening to Hop Li's stubborn refusal to accept good advice or to not having enough space in the crowded store. A drop of sweat trickled down the side of his face and he pushed his hat off his forehead and wiped his brow with his handkerchief.

Emma took the opportunity when TJ didn't speak to talk to Dr. Chung in Cantonese. As TJ listened to her, his body tensed, his head ached, and he felt as if a giant pair of hands squeezed his chest. He grew irritated at them, acting as if they had nothing better to do than chat the whole day. He took a deep breath, let it out slowly, and then did it again. His gaze wandered over Dr. Chung's head and came to rest on a small ivory statue of a Chinese woman on a shelf beside an urn of incense. The woman wore a long robe and a fancy headdress and held her head at an angle. He had no idea what the Chinese characters on her belly meant but for some reason the writing held his interest. He heard Emma and Dr. Chung talking as if from a distance and saw himself off to one side seeing Dr. Chung and Emma while watching himself staring at the statue. He found that he couldn't stop looking at the statue, that he'd lost the will to turn away. A part of him knew something was wrong, knew he should get up and leave. But his feet were rooted to the floor.

He felt a light touch on his forearm and heard Emma's voice, close. "Sheriff, Dr. Chung just asked you a question," she said and stared at him. "Oh my, what's wrong?"

Her touch and voice roused him. "What? Sorry." He rubbed his eyes with his hands. When he opened them, he found Dr. Chung's face inches from his. The doctor's large eyes peered at him through his spectacles. "Body too hot, Sheriff TJ. You all time work, eh? Too much work—no good."

"Are you feeling poorly, TJ?" Emma asked.

Dr. Chung took TJ's left wrist and gently placed it on a small black pillow, palm up. He placed three fingers on TJ's pulse and said, "Show tongue, please."

TJ pulled his hand back and forced himself to stand. His headache, a rhythmical pounding pain, had grown worse. He had to get outside. "No time now." He turned to Emma and said, "Let's go."

Emma touched his forearm again. "Please, one minute, Sheriff, I need to ask Dr. Chung something."

TJ turned away, without answering, sick to his stomach. Somehow he found his way down the narrow path to the door without bumping into a sack, pot, or basket. Once outside he squeezed into the space between Dr. Chung's pharmacy and Liberty Hall, leaned over, and threw up breakfast. He stayed bent over for a time waiting for the retching to stop, spitting and wiping sweat from his face and neck. When the nausea eased, he stepped back to the sidewalk and leaned against the front wall of Dr. Chung's store, gulping cool air. By the time Emma came out of Dr. Chung's, the nausea had gone and the tightness in his chest had eased. Except for the headache, he felt like himself.

Emma came up to him, tight-lipped and frowning. She reached out to touch his forehead but then quickly pulled her hand back as two middle-aged women approached the pharmacy. Emma said good morning and TJ touched the brim of his hat as they passed. When the women were out of hearing range, Emma gave him a long look and said, "Well, your color has returned. What on earth happened in there?"

"I'm all better, Emma. Don't fuss."

"Fuss? I am not fussing. But I am concerned. You were…you left us for a time in there. Do you realize that?"

"Afterwards, yeah, I did."

"Dr. Chung noticed it as well. Does this happen often?"

" No. Not often. It's nothin' serious…just sometimes when there's no space…I get to feelin' crowded. Makes me fidgety and I don't think clear. But it doesn't last long and fresh air cures it."

"Still, you should let Dr. Chung examine you, TJ. He is so knowledgeable. I trust his judgment completely. Perhaps…"

"Emma, I don't want to talk about it. I'm fine." He wasn't about to tell her of his affliction. It would only scare her off. And if word got out that Astoria's sheriff couldn't abide closed spaces, he'd be recalled.

Emma said nothing in response to his outburst. They walked on in silence for a block before he asked, "Well, what'd you find out after I left?"

"We talked about how to deal with difficult people. When Dr. Chung mentioned that Hop Li intended to kill a troublemaker, I remembered a ritual. I've never actually seen it practiced, mind you, so I don't know much about it."

"What is it?

"It's called beating the troublemaker. The practice empties the soul of hate so that harmony is restored to the supplicant. In his village, Dr. Chung told me of a favorite spot near a lake where a willow tree grows next to a large, flat rock. On festival days, villagers come there to perform the ritual. A wife made miserable by her mother-in-law, for instance, offers a sacrifice of food to the good spirits, the *kwai yan*. Then she leans an effigy of the mother-in-law, the troublemaker, against the rock and beats it with her slipper. Of course, the exercise must be done properly to have the desired effect. That's why Dr. Chung advised Hop Li to see a priest so that he would know what to do."

"You think he'll do that, go to a priest I mean?"

"Perhaps. I hope that…oh, it's all humbug and nonsense, I'm sure, and it's certainly not in keeping with Christian belief but…" she hesitated.

"But what?"

She pulled on his coat sleeve, stopping him. "I shouldn't admit to such thoughts, TJ, but if that nonsense prevents Hop Li from hurting or, God forbid, killing someone, well then I'm grateful. I don't care a fig that it's a pagan belief. There, I've said it."

The cool air, the expansive view of the waterfront and river, even the now overcast sky continued to serve as a tonic to TJ. With his headache all but gone, he felt optimistic, alive, and happy that this beautiful woman at his side cared enough for him to reveal what she considered a shameful thought. He offered her his arm and she took it.

43

Tuesday/Wednesday, April 20 & 21

A little after 11:00 am and in the midst of a steady drizzle, TJ boarded the Columbia for Portland. The steamer had an engine problem an hour out of Astoria and the air in the staterooms grew warm and stale. He ventured on deck for some fresh air but stayed only a minute as the drizzle and a swirling, cold wind pushed him back inside. Restless and grumpy, he needed to act but was cooped up in a stuffy stateroom with nothing to do but wait. To feel useful, he thought about Hop Li's choices in Portland. If Hop Li were thinking like a warrior, TJ figured he'd go straight to Purcell's office and fight Purcell right there. But even if Hop Li had taken Dr. Chung's advice and gone to a priest for help, he might reject the priest's counsel and still go after Purcell. TJ realized he didn't know Hop Li well enough to make a reasonable guess about what he would do. He decided to forget Hop Li and concentrate on getting the evidence on the sweetheart ring that would justify Purcell's arrest. He hoped to run into Hop Li before he did something stupid, but he couldn't chase all over Portland in the off chance he'd find him.

He checked into the St. Charles Hotel, and when the desk clerk handed him a telegram, he expected bad news because of the way his day was going. He ripped it open, read it twice, and then whooped in delight.

TJ,

Jeweler is Jacob Hoffmann. 733 3rd street suite 210. Warrant follows. Good Luck.

Silas

The startled clerk stepped back from the desk and an ancient bellman hurried over to ask what was wrong.

"Nothin' wrong. Just good news."

"If you'll just follow me, sir." The bellman bent down to pick up TJ's bag.

"Hold on a minute, will you?" TJ pulled his watch out and saw that it was 5:20. "What time do businesses close in town?"

"Most are open 'til six o'clock, sir. Is there something we can get you?"

"Nope. But you can stow my bag in my room." He gave the bellboy his key and a dime then walked out of the hotel at his marching-to-war pace.

He had no trouble finding the store, a cramped room on the second floor above a shoe repair shop. The jeweler told TJ that he did indeed replace a diamond, ruby and emerald in a sweetheart ring on Monday, April 5th and that his customer waited for the ring. The man had no trouble identifying Purcell from Sketch's drawings. TJ thanked him and left. Feeling on top of the world, he took the steps to the street level two at a time and, once on the street, gave a victory whoop that would have done Big Jim proud.

Next morning, he ate a breakfast of steak, eggs, and potatoes and checked with the front desk every few minutes for mail. The arrest warrant for Purcell didn't show up until after he was halfway through his post-breakfast cigar. He read the warrant and let loose another whoop, startling the same desk clerk of the day before. TJ stuffed the warrant in his coat pocket, left a quarter on the desk, and whistled as he headed out the door.

In contrast to yesterday's rainy weather, a bright spring day greeted him. The daffodils in the planters around the hotel entrance shouted their yellow at him. Even the colors in the adverts on the passing omnibuses seemed fresh and bright. He felt buoyant, full of energy, and wanted to run all the way to Purcell's office for no other reason than he felt alive on a good day. He hadn't felt this good since Lucy Ann had said yes.

He strode at his fast pace but when he happened to think of Lucy Ann he realized she hadn't been in his thoughts for days, maybe a week or more. He felt guilty but assured himself that he'd never forget her. How could he? Nevertheless the guilty feeling stayed with him and tempered his good mood.

He passed through the lobby of the Ainsworth bank building a little after 9:30 am and climbed the steps to Purcell's second floor office.

"Good mornin,' Mrs. Cramer," he said. He saw that the flowers and mourning cards were gone from Jane Thurgood's desk.

She studied him over her glasses for a moment. "Oh yes, the Sheriff from Astoria. Do you have an appointment, Sheriff?"

"I need to speak to Mr. Purcell but I don't have an appointment."

"Well, Mr. Purcell doesn't come in 'til late these days; he's so busy with his election. Would you care to leave a message?"

"No. Maybe I can catch him at home?"

" Oh, my no. He's up early and busy with meetings, I know that for certain."

"My business is urgent—you sure I couldn't track him down?"

"Well, I'm not sure how you'd find him. I suggest you wait here awhile, Sheriff." She slid her glasses off, leaned across her desk towards him and lowered her voice, "Urgent business, you say? It's doesn't have anything to do with that nasty affair yesterday, does it?"

Her air of conspiracy told him she knew something he might want to know. He leaned over the banister and said in a soft voice, "Well, I'm supposed to talk to him but that doesn't mean you can't talk to me—about yesterday or anything else."

"Well, if you're sure it's all right."

He nodded.

"It was a strange experience, Sheriff, the strangest I've ever had. Do you know, at one point I feared for my safety?"

"How so?"

"Well, Mr. Purcell and Mr. Chambers were at lunch and now that Miss Thurgood is no longer with us, I'm here alone. All of a sudden, these Chinamen burst in here, shouting and waving their arms around like madmen. Filthy clothes—ugh! And they smelled of garlic and whiskey and I don't know what. They simply would not take a seat like proper folk, climbing over the banister and crowding around my desk. They jabbered at me in that singsong of theirs. Just like a pack of monkeys! I couldn't make head or tail of it."

"Did they threaten you?"

"Not right away. But after a while I couldn't stand their gibberish and told them to leave. That's when this…this horrible creature shoved his face into mine and screamed, 'Talk Mr. Purcell, talk Mr. Purcell now.' His breath was so foul—I thought I'd faint. He frightened me, Sheriff, he truly did."

"What'd you do then?"

"I said Mr. Purcell wasn't here and to come back later. He didn't heed me, just pushed past me and headed straight down the aisle for Mr. Purcell's office. I yelled at him, I think, and ran after him. I put myself between him and the door to Mr. Purcell's office."

"Mighty brave of you."

"Never in all my years here has anyone been so rude and, well, he infuriated me. I just made up my mind. That fiend was not getting into Mr. Purcell's office. I tell you, Sheriff, it was a nightmare."

"So did the Chinee get into the office?"

"Well, no, he didn't. He kept his evil eyes on me for I don't know how long but then somebody from out front shouted at him. And this is the oddest part of the whole affair. All of a sudden the fiend backed away, even smiled. 'Leave now,' he said, and he did, thanks be to God. I don't mind telling you, Sheriff, I couldn't stop shaking when I talked to Mr. Purcell on the telephone. Mr. Purcell told me to lock up the office and go home."

"Did they say they were comin' back?"

"No. But you don't know what goes in their minds, do you? The police promised to leave a patrolman in the lobby of the bank for several days, just in case."

"They say why they wanted to see Mr. Purcell?

"No. And with all their yelling and screaming, I never found out. A disgusting race, Sheriff, nothing but savages. How anyone can believe those… animals might become Americans is beyond me. Mr. Purcell is doing God's work, Sheriff, preserving our country for Americans. Oh, I pray he wins the election next week, I truly do."

"Well, it's a mystery for sure, Mrs. Cramer. Anything taken?"

"Yes, and I'm just sick about it. Before I left, I had a last look around and noticed the missing photograph." She pointed to a pale spot on the wall where a photograph had hung.

"What photograph?"

She pulled a handkerchief from her sleeve and began to twist it as she talked. "The photograph that showed Mr. Purcell shaking hands with President Arthur the day the President signed the Exclusion Act." She wiped an eye with her hanky. "Oh, I feel just awful, Sheriff. Of course, I called Mr. Purcell right back and told him but he didn't blame me. Not at all. He's such a gentleman, you know." She put the hanky to her long nose and blew, honking like a goose. "That photograph is of no earthly value to anyone else. I can't imagine why they took it."

"All in all, a tryin' day for you, Mrs. Cramer, but you put up a good fight. I'd say you did yourself proud."

"Thank you, Sheriff. You're most understanding." She blew her nose again and looked at the paper in her typewriter.

"Now, what time did you say that Mr. Purcell comes in?" he asked.

"Most days, it's after 10:30." She looked at the clock on the wall beside her desk. "He could be an hour or more, Sheriff." She pursed here lips and then said, "Is it still raining?"

"Nope. Looks to be fair the rest of the day. Why?"

"Well, when it isn't raining, Mr. Purcell likes to walk. All the cherry trees along Oak Street are in blossom and wherever he begins his walk he finishes on Oak. There's a cafe, The Fireside, two doors down from the bank on Oak. They put tables outside on nice days. You could wait there rather than in our office."

"Well now, that's a good idea. You say he always comes down Oak?"

"Yes, Sheriff, he'll pass right by the cafe. He is most reliable, you know."

44

TJ took an outside table at The Fireside cafe with a clear view of both sides of Oak Street as far as the intersection at Fourth. He ordered coffee and then walked across the street to a Chinese grocery and bought an Oregonian. He glanced down Oak, saw nobody approaching, and returned to his table. He couldn't concentrate enough to read anything but headlines so made a show of reading for a minute or two before peeking over his paper.

The streets were nearly deserted of pedestrians, which may be why he noticed the two Chinese men in the empty lot next to the Chinese grocery. He took them for vagabonds hunting salvage and, after a glance, ignored them. But after five minutes of reading and checking the street for Purcell, he glanced back at the lot and noticed that the men looked fit and well fed. Whatever they were about, they worked with purpose. TJ turned back to his paper, checked the street for Purcell, and then looked over to the lot. The men had assembled a bench made of planks from supplies they'd brought with them.

The two now roamed the lot picking up scraps of paper, cardboard, pieces of wood, and dried weeds. They dumped the scraps in the center of the lot and then added pieces of the wood to the pile. The pile soon turned into a mound about four feet high and six feet round at its base. After a quick examination of the mound, they returned to the sidewalk and began hammering boards together.

Just then, an elderly Chinese man turned the corner at Third Street and shuffled towards the lot. Dressed in a black silk top with wide sleeves, a silk skirt, and a round, satin hat with high sides, the old fellow dressed like the priests TJ had seen in Astoria. Though thin and small, his gray eyebrows and queue gave him an air of authority. He carried a carpetbag and wore a necklace of black stones that swung gently from side to side as he moved. When the priest came abreast of the bench, he stopped and lifted his head to examine what the young men had done. An emblem, a long-necked bird stitched in white upon a square of green cloth, decorated the priest's chest. The priest and the young men talked for a time and then one of the helpers hurried off towards the riverfront while the priest went into the grocery store.

A well-dressed man rounded the corner on Fourth Street and walked briskly toward TJ. After a few seconds, TJ realized it wasn't Purcell and returned to his newspaper. When he next looked up, the priest exited the store with a bag of groceries and set the bag down on the sidewalk. From his carpetbag, he extracted a white bed sheet and spread the bed sheet over the plank table. He placed a bowl on the table and filled it with apples, oranges, and a dark fruit, dried figs maybe. On top of the fruit, he placed a pastry. Next, he retrieved a forked branch about five feet long from his supplies and shoved the sharpened end into the earth just behind the table. He hung a small painting from the fork of the branch. Thin strips of gold foil hung from the painting's frame. The foil twisted and sparkled with each puff of air.

TJ caught himself watching the doings in the lot too long and reminded himself to stay focused on Purcell. He checked his watch and discovered he'd been at the café for twenty minutes. He looked up and down the street for Purcell. Nothing. He turned back to his newspaper.

Wisps of smoke curled up from joss sticks burning in an urn underneath the painting and within minutes, the scent of pine reached TJ. The priest positioned a red glass candleholder next to the urn and then laid a bundle of paper money, tied with a ribbon, on the table. The priest lit the candle and then bowed from the waist several times while facing the painting. What had started out as a rough table with a bowl of fruit, a candle, an urn of incense, and a painting, had turned into an altar. TJ couldn't say when that change had taken place only that it had. A handful of Chinese men, too old for work that paid, stood with their hands clasped behind their backs and watched the proceedings from the boardwalk.

By this time, the assistant nailing boards together had finished his carpentry and had built something that looked like a rectangular tabletop about three feet wide and four feet long. He carried the tabletop across the lot and leaned it against the mound of scrap material, shoving bricks and rocks against its base to keep it in place.

More Chinese continued to gather in front of the lot, chatting, laughing, and poking each other playfully. They sounded to TJ like children waiting for a Punch and Judy show.

The assistant sent off earlier returned, followed by a much larger Chinese man wearing a wide straw hat, a clean set of blue cotton clothes, and fresh pair of rubber-soled slippers. The newcomer and the priest exchanged bows and then the newcomer took a paper bag the priest offered him. As the newcomer looked around the lot, TJ recognized Hop Li.

Shocked, TJ stood part way and almost called out but something stopped him. Hop Li's calmness, his clean clothes, and his respect for the priest, told TJ that Hop Li was part of the ceremony and wasn't about to kill anyone.

Hop Li lit the candle in the glass and knelt in front of the painting with his arms extended. He touched his forehead to the ground three times and then lifted the medallion from his neck and hung it on the forked stick. The priest and his assistants had retreated to the far side of the lot and sat crossed-legged with their backs against the brick wall of a stationery store. The old men on the sidewalk had moved too, aligning themselves so that some were at one end of the sidewalk near the grocery store while the remainder moved to the far side of the lot, near the stationery store. TJ had a clear view of Hop Li as he walked across the lot to the mound.

Hop Li took a piece of black silk from the paper bag and laid it against the tabletop. Stretching the silk here and there, he tacked it to the tabletop, adjusted it, and then re-tacked it. Finally, he stepped back and examined his work. A silhouette of a human figure appeared on the board, which looked like a gingerbread man without its decoration. Hop Li then pinned a tube of cardboard about two inches in diameter and a foot long at the neck of the figure.

Hop Li took off his hat, slippers, and shirt. He folded the shirt, laid it on the ground and put his hat on top of the shirt. He bowed to each of the four directions and then sat down cross-legged facing the figure. The grocer, a squat, round-faced Chinese with bowlegs, stood on the sidewalk, wiping his hands on a bloodstained apron and shouted something to Hop Li. Hop Li did not reply.

A beer wagon, loaded with empties, turned onto Oak from Third Street and TJ could hear nothing but the clanking of tubs and clopping of the hooves for the time it took the wagon to complete its journey down Oak. The wagon turned right at Fourth Street and in a minute, the only sound TJ heard was the squawking of crows as they chased one another. The crows quieted and TJ heard a soft humming but couldn't pinpoint the source. The humming grew louder, turned into a chant, and then he recognized Hop Li's voice. Hop Li picked up a slipper, shouted, "hah-yieee!" at the top of his lungs, and struck the figure in the chest so hard TJ's body jerked. Hop Li paused to catch his breath and then the humming began again, becoming a chant after a few seconds. The chant built in loudness until it ended in a high-pitched shout as he struck the figure again. For the first three minutes or so, Hop Li's chanting, shouting, and striking came in a flurry of quick, jerky actions but slowly it grew methodical and less savage, like the rhythm of an ocean wave, a buildup followed by an explosion as the wave broke.

TJ checked the street as far as the intersection of Fourth and Oak. Still no Purcell.

He turned back to the lot. Hop Li's back glistened with sweat and TJ wondered if Hop Li had to pray until he dropped. The waiter came out and asked TJ if he wanted anything else, interrupting his musings. TJ had used up the time a cup of coffee bought him so ordered coffee and a donut.

The chanting stopped as abruptly as it had begun. Hop Li walked back to the altar, bowed to the painting, picked up the candle and bundles of paper money, and returned to the mound. He scattered the money over the mound, knelt, and then touched his forehead to the earth. He set fire to the paper bag with the candle and stuffed the bag into the center of the mound. Within seconds, thick, dark smoke rose from the pile of scrap. Soon flames licked the edges of the tabletop with its gingerbread man. As the flames grew, the Chinese spectators cheered and clapped.

A white boy of ten or so, who had been watching from the boardwalk, darted into the stationery store and came back with a clerk. The clerk spoke to the Chinese man closest to him but the man ignored him, as did a second and third man. Giving up on the Chinese, the clerk sent the boy running into a clothing store next door to his, while he ran into his store. The clerk came out a minute later with a bucket of water. In his haste, the clerk tossed the water too soon and most of it struck Hop Li's back. Even when the water hit him, Hop Li remained facing the fire with his back straight.

Just then, the patrolman stationed in the lobby of the Ainsworth Bank came out and stood in the middle of the street with Mrs. Cramer beside him. He pulled his nightstick out and charged into the crowd shouting curses as he swung at the backs of the Chinamen. The Chinese scattered as fast as their old legs allowed moving just far enough to stay out of the patrolman's reach. After the Chinese scattered, the patrolman spotted the priest and his helpers who had remained in place.

Mrs. Cramer yelled, "There! That's them." She pointed a finger at the three Chinese. "That young one at the end—he's the fiend who accosted me. Arrest them," she shouted.

The patrolman, a beefy, big-bellied fellow, ignored her, marched across the lot and up to Hop Li.

"You there, Chinaboy, put out that goddamm fire."

Hop Li remained sitting and began his chant.

"You Chinee pisspot!" the patrolman shouted and put his brogan against Hop Li's shoulder and shoved. Hop Li toppled over but then returned to his cross-legged position with his back straight.

The patrolman stared at Hop Li, the fire, and the crowd, which by then had doubled in size. He spotted the boy running toward the fire with a bucket. "There's a good lad! Quick now!"

The boy emptied his bucket on the fire but as he'd spilled most of it as he ran, the small amount thrown on the fire produced nothing but a hiss followed by a cloud of smoke. The clerk returned with another bucket and this time his aim was true. The fire sputtered, hissed, and belched a column of smoke.

TJ stood up and glanced down the street but didn't see Purcell or anyone who looked like him. He turned back to the scene in the lot. The patrolman crouched over Hop Li, yelling for him to get up. Hop Li didn't move. The patrolmen raised his nightstick and hit Hop Li across the shoulders. He paused, nightstick raised, and yelled again. Hop Li still didn't move. The patrolman grabbed Hop Li's short queue and began beating him about the back and head with his nightstick. TJ jumped up and ran across the street, cut through the crowd, and up to the patrolman who, red-faced and breathing hard, raised his nightstick to TJ.

TJ held his coat open showing his gun and badge. "I'm a lawman. Can I give you a hand?"

The patrolman paused, looked TJ up and down, then at the Chinese spectators, several of whom had advanced into the lot with faces seething with hate.

"I ask this stinkin' lump of shit to get up three times, polite as you please, but he don't move, acts deef and dumb."

"I'm use to dealin' with 'em—let me try." TJ bent down and put a headlock on Hop Li. Blood flowed from a wound above Hop Li's left temple and welts dotted his back. Hop Li's eyes were shut so TJ put his mouth close to Hop Li's ear and, "Hop Li. It's me, TJ. I'll help you but you gotta listen close. Do what I say." TJ waited and felt blood drip onto his wrist and hand. He whispered his name in Hop Li's ear several times before Hop Li's eyelids fluttered and a frown appeared. TJ loosened his grip. Hop Li opened his eyes and blinked rapidly. He stared into TJ's face for a full second before he said, "Must burn all."

TJ looked at the still smoldering pile, the charred tabletop, and the human figure, most of which had burned. Only a patch at the center and a piece of the tube at the neck remained.

"It's pretty much burnt up, Hop Li. Your job is done. C'mon, it's time to go," TJ repeated what he said twice before he felt the stiffness leave Hop Li's body. He pulled Hop Li up while keeping a loose headlock on him. Before he turned him loose, TJ leaned in and whispered, "I'll come by, post bail, soon as I can."

TJ turned to the patrolman. "This Chinaboy won't be givin' you any more trouble. Now, unless you need somethin' else, I've got other business."

The priest and his helpers rose as one when TJ pulled Hop Li up and crossed the lot and stood behind Hop Li. The priest faced the boardwalk, head up, with his hands folded in front of him. The two assistants stood behind him in the same posture but with heads lowered. The patrolman nodded at the three Chinese standing one behind the other. "Them three ain't gonna be trouble. You go on." He pointed his nightstick at Hop Li. "What'd you say to that boy anyhow?"

"Oh, nothin' much. Just somethin' he wanted to hear."

The patrolman pulled Hop Li's hands behind his back and handcuffed him. The white boy ran out of the grocery store and handed a clothesline to the patrolman.

"Good lad," the patrolman said and tied the priest's hands behind his back, wrapped the clothesline twice around each of the helpers, pinning their arms to their sides. The patrolman then wrapped the line around Hop Li's waist, pulled the clothesline behind Hop Li, looped it around the handcuffs and tied it off. Holding on to the clothesline with one hand and waving his nightstick over his head, he shouted, "Giddy up."

The Chinese shuffled forward but they had taken no more than three steps when Hop Li called out in Cantonese. The Chinese spectators cheered and shouted back. The patrolman jabbed Hop Li's ribs with his nightstick. Hop Li lifted his head once more and shouted in English, "Guan Di fight for Chen Hop Li."

The spectators drifted off. TJ heard a cough close by, turned around, and looked into the tight-lipped face of Mrs. Cramer. "Well, Sheriff, it's over. Thank God." She wore a shawl over her shoulders even though the morning was mild. "Idol worship—in the middle of downtown—why, it's beyond words. Do you have any idea what that heathen flummery means, Sheriff?"

"Nope, can't say as I do, Mrs. Cramer. By the way, I haven't seen Mr. Purcell yet. You sure he's coming in today?"

"Oh, I should think so, Sheriff. After you left, I got to thinking that he might go home before he came in so I telephoned Mrs. Purcell and told her that the Sheriff from Astoria wanted to see him on an urgent matter. You did say urgent, didn't you?" She smiled, pleased with herself.

"Yep, guess I did." TJ looked over Mrs. Cramer's head, cursed to himself, and fought an urge to strangle her. His voice was strained when he asked, "Do you happen to know Mr. Purcell's home address?"

"Why, indeed I do. It's 1055 Morrison Street, just a block from the First Presbyterian Church. But there's no need to go to his home, Sheriff. I'm sure he'll hurry in as soon as Mrs. Purcell gives him the message." She turned and walked across the street to the bank building.

He went up to the altar and lifted Hop Li's jade medallion off the stick. One side had Chinese writing while the other had the image of a bald, fat, and smiling Buddha. The Buddha held a palm fan in one hand and carried a stick with a satchel attached in the other—the Laughing Buddha, according to Emma. He slipped the medallion into his pocket.

The unburned part of the tube at the figure's neck caught his eye. Curious, he pulled the fragment off the board and unrolled the tube. He stared at the charred remnant of a photograph, a remnant that showed part of a top hat, a frock coat, and striped pants. After what Mrs. Cramer told him, TJ now knew the men who attacked her had been after the photograph of Purcell and President Arthur, though he had no idea why.

Hop Li's ritual had earned him a beating and jail time but TJ hadn't heard an ounce of hate in his last words as he was marched off to jail. *Heathen flummery it may be but if it stops a murder, I'm all for it.*

45

T J ran up to a hack driver who'd just discharged a customer and gave him Purcell's address.

"How long to get there?"

The driver, a pint-sized man with a weathered face, knocked the ashes out of his pipe. "Well now, let's see...oh, I'm thinkin' fifteen minutes at least, sir."

"An extra two bits if you get me there in ten."

"The name's Finnegan, sir. And if it's speed you want, you picked the right man." Finnegan grinned at TJ, revealing a mouth empty of front teeth, and pulled his derby down. He flicked his whip and the calash sped down 4th Street towards Morrison Street. It was 11:45 by his watch and TJ estimated Purcell had about a 90-minute lead.

In less than twelve minutes, they pulled up in front of Purcell's home, a three-story mansion with a wrap-around porch and manicured yard. TJ asked Finnegan to wait and then went up the porch steps and rang the bell. A uniformed maid answered and said Mr. Purcell had left and that Mrs. Purcell wasn't seeing anyone. She started to close the door but TJ shoved his boot in the doorway and showed his badge.

"It's urgent, Miss. I need to ask Mrs. Purcell a few questions. Won't take long."

"I'm sorry, sir. But I'm afraid Mrs. Purcell has gone to bed. She's...well, she's not well."

TJ and the maid, a plump girl in her teens, stared at each other for a second before he asked, "Do you happen to know where Mr. Purcell is?"

She hesitated and looked down.

"I'm investigatin' a murder, Miss, so I need to know whatever you know."

"Well, all I know is he, I mean Mr. Purcell, left in a hurry. He took a suitcase with him and…"

"A suitcase. Did he say where he was going?"

"No. Just that he's goin' away for a spell."

"Do you think he told Mrs. Purcell where he was headed?"

"I don't think so, sir. They had this terrible row. I'm downstairs but I can hear them shoutin' and him cursin' and then I hear her bedroom door slam. Next thing, I hear him openin' drawers and bangin' around in his bedroom. Then he comes downstairs and calls after me."

"What did he say to you? Exactly."

"Is Mr. Purcell in trouble?"

"I just need to talk to him."

"He's mean to Mrs. Purcell. To me, too. Gettin' meaner all the time, seems like. Don't care a hoot if he's in trouble." She tilted her chin up and stared over TJ's head.

"Miss, please. What did he tell you?"

"Sorry. Well, he says he's goin' away for a time…let's see… oh, and he's stoppin' off at his club to arrange for the mail. And says to be sure and tell Mrs. Purcell to send his mail there. That's it, sir. That's all he said."

"What club is that?"

"I heard him mention it a time or two… let's see…the Oak…Tree… Oak Leaf. No, that's not it. Wait…" She turned around, hurried down the hall, and disappeared into a room. She came back with a torn envelope addressed to Paul Purcell from the Oak Grove Club. TJ wrote down the address and handed the envelope back to her. He wrote down his address at the St. Charles Hotel and gave it to her. "If Mr. Purcell comes home in the next day or so, please ask Mrs. Purcell to let me know."

"I will, sir."

"Thanks, Miss. You've been a real help."

"The Oak Grove Club, Finnegan," he said as he climbed into the hack. "Can your nag run any faster?"

"Is it another two-bits you're offerin'?"

"It is."

"Hold on, me boyo." Cracking his whip and shouting with glee, Finnegan drove hard down 11th Street. As the calash took the corner at Taylor, it went up on one wheel. Finnegan swerved around a slow moving hearse and cut back at the last second to avoid running into an ice wagon. The driver of the ice wagon shook his fist at him but Finnegan glanced back at TJ and laughed. TJ laughed too. He liked the man's willingness to take risks and when Finnegan slowed to take the next corner, TJ shouted, "Don't slow, man, keep pushin' it!"

At West Park, they turned south and within two minutes the hack pulled into the curved gravel drive of the Oak Grove club. The row of Greek columns along the front of the building gave it a stern, business look, like a government building, and it didn't strike him as a place to go for fun. He asked Finnegan to wait.

TJ didn't get but three steps inside the lobby before a stout man with flabby cheeks left off talking to a couple and hurried over to him.

"Sir?" he said, as he took in TJ's worn Levi's, Pendleton shirt, off-the-shelf sport coat and no tie. The tone of voice, the tilt of the head, and the look in that one-word question told TJ that however important his mission, he shouldn't have come in through the front door. The headwaiters at the Occident and other fancy restaurants gave him that same "you-don't-belong-here" look but he enjoyed watching headwaiters squirm as he pushed by them and sat where he pleased.

"You the manager?"

"Yes. Henry Tuttle. What can I do for you, sir?" A foot shorter than TJ, Tuttle rose up on his toes when he spoke.

"I'm Sheriff Stone, Clatsop County. I'm looking for Paul Purcell. Heard he was here earlier."

Tuttle frowned. "That may be, but Mr. Purcell isn't here at the moment. However, if you care to leave a message, I'll see that he gets it."

"My message is personal. Understand he left some instructions with you. Where does his mail go, better yet, where'd he go? And I'm in a hurry, Tuttle."

"I'm sorry, sir, I'm afraid that information is confidential," Tuttle said through a stiff smile.

A well-dressed couple approached them and stopped a few feet away, waiting for the two men to finish speaking.

"I'm goin' after a fugitive wanted for murder, Tuttle, so nothing's confidential. And aiding a fugitive is a felony, earns you a good spell in prison. Now, you best talk," TJ said in a voice louder than necessary. The woman scowled at TJ and the couple retreated a few yards.

Tuttle, eyes wide at the mention of prison, took a step towards TJ and whispered, "Please, Sheriff, there's no need to raise your voice. If you'll just wait over there..." he pointed to a chair by the coat check cubicle, "I'll be right back." Tuttle scurried off and disappeared around a corner. In a minute he came back and handed TJ a slip of paper with an address: House of Lum, 763 Second Street. See Limpy Lum.

As he walked by the couple on his way out, TJ tipped his hat to the woman. She pinched her lips together and turned her back on him. Outside, he found Finnegan with his derby pulled over his eyes. "Wake up, Finnegan. We're movin' out."

"Are we still in a hurry, sir?"

"We are. And there's another two-bits in it." He gave the address to Finnegan and climbed in the calash.

Once the hack cleared the Oak Grove's driveway, Finnegan cracked his whip and yelled, "Giddup!" The calash picked up speed and raced down Main to Second Street. They turned north toward the business district and Finnegan encountered wagons, drays, buggies, and pedestrians forcing him to slow. By the time they reached Morrison, the hack had slowed to a crawl while Finnegan scanned buildings for Lum's address. After crossing Alder, Finnegan pulled over in mid-block. "We're well past your address, sir, but I saw nothin' like it at all. The heathens do away with some numbers, you know, ones they don't take a likin' to. It's all pagan nonsense but it makes for a devil of a time findin' places. Anyway, I'm afraid you're on your own now."

"Thanks, Finnegan. You did fine, just fine." TJ handed him two dollars.

The driver touched his derby with his whip hand and said, "Good day, sir. And best of luck catchin' whatever it is you're chasin.'"

TJ assumed he must have been in Portland's Chinatown before but, in looking around, realized he hadn't—he'd only been by it on his way elsewhere. The covered sidewalks with balconies that extended over the sidewalk were new to him as were the sidewalk stalls. He hurried to an open-air market where pieces of fish hung on a line to dry and showed the vendor Lum's name and address. The man looked at the address, smiled, and then shrugged his shoulders. Frustrated at losing more time, he hurried on towards Morrison Street.

He slowed as he approached Morrison, studied the addresses, and noticed the numbers were lower than the address he wanted. He glanced around for someone to question but saw only Chinese faces.

Across the street, he saw what looked like a temple and figured maybe one of the priests or assistants would speak English. He crossed the street and stepped into the dark interior of the temple's foyer. A young man wearing a plain brown robe came up and bowed. The assistant recognized the name, Lum, and motioned for TJ to follow him. They walked a little ways back toward Alder Street and stopped in front of a store with a trunk, chest, and two large vases in the window. The only English on the window said in small letters: House of Lum, Importer of Oriental Goods. TJ swore as he compared the address of the store, 736, to the one on the slip of paper, 763. The manager had switched the last two numbers. His watch said 12:50 and he figured stumbling around Chinatown had cost him twenty minutes.

46

The aisles inside the House of Lum were crowded with baskets, chests, vases, nested tables, umbrella stands, and knickknacks. Tapestries, paintings and scrolls covered every inch of wall space while cheap paper lanterns and a few expensive wood ones dangled from hooks in the ceiling.

A young Chinese man dressed in a simple black gown approached. "Yes sir?"

"I need to see Limpy Lum."

"Master Lum busy. Maybe I help?" He offered TJ a well-practiced smile.

"No. I need him. Please get him."

The clerk steered him to a bench. "You wait, please." He bowed and made his way to the back of the store and climbed a flight of stairs to an office. After another long wait, the clerk returned followed by an older man. The man's left leg was shorter than his right causing his body to dip to the left as he walked. Lum wore a red vest with gold trim over a green silk robe and a black skullcap. The clerk bowed to TJ then stood off to the side.

Limpy stopped a good ten feet from TJ, inclined his head a fraction, and slipped his hands into the sleeves of his gown. His eyelids drooped, the left more than the right, and gave him a sleepy look.

"I'm Sheriff Stone, Clatsop County, and..."

Limpy shook his head from side to side and said, "No English."

TJ slowed his words and spoke louder. "I'm looking for a man, Paul Purcell..."

Limpy shrugged and turned to leave. TJ walked up and grabbed his shoulder.

Limpy stopped, looked from TJ's hand to his face, and then said something in Cantonese.

The clerk listened to his boss then turned to TJ. "Please. You go now. Master Lum too busy man." He bowed low.

"What? Listen, you tell your too-busy master I'm searchin' this store, one way or the other. If I have to get a warrant, official papers, then when I come back I won't be too careful when I search, might break something. Now, do I search the easy way or the hard way?"

The clerk nodded but continued to stare at him. TJ grabbed his collar and pulled him close. "Go on. Tell him what I said." TJ came close to stuffing the clerk and his boss in the waist-high vase next to him but after a long second turned the man loose. The clerk's hands trembled as he clutched his knees and bowed three times to TJ. When the clerk finished translating, Limpy said a few words but kept his droopy eyes on TJ.

The clerk bowed again and held the bow as he translated. "Master Lum say if search, must show paper."

Without another word, Lum turned and limped back towards the stairs and his office. TJ swore and deliberately knocked over a basketful of umbrellas on his way out. He stood outside the store, letting his blood cool, and his stomach settle. He hadn't been that far behind Purcell—maybe two hours—but when he got back with a warrant Purcell would be gone for sure from Limpy's if he'd been hiding there.

He crossed the street and started walking back towards Morrison. He'd been so caught up in the chase that he hadn't thought what to do if Purcell evaded him. He imagined Doc waving his pipe at him and saying, you're making a move with no idea where to move. Take some time to think before you go charging off.

He found himself next to the vegetable stand across the street from the temple. He backed up to a building front to let people pass and looked across the way. He hadn't noticed the temple's exterior earlier and was surprised now at its strange and lavish decorations. Scrolls and lanterns hung from the ceiling of the third floor balcony while two gods, at least seven feet tall, guarded the glass door entrance on the recessed second floor balcony. The gods wore bright-colored robes with tiny mirrors sewed on to catch the sunlight. Over their robes, they wore aprons encrusted with spangles and baubles resembling jewels. The stern-faced gods each held up an arm as if waving to those passing below.

He turned his thoughts back to Limpy and realized that, even in their brief encounter, he'd learned something important. Limpy's lack of respect for him meant that Limpy had no fear of the law and that in turn probably meant Limpy had an arrangement with the police.

As Police Commissioner, Purcell had a big say in appointing the chief, which probably meant that the chief was in Purcell's pocket. If the chief couldn't be trusted, could any of his men? Probably not and it meant TJ was on his own. That possibility weighed on him and, for an agonizing few seconds, he questioned his decision to leave Big Jim and Sketch in Astoria. TJ had to get Purcell before the man became a senator because a senator could dispense many more favors and on a grander scale than a police commissioner. He knew his chances of catching Purcell before the election next week were slim if he had to do it by himself.

An omnibus from the Merchant hotel roared by and brought him back to the present. He needed to do something, anything, just to get a sense of movement so he turned around and headed for the central police station on Oak Street, four blocks ahead. As he walked, he planned his next move. He had to get that search warrant but a search would be more effective if he had a translator. A translator could get things out of Limpy that TJ couldn't, by noticing Limpy's tone of voice when he spoke, for instance. But the only Chinaman he knew in Portland was Hop Li and he was in jail. He decided to post Hop Li's bail and go after Limpy first thing tomorrow.

But getting help from the police was another matter. Somehow he had to convince the chief to help him catch the man who probably gave the chief his job.

47

He'd skipped breakfast so stopped at a food cart on Washington Street and bought a Polish sausage in a roll with sauerkraut. He ate as he walked and thought of how to approach the chief. After mulling over several approaches he decided to trust him since he hadn't heard any scandal about the man.

He finished his roll and sausage as he came up to Portland's police headquarters at the corner of Second and Oak. In spite of its ornate trimmings and arched windows, the large, three-story masonry building looked as much a fortress as his castle-like jail building in Astoria. He'd been inside once when he transferred a prisoner from Astoria to Portland and knew that the main floor housed the captain's office and the men's jail. What happened on the second and third floors was still a mystery.

TJ climbed the stairs and showed his badge to a gray-haired sergeant at the front desk. The sergeant's lips were turned down at the corners as if disapproving of TJ even before he said a word.

"Who you lookin' for?" the sergeant asked.

"The chief."

"Second floor. Turn right at the top of the stairs, go past the commissioner's office, first door on the left."

TJ heard the words, "commissioner's office," and a knot formed in his gut. The chief and Purcell had offices next to each other. More than ever he believed he was on a fool's mission. The knot in his stomach spread to his chest as he passed the open door of the commissioner's office. He didn't think Purcell would come here but stuck his head in the doorway anyway. "Is the commissioner in?"

A large, gray-haired woman with a kind face said, "Commissioner Purcell only comes in the first and third Mondays for meetings. But I'd be happy to give him a message, sir."

TJ shook his head, no, thanked her and left.

The chief's door was open so TJ knocked on the doorsill. A strong, bass voice called out, "Come on in."

The chief had a thick chest, broad shoulders, and a belly that rivaled the one TJ saw on the Laughing Buddha. And his office was as oversized as he was. A Persian rug covered the floor underneath his desk, a huge oak piece with carved legs. Brass spittoons, polished to a high sheen, sat on the floor on either side of the desk. A bronze statue of an angel with her wings spread stood in a corner on a pedestal.

"Afternoon, Chief. Sheriff TJ Stone, Clatsop County." He stuck his hand out. The chief shook it with a firm grip.

"Tom Gorman. Have a seat, Sheriff." He turned his head and spit a stream of tobacco juice into the spittoon on his right. "You're a ways from home, Stone. What brings you to Oregon's first city?" The skin under the chief's mouth jiggled as he chewed on a wad of tobacco. TJ regarded the chief's belly and vowed to start chopping the firewood for his office and jail instead of hiring it out.

"Well, I'm lookin' for help—two patrolmen at least—and it'd be great if I could have them by tomorrow. That's the first thing…"

The chief held up his hand. "Whoa, back up. Why are you askin' for help and what's the hurry?"

"I'm huntin' a fugitive. I got word that a Chinee by name of Limpy Lum has him or knows where he is. I paid Lum a visit but he claims not to speak English. The son of a bitch knows the law, though. Told me I need a warrant to search his place."

Gorman grinned. "Limpy. Mighta known. Yeah, he knows our laws real good. On top of which he always seems to know when we're comin.' He's into gamblin,' crimpin' and runs two whorehouses none of which makes him of special interest." He leaned forward and smiled. "But I got reason to believe the little shit is sellin' opium that ain't goin' through customs. Now, that's a whole different story—that's federal. Don't know where he keeps his stuff—we've searched his store and dives from top to bottom but so far, no luck. You want a donut? Coffee?"

"Just ate, but thanks. How long you been after Limpy?"

"Little over a year. And if you're wonderin' why it's taking so damm long there's couple reasons. Limpy's crafty—puts extry turns and doors in the passageways of his gamblin' joints. By time we knock three or four doors down, he and his pals is back home eatin' supper. And to pile on the agony, we got a spy in the department givin' him notice when we're gonna raid. But I'm a patient man, Stone, I'll get him." He spit a stream of juice into the spittoon on his left, most of which hit the target. "But back to your problem. Limpy knows you're comin' back so if your man was at Limpy's he ain't now. And all right, so you got a warrant—it don't mean Limpy is gonna speak English all a sudden."

"Still, Limpy knows where my man is. I aim to push him, let him know what happens to a fella when he aids a fugitive. That's why I need a translator."

"A translator?" Gorman shifted his chew from one side of his mouth to the other.

"Yep. And I've got one in mind. One of your boys arrested a Chinaboy today, one Chen Hop Li. Any chance I could get him released to my custody now for two, maybe three days?"

"You talkin' about that crazy John started a fire on Oak Street?"

"Yep. Only he was just burnin' a pile of scrap in an empty lot—some kind of Chinee prayer service. I saw the whole thing."

"Why you want this John? Plenty translators in Chinatown, other places."

"He speaks our lingo better that any Chinee I know. Plus I trust him."

"Well, suit yourself. But your boy needs to be arraigned and his bail set. Can't get him out before then—but you know that."

"Yep. So I'll see Hop Li tomorrow then."

"Must be some real bad fella for you to chase him all this way. What's he done anyway?"

"He's wanted for two murders."

"Uh-huh. So...he kills in Astoria and skedaddles to Portland. Is Portland home to this boy? Could be I know him."

From time to time after he sat down, TJ had looked over the photographs of Portland big shots lining the wall behind the chief. In one, a smiling Purcell stood next to a dour-faced chief.

"Yeah, you know him all right. And Portland is his home. I'm after Paul Purcell."

Gorman's jaws stopped in mid-chew and he stared open mouthed at TJ. "Come again?"

"You heard right. Paul Purcell."

"Well now, the name ain't all that uncommon. Could be you boys in Astoria got the wrong Purcell. That possible?" The chief looked at him hard.

"Nope. I'm after Police Commissioner Purcell, the fella runnin' for the U.S. Senate."

Gorman continued to look at TJ hard but didn't say anything for a few seconds. Finally, he put up his hand up signaling TJ not to speak, pushed back his chair, got up, and shut the door to his office. He came back to his desk, sat down with a sigh.

"All right Stone, let's hear what you got."

TJ gave a brief account of the murders, the evidence against Purcell, and finished by saying he had two reliable witnesses who put Purcell in Astoria the weekend of the murders. It would only complicate things, TJ thought, if he told the chief his witnesses were Chinese so he didn't. TJ pulled the warrant out of his pocket and slid it across the desk. The chief read it while his jaws massaged his chew, slow and deliberate.

"Shit," Gorman said and shook his head slowly from side to side. "Anybody besides me know you're in town, know why you're here?"

"Well, my deputies and the DA in Astoria know. In Portland, his wife and his secretary know I'm lookin' for him but don't know why, leastways, I don't think they do."

"Purcell up for double murder. I'll be goddammed." He spit a stream of juice into the right spittoon and wiped his mouth with the back of his hand. "You're goin' after a big fish, Stone. You know what you're in for?"

"What I know is that if I don't bring him in before the election and he wins, I'll be tryin' to take down a U.S. Senator."

"And you'll lose." Gorman ran his hand over his droopy mustache. "When word gets out, papers be over us like flies on shit. Be hell to pay if you're wrong. You'll be lookin' for work in a week. Me too, if Purcell finds out I helped you—hell, that ain't right either—I mean when he finds out. 'Cause he damm sure will if I let you have a couple of my boys. He's got friends, Stone, powerful friends, but you know that, right?"

"Are you one of them?"

The chief stopped chewing. "You accusin' me of something, Stone?" His brow furrowed and a patch of red slowly crawled up his neck and spread to his cheeks.

"Nope. Just askin' if he's a friend of yours."

The chief locked eyes with TJ then a smile started at the corners of his mouth and slowly widened until he broke into a chuckle. "You're a brassy son of a bitch. What makes you think me and Purcell is pals?"

TJ pointed to the photograph of Purcell and the chief.

"Oh, that. That's the day I got this job. Yeah, well, things ain't always how they look. But guess only a fool is gonna believe I don't owe him. Well, truth to tell, I did. Once. But that debt's been paid, paid in full. In fact—no, goddammit, enough said—you know all you need to know. Satisfied?"

TJ thought about what the Gorman said. A man didn't confess to being owned by a boss and, in the next breath, say he was through with the boss and then lie about it.

"Your word is good enough for me," TJ said.

The chief swiveled back and forth in his chair, his smile gone. "But dammit to hell, Stone, if you don't get him and he gets elected, what then?" He stared at the ground, speaking as much to himself as to TJ. "Won't matter a tinker's damm what I done for him."

"Won't come to that. I'm gonna put him away. Be easier with your help but with or without it, I'll get him."

"So you say." He stared over TJ's head and rubbed his eyes with his hands. "Shit. You've dumped a mess on my desk, Stone, a goddamm mess."

"He's not a senator yet and he's not gonna be. I aim to catch him tomorrow and for sure before the election. Like you said, the story will make all the papers and come next Tuesday, Purcell couldn't get elected keeper of an outhouse."

"Purcell..." He let the air out of his lungs as if he'd just taken a shot to the belly.

"Now, who do I see about gettin' a search warrant?"

Gorman didn't seem to hear him. He got up, walked over to a tall window, pulled the curtain aside, and looked out. "Purcell...sweet Jesus." He muttered and continued to stare out the window. Finally, he turned and faced TJ. "Listen Stone, what I said a while back—it's true. I don't owe Purcell—now. But could be he thinks I still do. He's gonna tell me to get in your way, do what I can to stop you. Now, I can't blame you none if you think I'll do his biddin.' I'm tellin' you I won't."

"Good. Now, about that warrant..."

Gorman wagged his finger at TJ. "Hold on. I ain't finished. Thing is, Stone, I like my job. We've knocked some of the cussedness out of Portland since I took over. Me and my boys are doin' some good here. I can't afford an enemy as big as Purcell."

"I don't take your meanin,' Chief."

"You got balls, Stone. Could be you'll bring him in...but see that's what's botherin' me, the 'could' part of it. Even if I gave you six of my best, it's far from a sure thing—he's smart, knows how we work. Nope. And if you don't get him before the election, I can't have him knowin' I helped you. Too risky. I won't get in your way but you'll hafta bring him in on your own. Understand?"

"I think so. You're sayin' even if you don't owe Purcell, you can't afford to rile him 'cause if I don't nail him, he'll nail you. Guess I oughta thank you...but seems a funny thing to thank a man for tellin' me he's not gonna help me." TJ stood up and put his hat on. "This not helpin,' it include not tellin' me who to see about gettin' a warrant?"

"Like I said, you're on your own. And I don't want to see you back in my office 'less you walk in with Purcell in shackles, clear?"

TJ nodded. "Thanks for, well, thanks for tellin' me how you stand, Chief."

"Yeah, sure. And Stone, if anybody asks, you don't know me and I didn't help you." He dismissed TJ with a nod.

As TJ walked downstairs, he went over what he'd learned. Gorman's anger and frustration over not catching Limpy with the smuggled opium seemed genuine and told TJ the chief was on the up and up, at least as far as Limpy was concerned. And since Gorman admitted he had a spy in the department tipping Limpy off, the spy wasn't Gorman—unless he was a much better actor than TJ thought.

But Gorman had refused to help. TJ was on his own. What TJ couldn't understand is why Gorman thought that TJ and six patrolmen couldn't find Purcell before the election. Maybe since he couldn't catch Limpy in over a year, the chief believed the odds favored Limpy outsmarting everyone at least until after the election.

Downstairs, TJ stopped at the front desk and read the sergeant's nameplate.

"Where's a lawman go to get a warrant, Sergeant Dunn?"

"You the man from Astoria, right?" Sergeant Dunn looked him up and down.

"That's right."

"Got a cousin lives in Astoria. Gillnetter. Works outta Kinney's Cannery. Denny Sullivan's the name. Don't suppose you know him?"

"Sure, I know him. Good fisherman, easy to work with is what I hear. I used to be a gillnetter before I took this job."

"You don't say? Why'd you quit?"

"A run of bad luck—it's a long story." TJ wanted to ask about the warrant again but in studying the sergeant's face, he realized that beneath the grumpiness, the sergeant wanted to talk. TJ listened as Dunn talked about his last fishing trip where he'd landed two thirty-pound Chinook in less than an hour. Finally, after agreeing that the best salmon is cooked naked and not too damm long, TJ said he needed that warrant sometime today.

"Ah well, why didn't you say so? Police Judge is second floor. Turn left at the top of the stairs. Judge Daly is first door past the police court—you can't miss it."

"Thanks, Sergeant. Any messages for Denny?"

"You tell that rascal it's past time for a visit."

"I'll do that," TJ said. As he climbed the stairs for the second time TJ wondered if the Police Commissioner had anything to do with appointing the Police Judge.

48

Thursday/Friday, April 22 & 23

Judge Daly wasn't surprised that Purcell was a wanted man only that the scalawag, as he called him, was wanted for murder rather than fraud and bribery. He granted the warrant without a lot of hemming and hawing. Daly's face and bearing spoke of strong character and, more to the point, the judge didn't like Purcell.

"Judge, what can you tell me about Chief Connelly and Purcell."

Daly looked up and smiled for the first time. "You want to know if Purcell owns the chief, eh?"

"Yep."

"Well, there's no getting around it, Sheriff, the chief's job is political. With every election there's a good chance we'll get a new chief. But Gorman is better than most. I wouldn't be too hard on him."

TJ left Daly's office about 5:30 and since he couldn't get Hop Li out of jail until the next morning, he decided to go back to the St. Charles for dinner and an early night.

The next morning in Police Court, Hop Li was charged with disturbing the peace and refusing to obey a lawful order. He pleaded not guilty. Judge Daly set bail at one hundred dollars and the trial date a month ahead. TJ posted a ten-dollar deposit, thanked the judge, and left.

As Hop Li and TJ waited under the covered landing of the police building for a break in the rain, the sun poked its face around the edge of a cloud and lit up a strip of rain across the street. At the sight of the sparkling rain, Hop Li shouted, ran down the steps, and turned his face to the sky, laughing, rubbing his face, and gulping rainwater. TJ laughed as he watched Hop Li tasting freedom. He ran down the steps and pulled Hop Li under the awning of a nearby bakery.

"You keep promise, Sheriff TJ. Ten thousand thank you. Portland jail stink like hell. All same like you jail." He grinned.

TJ chuckled. "Yeah, guess all jails stink. How's your head?"

"Head hurt but better soon. So, Hop Li free?"

"You're free until your trial."

"So, go jail again?"

"I don't know. Lots can happen in a month. I'll tell the court you were prayin'—not tryin' to burn anything down." TJ reached inside his coat pocket, pulled out the Laughing Buddha medallion, and gave it to Hop Li. Hop Li yelped with joy and put the medallion around his neck. He grabbed TJ's hand and pumped it without letting go. TJ started laughing and Hop Li joined in.

Hop Li waited until a wagon loaded with gravel rumbled by and then asked, "So, why you come Portland, Sheriff TJ?"

"Well, I'm after Purcell but I need some help and wondered if you…"

"What do?"

"I need to question a Chinaman. I'd like you to translate."

"Translate? Yes, honor help Sheriff TJ."

"Thanks." TJ supposed the exorcism ceremony Hop Li went through had drained all hate of Purcell out of him. But were the effects permanent or did they fade in a day or two, like a Sunday sermon? He didn't know and didn't want Hop Li jumping Purcell as he had Kephardt and maybe getting killed. "Listen to me close, Hop Li. After we're done talkin' to this fellow, I want you to stay back, keep out of the way. If trouble starts, you don't fight. Understand?"

"Yes, understand. No fight," Hop Li said with his eyes glued to the pastries and cakes in the window of the bakery. "You hungry, Sheriff TJ?"

"Didn't they feed you today?"

"Wah! One bowl mush. Good for boy, not Hop Li. So, maybe eat, walk same time?" He grinned and pointed to a coffee cake.

"All right, but something more than sweets. C'mon, I know just the place." They stopped at the cart selling the Polish sausages and rolls. TJ bought two for Hop Li and one for himself with extra sauerkraut. They ate without trying to talk and when Hop Li finished, TJ asked, "Do you know a fella by name of Limpy Lum?"

Hop Li said the name and nodded. "Yes. Limpy Lum rich, big boss."

"Well, I don't care how big a boss he is, he's gonna help us." Without thinking about it, TJ had picked up his pace and Hop Li ran a few steps to catch up to him.

"Why Limpy help?"

"'If he doesn't, maybe I'll shut his store down or send him back to China. Depends how mad he makes me."

Hop Li smiled. "Hah! Sheriff TJ joke, yes?"

"No. No joke, Hop Li. I mean to get that son of a bitch Purcell today."

Hop Li looked solemn and didn't say anything for a minute but then pulled out his Laughing Buddha and rubbed its belly. "For good luck," he said and stuffed it inside his shirt. After another minute, he said, "Also pray Guan Di, god for war, for justice. So, we catch sonbitchee for damm sure!"

49

Friday, April 23

At the House of Lum, they found Limpy sitting in a wingback chair, sipping tea from a tiny cup. His clerk stood behind him, available but out of sight of his boss. TJ handed Limpy the search warrant and Limpy gave it to his clerk. The clerk read it, said something to his boss, and then gave it back to TJ.

"All right Lum, you know what I want. Where is he? I'm not leavin' 'til you tell me." As Hop Li translated, TJ tried to read the headman but couldn't see past the immobile face and droopy eyes. After some back and forth talk, Hop Li said, "I say you no give up. He no help, you close store. He lose much money."

Limpy set his teacup to one side, didn't say anything for a second or two, and then raised his hand to shoulder level without looking at his clerk. The clerk put an unsealed envelope in Limpy's hand and without looking at TJ, Limpy handed him the envelope. TJ opened it and whistled. He handed the envelope to Hop Li and said, "Count it out, Hop Li."

Hop Li counted the bills twice and then said in a solemn voice, "Fifty dolla, hnnnn!"

"That's my salary for a month," TJ said as he took the envelope from Hop Li and tossed it into Limpy's lap. If the headman could afford a bribe this large, TJ realized, Purcell had to be a gold mine for him.

Limpy looked at the envelope in his lap but didn't say anything. He reached out and the clerk put another envelope in his hand. Limpy handed this envelope to TJ, again without looking at him.

TJ felt the fat envelope but tossed it back without looking inside.

Limpy smiled, showing a mouth full of stained teeth, and then picked up both envelopes, said a few words to Hop Li, and held both envelopes out.

"Limpy say, this one, last one," Hop Li said.

TJ shook his head from side to side and didn't take the envelopes.

"Eh?" Limpy said and looked at TJ for the first time.

TJ should have expected a bribe—it's how a headman like Limpy or Wing operated. But even more than the attempted bribe, it was Limpy's offhand manner that offended him. He could see that Limpy expected him to bargain but, in the end, to take the money. To Limpy the bribe was an ordinary transaction, as ordinary as mailing a letter or buying a loaf of bread. Up until TJ refused the last offer, Limpy had treated him with no more respect than one might show a drummer of patent medicine.

"Goddammit. Tell him I'm not for sale. I want Purcell and he's got three seconds to make up his mind to help me. After that I'm arrestin' him for attemptin' to bribe a lawman. And in case he's wonderin,' it means a long time in prison. And when he gets out, it means he's goin' back to China." TJ's face felt warm and he clenched his jaw. Limpy watched TJ with growing interest and when TJ stopped talking, Limpy nodded. Hop Li translated about half of what TJ said before Limpy waved his hand in annoyance, as if brushing off a fly. He clapped and the clerk came out from behind the chair and bowed. Limpy spoke at length while his clerk nodded and bowed throughout the monologue.

"What's he sayin,' Hop Li?"

"He tell servant to watch over store. He say, we go now. Not know when come back."

"Where are we goin'?" TJ asked Hop Li.

Hop Li repeated the question to Limpy. Hop Li's brow furrowed as he listened to the reply. "He say we take walk, see Limpy friend."

"Friend?"

"Yes," Hop Li shrugged, "Also, not understand."

"Listen Hop Li, you tell him I'm not chasin' all over the place. He's to bring Purcell to us. And tell him again what happens if he doesn't."

Limpy's right eyelid spasmed twice as he waited for Hop Li to stop speaking. When Hop Li finished, Limpy barked an order to his clerk who ran up and took his cup and saucer. The headman turned to Hop Li and spoke at length.

"He say, Purcell not stupid, no come us. Purcell wait, we go him. Limpy say he make plan. Catch Purcell all same like hungry fish. Limpy say, must have patience."

Limpy stood up, dismissed his clerk, nodded to TJ, and then started walking towards the front of the store. Limpy stepped outside and waited for Hop Li and TJ to catch up. They walked three doors down from Limpy's and went into a store that appeared vacant. Unlike other stores on this street, its large store window was empty of bric-a-back or furniture. A black curtain formed a backdrop for a red and white porcelain vase that held a single twig with blossoms. A few blossoms from the twig had fallen onto the black silk draped around the base of the vase.

They stepped into a formal parlor, its only decoration a golden Buddha perched on a fragile side table. A bowl of joss sticks burned next to the statue filling the parlor with a smoky haze and the aroma of jasmine. Limpy walked up to a door and knocked lightly with the back of his hand. He waited and when no one answered, he turned to Hop Li and said something.

Hop Li said, "We go now."

"What is this place, Hop Li?"

"When Chinaman die, make plan for bury here. Also make box…not know English word…put Chinamen in."

"Coffins? A box to bury someone in."

Hop Li nodded.

TJ was confused and puzzled. "Ask him why we came here."

Hop Li turned to ask the headman, but Limpy had started walking down a short hallway and said something over his shoulder.

"We go basement now," Hop Li said.

At the word basement, TJ's chest tightened and his face grew warm. Somehow, he'd allowed Limpy to dictate where they were going and the conditions under which they would meet Purcell. TJ liked to lead rather than follow and hated being dependent on someone he didn't trust. Limpy stood at the end of the hallway holding one door of a set of double doors open. With one hand on the butt of his gun and the other on a railing, TJ followed Hop Li down a flight of stairs. As he descended, TJ started to sweat, his chest tightened even more, and his mouth felt dry. But just before he reached the bottom step, he smelled fresh cut cedar, an outside smell. A row of basement windows and several overhead lamps made for a brightly lit workshop, which eased his anxiety.

Shelves along one wall of the basement held bottles, cans of glue, clamps, and assorted scraping tools while seven-foot long slabs of rough cedar stood upright in cribs along the opposite wall. An unfinished coffin resembling a six-foot long bulbous tube with flanges at both ends sat on the floor waiting to be sanded and lacquered. Three completed coffins lay on a pallet close to the rear wall.

Just to the side of the stairs, a shirtless carpenter sat on a stool and smoothed the rounded side of a cedar slab with a jackplane. Thin but with wiry muscles, the young Chinese paused in his work to nod at Limpy. Limpy said a few words to Hop Li then went over to the carpenter.

"Why'd we stop here, Hop Li?"

"Limpy say, one minute, then go Purcell." He nodded towards the carpenter. "Limpy tell carpenter, sorry, no fan-tan today. Limpy run fan-tan game—for rich men."

He noticed the carpenter eyeing him as Limpy talked to the young man. Limpy finished and the carpenter got up from his bench and headed for the stairs. As the carpenter climbed up the stairs, he called out something that made Limpy laugh.

"What he'd say, Hop Li?"

"He say, you too tall, break neck when go tunnel," Hop Li shrugged, "not understand."

"Tunnel?! What tunnel?" He shouted. He'd never been in a tunnel and the thought of going in one caused his guts to churn. "What the hell's goin' on, Hop Li?" TJ undid his holster strap and rested his hand on the butt of his Colt.

Hop Li shrugged again. He didn't seem worried and acted as if each wrinkle Limpy tossed at them was simply another challenge in a childhood game of follow-the-leader.

"Can we trust him, Hop Li?"

Hop Li paused before answering, "Limpy no buy Sheriff TJ like other policeman. Maybe Sheriff TJ put Limpy in jail, send back China if no help. I watch Limpy face, eh? He worry like hell, hnnnh!" Hop Li nodded. "So, maybe trust…maybe."

Limpy said something sharp to Hop Li. "We go now," Hop Li said.

"Go? Go where? Goddammit, Hop Li. That's it. I've had enough." TJ pulled out his gun, cocked it, and aimed it at Limpy. "All right. Where is he? And speak English, you son of a bitch, 'cause I know you can."

Limpy stared at the gun and raised his arms. He spoke slowly to Hop Li.

Hop Li translated as Limpy continued to speak. "Limpy say, no need gun. Follow him. No talk, no noise. Maybe ten minute. We go room, secret room. Limpy bring Purcell to us."

TJ eased back the hammer. "Tell him again I don't work for the Portland police. If he tries any tricks, I'll use it. Tell him that."

When Hop Li finished translating, Limpy nodded, lowered his arms, and then picked up a lantern hanging from a peg on the rear wall. Limpy pushed aside the pallet on rollers holding the three coffins, revealing a canvas that covered the brick wall. Limpy pulled the canvas aside and exposed a hole about three by four feet. He motioned for them to follow and went through the hole.

"Hah?" Hop Li muttered and looked at TJ, obviously as confused as TJ.

TJ couldn't see anything on the other side of the dark hole. Sweat trickled down his armpits and he felt sick. He swallowed several times, fighting the nausea, and kept a sweaty hand on his gun. Just before he went through the hole and disappeared into the darkness, Hop Li looked back at TJ and grinned as if to say the game had become more interesting.

TJ hadn't counted on this, hadn't counted on going into a hole or tunnel or whatever the hell it was. His heart raced and his guts, already tight, tightened into the familiar hard knot.

He tried to control his body by talking to himself but it didn't help. Sweat dripped off his forehead and every nerve in his body screamed at him to turn back.

50

Friday, April 23

TJ followed Hop Li and found himself in a tunnel not much over five feet high, preventing him from standing upright. They were enveloped in darkness except for light that leaked around the edges of the canvas door. Limpy lit the candle inside the lantern. The candlelight passed through the metal-filigreed sides of the lantern, casting shadows that snaked across the dirt floor and nearby brick wall. Tiny bells at the corners of the curved-roof lantern tinkled when the lantern moved.

After a dozen steps, TJ bumped into a support timber and, in reaching out to steady himself, touched a wet spot in the wall and an insect, a cockroach probably, scurried over his hand. He yanked his hand back. Drenched in sweat and close to vomiting, he squatted and put his head between his knees. The smell of dank earth reminded him of being locked in his coal cellar and the memories came back, memories of being sick and alone, and of a blackness that clung to his skin after a time like a wet sheet after a fever sweat. Dizzy, he closed his eyes. Images of his father filled his head. He smelled Dad's fish stink, whiskey breath, and the coal. He could see Dad's face as clear as if he were standing over him now—lips curled up, face white with anger, looking at him like he was wrong for living. Then the words—'coward,' 'useless,' 'never amount to a thing'—exploding out of Dad's mouth. The words didn't fit but they stung all the same, stung worse than a whipping. He wanted Dad to hurry up, get the yelling over, get to the hitting. But there was an order to it—words and curses first, then the hitting, like a summer storm with thunder and lightening coming before rain. The hurt from the beating gone in a day or two but the meanness in the words—the goddammed words—stayed with him. He never got used to the words.

"Sheriff TJ?" Hop Li leaned down and touched TJ's shoulder.

TJ lifted his head. He was in a tunnel, not a coal cellar. "Yeah, yeah. I'm all right. Let's move on."

He decided to count his steps in case he had to backtrack without a guide and, just as important, to keep his mind off his body. After only a dozen paces, he felt his chest being squeezed, felt a presence, a thing, taking the air meant for him. The back of his shirt was wet and nausea enveloped him. It's like old times, he thought, hard to breathe, guts ready to heave, head burning up, and skin hot and itchy. Same goddammed feelings. But you got to fight it, TJ. You can't puke down here, not in front of the Chinee. You show fear in front of Limpy and he'll use it to beat you.

They walked hunched over for another twenty steps and then made a sharp turn to the left. Another thirty steps and they came to a wide space, a chamber about the size of a living room and with enough headroom for TJ to stand up. He felt cool air move across the top of his head and this along with the increased space, eased his symptoms.

Directly in front of him, the tunnel continued on but the light from Limpy's lantern didn't reach far enough for him to see more than three or four feet so he didn't know how far the tunnel extended. To his left, the wall curved out in a semi-circle and he saw a large statue of a Chinese god, like those on the balcony of the Portland temple, set into a niche in the earth wall. The god held a flywhisk in one hand and carried a sword in a scabbard over his shoulder. A makeshift altar, a wood box with a lit votive candle, stood in front of the god.

Opposite the statue, a three-foot wide strip of canvas covered the wall from ceiling to floor. Limpy shoved the canvas aside and invited them into a small room. A candle in a sand-filled tin can sat on a table in the center of the room and provided enough light to see the room's furniture: a pot belly stove, a wood water bucket, two chairs without backs, a dirty mattress on a pallet, and several saw horses. A shelf above the stove held pots, dishes, tins of food, a toolbox, and bottles with stoppers.

Even though TJ didn't see a window, the flame of the candle flickered so the room had to be vented. In spite of the vent, the cloying aroma of opium filled the room, triggering another wave of nausea. Swallowing a half-dozen times, he tried to calm his stomach but couldn't. He left the room, crouched down in the tunnel, and lowered his head. Limpy and Hop Li came out and stood over him.

"You sick?" Hop Li asked.

"Opium stink. Be all right in a minute."

Limpy and Hop Li talked back and forth and then Limpy pointed across the way to the statue. Hop Li nodded and said, "We wait, behind

Lü Yen, eh? Purcell come, that way." He pointed in the direction opposite the one they'd come.

Limpy walked Hop Li over to the statue and said a few words to him. Hop Li nodded and squeezed in between the statue and the earth wall. TJ stood about midway between the statue and the entrance to the room but couldn't see any part of Hop Li. Anyone coming towards the statue from the far tunnel wouldn't be able to see him either. Limpy nodded at TJ and he slid in next to Hop Li. The statue was large enough to hide them both. TJ peeked around the shoulder of the god, and found he could see the canvas door and the tunnel from which Purcell would come.

Limpy snuffed out the candle on the altar then went into the room and put that candle out. The filigree lantern now provided the only light and when Limpy emerged from the room, the ceiling and walls of the tunnel crawled once again with tongues of light. Limpy nodded once in the direction of the statue and then disappeared down the far tunnel. The smell of opium was still strong and kept the storm churning in his stomach. He swallowed repeatedly and forced himself to think of Tug and the river. He came close to vomiting twice but gradually the waves grew less frequent, less intense.

"China have eight immortal," Hop Li whispered. "Immortal all same like god. *Lü Yen* number one immortal. Sword magic, hide *Lü Yen*, so easy kill enemy. Good omen, Sheriff TJ. Sonybitchee no see us."

"Hop Li, when Purcell comes, you stay put. Understand?"

"Yes. Understand." Hop Li rested his head against the back of the statue and caressed the scabbard with his hands. Suddenly, he pulled back. "Hah...?" he muttered.

"What?" TJ's hand went to his gun.

"Opium. Here. Inside *Lü Yen*," Hop Li said and led TJ's hand up the back of the statue until he felt a crack in the wood.

"Smell," Hop Li said.

TJ put his nose up to the crack, sniffed, and jerked back at the sharp, sickening sweet odor. Retreating as far as he could from the statue, he spent a minute taking slow, deep breaths allowing the nausea to ease before returning to his hiding place.

"Well, we found Limpy's opium cache. Wonder how this thing opens," TJ said.

"Men come soon, Sheriff TJ. We not talk now."

Except for Hop Li's steady, slow breathing, it was quiet. And ink black. TJ recalled the silence and blackness that tormented him as a boy. Either one by itself didn't bother him so much but after the cellar door lock clicked shut and Dad left, there was nothing but the silence, the blackness, and it—a presence he never saw, only felt. All the same, he knew as sure as he was alive, that it was too. The thing came to life in the silence and blackness, fed off it, got heavier with each second, squeezing him, taking the air in the cellar. If he slept, it'd get him, he knew that too. So he talked to himself, prayed, told stories, until morning light when the door opened and Sis called down, "He's gone. You can come up now."

Dammit, could use Sketch or Big Jim now. Stop it. They're not here. Forget it, TJ, you're on your own.

The air behind the statue grew thick, humid, and the thing started to squeeze his chest, gaining strength. His breathing grew shallow, the muscles in his neck and shoulder tightened, his stomach a volcano about to erupt. Could he keep his affliction from reaching the last stages until Purcell got here? He put his hands on his knees and lowered his head. *Forget your body. You got one job now. Putting the cuffs on Purcell.*

A rustling sound came from somewhere near the ground. He stilled his breathing and strained to see. Something ran on to his boot, tugged at the bottom of his Levis. He kicked out and struck the thing. Screeches shattered the silence. The rat felt heavy when he kicked it, closer to the weight of a small dog. Fingers of cold ran down the back of his neck and he shuddered at the thought of a tunnel full of dog-sized rats. He turned his head this way and that, listening for any sounds, human or rat, but heard nothing.

Hop Li made a shushing sound when the rat screeched but otherwise didn't speak and didn't move. How did he stay so calm? He wanted to hear Hop Li's voice again, anything to break the silence, but he had no reason to talk and felt weak for wanting to. He took a deep breath and leaned back against the earth wall. When he closed his eyes, he saw Dad's face, drunk and raging, just as clear, as fearsome, as when he was eight.

Hop Li clicked his tongue. TJ quieted his breathing and heard the tinkle of lantern bells. He turned to where he guessed the men would come and didn't have long to wait before he saw the dancing light of the lantern. Seconds later, a Chinese man he didn't recognize appeared carrying Limpy's lantern. A large man with a beard followed. He walked hunched over and wore a slouch hat pulled down tight. Another young Chinese man followed the large man. The three filed into the room across from TJ and Hop Li but in less than a minute, the two Chinese came out. The man with the lantern nodded once towards the statue and then the two left in the direction they'd come.

TJ waited until he could no longer hear the lantern bells then stepped out from behind the statue. The candle inside the room had been lit and light leaked out around the edges of the canvas, providing direction. TJ heard footfalls behind him. He reached out, caught Hop Li by the arm, and shoved. Hop Li retreated but TJ didn't know how far.

When he heard no sounds from Hop Li's direction, TJ drew his gun. He moved across the dirt floor with slow steps, feeling for rocks or holes with the tip of his boot before shifting his weight. To avoid crossing the strip of light at the edge of the door, he moved on a path that took him to the side of the door. He reached the wall, held his breath and listened for sounds inside the room. Nothing. He pushed the canvas aside, tucked and rolled on his shoulder, and came up in a crouch, gun pointing at the candle.

Purcell jumped up from his chair. "Christ!" Purcell's eyes locked onto the gun. "Stone! You damm near gave me a heart attack."

"Put your hands on the table."

"Why?" Purcell hadn't moved.

"I said put your hands on the table." He waited until Purcell complied then said, "You know why I'm here. I'm arresting you for the murders of Jane Thurgood and Wah Fong."

"An impressive entrance, Stone. But totally unnecessary—I'm not armed."

"Uh-huh. Open your coat...slow now."

Purcell took one hand off the table and opened his coat. TJ didn't see a holster or a gun in Purcell's belt or a bulge in his inside pocket.

"Goddamm that Limpy. Should have guessed he'd snooker me," Purcell said with a smile.

"All right, now turn around." He kept his gun aimed at Purcell's chest.

"Anything you say, Sheriff." Purcell tilted his head, seeming to study TJ, as he slowly turned. Something wasn't right. TJ didn't know what but his guts told him that everything about Purcell's voice and manner was wrong. The next instant he realized that Purcell didn't have the look of a defeated man—he didn't look worried. A yell came from the tunnel outside. Before he could turn around, he took a blow to the back of his head. Pain consumed him. He felt himself falling, the gun slipping from his hand, and then nothing.

51

T J woke to a hospital stink and a head throbbing with pain. It hurt even to think about opening his eyes. The pain in his right elbow kept him from moving that arm. He made a fist with his left hand and lifted it a few inches without pain. He tried lifting his legs an inch or so but his boots felt as if made of lead. That bit of movement wearied him and he rested. When he felt up to it, he moved his good left hand out to the side. After a few inches, it bumped into something solid. Fingertips felt wood, rough-cut, as far he could reach forward and backward. He reached under him, ran his fingers over wood and caught a splinter. He lifted his hand straight up and, again after only inches, bumped into wood, a two by four this time. He traced the two by four from left to right and found planks of wood nailed at right angles to the two by four.

With growing panic, he stretched his leg and pointed the toe of his boot out and it touched a hard surface after an inch or so. He lifted his foot up and felt another two by four. Quickly, he reached out to his left, then above, then to his right. Nothing but wood as far as he could reach. Refusing to believe what his fingers told him, he repeated the search, this time moving from right to left but only got another sliver for his efforts. He forced his eyes open. Dark, dark as forever, and the only sound came from his shallow, quick breaths.

Can't be. No. Jesus, God no! They nailed you up in a box! A coffin. Bastards!

His heart slammed into his chest, the muscles in his neck tightened, and he fought for air. The food in his stomach wanted to come up and he tried to swallow but had no saliva in his mouth. He yelled but the sound came out weak, as if far away. He tried to yell again but his stomach couldn't hold out. He turned his head to the side and puked the meal he'd eaten earlier: sauerkraut and sausage. Again,

306 |R i c h a r d   B .   P o w e r s

and again, and again, he puked. The stink of his vomit kept him puking until he thought he'd never stop. Vomit covered the collar of his coat, the front of his shirt, down his right side, and his coat sleeve. He turned his head but couldn't get away from the stink. About when he decided he'd rather die than keep on puking, the waves of nausea subsided. His shirt and underclothes were soaked in sweat and he couldn't stop shivering. Even so, he felt better.

He reached up, and banged on the lid with his fist, hitting with energy fueled by terror. He heard a voice. Someone was out there. Footsteps padded toward him. A piece of wood slid across the top of the box just above his chest. A pause, then another piece of wood was pulled out from further down. The lid of the box slid open part way. A triangular Chinese face with sharp cheekbones stared at him. He raised himself a few inches and tried to speak but a hand pushed him back down. The hospital stink was sharp now—ether. The cloth came at him, covered his nose and mouth. He pulled back, grabbed at the hand, twisted his head this way and that but his muscles were weak, useless. His body relaxed and he dropped his hand.

He woke up later with a terrible thirst. He reached up, banged on the lid and screamed. Nobody came for what seemed like an hour. Exhausted, he stopped yelling and within minutes the locking boards were pulled out and the top opened part way. The same face but this time the hand held a tin cup.

"Water," the man said.

He raised his head, tilted the cup to his lips, and took a sip. That first sip felt so good that he drank without stopping, spilling some of the precious water. The guard took the cup back, put the lid on, and slid the locking boards into place. The darkness covered him again, and he felt the weight of it, worse than before. He took a deep breath, and then let it out slowly. It felt good to do that and he continued to breathe, deliberate and slow, until the tightness in his chest eased and his hands stopped shaking. He told himself he had to focus, to find a way out. He turned his head to the left, away from the vomit, and felt a thin stream of cold air on his forehead. He stretched his head back as far as he could and saw a faint light coming through two holes above him. Air holes. He could breathe in here, as long as he didn't tighten up. Not a sound came from the room and he strained to catch a whisper, or hear a chair creak, anything, but after five or six minutes of silence, he panicked.

Shit. They've gone. Left you shut up in here. Can't stay in this box. Got to get out! NOW! Goddammit.

He yelled but his voice, hoarse from the vomiting, came out puny, no more than a squeak. He made a fist and rapped on the lid with his knuckles. Waited. Nothing. He let his hand fall back to his side and breathed in deep, let it out, lifted his shoulders. They were heavy, too heavy to hold up and he sank back. As soon as he relaxed, he realized that the pain in his head and elbow had lessened, the nausea was tolerable, and he no longer felt cold.

When he went to raise his arm to knock again, it didn't obey. Something wasn't right. He felt good inside. Too good. Part of him wanted to hold onto that good feeling, a relaxed, happy, feeling, like the feeling he had after making love to Lucy Ann. Another part of him wanted to push the feeling away. Didn't trust it. That part wanted out of this box, that part said fight it, don't sleep, don't give in. But he couldn't help it. He let go, closed his eyes, his breathing slowed, became shallow, and he drifted into something like sleep.

He saw things as in a dream but when he wiggled his little finger, he felt it move so knew he wasn't asleep. But he wasn't awake either. In his dream, a palomino raced around an open field on a summer's day. A beautiful animal that made him think of Emma and the grace with which she moved. The horse leapt as if to jump over a fence but then kept right on going, flying up into the sky. He went with the horse and saw it turn into a cloud in a purple sky, a purple so deep and pure, it seemed as if he could feel it. He saw other colors too and didn't realize colors could be so strong, so intense, and so pleasurable to look upon. He saw a red ball next that seemed to be made of glass like a paperweight, but when he touched it, it was soft and furry like the pelt of a rabbit. What he saw and felt wasn't right, didn't make sense, but it didn't bother him; he liked the images, liked how they made him feel.

He woke up with a thirst worst than before and his head ached all over, not just from where he'd been hit. He smelled his vomit, the ether, and then remembered. Panic hit his stomach with the force of a punch. Heart kicking like a rodeo bronco, he retched and brought up nothing but a trickle of thin gruel. He felt weak, helpless. And even after nothing came up, the retching didn't stop, which added to his misery.

Can't give in, TJ. Cup of water had something in it. Slow your breathin.' Mind outside, on the river, sunny day, you and Tug headin' to the Shoo-fly drift. Emma, God bless you. Maybe this is it. How it ends. Wish I'd told her…dammit, what are you doin'? Christ, man! Stop! Won't get you out of here, wallowin' in sorry. What about Hop Li? Poor bastard. Got nothin' but trouble from knowin' me. Not right…stop! You're doin' it again. Gotta get out of this goddamm coffin. Think, TJ. What would Doc say?

Doc sat behind his desk at his coroner's office and his index finger pointed at TJ. *How come you're still alive? If they wanted you dead you'd be dead hours ago. Seems to me they want you out of the way and only that. So they Shanghai you and Limpy gets paid double for you. Once from Purcell and again from a ship captain for a strong hand.*

He screamed and kicked at the sides of his prison, which brought a guard, the opening of the box, and the rag full of ether. The sequence of waking up in a panic, lashing out, and the coming of the guard repeated several times but he had no idea how often. And with no way to measure the passage of time, he had no idea how long he'd been shut up. He felt himself drifting again and let the feeling take him where it would.

When he was fully conscious again, he smelled something sweet and felt a weight on his chest, an orange, sliced in two. He grabbed a piece, bit into it, and, Oh God but it tasted sweet. It wasn't until the juice dripped from his hand onto his neck that he wondered if the orange had something in it. Cursing his stupidity, he put the other half to one side and counted to one hundred. During his count, he didn't feel any of the sensations he'd felt earlier so he picked up the other half, sucked out the juice, and ate the inside.

Sometime during one of his wake times, he didn't remember when, he'd felt for his holster and gun and found them gone. Now, he reached up and patted his shirt where his badge should be. Gone. He felt his vest pocket and found no watch. Moving his butt back and forth, he felt an empty back pocket. Wallet gone.

So what'd you expect? The shits. But wait…they left my boots on. Tug's knife! Maybe…

He pushed his right boot forward until the toe touched the back of the box then bent his ankle. He felt the leather sheaf and knife push against his leg. His heart leapt and he almost shouted. Just then, a guard with a gruff voice said something and his partner answered. TJ's guts knotted and he held his breath. Someone pulled a chair or stool off a table and the two talked back and forth. TJ let his breath out and eased his leg back to the floor of the box without a sound. Outside, he heard tiles dumped onto a table. The gruff voice talked while the other man slurped soup or tea.

Tiles clicked on the table for a time then a guard shouted in glee. Dominoes, TJ guessed. So far, he'd heard only two voices; the gruff voice and a higher pitched one. He let his head sink back, his legs relax, and tested his right hand by making a fist then opening it—the pain in his elbow was still there but tolerable.

He twisted his torso to the left, pressed his butt against the wall, and scrunched his head and shoulders towards his knee. As he made this last movement, his right shoulder scraped the top of the box, making a noise. He froze and listened. A tile slid on the table. Someone grunted. Another tile slid. The guards seemed lost in their game. He realized he'd been holding his breath and released it. After a second or two, he reached his arm and shoulder forward and brought his knee up until it brushed the other side of the box. He touched the top edge of his boot with his middle finger. Not far enough. Sweat ran down his forehead into his eyes, stinging them.

With his neck and head bent forward, he sucked his stomach in and pushed his butt hard against the side. The middle and first fingers touched the top of the knife's handle. By design, the knife fit tight. He tugged and his fingers slipped off the handle. He jerked reflexively and hit the back of the box with his boot. He froze, listened. The guards talked and then tiles were pushed around the tabletop. They must be used to sounds coming out of the box by now, he thought.

With his next attempt, he got the tips of two fingers on the handle. He twisted instead of pulling and the knife moved. But with the twisting movement, his hand started to cramp. He lifted his fingers and let them hang at his side. In a minute, he took hold of the handle again, twisted and pulled. The knife moved towards him but, again, the awkward position caused his hand to cramp. He relaxed, closed his eyes, and thought of Emma, saw her face as he told one of his Finn or Swede jokes, saw the way she'd turn her head to one side and burst into laughter, not so much at the joke but at his pleasure in telling it. When she was happy, her eyes grew wide and soft, her face glowed. It lit up his insides to see her happy, gave him a jump-over-a-fence feeling.

Never thought you'd feel like that again, did you? You've been a fool, TJ. That's right, a goddamm fool. When you get outta here, first thing...hold on...you mean if, don't you, if you get out of here...stop it...forget what if...think about now.

He curled up again and stretched his arm towards the boot, middle finger on top of the handle, further than before, and pressed down, gently. He edged the tip of his first finger under the handle. It felt secure. He twisted the handle a touch and pulled. The knife slid forward. His wrist cramped this time and he felt the pain all the way to his elbow. Couldn't keep holding the handle like this. He loosened his grip and wiggled his thumb, easing the cramp. The muscles in his right calf shook and were close to cramping.

Sweat ran down his arm onto his hand and fingers. For some time, he'd resisted the urge to piss but he couldn't hold off any longer. He let go of the handle, wiped his fingers on his shirt, and unbuttoned his fly. The seat of his pants and his underwear were wet and he realized he must have pissed in his pants while sleeping. He let go and piss trickled through the cracks in the boards. He heard it splash on the floor and realized the box was raised off the floor, supported by boxes or sawhorses. Outside, tiles clicked in a one-two-pause rhythm, the guards speaking only after a break in the rhythm.

He hunched up again and this time the tip of his thumb went under the handle. He twisted the handle, pulled with a steady pull, and the knife came out another half inch. His wrist screamed at him to stop but he crept further down the handle with his thumb and finger. The knife came out further, maybe another inch.

Too damm slow. It'll take forever this way....shit.

He took his fingers off the handle, shook them, and took a long breath. A sharp pain shot through his neck and shoulders. Couldn't stay hunched up like this much longer. His entire body would cramp soon and he wouldn't be able to relax his muscles without thrashing around. And that would bring a guard.

He got a fresh grip as before and pulled. The knife slid and slid and then—came out. Out!

He untwisted his body, gripped the knife with both hands, and sank back with his heart racing. He wanted to shout in victory but his body needed attention. Leg, arm, and shoulder muscles were stiff and sore; pain from the blow to his head came back; and the vomit stink had new life, bringing on flutters of nausea. He needed rest, an undrugged sleep. Exhausted, he tried to think where to hide it, somewhere he could reach quickly. But he couldn't think—he wanted to sleep. His eyelids grew heavy, he felt sleep coming on.

Hold on. Not yet. Get it out of sight.

He found space between two buttons on his shirt, slipped the knife inside, and then rolled his body to the left. The knife slide down by his left hip. When he lay flat again, part of his back and hip rested on the handle. If he moved in his sleep, the blade might cut him but he didn't care. He needed to feel it, to know it was there. In less than a minute, he fell asleep to the sounds of tiles hitting the table.

52

Sunday, April 25

He woke to the sound of voices and the smell of cooking; onions, spices, and meat. His stomach rebelled at the odors and he vomited, bringing up bits of orange. He felt chilled and shivered after the retching stopped. He moved his arms and legs up and down and from side to side to warm himself.

In the room, he heard a new voice, a voice full of confidence. He knew that voice but something wasn't right—the voice spoke Chinese. Someone dragged a chair or stool towards his box.

"Good morning, Stone. You don't sound well. Rough night?" The voice said.

"Purcell!"

Purcell chuckled. "That's right. Another little surprise, eh?"

TJ forced himself to concentrate. *Purcell speaking Chinese. Christ, what next? And why is he hanging around? Think, TJ. He wants something, but what? Wants to gloat for one thing. So let him, keep him talking. Find out what he's up to.* TJ turned his head in the direction of Purcell's voice so that he didn't have to shout. "What you aim to do with me?"

"Haven't you guessed? You're going on a little trip. Any preferences?"

"Go to hell." As soon as the words left his mouth he knew he'd made a mistake.

"Now, now. Here I'm offering you a choice and you spurn my offer. Perhaps I should leave?"

"No! I'm listenin.' What's the offer?"

"That's better. Well, the Eastern Star departs next Saturday for Hong Kong with stops at Yokohama and Hangchow. The Far East will be good for you, Stone, teach you patience if nothing else."

"Christ. No. That's more than a week away. Can't stay in this goddamm box that long."

"You have a roof over your head, no work to do, and a chance to catch up on your sleep. What more do you want? Besides, today's Sunday which means it's only a six-day wait. Time will fly by in that little house of yours."

"You…" He stopped himself. "What else is there?"

"Ah, very good, Stone. You're learning restraint—an admirable trait in a lawman. Now, let's see…yes, there's the Jane Barnes bound for Sidney, Australia. It leaves Thursday afternoon, three days from now. How's that suit you?"

"Better. It's three days I'm not rottin' in here."

"Well then, it's settled. The Jane Barnes it is."

Purcell liked lording it over him, TJ realized, and told himself to encourage him. "I'm still wonderin' about a few things, Purcell. I can't stop you now, so how about answerin' a couple of questions."

"Well, well, always the lawman, eh?" Purcell paused and then said something in Cantonese to one of the guards. "All right, Mr. Sheriff, ask away. But I haven't had my breakfast yet so, if you don't mind, I'll eat while we chat."

A pot scraped on the stovetop and the next thing he smelled meat and onions up close. He retched for a time without bringing anything up.

"Touchy stomach you have there, Stone. You ought to eat something to settle it. This pork is a bit fatty for my taste but the scallions and fried rice are not half bad."

At Purcell's mention of pork, TJ gagged and retched for another ten seconds.

Purcell waited for the retching to stop and then said, "A long sea voyage is just the thing for digestive ailments or so I've been told. But now, you had a couple of questions."

"Why'd you kill her?"

"You disappoint me, Stone. Thought you'd have figured that out by now. But you didn't meet her, so perhaps that accounts for your ignorance. Well, behind that pretty face and sweet manner was an ambitious whore. She betrayed me. Spied for that prick Jameson—slept with him to boot. She had the gall to threaten me. Imagine! Said if I didn't marry her, she'd say the baby was mine. Couldn't have that—publicity would cost me the election." He took a few bites, chewed, and then put his mouth close to the air holes. "Nobody threatens me, Stone, nobody." He ate for a time and then continued. "Anyway, she had the morals of a cobra. World's better off without her—though I must confess to missing our little love bouts. My God, what a woman! Could bewitch a man with one look."

"And the grocer?"

"Ah yes, Wah Fong. Always liked him, too. But he made the arrangements, showed us our room. Even if he couldn't testify against me, he knew too much."

"What about her hands? Why'd you cut them off?"

"You said a couple of questions—that's four. Sorry."

"What you afraid of, Purcell? Nothin' you say is gonna come out." TJ considered a man who cut off a woman's hands for whatever reason strange, not right in the head. He tried to soften his question so as not to provoke him. "Maybe in the heat of the moment you did something you wish you hadn't. You carryin' some shame over what you did? Is that it?"

Purcell drank something, smacked his lips, then silverware clanked on the tin plate and he called out to the guards. To TJ he said, "Shame? Ha! You don't know me, do you? The explanation is mundane, nothing like what you're imagining, and nothing like those amusing reports in The Star. Mind if I smoke?"

Purcell didn't wait for TJ to respond before lighting a cigar and puffing hard for a few seconds. Soon, smoke slipped through the air holes and filled the inside of the box. The aroma of a good cigar ordinarily gave TJ pleasure but now only brought on a bout of retching.

In between heaves, TJ said in a hoarse voice, "So why cut off the hands?"

"Let's see, where was I? Ah, yes, Fong's place, our love nest. I hadn't planned things, Stone, so didn't know what to do with the bodies. Then it came to me. What if Fong or Jane had walked in on a Chinee burglar that night? An inspired plan, yes, but here's the best part. You listening? I asked myself not what a Chinee burglar would do but what the God fearing people in Astoria would suspect him of doing. Their worst fears come to pass, eh?" He stopped, took a long draw on his cigar and exhaled. More cigar smoke streamed into the box.

"So I took Fong's money and that assassin's dagger he was always going on about. A burglar would take Jane's rings, too—they looked real enough. But by the time I thought of the rings, her hands had swollen and I couldn't get the damm things off. So what would my heathen do? Why he'd cut off her hands and take them along to work on later. So that's what I did. Once you understand the premises, Stone, it follows. Simple logic."

"Christ, how could you..." He stopped himself. "I mean you had feelings for her, didn't you?"

"You're not thinking, Stone. She was dead. Of what use were her hands? Now, do you want to hear the rest of my story or not?"

Don't judge him, TJ scolded himself, tell him what a clever boy he is. "Yeah, let's hear it. I have to admit I'm learnin' a thing or two."

Concentrating on the details of Purcell's story helped take his mind off his body and the box. "So, puttin' her hands in that retort tank at Jameson's—how'd that come about?"

"Opportunity, Stone, and a stroke of genius, nothing less. I left Fong's with the dagger, a box with my Chinee clothes, and the hands wrapped in butcher paper just like a pair of lamb chops. A nice touch, I thought." Purcell chuckled.

TJ wanted to curse but held his tongue. Purcell didn't have feelings about people like most folks—something missing in the man. "Yeah, that was slick. Last thing I'd expect to find in a package."

"Of course."

"So after you left Fong's?"

"I had one thought—to get back at that ass-wipe Jameson. But I didn't know how yet. Then I happened upon this big Chinaboy at a tea stand. I knew right off that my robe would fit him or be close enough. And when the Chinaboy told me he worked at Jameson's, my cup runneth over. Seemed too good to be true. But then the gods favor some mortals and yours truly is one of them. So I offered to pay him to keep the box for me—gave him some cock and bull story and he bought it. But Hop Li is a greedy bastard and what's worse, insolent. The whelp argued with me, forced me to pungle up another dollar fifty. Infuriating. I came close to slapping him. Can't abide a menial who tries to rise above his station."

"So you left him with the box of clothes and went to the cannery. How come nobody saw you?"

"The strike. Remember? Nobody at Jameson's that night except a night watchman and I'll wager he was asleep in the upstairs office. As I said, the gods smile upon me, Stone."

"I expect you wrote that Chinee message on Jameson's tank, which pointed to a Chinee killer. Derailed my thinkin' for a good spell."

"One of the few times I've found a use for my written Chinese. But now it's my turn to ask a question. You almost hung Hop Li for me. Why didn't you?"

"Well, too many things weren't right. Take that Chinee writin', for instance. Folks that know said it looked like a beginner wrote it. And the opium in Fong's safe? Any Chinaboy would take that—it's as good as cash in Chinatown."

"Ah yes, the opium. I didn't take it because I hate the stuff. An oversight, in retrospect. But you intrigue me, Stone, perhaps I've underestimated you. What else led you away from Hop Li?"

"All this talkin' has made my throat dry. Any chance of gettin' a wet towel and a cup of water, plain water that is?"

"Don't fancy the opium, eh? Most times, Limpy Shanghais a man straight away but we had to stow you 'til we had a deep-sea ship available. The coffin was my idea, the opium and ether Limpy's." He chuckled. "You've piqued my curiosity about Hop Li so you've earned your cup of water, plain." He said a few words to the guards.

Within seconds, the locking boards slid off, the lid opened, and a new face, round and with thick lips, handed TJ a wet rag and a cup of water. TJ took a sip and drank, slowly at first, and then gulped it down. He handed the cup back and then wiped the stale vomit from his chin, neck and throat with the rag.

The guard put the lid in place and then TJ said, "Well, the jewels we found at Fong's set me to wonderin.' I asked myself why they were left behind."

"And what did you conclude, Mr. Detective?"

"Well, I figured the jewels were the killer's and he left them 'cause he didn't know they were missin' 'til later. Since you and Jameson were the main suspects, I asked what a fella would wear with jewels in it. A ring was a good bet. A jeweler put us on to sweetheart rings."

"Not bad for a hick Sheriff, Stone." A chair scraped the floor. "Well, it's been fun but I have to go."

"Wait, one more question. Somethin' been botherin' me for some time now."

"Ask away but be quick about it."

"You been goin' on about how the Chinee steal white man's jobs and we ought to ship them back to China. Yet, you speak their lingo and seem to get on fine with them. Hell, Limpy's even helpin' you escape. Doesn't make sense."

"It doesn't make sense because you don't know me. The white man in these parts is terrified of losing his job to a coolie. After I give my little talk, men know that I'm on their side, that I'll fight to rid this country of heathens so that the white worker can keep his job. Politics is all about now, Stone, all about what's practical."

"But seems to me you're sellin' hate just like the Knights. They don't seem bent on much other than killin' and destroyin.' How's that help you?" TJ took the chance on asking a question that might anger Purcell but he wanted to understand the man's thinking.

"Hate is useful, Stone—it's a force, don't you see, like an ocean wave. And if you know what you're doing, you can use that wave, guide it any way you want. The Chinee talks funny, works for less than the white man, wears a pigtail, worships idols, and lives on next to nothing. In other words, he's easy to hate." Purcell's voice sounded warm and confidential, as if he were advising a younger colleague. "The Chinee are made to order for me."

"But the Knights lynched Fatt Luk and damm near caused a riot—not you."

"Quite right." He chuckled.

"You sayin' you sicced them on us?"

"Who else? Your pal, Kephardt, was a godsend, coming to Portland when he did. The man's a plodder, no imagination whatsoever. But he's a bulldog, tireless, and, best of all, takes orders well. I needed an engine, a locomotive, to get things moving. Kephardt and his Knights were my engine." He chuckled again. "I told Kephardt about Hop Li, the strike at Jameson's, and gave him a little money. Christ, you should have seen him when I told him the Chinese Benevolent Association had hired a good defense lawyer for Hop Li—damm near ripped the hinges off my door on his way out." Purcell smoked for a time. "And Kephardt was doing so well before you locked him up too. Pity." His voice took on a hard, flat tone. "But you'll be gone soon, gone for good, while I'm riding the Chinese question to the United States Senate." He started laughing and kept on until the laugh turned into a cough. He drank something and the coughing stopped.

"Sounds like there's some wrath to your feeling' about the Chinee."

"Wrath? Ha! Wrong again, Stone. My father was a missionary in China—had his heart set on me taking up his mission work. I had private schooling, the best of tutors, all to mold me in his image. But by the time I was twelve, I knew what I wanted and it had nothing to do with saving heathens. I had to run things, you see, even as a boy." He puffed on his cigar then leaned in and put his mouth close to the air holes. "It's all about power, Stone, nothing else. Only power matters. With power comes money, women, and privilege—in short, the best life has to offer. And I deserve the best things in life, don't you see?" He stopped to take a long pull on his cigar before continuing. "I have nothing against the Chinee. On the contrary, they've been most useful."

The chair scraped on the floor and Purcell said something to the guards.

TJ put his mouth close to the air holes and shouted, "What you plan to do with Hop Li?"

"Well, well. Do I detect a Chinee lover under that tough hide?"

"Just curious."

"Oh, you'll probably cross paths in some Chinee port in a year or two. You might even bump into that livery boy—what's his name?"

"You mean Slim, the one rented you the buggy?"

"That's the one. Well, ta ta, Sheriff. *Bon Voyage*." Purcell and one of the guards left.

53

Monday, April 26

After Purcell left, TJ listened to the voices in the room for what he guessed was five minutes and heard only two voices so felt confident only two guards remained in the room. He eased Tug's knife out of his shirt. So far the guards had opened the lid on TJ's right side and both men who gave him ether or the cup of water reached toward him with their right hand. He saw how he might attack that guard but then the other guard would be all over him in seconds. He told himself to plan one step at a time and concentrated on the knife.

It had to be hidden when the guard opened the lid but where? He put the knife up his coat sleeve, point down, wiggled his wrist and let the handle slip into his hand. But the next three times he tried the maneuver, the blade caught on his shirtsleeve or didn't drop down without a lot of wiggling. Won't work, he realized, and allowed his body to relax. Doc's voice came to him as he massaged his wrist and fingers: *Don't make it so hard to get the knife. You got surprise working for you. Use it.*

He slid the blade of the knife under his thigh, kept his hand on the handle, and rested his left arm over his stomach so that his left hand hung loosely over his right. He pulled the knife out from under his thigh a few times and it slid out easily.

In the room outside, a kettle whistled, and someone poured water into cups. To his surprise, his stomach felt settled enough to take food. He pushed the knife all the way under his thigh and yelled, *sihk*, the Cantonese word for "eat." A chair scraped the earth floor and soon after, he heard the familiar sound of wood sliding across the top of his box. The lid opened part way and the round-faced guard held a wooden bowl out so that TJ had to reach up and take it with both hands.

TJ rested the bowl on his chest, tilted his head up, and ate the rice, pork fat and scallions with his fingers. His supine position made feeding himself awkward and he spilled food on his chest but what he did manage to eat lifted his spirits. He finished, handed the bowl to the guard, and then made a drinking motion with his hand. The round face grunted and came back with a dipper of water.

He took a sip, paused, and asked, "Opium?"

The guard shook his head, no.

The man could be lying but he drank anyway since he needed water. He noted that the guard took the dipper with his right hand while his left rested on the edge of the box. The guard dropped the lid in place and slid the locking boards over the lid. Next he heard the click-click of the tiles.

A minute passed with no sensations of floating or dizziness and he knew the water had not been drugged. He stretched his legs until his boots touched the back of the box and then lifted his fists until his knuckles touched the lid. He repeated the sequence several times, relaxing after each tensing, and found that though his muscles were stiff and sore, he could move all parts with only minor pain.

You're as ready as you'll ever be. You've got surprise, the knife, and fast hands. Anything else? That rag of ether. If you grab that, you can use it on them. Ether. What Doc say about it? Got to be careful with it. Why? Don't recall. Damm.

He slid the knife out of his shirt and tucked it under his thigh. Heart racing, he took a deep breath and let it out slowly. But before he called out, someone moaned. He froze. A second moan, louder, followed. Someone banged against wood and shouted. He recognized Hop Li's voice. He was shut up too. One of the guards shouted back and the room grew quiet for a few seconds. But then Hop Li yelled louder and knocked against the sides of the box with his fists. A chair slid on the floor.

He waited until he heard the top of the other box being opened and then he banged on the lid of his box, kicked the sides, and yelled at the same time. A voice shouted a Cantonese term he knew, dogface, and a second chair scraped the floor. In seconds, he smelled ether. He filled his lungs with air, slowly exhaled, and then rested his arm on his stomach.

The boards slid across the top, the top opened part way, and the round-faced guard extended his hand with the cloth soaked in ether. TJ grabbed the man's right wrist and pulled. The man shouted and his head came forward. TJ shoved the knife into the soft spot below the Adam's apple. The blade went in more than halfway. The guard screamed and then lunged for TJ's hand. TJ twisted the knife once, let go of it, and then yanked the cloth out of the guard's hand. He still held the guard's right wrist with his left hand and as the man pulled against him, he let the guard's backward pull take him up. As TJ pushed off with his legs, the box tipped sideways and fell off its support. TJ and the box landed on the guard's head and chest. The man screamed as the blade sank deeper into his throat.

Before TJ could get up, the other guard kicked the box aside, jumped on his back, and had an arm around his neck. TJ pushed onto one knee, got both feet under him, and scooted backwards. Both fell with TJ landing on top of the man. The guard squeezed TJ's throat. Arching his back, TJ slammed his elbow into the man's stomach and the guard's grip loosened. TJ rolled off and held the ether cloth over the guard's mouth and nose. The man grabbed TJ's wrists, twisted and jerked his head back and forth, and tried to buck TJ off. TJ lay across the man's chest, using his weight advantage to keep the cloth over the man's face. In half a minute, the guard's hands let go, his eyes closed, and his head rolled to the side.

The other guard sat with his legs splayed out and his back resting against the wall. Blood pulsed from his wound and drenched his shirt. The guard was trying to ease the knife out of his throat when he saw TJ coming and crawled towards the table. TJ caught up with him, pushed him to the ground, and turned him over. He held the ether cloth over the man's face until his eyes closed and his body went slack. TJ pulled the knife out. A soft gurgling sound escaped the mouth and bright red blood poured from the wound. He wiped the blade on his pants and slipped the knife back in his boot. Returning to the other guard, he draped the ether cloth over the man's nose and mouth. He glanced around the room, saw Hop Li's box against the back wall, and shouted Hop Li's name. Hop Li didn't respond.

TJ took a step toward Hop Li's box but then became light-headed. He gripped the edge of the table with shaking hands, waiting for his breathing to slow and his heart to stop racing. He found the water bucket and drank three dippers of lukewarm water. He poured water over his head and wiped his face with the dirty towel he found on a peg. Inside the food chest, he found vegetables, a sack of rice, a bag of apples and another of oranges. He stuffed two oranges into his coat pocket, straightened up, and again called Hop Li's name. Hop Li still didn't respond.

Have to keep moving. Can't wait around for Hop Li to wake up. Get some help and come back—that's the smart thing to do.

"Nope. Can't leave him," he said aloud.

The lid of Hop Li's coffin was open and the ether cloth rested on Hop Li's shoulder. TJ stuffed the cloth in his pocket and pushed the lid all the way off. He shook Hop Li and shouted his name. Though Hop Li's eyelids fluttered and his head moved, he didn't wake. TJ tipped the box towards him, held on to Hop Li's shirt and, using his knee as a support, lowered Hop Li to the ground. He put his arms under Hop Li's shoulders, dragged him through the canvas door, and down the tunnel about five paces. He stood up and thought over his next move.

If Hop Li didn't wake up, he'd have to carry or drag him through the tunnel to the basement of the funeral parlor. And what if new guards showed up? He reached for the gun at his side and felt its absence with a sinking feeing in the pit of his stomach. With a pounding heart and a knot in his stomach, he went back into the room to search for his gun.

The guard with the knife wound looked dead or dying and the other guard hadn't moved. He searched under the dirty mattress and the shelf over the stove but didn't find his gun. The shelf above the stove held a bottle of cooking oil, tin cups and plates, and a shoebox with candles, matches, and strips of cloth. A leather case hung from a peg on the wall opposite the stove. He found a stoppered bottle inside the felt-lined case. When he pulled the stopper out, the odor of ether struck him with the force of a blow. He stoppered the bottle and hung the case up. It was of no use to him.

He noticed the coal oil lantern and realized he needed it. As he reached for the lantern, the flame flickered and suddenly he remembered why Doc said you had to be careful with ether. If the fumes got too close to a flame, there'd be an explosion; an off-season Fourth of July is how Doc put it. He thought of all the wood and sawdust in that Chinese funeral parlor and realized the ether might be useful after all. He put the strips of cloth from the shoebox in the case with the bottle of ether. The box of matches he wrapped in a towel, shoved the towel inside his shirt, and looped the handle of the ether case through his belt.

Back in the tunnel, he paused and listened. All quiet. He bent over Hop Li, shook him, and called his name. Hop Li moaned, opened his eyes briefly, but then closed them.

"Hop Li, wake up. You've got to walk on your own, you hear?"

But Hop Li showed no sign of having heard and TJ reconciled himself to carrying Hop Li through the tunnel.

A screech startled him and he jumped to his feet. Only a rat, he thought. But the sound came from the direction in which Limpy's men would come. He told himself the sound didn't mean anything but the rush of adrenaline he felt gave that the lie.

He got down on one knee, put Hop Li's arms over his shoulder, and shifted his body so that Hop Li's chest lay across his back. Another sound. He froze and heard nothing more. He got up part way, grabbed Hop Li's wrist with one hand, and put the lantern ring in his mouth. With one hand free to steady him, he walked bent over like a miner for thirty paces before the muscle burn in his legs forced him to stop. He put Hop Li's weight at 160 pounds at least. "You're too damm heavy, Hop Li. Time to carry your own weight. You listenin' to me?" He said aloud.

Carrying this much weight stooped over was harder than he expected. The hope he felt earlier was replaced by the familiar knot in his gut that said you're not getting out, you won't see open space and blue sky again. He let Hop Li slide part way off his back and caught his breath. Again, he thought he heard something, voices maybe, in the tunnel behind him.

He looked at Hop Li's body and believed for a second that if he wished hard enough, he could revive Hop Li, make him wake up and speak. But then he realized his foolishness, spit on his hands, and shifted Hop Li's body onto his back. Fighting the cloud of doubt in his head, he pulled at the ground with his free hand and drove forward with his legs another twenty paces. Gasping for air, he eased Hop Li off his back.

From the tunnel behind him, he heard a shout and then loud voices. The new guards had found their comrades. He asked himself what he'd do if he were in their place. If there were two men, he reasoned, one would run back to Limpy with the news while the other would wait in the room or he might come after him. But if TJ were the man left in the room, he wouldn't go after two men in a dark tunnel, especially after seeing what happened to the guards. So the new guards would probably wait for more men before coming after them. But he realized his thinking was laced with a good dose of wishful thinking.

Hop Li's eyes opened and he grunted when TJ said his name. TJ shook him and Hop Li lifted his head, mumbled, but then his head lolled back. TJ covered another fifteen paces before he stopped, wiped the sweat from his face, then tied his sopping wet handkerchief around his neck.

After a rest, he picked up the lantern, looked up and then froze. Not more than six feet ahead, a solid wall faced him. With mounting panic, he lifted the lantern and moved it around but saw nothing but wall. *A goddamm, dead-end! Can't be. What the hell happened?*

54

T J stared at the wall in front of him and realized he must have taken a wrong turn. But then he heard Doc's voice. *You came this way. Calm down and take a close look.*

He walked towards the wall. After several paces, the lamp illuminated the opening where they'd taken a sharp turn.

Voices, faint but excited, came from the tunnel behind him. He put the lantern ring back in his mouth and pulled Hop Li up on his back. Pain shot down the sides of his jaw into his neck and shoulders. He pushed ahead but moved too quickly, stumbled, and fell.

Can't hurry a dead weight of 160 pounds—not hunched over. Slow and steady, TJ, slow and steady.

He made it around the turn and for another ten paces. He stopped, gasping for air, and looked back the way they'd come. No flickering light, no sounds. Nothing. Earlier he reasoned that one man would run back to Limpy while the other stayed in the room. But what if more than two men had come in relief?

Stop thinkin' about what-ifs, TJ. Concentrate on what you got to do.

He held the lantern up but could see only darkness after about six feet. "Goddamm tunnel is never gonna end," he muttered and cast a glance at Hop Li, wanting him to answer, but Hop Li remained mute. "Don't know about you, Hop Li, but I need some fresh air and sunshine."

With Hop Li up on his back again and the lantern in his free hand, he wobbled and staggered three or four paces before going down on one knee. His balance wasn't good like this, the lantern in his hand instead of his mouth, but his jaw needed a rest. With his arms and legs burning, he moved only three paces before stopping. His body told him it couldn't do any more.

"Been for nothin,' if you stop now," He said aloud. "Think of Purcell braggin' on how he outfoxed a hick Sheriff. You like the sound of that, Hop Li? Me either."

He pulled Hop Li onto his back and picked up the lantern, moved three paces, rested, stumbled forward another two paces, and rested again. He saw a dim light ahead and recognized the entrance to the funeral parlor. Close now, he told himself, and though he moved as if through mud, he made another five paces before stopping and letting Hop Li slide off him. Fighting for every breath now, he picked Hop Li up by the shoulders and walked backward, dragging him a few paces before he lost his footing and fell on his rear. He looked over his shoulder. The entrance to the funeral parlor was three yards ahead. He whispered Hop Li's name in his ear. Hop Li opened his eyes, frowned, trying to focus.

"It's me, Hop Li. Sheriff TJ." He eased Hop Li into a sitting position. Hop Li said a word in Cantonese with a shaky voice.

"Wake up Hop Li! C'mon, wake up!" TJ shook Hop Li's shoulder. Hop Li blinked a few times, turned his head to spit, and stared at TJ for a full second before saying, "Sher...iff T...J! Wha...happen?"

"Later, Hop Li, we'll talk later. Let's get you up." TJ stood, grabbed Hop Li under the shoulders, and pulled him upright. TJ draped one of Hop Li's arms over his own shoulder and then put his arm around Hop Li's waist. Staggering like two drunks, TJ propped Hop Li against the wall and then went back to pick up the lantern. He put the lantern down next to Hop Li and leaned against the wall. He closed his eyes and listened for sounds from the tunnel behind him but heard nothing.

"Can you stand by yourself?" he asked and backed away from the wall. Hop Li took a step towards him then started to fall. TJ caught him and propped him against the wall.

"Sick," Hop Li said, then turned against the wall and vomited. In a minute, he stopped retching and wiped his mouth with his sleeve. TJ went up to him. "We're goin' in that basement, Hop Li. Can you walk by yourself?"

Hop Li nodded and stood up as far as the tunnel allowed. TJ picked up the lantern and then put his free arm around Hop Li's waist. They moved towards the entrance with unsteady steps. As they grew close, TJ heard the sound of a handsaw but no voices. Maybe only one man between them and freedom. The thought triggered a surge of adrenaline. He untied the thong holding the ether case to his belt and loosened the stopper. He slid Tug's knife out of its sheath and stuck it under his belt buckle. The carpenter in there wasn't expecting trouble, probably wouldn't have a gun. But the man had a hammer, a crow bar, and knives. So it came down to the ether. If he poured ether on a pile of sawdust and put a match to it, the pile would ignite in a flash and the basement would turn into an inferno if allowed to burn.

"Time to go, Hop Li," TJ said and held the canvas door open, pushed the pallet of caskets aside, and helped Hop Li through the opening. Sunlight streamed into the basement from the windows at the front and TJ blinked repeatedly trying to see in the bright light. When his eyes adapted, he saw the carpenter standing motionless at a front workbench with a saw in his hand. The man was shirtless, his leather apron tied at the waist. TJ took note of the tattoos on the carpenter's muscular shoulders and biceps. As close to exhausted as he was, he knew he couldn't best the carpenter in a fight. TJ held the bottle of ether in one hand and the lantern in the other. He opened his coat and showed his knife.

"Speak English?" TJ asked and took a step towards the man.

The man dropped the saw and stepped behind the workbench, his eyes locked on TJ.

"I'm not lookin' to hurt you. We just want to go outside. Savvy?" TJ took two more steps toward the man.

The man turned and bolted up the steps.

"Shit. He's probably goin' for help. Go over and stand next to those stairs."

Though his steps were unsteady, Hop Li reached the stairs without falling. "What do?" he asked.

"I'm goin' to start a little fire. Could be things get out of hand and it turns into a big fire. If that happens, I want you to get up those stairs as fast as you can. Don't wait on me. Understand?"

Hop Li frowned and asked, "Why make fire?"

"Well, the fire is to show I mean what I say—if they don't let us go, I plan to burn the place down. But I'm bettin' they won't risk their building just to keep us locked up. It's a gamble, Hop Li, but I don't know what else to do."

"Gamble, maybe live; no gamble, we go in box, all same die. So, gamble best way."

TJ blew out the candle in the lantern and then set the lantern on the floor. Next, he pushed sawdust into a small pile with his boot and after he had a mound about a foot deep and two feet wide he poured about half the ether in the bottle on the pile. After putting the stopper back, he put the bottle of ether within easy reach on an unfinished coffin. Then he took the towel with its box of matches from inside his shirt.

Within a minute a thin, middle-aged man with a wispy beard appeared followed by the carpenter carrying a six-foot staff. The older man, probably a boss or owner, wore a black gabardine tunic with frog buttons, spectacles, and a soft felt hat. The boss inspected TJ and his eyes grew big. He made soft clucking sounds with his tongue.

At that moment TJ became aware of how he must look: coat caked with dried vomit, pants soiled with piss, shirt soaked in blood, and hair matted and dirty. TJ could smell the stink of his body so he suspected the boss could too. He and Hop Li must look like desperados ready to do God knows what to them.

"We won't hurt you. Just step aside and let us leave," TJ said in a soft voice.

Hop Li started to translate TJ's words and the boss gave a start, so engrossed had he been in studying TJ that he appeared not to have seen Hop Li. The boss turned and acknowledged Hop Li with a bow. The two talked back and forth for a time.

"What'd he say, Hop Li?"

"Say, if we fight, Lu-fan fight us. Lu fan best fighter, so Lu fan win. Best way, we no fight, wait for Limpy."

"Like hell. Tell him I'll burn the place down unless they let us go."

While Hop Li translated, TJ lit a match, waited for the flame to spread to the matchstick, and then dropped the match on the pile of sawdust. There was a whoosh and the sawdust erupted in flames. The boss shouted, ripped off his tunic, and started for the fire. TJ pulled out his knife and stepped in front of him. The older man halted, looked at the knife, then at TJ, frowning and mumbling to himself. The boss said something over his shoulder to Hop Li.

"He ask, what you do," Hop Li said.

"Tell him, I meant what I said. This place will be nothing but ashes if he doesn't let us go." TJ dripped a small amount of ether over the coffin next to him.

Both boss and carpenter watched TJ wide-eyed with horror. The boss shouted to the carpenter before Hop Li finished translating. The carpenter took off his apron and started for the fire. TJ turned, pointed the knife at the man, and yelled, "Stop!"

The carpenter halted but didn't retreat. Looking back and forth from TJ to his boss, the man waved his apron back and forth while shouting to his boss. By now, smoke had risen to the ceiling and had started to descend, filling the basement with an acrid smell. TJ stuck the knife in his belt and held a match next to the matchbox as if to strike it.

The boss glared at TJ, nodded, and waved for them to leave.

"Go on, Hop Li. Get out of here. Wait for me on the street." He watched Hop Li climb halfway up and then slipped his knife back in his boot. He backed away from the two Chinese, dripping ether on the sawdust-covered floor as he retreated. As he climbed the stairs, he saw the carpenter run to the burning pile and cover it with his apron. The boss grabbed a broom and swept sawdust away from the smoldering fire. TJ pushed open the doors at the top of the stairs, hurried through the parlor, and out the front door.

Once outside, he realized he was walking hunched over as if still in the tunnel. He raised his arms over his head and stretched. Outside meant space to stand up, space to move in any direction, space to run down the boardwalk, and space to dance in the street if he had a mind to. Outside meant fresh air, sky, and sunlight. He took in a lungful of air and with it the smells of the city: horse dung in the street, meat cooking on a brazier nearby, the tang of the Willamette River three blocks away. Light hearted, he couldn't stop smiling and whooped with delight.

He found Hop Li leaning against a railing outside a fortuneteller's tiny stall a block from the funeral parlor. He took the oranges out of his pocket, bit into one, and held the other out to Hop Li who stared at it without taking it.

"Go on, eat. It'll settle you're stomach," TJ said. Hop Li took the orange, bit off a chunk of skin and then sucked the juice.

After finishing his orange, TJ looked off to the east and feasted his eyes on the snow-capped peak of Mt. Hood. The mountain had never looked so beautiful, so large, so present. Its permanence comforted him. After a time, the fortuneteller's spiel brought him back to the moment. The fortuneteller would shake a can holding thin bamboo sticks, jabbering away like a hungry blue jay as a potential customers approached.

TJ smiled at the fortuneteller's antics but as he watched the fellow, the good feelings of a moment ago were replaced by a feeling of being used up. Of a sudden, he lacked the energy and will to move. He felt safe standing here and part of him wanted to hang on to the safe feeling. But with a sudden shake of the head he freed himself. "We got to get movin,' Hop Li."

"Where go?" Hop Li said. He stared down Second Street as he shoved the remainder of his orange in a pocket.

"Police station. It's on Oak Street, about three blocks from here. Can you make it?"

Hop Li didn't respond and continued to stare down the street. TJ followed Hop Li's gaze. About a block and a half away, four Chinese wearing leather leggings laced to the knees came towards them.

"Those men, Limpy men. Go temple now," Hop Li said.

"Wha....we need the police—not any damm temple."

"Master Sung say, need help, come temple. So, we go temple." Hop Li started walking up Second Street, away from the Portland Police station.

55

T J and Hop Li reached the temple and stepped into the foyer but no one came out to meet them. Hop Li sat down, took off his slippers and placed them next to a row of slippers at the side of three steps leading into a large hall, the place of worship. He pointed at TJ's boots and said, "Please, take boot off, Sheriff TJ."

"Whaa…? Godammit, Hop Li, we don't have time for monkey business."

"Respect necessary. No shoe in temple."

"Christ!" He yanked his boots off, slipped Tug's knife out of his boot, and stuck it under his belt. He set his boots down next to Hop Li's slippers.

TJ followed Hop Li up the steps onto a hardwood floor waxed and polished so often that he had to take small steps to keep from slipping. As his eyes grew accustomed to the dim interior, he made out a center altar with a statue of a god sitting on a horseshoe-shaped throne. A female god beamed a smile at him from an altar on his left. TJ caught movement in his peripheral vision and saw an old man kowtowing at an altar to his right. The old man prayed to a god with a white-painted face and a streak of black that ran over his eyes and down his cheeks. The corners of the god's mouth turned down as if he'd just bitten into a lemon.

Hop Li paused and whispered, "That *Jung Ji,* God for dead people. When man die, *Jung Ji* call spirit for judge."

"Spirit is what we'll be if we don't get to a hidin' place soon."

Incense smoke from several bowls of joss sticks filled the room with the aroma of Eucalyptus.

Hop Li slowed in front of the center altar and announced, "That one, Jade Emperor. China name, *Yü Haung.* Boss God." A dragon crouched on one of *Yü Haung's* knees and fixed TJ with a marble-eyed stare. A phoenix glowered at TJ from the other knee.

"Yeah, yeah. Keep movin,' Hop Li." TJ glanced up at the calm face of the Jade Emperor and decided that if he were a praying man, that would be the god he prayed to.

Hop Li continued down a side aisle and stopped next to a narrow door. He knocked, the door opened, and the assistant TJ talked to earlier poked his head out. Hop Li bowed and spoke in an excited voice. The assistant smiled and then invited them into the temple's living quarters.

As they entered, another young man, wearing an apron over his coarse brown robe, looked up from washing bowls in a basin on the stove. The old priest sat at a rough wood table with a cup of tea and squinted at his guests. When Hop Li drew close, the priest shouted and opened his arms wide. With some difficulty, the priest rose and the two exchanged bows with Hop Li bowing from the waist. As he studied TJ, the priest's face lit up in recognition. TJ recognized the priest as well, smiled, and stuck out his hand. The priest took it and held it for a time rather than shaking it.

Hop Li started talking and kept on with no sign of pausing. Even TJ noticed Hop Li spoke too fast. The priest smiled and held up his hand stopping Hop Li's monologue. He put an arm around Hop Li's shoulder, said a few words, and then spoke to his assistants. The assistant at the stove, a sturdy fellow with large hands, bowed to the priest, took off his apron, and hurried out.

"Where's he going, Hop Li?"

"Baakgap go out front, tell Limpy men Master Sung too busy. Later, Master come out, bring guest."

"Guest? What guest?"

"Sheriff TJ, Hop Li, guest."

"He's givin' us up!? That's it, Hop Li, we're leavin.'" TJ turned towards the door.

"Wait Sheriff TJ!" Hop Li grabbed TJ's arm. "Master Sung help. I know this."

"What's he gonna do? Tell me, for Christ's sake."

The priest stood between Hop Li and TJ, looking from one to the other as the two friends argued. Hop Li turned to the priest and spoke rapid-fire Cantonese. The priest nodded, smiled, and this time let Hop Li finish. The priest kept his eyes on TJ as he spoke.

"Master Sung say, sometime fight necessary, sometime not necessary. In temple, fight not necessary." Hop Li shrugged as he said, "Master ask, what happen we not fight?"

"Not fight? What the hell is he sayin'? They'll lock us up in those goddamm coffins, if we don't fight."

The priest poked Hop Li in the ribs and Hop Li translated.

Hop Li listened to the priest's response and then translated for TJ. "How know what happen when not fight? Maybe big surprise."

"But they're under orders from Limpy," TJ said.

The priest answered and Hop Li translated. "Men always obey Limpy? Sheriff TJ think Limpy god? Maybe men not listen Limpy this time."

"I didn't say Limpy is a god. Shit, Hop Li this isn't getting us anywhere. We got to find a way out of this mess."

Hop Li translated only a few words before the priest hushed him with a wave of his hand. Master Sung held his right hand over his heart and when he finished speaking he bowed to TJ.

"Master Sung say no man all evil, all good. Limpy men sometime forget where come from. So Master tell story, men remember. When men remember, they not fight." Hop Li pointed to Tug's knife in TJ's belt. "Master say, knife not necessary."

TJ didn't know what to say and had used up the little energy he had. His legs felt heavy and the orange he'd eaten a while ago only reminded him how much he needed food. He also needed rest and a wash-up. Hop Li trusted the priest and the priest had been willing to go to jail for Hop Li. TJ admitted the old fellow might know something he didn't. "All right. Let's try it his way," he said and leaned his aching body against the wall.

The other assistant, smooth-skinned and with a scholar's wide forehead, followed the priest to a part of the room furnished with a cot, a small trunk, and an open closet. The assistant opened a plain, bamboo screen and placed it in front of the closet. From behind the screen, the priest talked to Hop Li who listened with head bowed.

"Dammit, Hop Li. What's he doing? We're runnin' out of time." TJ suspected Limpy's men would storm in any second. He and Hop Li could not take on four men.

"Master Sung say, no worry. Patience."

In spite of the priest's assurances, TJ didn't feel safe. The priest meant well but did he really know Limpy? TJ wrapped his fingers around the handle of Tug's knife, taking comfort in the familiar feel.

Ten minutes later, the priest entered the kitchen dressed as he had when he escorted Hop Li to the troublemaker ritual; three-quarter length black silk coat with an egret embroidered in white silk on his chest and a necklace of black stones. The assistant trailed the priest and carried the round satin hat with the pheasant feather sticking out the back. Master Sung halted in the middle of the room and the assistant placed the hat on the priest's head.

"Why's he wearin' that fancy getup, Hop Li?"

"Master Sung also official. Necklace have one hundred eight stone. Only big official all same like Master Sung can wear necklace, coat. Respect necessary for official. All Han know this."

TJ thought the priest's vestments too large by a size at least. With his oversized clothes, ears that stuck out from his head, stooped posture, and saucy hat, the old man looked like more like an elf than a priest. The assistant held the door open and the priest motioned for TJ and Hop Li to follow.

In the hall of worship, the gang leader stood with his hands on his hips and shouted at Baakgap, who took the onslaught without moving or answering back. Three men clustered behind the leader, arms folded across their chests. The priest approached the group, held up his hand, and said a single word. The leader turned from Baakgap and shouted in triumph when he saw Hop Li and TJ.

Hop Li nodded at the leader and said, "That man name, One-Ear. One-Ear, bandit—kill three soldier back home. Also kill farmer. Not know how many. One-Ear work for Limpy now."

The leader was no taller than his companions but powerfully built. His left ear had been cut off and, though he could have hidden the scar easily with his queue, he'd tied his hair so that it was visible. One-Ear and his men dressed alike in coarse blue cotton tops, baggy pants, leather leggings, and heavy wooden-soled slippers.

One-Ear drew a long knife from the sleeve of his shirt and raised it over his head. His men drew their knives. TJ slid Tug's knife from his belt, stepped away from the group, and faced the gang leader. One-Ear crouched and turned towards TJ but before either made a move, Master Sung stepped between them. The priest turned to One-Ear with his hand raised and spoke in a voice so soft that TJ could just hear him. Even so, at the priest's words, One-Ear straightened from his crouch and lowered his knife. As the priest continued his talk, One-Ear shook his head and grunted. At one point, he pulled his lips back and bared his stained teeth, perhaps trying to intimidate the priest. But though he'd been yelling at Baakgap earlier, the gang leader said nothing to the priest. TJ noticed that the arms of the accomplices hung at their sides, knives pointed at the ground.

The priest lifted his arm in a sweeping gesture taking in the gods at the three altars. His arm came to a stop in front of the Jade Emperor. For an instant, the eyes in *Yü Haung*'s large head seemed to stare into TJ's eyes but as he continued to look, *Yü Haung's* gaze appeared to shift so that the god stared over TJ's head.

At this point, the priest lifted his head and spoke directly to the men behind One-Ear. The oldest of the three said something that brought a nod from the priest. The three accomplices huddled, whispered among themselves, and then slipped their knives up their sleeves. The eldest of the three said something to the leader who pulled his lips back, turned his head to the side, and spit. TJ watched amazed as the three accomplices turned around and walked out.

"What's goin' on, Hop Li?"

"Master Sung say many thing. Not easy translate."

"Well, I'd need to know—are they comin' back or not?"

"Master say, temple for worship, no kill. Master know those men…" Hop Li pointed to the backs of the departing men…"men belong *Seiyup* Company. Master also *Seiyup*. *Seiyup* live same place, Guangdong, China. Master say, come temple for kill, bring shame family, shame ancestor, shame *Seiyup*. Any one kill in temple, Master Sung lose honor also. So if any man die today, Master Sung must die first."

TJ couldn't believe what Hop Li just said. "Are you sayin' Master Sung is willin' to die for us?"

"Yes. Master Sung also say, Sheriff TJ, Hop Li, guest. Priest duty protect guest."

TJ slid his knife back in his belt and said as much to himself as to those around him, "Well, I'll be dammed." The priest didn't know him but was ready to die to protect him, a barbarian in the eyes of most Chinese. The priest lived by an impossible set of rules that TJ had encountered only in the stories of the saints and martyrs that his Mom read to him as a boy.

The priest finished speaking and slipped his hands into the sleeves of his coat. One-Ear glared at the priest, pointed his knife at TJ, and said something in anger. He then slid his knife up his sleeve, handle first, and stomped out of the temple. The wood soles of his slippers banged against the hardwood floor, shattering the peace of the hall. The priest said something to the back of the retreating gang leader, which made Hop Li smile. Hop Li translated, "Master Sung say, please come back. One-Ear welcome. But leave anger, slipper at door."

Back at the temple's living quarters, Baakgap picked up a bucket of water, a brush, and a bar of soap and led TJ into the small garden at the back of the temple. Baakgap handed TJ the soap, rubbed his hands over his face, under his arms, over his body, and between his toes with such vigor that TJ laughed. Baakgap left, TJ shed his clothes, and scrubbed himself down three times before he felt free of vomit stink. Baakgap returned with a towel, robe, and gunnysack. TJ dried himself and put on the robe, while Baakgap stuffed TJ's filthy clothes in the gunnysack. The end of TJ's robe fell to a few inches below his knees and when he walked back into the kitchen, Hop Li erupted in laughter. The priest and the scholarly assistant tried to suppress their smiles but couldn't.

"What's so damm funny?" TJ asked, at which Hop Li doubled over laughing. "All right. All right. It's your turn, Hop Li," TJ said.

Hop Li followed Baakgap outside and returned in ten minutes in a robe that fit. Wearing a huge smile, Hop Li bowed from the waist to the priest and the priest invited them to sit at his table.

"First off, Hop Li, thank Master Sung for gettin' rid of Limpy's boys—not many men, Chinee or white, would have done what he did. I'm much in his debt."

Hop Li turned, bowed, and spoke a few words. The priest bowed to both men in turn.

"But we're not out of the woods yet. What did One-Ear say before he left?"

"He say, wait outside. Kill barbarian, Han dogface, when leave temple."

"Yeah, I expected that. Well, what now? Any ideas?"

Hop Li turned to speak but the priest held up his hand, said a few words, and smiled.

"Master Sung say eat first, plan later."

The two famished guests didn't have to wait long before the scholarly assistant placed a steaming bowl of rice with sliced carrots and bits of fish in front of them. The assistant served the priest a pot of tea, and then, since TJ and Hop Li had taken their stools, the assistants sat down on the floor next to the stove and sipped tea. Even eating with chopsticks, TJ wolfed down his meal as fast as Hop Li. At first, the priest clucked his tongue at the speed with which his guests ate but when both looked up from their empty bowls at the same time, he threw his head back and laughed. The priest said something to Baakgap who jumped up and refilled their bowls. When they'd finished eating, the priest poured cups of tea all around. For a time, nothing but the sound of slurping and satisfied sighs filled the kitchen.

While TJ sipped his tea, he thought back to when he'd bailed Hop Li out of jail and asked for his help with Limpy. "Sorry, I got you into this mess, Hop Li. Wasn't your fight."

"Wah! Sheriff TJ help me. So, honor help Sheriff TJ." Hop Li finished his tea and spoke to the priest. The two talked back and forth and TJ noticed that Hop Li's grunting grew more enthusiastic over time. Hop Li turned to TJ after a pause in the conversation and said, "I ask Master how leave temple, go police. Master say, Limpy men wait in front. Also wait behind, in alley. So, not possible leave temple."

"Not leave? What if those boys out front change their minds, decide to finish us in here. We need to get to the police station. Tell him that." He chewed on his mustache. Though his respect for the priest hadn't decreased, TJ thought the priest didn't realize that their troubles weren't over. As Hop Li and the priest talked, TJ rose and paced the small kitchen.

When the priest paused again, Hop Li turned and said, "Master say, no necessary leave temple. Maybe police come temple."

"Wha…? Why would they come here? And how would we get a message to them? Nope. Not possible."

"Sheriff TJ write message, Baakgap take police station. Baakgap best *bāguà* fighter. Limpy men no stop Baakgap."

TJ spoke his thoughts out loud, "All right, let's say we get a message out. The chief is afraid of Purcell, Hop Li. He wouldn't help me before. Why would he help me now? Nothing I say could …hold on…wait just a damm minute." He thought of the crimes Limpy committed against him and Hop Li: attempting to bribe a lawman, kidnapping—two counts, and harboring a fugitive. The chief could put Limpy away for years and when Limpy got out, immigration would ship him back to China. TJ recalled how much the chief wanted the little bastard. By God, it might work.

TJ said, "I need pen and paper, Hop Li. I think we just found our ticket out of here."

56

Monday, April 26

TJ hunched over the table and wrote a note to Chief Gorman. He scratched out a line, crumpled up the note, his fifth, and threw it on the floor. He grabbed a fresh sheet of paper and started again. He finished, read over the note, and nodded in satisfaction. He looked up and discovered that Hop Li had picked up his discarded notes, smoothed out the paper, and stacked them in a neat pile on the table.

"Hop Li, what the hell you doin'? Those are to throw away—they're no good."

"Chinamen respect word, writing. No throw away."

"You keep all this paper? What do you do with it?"

"Each moon Ming Wat, Master Sung student, burn all paper with writing, put ashes in river. Best way, respect writing."

"Seems considerable trouble to take over trash paper. But then I'm learning' you Chinee have a whole different way of seein' things," TJ said and asked Hop Li to send Baakgap in.

Hop Li went into the garden where Baakgap guarded the back entrance to the temple and the two came back within a minute. The big man stood at the table, arms crossed over his chest, ready for the next emergency.

"This note is for Chief Gorman, Hop Li. Nobody else. Tell Baakgap to go to the chief's office and give it to the chief himself. Understand?"

"Yes, understand," Hop Li said and turned to Baakgap who grunted each time Hop Li paused in giving instructions. When Hop Li finished, Baakgap nodded once and then looked at TJ. TJ realized that he hadn't heard Baakgap speak English. He turned to Baakgap and asked, "Can you speak English?"

Baakgap smiled at TJ but didn't say anything. Hop Li put the question to the big man in Cantonese.

"No sabbee," He said and then added, "Tankee moochee."

"Ask him to say, 'I need to see Chief Gorman.'"

Hop Li turned to Baakgap and translated.

Baakgap straightened his shoulders, spoke in a loud voice, and grinned in satisfaction when finished. TJ hadn't understood a word. If Baakgap couldn't make himself understood at the front desk, the sergeant would ignore him or, if Baakgap persisted in trying to speak, would kick him out. He tapped his pen on the table in frustration and then wrote a second note.

This note said the Chinaman Baakgap had a message for Chief Gorman from Sheriff TJ Stone and that said Chinaman was to deliver it himself. TJ told Hop Li the second note was for the policeman at the front desk. Hop Li translated and then gave both notes to Baakgap who stuck the note for the chief up his right sleeve, the other up his left. He bowed to each man and then grabbed a thick, six-foot staff before he went out.

The priest emerged from behind the curtain where he'd been resting. He and Hop Li conversed and when they finished, Hop Li announced that he and Master Sung were going to the garden. "Master Sung say maybe have job. Hop Li luck change, eh?" He smiled and followed the priest out the back door.

TJ sat in the kitchen letting the cup of tea in front of him grow cold. Twenty minutes passed with no word from Baakgap and, for what must have been the tenth time, TJ went over all the things that could have gone wrong: Baakgap might have given the note intended for the chief to the sergeant at the front desk; or Limpy's boys might have ganged up on Baakgap, beat him senseless, and left him to die; or an irritable front desk sergeant could have thrown Baakgap out without bothering to read the note. TJ paced the floor, circling the small table, two or three times before sitting down again. He'd gone without a cigar for three or four days now and was desperate for a smoke. He chewed on his mustache trying to put thoughts of a cigar and disaster out of his mind.

After another fifteen minutes passed, he concluded that Limpy's boys must have gotten to Baakgap. With a sigh, he got up and started for the back door to call Hop Li in. But before he reached the door, a booming Irish voice called out from the main hall, "Is there a Sheriff Stone in the house?"

TJ stuck his head out the side door and yelled, "In here." He opened the back door and shouted, "Police are here, Hop Li. Let's go."

Hop Li and the priest came into the kitchen just as two patrolmen burst in. The younger, a lanky Scandinavian with ruddy cheeks, stood behind a sergeant, a redhead with a handlebar mustache and a stomach already shaped by a daily quart of beer. The sergeant stared at TJ with his mouth hanging open. "Jesus save us!" he muttered as his gaze came to rest on TJ's bare lower legs. "What have we here?"

TJ approached the sergeant. "Forget the damm robe, Sergeant. I'm Sheriff Stone, Clatsop County." He extended his hand.

The sergeant hesitated but then shook TJ's hand. "Have you converted, Stone, is that it? For the love of God, man, tell us you're not a heathen."

"I'll tell you all about it in due time, Sergeant. Right now I need to get to my hotel and into my own clothes."

"Ah, well now, that we can't do. The chief was crystal clear, he was. Straight back to the station with you and not so much as a look at Limpy's boys if we run into them. But we'll have no trouble from the likes of them. Three or four scruffy heathen scattered to the four winds as we drove up in the paddy wagon, didn't they Alvord?"

"Ya. They run away too," Alvord said.

"Well, I'm not goin' to the station wearing this." TJ looked down at his bare lower legs.

"I have me instructions, Stone. Sorry."

TJ shuddered at the thought of parading around in this knee length robe. If he showed up at police headquarters in this robe, he'd be laughed out of the station house.

"What's your name?" TJ asked.

"Kevin Doherty. But why are you wantin' to know?"

"Well, Doherty, put yourself in my place. Would you report to your chief lookin' like this?" TJ tugged at the sleeve of his robe and then nodded at Alvord who had not taken his eyes off TJ or stopped smirking. "Your partner is so taken with my outfit he hasn't heard a word I've said."

Doherty glanced at Alvord. "You've bewitched the lad with the look of you. Well, there's no denyin' the fact, Stone, you're a sight to behold, a lovely sight indeed." He paused and grinned at TJ.

TJ said, "If you boys are finished laughin,' I'd like to get movin.'"

Doherty turned to his partner. "What'd think, Alvord, do we take him in as is or do the decent thing?"

Alvord shrugged but didn't stop grinning.

"And just how long will it take, this changin' of the gown?" Doherty asked.

"I'm at the St. Charles. Shouldn't take but ten minutes once we're there."

"All right then. The St. Charles it is."

TJ turned to Hop Li. "Let's go."

"No. Hop Li stay temple."

"What? But why? You can't…what the hell will you do?"

"Plenty work here. Work garden, fix fence. Master Sung feed, give bed. Also study *DaoTeChing* with Baakgap, Ming Wat. So, all time busy.

"You've got your trial next month. Don't forget that."

"No forget."

"I'll be back for the trial, Hop Li. With all you've done for me, for the law, I expect the judge to go easy, a fine maybe but no jail time. By the way, how will you live?"

"No need money. After trial, find job."

"You've been a help to me, Hop Li, a big help. Thanks." TJ extended his hand. Hop Li pumped TJ's hand up and down a half dozen times.

Doherty opened the door and pushed Alvord out. "All right, Stone, time to go."

TJ picked up the gunnysack with his clothes, turned to the priest, and said, "Master Sung, you and your boys saved our skins today. Many thanks." He started toward the door.

"Wait!" Hop Li reached inside his robe and pulled out the Laughing Buddha medallion. "For Sheriff TJ," he said and held the necklace out to TJ.

"I can't take that—it's yours. You need it."

"No need now. Master Sung know many thing, know…" He tilted his head up, eyes searching the ceiling, and then said, *"wu wei*…not know 'merican word. But Master Sung help Hop Li beat troublemaker. So now Laughing Buddha help Sheriff TJ. Please, you take, yes?" He smiled and continued to hold his arm out. TJ took the necklace.

Hop Li bowed from the waist and held the bow while TJ tucked the necklace inside his robe. Though the medallion wasn't cold, a shiver ran down TJ's spine as it came to rest against his skin and for a few seconds he felt a tingling, an energy, flowing through his body. He told himself he was imagining things, that what he felt was nothing but the sensations of a tired body.

Hop Li straightened up and smiled. Although Hop Li's physical features seemed the same to TJ, something about him had changed— he'd become a person, not just a Chinaboy. TJ paused then bowed from the waist and held it for a second just as Hop Li had. It was the first time he'd ever bowed to any man or any thing and, though he felt clumsy and strange, he also knew that the bow expressed his feelings to Hop Li as nothing else could. The bow was more than a thank you; it acknowledged Hop Li as friend and equal.

"Ah, for the love of Jesus, Stone, are we leavin' today at all?" Doherty asked.

"See you in a month, Hop Li. All right?"

"Yes. Hop Li send ten thousand prayer *Guan Di*, Sheriff TJ catch sonbitchee."

TJ and the patrolmen stopped in the foyer so that TJ could retrieve his boots. "Supposed to take your shoes off before you go in the temple, Doherty."

"You don't say? Ah, that's all well and good for the heathens, I suppose, but it doesn't hold for the rest of us."

"Nope. It holds for everybody."

57

Tuesday, April 27

T he next day, TJ woke up in his room at the St. Charles to the delicious feeling of clean sheets on his well-scrubbed skin. But then he thought of Purcell and instead of lingering in bed as his body begged him to do, he yanked the covers off. As he shaved, Doc's advice of looking at the board from the opponent's perspective popped into his head. Purcell wouldn't return to his hideout after he learned his prisoners had escaped. Where would he go? He hadn't taken a steamer to Washington Territory or elsewhere when he first heard TJ was on to him. He hid out in Limpy's tunnels. Why? But as soon as he asked the question, he knew the answer—Purcell couldn't turn his back on the power that came with being a U.S. Senator. From past elections, TJ knew that it might require forty or more ballots to elect a senator. Both Jameson and Purcell had to be in Salem next week to shore up wavering supporters and to tempt potential defectors with bribes. "That's it, Doc!" He said aloud, "He's in Salem or on his way there."

TJ put on a clean shirt, Levis, and his freshly cleaned coat. He stopped at the hotel's front desk and picked up a package from Sketch. Inside the thickly wrapped box he found everything he'd asked for: a Smith & Wesson .45, a holster and gun belt with twenty cartridges, a copy of Purcell's warrant, a sheriff's badge, handcuffs and key, and an envelope with fifty dollars. TJ chuckled as he read Silas's note.

Be advised your telegram asking for sheriff's toolkit spawned considerable rumor & betting. Smart money says you've fallen for a soiled dove & lost money & dignity. Have a five-dollar wager myself. Get back pronto & settle issue.

With impatience and more than a little curiosity,
Silas

He strapped on the holster and gun, pinned on the badge, and stuffed the handcuffs in his back pocket. The weight of the gun at his side felt good and for the first time in days he felt fully dressed, or almost, as he had no hat. TJ turned to leave but the clerk called him back. "Sir, almost forgot—this came for you last night." He handed TJ a scented note written on cream-colored stationery.

Dear Sheriff Stone,

Paul came by this morning and asked to stay the night. I begged him to tell me everything—I have no doubt but that he is in serious trouble. But once again he refused. I can no longer countenance his refusal to confide in me and asked him to leave, which he did. If you need to see me, I will be staying at my father's home (Jay P. Hathaway) for a time. Before Paul left, I learned that he planned to take the first steamer to Salem Sunday morning.

I pray God can forgive him—I cannot.

Frances S. Hathaway

TJ asked the clerk when the first steamer left for Salem.

"Let's see…" the clerk checked a schedule, "looks like 7:15 from the Stark Street dock."

Both men looked at the large grandfather clock next to the coat closet. The time was 7:03.

"You might make it," the clerk said.

TJ put thoughts of breakfast out of mind and darted out of the lobby onto Second Street. Running easily, he rounded a corner onto Front Street and came on a sprinkler wagon pulled by four Percheron. He yelled and jumped out of the way of the lead team. Water from the wagon's sprinklers sprayed his boots and the bottom of his pants. He picked up his pace—nothing or no one would stop him today. He reached the dock just as the steamer whistled a long blast. He shouted and waved his arms at deckhands who were pulling up the gangplank. The men looked at him, each other, and then lowered the gangplank. TJ climbed on board and a crewman asked for his ticket.

"Didn't have time to buy one."

The deckhand pointed him to a man in an officer's uniform.

"Where to?" The officer asked.

"What's your first stop?"

"Milwaukee, in about twenty minutes."

He realized that he might not locate Purcell before the steamer got to Milwaukee. "And the next stop?"

"Oregon City." The officer gave him a puzzled look.

"Oregon City then—and make it a round trip." He paid the $3.00 and got directions to the gentleman's smoking cabin. He decided against telling the captain why he was on board. It wouldn't do to have the captain running around scaring folks and spooking Purcell into doing some fool thing like drawing a gun in a compartment of women and children. Purcell smoked cigars and sooner or later he'd wander into the smoking cabin. He'd take him there.

Another long blast announced the steamer's departure and the deck shivered as the engines powered up and the City of Salem got under way. TJ picked up the morning Oregonian at a newsstand on the lower deck and then climbed to the top level where he exited onto the hurricane deck.

A stiff, cold breeze off the Willamette had emptied the deck of all but a young couple who took no notice of him. He sat down in a deck chair a dozen yards from the port door of the smoking cabin. TJ opened his paper and held it so that by shifting it a little to one side or the other, he could see both outside doors to the cabin as well as the inside door that connected the cabin to the dining saloon.

The steamer docked at Milwaukee to take on a family of four and got underway ten minutes later. TJ guessed those boarding at Portland would be finished breakfast soon and within five minutes, four men entered the smoking cabin from the dining saloon. The men had only just settled into their seats when another man entered the cabin with a newspaper under his arm. The man's wide brimmed hat hid most of his face but he was about Purcell's height and build and sported muttonchops like Purcell. TJ waited for the man to light his cigar and open his newspaper then got up, walked over to the door, and opened it. The man looked up from his paper as TJ entered.

"You!" Purcell dropped his newspaper and rose part way out of his chair.

"Mornin,' Purcell."

"But how…? Oh, of course. Frances. Shit." Purcell sank back into his chair.

"You gonna make this easy?" TJ put his hands on his hips and showed his gun.

Purcell glanced around the room. Two old timers smoking pipes sat in one corner, a youth with a scraggly beard sprawled on a piano bench with a cigarillo, and a well-dressed, fat man sat across from the old timers, smoking a double corona cigar. All eyes were on TJ and Purcell. The only sound came from the rumble of the engine and the chop of the buckets as the City of Salem churned upriver.

TJ spoke to the room. "I'm Sheriff Stone and I'm arrestin' this fella. I'd appreciate it if you'd all leave the cabin for a spell."

The old timers got up right away but before they took two steps, Purcell said, "This man is an imposter. He's Frank Kelly, a notorious criminal, and out for revenge. He believes me responsible for his brother's death." Purcell spoke in his best orator's voice.

Even TJ was taken aback at Purcell's brazen lie and couldn't think what to say for a second. Finally, he said, "That's a damm lie. The son of a bitch can't open his mouth…"

"Well, somebody's lying," the youth smoking the cigarillo interrupted him. He turned to Purcell. "And just who might you be, sir?"

"I'm Paul Purcell, Portland Police Commissioner." Purcell removed his hat and smoothed his hair down.

The fat man said, "Why, by God, I recognize you, sir. Indeed, I do. You talked on the Chinese question at the Elks Club. A damm fine talk too, in my opinion. I'm Jay Loomis, Loomis Department Store, at your service, Commissioner."

"Thank you, Mr. Loomis," Purcell said and nodded in turn to the others.

Nobody spoke and in the silence the creaking of the overhead lantern grew louder as it swayed in its cradle. TJ sensed that the bystanders had accepted Purcell's lie. "This man is Paul Purcell all right but he's wanted for murder in Astoria. I'm Sheriff of Clatsop County."

Loomis spoke up, "You say you're a sheriff, mister. Prove it."

TJ cursed to himself. Limpy's boys had taken his wallet with his identification and he'd forgotten to ask Sketch for another identification card.

"My wallet's been stolen…goddammit…you'll have to take my word for it. I'm a lawman."

"You're wrong, mister, we don't have to take your word for a damm thing," Loomis said, standing up. TJ kept his eyes on Purcell who clutched the arms of his chair.

"I think it time we called the captain," Loomis said to the room.

Purcell nodded to Loomis and said, "Quite right, Mr. Loomis, call the captain and a couple of stout lads as well. We don't want this scoundrel getting away."

Loomis started for the door.

TJ couldn't risk the captain siding with Purcell. He drew his gun, pointed it at the ceiling, and said, "Hold it. Nobody's goin' anywhere. I've got a warrant for this fella's arrest right here." TJ tapped his chest. "That oughta prove I'm tellin' the truth."

"Let's see it," Loomis said.

TJ shifted the gun to his left hand and pulled the warrant from his inside coat pocket with his right hand. He turned slightly to give the warrant to Loomis, taking his eyes off Purcell for an instant. Purcell lunged and rammed TJ's chest with his shoulder. TJ fell into Loomis who tried to keep from falling by grabbing TJ. Loomis fell to the floor, pulling TJ with him. With a curse, TJ untangled himself from Loomis and jumped up in time to see Purcell running towards the stern.

TJ ran outside and looked aft but didn't see Purcell. A waist-high chain with a 'Crew Only' sign blocked access to the afterdeck. TJ stepped over the chain while holding his gun level.

A farm tractor, its top half covered in canvas, was lashed against the rear wall of the smoking cabin. Some space existed between the wall of the cabin and the tractor but it looked too small for a man of Purcell's size to squeeze into. Still, he'd learned caution in his short time as a lawman so he bent down and looked into the space. Nothing. He looked at the lifeboat next. The cover was lashed down.

Within seconds, the cloud of mist sent up by the huge wheel wet his face. The deck vibrated with the engine and the force of the buckets as they chewed up the water. Spray from the wheel kept this part of the deck wet and, as he took a step, he knew it'd be impossible to run here without slipping.

The noise of the buckets as they tore into and spit out the water drowned out most sound. Still he heard something, a clump somewhere behind him. He spun around and saw Purcell coming at him with a fire axe. The blade overshot the mark but the handle struck his gun hand. The gun flew out of his hand, skittered across the deck, and went over the side. He screamed and grabbed his throbbing wrist with his left hand.

"You're finished, hick," Purcell shouted. Purcell lunged and swung the axe but slipped on the wet deck and went down on one knee. TJ rolled to the side, got up, and, with eyes darting left and right, scanned the deck for a weapon. Purcell regained his balance and stalked TJ with short steps.

"This is stupid, Purcell. You can't escape—it's over," TJ shouted as he continued to back up. TJ's foot bumped into a coiled mooring hawser with a loop at the end. Without taking his eyes off Purcell, he reached down, found the loop, and then slid his left hand down the hawser about two feet. Purcell swung the axe in a wide arc. TJ jumped to the side, lifting the line up to protect him. The blade glanced off the line but the flat of the blade struck TJ in the back of the shoulder. TJ went down with the force of the blow, yelling as he fell. In spite of the pain, he tucked and rolled several feet.

"Not for me, hick, for you. It's over for you," Purcell yelled.

Back on his feet, TJ stepped into Purcell and swung the loop at his head. Purcell took the blow in the face as he swung in panic. The blade went over TJ's head. TJ swung the hawser at Purcell's legs next. Purcell jumped, dodging the line, but slipped and fell, dropping the axe as he hit the deck. TJ kicked the axe away. As Purcell scrambled up to his knees, TJ hit him in the chest. Purcell fell back, grabbing the loop of the hawser as he did. Purcell pulled himself upright and then put his arm and shoulder through the loop. TJ yanked and then pulled but couldn't break Purcell's grip.

"One way or the other, Stone, you'll die today," Purcell screamed and pulled with adrenaline fueled by rage. Several feet of line slipped through TJ's hands before he regained his grip. The pain in his wrist and shoulder kept him from pulling with full strength. He realized he couldn't win a tug of war so let go of the line and charged.

When TJ let go of the line, Purcell flew backward. Still clutching the line, Purcell hit the rail and tumbled over. One of the paddles snapped his head backward and then the wheel pulled him down. Purcell hadn't let go of the line and the line hissed as it payed out across the deck. Reaching its end at the cleat, the line tightened, and then bounced around like a live eel as the paddles battered it. A crewman, shouting curses, ran past TJ and up to the wheel.

TJ roused himself, ran up to the crewman, and shouted into the man's ear, "A man went overboard, into the wheel."

The crewman turned, cupped his hands around his mouth, and hollered, "Man overboard!"

Other crew repeated the call and, within seconds, the pilot blew five short whistles, the engines powered down, and the City of Salem slowed. One crewman grabbed a life preserver and tossed it over the port rail while another threw one over the starboard rail. With two short and one long whistle from the pilothouse, the wheel reversed several revolutions. A long whistle blew and the sternwheeler came to a full stop. While anchors were lowered, crewmen leaned over the rails craning their necks to search the foaming water. Within a minute, a crewman shouted, "There! Just starboard the wheel."

TJ ran to the starboard rail and looked down into the now wake-less water. The line was held tight by something in the water. On both sides of the smoking cabin, onlookers gawked from behind the chains that restricted passengers from the afterdeck.

"Clear the way, goddammit," A steam organ voice bellowed. The voice belonged to a short but solidly built man in his mid-forties who pushed through the crowd, strode up to the railing, and looked down at the taut line. He gave orders to lower a dinghy, and then walked over to TJ.

"I'm Captain Hauptman. This area is restricted to crew. You mind telling me what the hell you two were doing here?"

"It's a long story, Captain. I'm Sheriff TJ Stone and the man overboard is wanted for murder."

Captain Hauptman looked TJ up and down. "Stay where you are until I'm finished here. Understand?" The unblinking stare of his gray eyes let TJ know who was in charge.

TJ nodded.

"We'll talk later—I need answers."

The crew of the dinghy came along side the steamer and hoisted Purcell's covered body on board. TJ followed the captain down to the lower deck where the dinghy crew stood around the body. One of the crew stepped forward and reported that the line had wrapped itself around Purcell's neck. The captain nodded and the crewman lifted the canvas, revealing Purcell's head and shoulders. The skin had been scraped off one side of his face, an eye forced out of its socket, and the skull split open so that brain matter pushed through.

"My God…" The captain muttered. TJ would have been hard pressed to identify Purcell from the butchered face. Feeling queasy, he turned away. He'd hated what Purcell had done and, for a time, hated the man when he taunted him as he lay in his coffin. Even so, he never wanted to kill him. From the time he became a lawman, he wanted to show people in Astoria that the law worked for everyone. He believed he could do that with this case. Purcell was a professional, with money, influence, and, in the eyes of many, well respected. Always, in his mind's eye, TJ saw himself bringing Purcell back to Astoria in handcuffs and testifying at his trial in front of a packed courtroom.

But looking down on that mangled face, he realized he didn't feel victorious or righteous or justified or any of the things he'd imagined he'd feel when he captured the bastard. He felt pity, yes, but also anger. Purcell was dead—what was there to be angry about? But then, as he followed the captain up to his cabin, he realized the reason for his anger: Purcell's death had cheated him of victory and cheated the decent folk of Astoria from seeing the man humbled and punished, as he ought to have been. He recalled the meaning of the Chinese writing on that tank, 'death settles all debts,' and asked himself if it were true in Purcell's case. He thought of Wah Fong, Fatt Luk, and Jane Thurgood—lives cut short by Purcell's lust for power. No, he concluded, the proverb didn't hold for Purcell: the man died leaving behind debts that would never be repaid.

58

Tuesday, April 27

Captain Hauptman sat down at a narrow pine desk, took out a piece of paper, and dipped a pen in the inkwell. "Now, who went into the river?"

"Paul Purcell."

"You don't mean the police commissioner?"

"I do. He murdered two people—three if you count provokin' a lynchin.'"

The captain held out his hand. "Let's see the warrant."

TJ handed him the warrant and the captain examined it closely before giving it back. "This looks legitimate. But dammit, Sheriff, I'm bothered by how you did your job."

TJ shrugged. Dead tired and with his wrist and shoulder throbbing with pain, he didn't feel like explaining his actions to man or God.

"You went after this man by yourself. Why?" Hauptman tilted his head to the side and tapped his fingers on his desk.

"A long story, Captain. If it were up to me, I woulda had a patrolmen or two with me but it wasn't up to me."

"But why in God's name didn't you ask for my help? It's what an experienced lawman would have done, seems to me." One side of his mouth twisted up in annoyance.

TJ didn't have an answer for what now seemed like a stupid decision and said nothing.

"A witness said the man came at you with an axe. Why didn't you shoot him?"

TJ opened his coat and showed the empty holster. "It went overboard in the fight."

"You lost your gun? Good God, man, how long have you been Sheriff?"

"Seems like too long today—but if you're countin' years, it's a little over two."

"I see." He pursed his lips, seemed about to ask another question but didn't. He stood up. "I don't know if you take advice, Sheriff, but on the off chance you do, I'll offer some. Spend some time with a lawman that's been around and then heed what he says. You might live another two years if you do."

"I'll think on your advice, Captain," TJ said without enthusiasm. "But right now, I could use some time alone."

Hauptman stood up, went over to the door, and knocked once. The crewman stationed outside entered.

"Riley, find a cabin for the sheriff and make sure he's not disturbed." Captain Hauptman extended his hand. TJ started to reach for it but then stuck out his left hand.

The captain's mouth twitched at the corners in a near smile. "Well, you've had yourself a full day, Sheriff. Guess you're earned a rest."

Once inside the cabin, TJ lay down on a bunk and tried to sleep but couldn't. To keep his mind off the pain in his wrist, he thought about what Purcell did in an attempt to understand him. When Purcell spoke to the fishermen's union at Liberty Hall, TJ thought the man believed that the Chinese should be sent home for the good of the country, like Marvin Kephardt. Kephardt was a thug but the man believed in his cause—he fought to keep jobs for the American workingman. Purcell used the same words, the same logic, as Kephardt but the words and logic served only Purcell's aim of becoming a senator. Whether the Chinese were sent home or stayed was as little moment to him as what he named his dog. The words stupid and senseless came to mind when he thought about Purcell's life.

The City of Salem blew for the landing and within ten minutes docked at Oregon City. TJ came out of his cabin to find a dark sky and raindrops splattering the deck. By the time the Oregon City passengers disembarked, the rain had turned fierce, coming down in wind-driven sheets. The captain handed TJ a slicker and they hurried ashore to the waiting room of the Oregon Railway & Navigation Company. Minutes later, four crewmen, their slickers dripping rainwater, lumbered into the waiting room carrying Purcell's body wrapped in canvas.

TJ didn't feel like talking and the captain wasn't a man for chitchat so they sat in agreeable silence. After twenty minutes or so, a doctor pulled up outside the waiting room and the captain briefed him on what had happened. After he finished talking to the doctor, he shook hands with TJ, wished him luck as a lawman, and then followed his men up the City of Salem's gangplank.

Dr. Chaney examined Purcell's body and filled out some papers. "I've written a temporary death certificate, Sheriff, but since the death occurred in a fight, we'll need to perform an autopsy. What are your plans?"

"I'm taking him back to Portland on the 2:45 steamer. The fellow in the steamer office said we could store him in Nolan's ice house 'til then."

"We're off to Nolan's then. And I'll try to scare up a cooling basket for your trip back."

"Thanks. Now, if you got time, I could use some help with this wrist." TJ extended his arm toward the doctor.

The doctor lifted TJ's hand, twisted it slightly, and then pulled the wrist joint with his fingers. TJ winced at the doctor's prodding.

"What happened?"

"It took a blow from an axe handle."

"Uh-huh. Well, it feels broken. After we see to the body, we'll go back to my office for a close look."

At his office, Chaney examined TJ's wrist as well as his shoulder and rendered a verdict: one broken wrist, one bruised shoulder. Chaney offered him two fingers of whiskey before he started to manipulate the wrist. TJ said no to the whiskey, clamped his jaw tight, and didn't howl until the third pull on his wrist. The doctor put a splint on the inside of the wrist joint and then put a cast on the wrist from hand to elbow, leaving only thumb and fingertips to the middle knuckles free. TJ wiggled his fingers and turned his arm this way and that. "Don't believe I can shoot with this hand, Doc. How long I have to wear this?"

"Oh, ten to twelve weeks. And I wouldn't rely on that hand for some time after that if I had to shoot a bad man."

As he walked out of the doctor's office TJ reminded himself that if trouble came, he always had Sketch and Big Jim. But he'd think about that later. *It's over. My job's done. Time for a good cigar.*

The clerk in Samuels's Haberdashery said the Great Western was Oregon City's finest hotel and, for once, it wasn't a lie. The walk-in humidor of the Great Western was twice the size of TJ's bedroom and the aroma of fine tobacco made his mouth water. He paid 25 cents for a *Romeo y Julieta*, the best Cuban there, and stepped outside into a glass-covered patio. He took a table set with white linen, a vase with a yellow rose, and silverware fit for the hands of giants. TJ bit off the end of his cigar, struck a match, waited for the sulfur to burn off, and brought the flame close to the tip. He took a few short pulls and drew the flame into the cigar while rolling the cigar back and forth until it had an even burn. He took a long pull, blew a smoke ring, and ordered a pot of coffee from a squirt of a kid in an oversized waiter's coat.

"Somethin' to eat, sir?" The waiter's eyes stayed on TJ's cast.

"And spoil this?" TJ asked and lifted his cigar. "Not a chance, son."

"I knowed ya was a lawman, sir, 'cause I seen the badge. But that arm...I mean...how can ya shoot and fight with your arm like that?"

"Don't know. But I'm about to find out." The boy was nosy but TJ didn't let it bother him.

"Un-huh. Sir, if ya don't mind my askin'...uh...how'd it happen...I mean...did ya hafta shoot someone?"

"Had a fight with a bad man. But I didn't shoot him. And to answer your next question, he got the worst of it."

The boy flipped his towel over his shoulder. "Well, seems a hard life—bein' a lawman I mean."

"It can be, son, it can be."

The rain had stopped by now and storm clouds were drifting northeast towards Pendleton. A burst of sunlight lit up the patio and he looked up, taking pleasure in the warmth of the sun on his face. The good feeling he got reminded him of the good feelings he'd had as a fisherman. When he and Tug had set out for the Shoo-fly drift with a late afternoon sun warming his face, he felt right with the world. Part of that good feeling came from the freedom of the life—no boss telling you where to fish or how long to stay out. The possibility of a good catch, that too was part of the good feeling. And when he and Tug come back to the cannery with the *Lucy Ann* filled to the gunnels with Spring Chinook, well, he couldn't imagine a better life.

He asked himself why he'd quit the fishing life. Even in a poor season, he'd made enough to get by. Fishing could be dangerous, sure, but look what he just went through: two head bashings, buried in a coffin, almost Shanghaied, and damm near killed.

What for, Doc, what the hell for?

He smiled as he thought of how Doc would probably answer. *Having second thoughts, are we? You'd like some other fool to take on the life of a lawman, is that it? Somebody like Turk, maybe, who'd uphold the law just fine for those who could pay. You could go back to fishing. Be an easier life.*

TJ scratched an itch on his chest, felt the Laughing Buddha medalion, and thought of Hop Li. Hop Li had purged hate from his heart without having to fight or kill. How did the priest convince Hop Li to do that troublemaker ritual? And by what magic did the priest change the minds of Limpy and his men? TJ had a glimpse into a world where a man bent on killing could be defeated without violence and he wanted to know more about that world.

A shadow fell across his table. He looked up to see the boy waiter hovering nearby with a pot of coffee. TJ pushed his cup forward and the boy filled it.

"You want somethin' else, sir?"

TJ looked up at a blue sky and felt the sun's warmth again. Greedy for more warmth, he turned his face full to the sun. As the waiter continued to stand by the table, TJ realized the boy expected an answer. "I don't need another thing, son. I'm feelin' as fine as I have a right to feel."

The waiter left. TJ picked up his cigar, glanced at the label, *Romeo Y Julieta,* and thought of Emma. It had been a while—weeks it seemed—since he'd talked to her. Word would be all over Astoria soon that Purcell had been killed and she'd worry herself dizzy over him and Hop Li. He had to tell her they were alive and well. And then he remembered Mrs. Purcell. She needed to hear what had happened to her husband from him, not from the newspapers.

He told the waiter to keep his coffee warm and got directions to the telegraph office. He telegraphed Mrs. Purcell that her husband died in an accident and asked her to bring a carriage to the Stark Street dock to meet the afternoon steamer. Then he sent the following telegraph to Emma at the parsonage:

It's over. Hop Li and I banged up some but we'll live. I'm ready for dancing lessons if offer still holds.

He wanted to add "Love, TJ," but didn't feel right saying such a thing in public before he said it in private so he just signed it "TJ." He left the telegraph office glowing with pleasure at the thought of seeing Emma, the pain in his wrist forgotten for the moment. It was not yet noon with plenty of sun left in the day and he planned to get his share.

SELECTED BIBLIOGRAPHY

Barlow, J. & Richardson, C. (1979). *The China Doctor of John Day*. Portland, OR: Binford & Mort.

Beatty, L. (1999). *Lillie Langtry: Manners, Masks and Morals*. London: Sinclair-Stevenson, Ltd.

Brough, J. (1975). *The Prince and The Lily*. New York: Putnam Adult.

Chan, S. (Ed.) (1991). *Entry Denied: Exclusion and the Chinese Community in America, 1882-1943*. Philadelphia, PA: Temple University.

Friday, C. (1994). *Organizing Asian American Labor: The Pacific Coast Canned-Salmon Industry, 1870-1942*. Philadelphia, PA: Temple University.

Gault, V. (1988). Then and Now: Contract men vital to Astoria. *The Daily Astorian*, February 12,

Hsu, F. L.K. (1948). *Under the Ancestors' Shadow*. New York: Columbia University

Hsu, F. L.K. (1983). *Exorcising the Trouble Makers*. Westport, CT: Greenwood Press.

Karin,J. A. (1948). The Anti-Chinese Outbreaks in Seattle, 1885-1886. *Pacific Northwest Quarterly. 39*, 103-130.

Karin, J. A. (1964). The Anti-Chinese Outbreaks in Tacoma, 1885. *Pacific Historical Review, 23*, 271-283.

Mccunn, R. L. (1979). *The Illustrated History of the Chinese in America.* San Francisco: Design Enterprises.

Mccunn, R. L. (1979). *Chinese American Portraits: Personal Histories 1828-1988.* Seattle: University of Washington.

McKeown, M. F. (1948). *The Trail Led North: Mont Hawthorne's Story.* New York: Macmillan.

Penner, L. (1990). *The Chinese in Astoria, Oregon: 1870-1880.* Penner, Rt. 3. Box 525, Astoria, OR 97103.

Pfaelzer, J. (2007). *Driven Out: The Forgotten War Against Chinese Americans.* New York: Random House.

Spence, J. D. (1996). *God's Chinese Son: The Taiping Heavenly Kingdom of Hong Xiuquan.* New York: W.W. Norton.

Tetlow, R. T. (1975). *"The Astorian."* Portland, OR: Binford & Mort.

Wiltshire, T., Gross, B. & Chung, K.K. (1990). *Echoes of Old China.* Hong Kong: FormAsia Books.

Wong, M. R. (2004). *Sweet Cakes, Long Journey: The Chinatowns of Portland. Oregon.* Seattle: University of Washington.